MY MOTHER'S SECRET

Sanjida Kay is a writer and broadcaster. She lives in Bristol with her daughter and husband. She's written two previous thrillers, *Bone by Bone* and *The Stolen Child*.

MY MOTHER'S SECRET

Sanjida Kay

CORVUS

Published in trade paperback in Great Britain in 2018 by Corvus, an imprint of Atlantic Books Ltd.

10 9 8 7 6 5 4 3 2 1

A CIP catalogue record for this book is available from the British Library.

Trade paperback ISBN: 978 1 78649 252 4
E-book ISBN: 978 1 78649 253 1

Printed in Great Britain.

Corvus
An imprint of Atlantic Books Ltd
Ormond House
26–27 Boswell Street
London
WC1N 3JZ

www.corvus-books.co.uk

MIX
Paper from
responsible sources
FSC
www.fsc.org   FSC® C117931

To my mother,
Rosemary O'Connell

'If I were to marry you, you would kill me.'

Reader, I married him.
Jane Eyre by Charlotte Brontë

PROLOGUE

'Did you know my name means God?'

She shook her head and the movement made her forehead throb, her vision blurring into ultramarine and plum. She winced.

'So I'm kind of a superhero.'

'Like Spider-Man?' she asked, smiling in spite of the pain.

'Yeah. What do you think my superpower could be?'

The child knelt on the floor beside the camp bed and stared into her eyes. His own were large and dark as treacle. He was so close, she could see how long and thick his eyelashes were, and smell the cream Arjun must have put in his hair to try and stop it standing on end. The boy was going to be a heartbreaker when he grew up.

'Can you fly?'

'All superheroes can fly,' he said scornfully.

A little light spilled into the room from round the edge of the door, which was ajar; it was just enough to see the boy. There were no windows and Arjun had turned off the lamp when he left. She rolled gingerly onto her back and closed her eyes. The darkness was soothing.

'Maybe you could be invisible.'

'That's not very exciting,' he said.

'Is this where you sleep?'

'Sometimes,' said the boy. 'If Daddy's working late and there's no one to look after me. My mummy's dead,' he added, matter-of-factly.

'I'm sorry, Dev,' she said, taking his small hand in hers.

'That's okay. She'll come back. Maybe as a horse. She loved horses.'

He was only six, she thought. How could he hope to understand death?

'Perhaps your superpower could be to talk to horses?' she said.

'Lizzie?

'Yes?'

'Are you going to die, like Mummy did?'

'No, Dev, I've just got a really bad headache. I had a funny turn in the shop, so your daddy said I could lie down for a little bit. I'll be better soon.'

For a couple of minutes the child said nothing, and she was aware of how loud his breathing was, and the strange smell of the room: of damp in the walls and dust, curry powder and laundry liquid. She gradually realized that something was happening on the other side of the door; there were raised voices and then a bang, as if a fist had pounded against something: a shelf maybe, or a table. The child jumped and his breathing sped up. He gave a little whimper.

'He's been here before,' he said. 'I saw him.'

'Who has?' she asked.

'The bad man,' he whispered.

She forced herself to sit up, swing her legs round. She pressed her hand against her forehead; her skull felt as if it was being crushed in a vice. The child had disappeared into the darkness. She stood and swayed; the floor lurched like the deck of a ship; nausea threatened to overwhelm her. She squinted towards the door and saw Dev standing, peering through the chink, his hair haloed by the light.

Whoever was on the other side was shouting and there was a loud crash and the sound of hundreds of cans falling, of glass shattering. She forced herself to walk over to Dev. The yelling and swearing grew louder. She gripped the boy's thin shoulders and tried to pull him away from the door. He resisted. She looked around, but there was no other way out of this room. Arjun was asking whoever was with him to leave; he said he would call the police. She tried again to get Dev away, but he grabbed hold of a shelf and she thought it might topple, or he would cry out and give them away. Instead she hugged him closer to her; she could feel the beat of his racing heart, the tremor in his body.

Through the crack in the door, she could see a man. He was large, well over six foot tall, and broad. He was dressed in black. He had a tattoo, like a blurred tear on one side of his face, and his head was shaved. He was shouting at Arjun, destroying his shop, overturning shelves and smashing bottles. Each time something crashed on the floor or was hurled against the walls, she and the child flinched. And then he stopped. He looked towards them. She shrank back, still gripping the boy.

Someone, barely inches away from her, on the other side of the door, spoke. His voice was thin, reedy, almost refined. The man with the tattoo was listening to him. His chest was heaving, but he'd stopped tipping over the shelves. The other man continued to speak in a low and soothing tone. It was going to be okay, she thought, they would leave.

'Now, Mr Kumar, I don't like my people to be unhappy, but equally we cannot let this slide, can we?' he said.

She should phone the police, she thought, she ought to take this chance before anything worse happened. She let go of the boy. Her mobile had been in her rucksack, but she didn't know where Arjun had put it. She hoped he'd brought it in here and he hadn't left it out there. She went back to the camp bed in the corner and ran her hands over the floor. She felt grit and dust beneath her fingertips, but she couldn't see or feel her bag.

The man with the soft voice was still speaking to Arjun, but she was too far away to make out the words. She crouched on the camp bed and felt the strap of her rucksack. It had fallen down the back and was wedged between the metal frame and the wall. She pulled it up and rummaged inside for her phone, but she couldn't find it. She glanced over her shoulder and saw the outline of the child. He was too close to the door. Frantically she searched again, and then tipped the contents onto Dev's Spider-Man duvet. It was there, she'd got it! She switched the phone to mute, so the men wouldn't hear the click of the keys, and started to dial.

There was a sickening thud, like the sound of a cricket bat hitting a watermelon, and Arjun screamed. The boy gave a cry. She ran to him, her fingers slipping from her phone. But she was too late.

The man on the other side of the door had heard him. Or maybe he had known the boy was there the entire time. She saw his arm – he was wearing an expensive navy suit and a white shirt with gold cufflinks – shoot through the gap in the door. He seized the child by the hair and pulled him into the newsagent's. And in that brief moment, as the door swung open and shut, she glimpsed the expression on his face, and she saw the knife.

EMMA

It's as if we've stepped into a Constable painting, a bucolic vision of England. There's a single oak ahead of us in the heart of the valley; the grass is lime-green and the steep sides of the Cotswold escarpment are covered in dense woodland. Even though it's May, the sky is shale-grey; there's a brooding mass of clouds on the horizon.

'We could have parked right there! Why did you make us walk all this way?' Ava whines.

'Because you'll appreciate it even more,' says Jack.

Stella snorts. 'Yeah, like anyone but you is going to "appreciate" a mouldering old church.'

'It's so creepy. I don't like it,' Ava says.

I have to admit, the lowering sky and the dark green of the trees surrounding us make me feel a bit hemmed in.

'I've been bitten!' she shrieks and jumps about, slapping at her ankles.

'I did see a horsefly back there,' I say.

'It's probably nothing. Just a scratch,' says Jack.

'Let me have a look.' I turn Ava's slim calf in my hands.

Sure enough, there's a large red lump starting to form above her ankle bone.

'Don't worry, I've got some ointment,' I say, sliding my backpack off my shoulders.

Stella rolls her eyes.

'Of course,' says Jack, 'your mum is prepared for anything. Break a leg, and she'll wrap you in her space-blanket while we wait for mountain rescue on speed-dial.'

'You're kidding, right?' says Stella. 'A *space*-blanket.'

'I do have a space-blanket, as it happens. You never know when you might need one . . .' I rub antihistamine into Ava's leg and she stops whimpering. 'It's so light, it would be stupid not to bring it.'

'I told you,' says Jack.

'Oh my God, you are insane.'

'We could use it to fly to the moon,' says Ava.

'Jesus, Mum, the Taliban carry those things to stop the US spying on them with thermal cameras,' says Stella.

'Multi-purpose,' murmurs my husband.

I finish putting away my first-aid kit. Ahead of us are a tiny stream and the remains of an old bridge.

'Look! The people who once owned this place probably swept down here in their coach and horses, right over that bridge and up to the big house,' I say brightly.

'Like, that's even interesting,' says Stella.

There's a sign saying the ruined bridge is unsafe. A round, stone ball lies to one side, as if it has tumbled from the crumbling turrets. It's now half-obscured by long grass. There's a cowpat next to it. We head to the right; buttery-coloured Cotswold stones poke through the soil.

I start singing 'Follow the Yellow Brick Road'.

'Spare me,' mutters Jack under his breath, striding ahead of us. He's smiling, though.

Ava joins in with the chorus, and we keep singing and she forgets to moan as the hill curves steeply upwards.

I don't have my husband's strength or resilience in the face of concerted opposition: I would never have managed to drag a fourteen-year-old and an eleven-year-old out of the house when they'd much rather be Snapchatting (Stella) or practising ballet (Ava). So I'm pleased Jack's cheerily ignored any opposition to his plans, as he normally does, even if it means visiting yet another church. We haven't been to see this one in a while, but sadly there's no cafe nearby that the girls and I can escape to.

I'm out of breath. I really should lose some weight, I think, as I always do when Jack is marching us up some hill. He's as fit as a flea. He goes to a posh gym in town and does kettlebells and something called HIIT in his lunch hour.

At the top, there's a mansion that a family actually lives in, rather than opening it up to the public and allowing the whole world to traipse through the living room to raise money to repair the roof, plus a walled garden with stables and greenhouses that are also off-limits. The church is open but to reach it you have to walk round in a loop and double-back to give the owners a modicum of privacy. I get distracted by a lily pool and stop to take some photos on my phone. It's surprisingly dark: there's a thick hedge behind me, and beech trees overhead. I imagine this must have led to the main driveway for the house at one time. I lean over the fence, the metal cold against my stomach, and try and get a water lily to fill the frame in my camera. When I finally manage to take a halfway decent photo, I look up, ready to show Ava.

She's gone. I can't hear her or Stella and Jack, either. There's the faint smell of horses and leather. It's silent. It appears darker than before. The first spot of rain hits my cheek. I look round, but the narrow path is empty of walkers or my family.

I start jogging and call out, 'Ava? Stella?'

I still can't see them. The path grows narrower, the trees tower over me and it's impossible to see over the hedge. Shrubs encroach. Something snaps across my face, stinging my cheek. I cry out. It's a branch. I feel as if I'm in a tunnel. I run faster. A black shape explodes out of the bushes and I jump back. It's a blackbird, disappearing into the wood in a flurry of feathers. I can't breathe. There's no sign of them, no sign that anyone else even passed this way.

I start screaming their names, over and over, the names of my family, my loved ones, the people I cannot live without. My heart is beating so hard it's painful.

I must have missed the turn for the church, because now I'm on a wide driveway flanked by those giant beech trees, last year's masts crunching beneath my feet, and the house is behind me, the windows shuttered against tourists. There's still no one else around. No walkers. No one appears at the window. I can't stop shouting; the silence will choke me. I feel as if my chest is in a giant vice that's squeezing my ribs. I run to a fence and look down into the valley. There's a girl on horseback a long way below me. She isn't even aware that I'm up here, shouting for help. The path twists to the left, away from the fields, and disappears into a dark thicket of laurels. Is that where they are? I'm frozen. I don't know where to search next, what to do.

And then Jack is running towards me. He puts one hand on my shoulder and looks straight into my eyes.

'Take it easy. Deep breath. In. We're all here. We're safe. Breathe out.'

I see the girls peeking round a trellis draped with pink tea roses. Their faces are white. They're fine, though, just as Jack said they were.

Once I've stopped hyperventilating, Jack folds me in his arms.

'We were inside the church,' he murmurs in my ear. 'You know I'd never let anything happen to them, don't you?'

I nod, and pull away. Ava comes and flings her arms around my waist.

'Are you all right, Mum? I'm sorry, I shouldn't have left you. I thought you saw . . .'

'It's okay,' I say. 'It's my fault, not yours. I should have kept up.'

Stella scowls at me. 'You screamed the whole bloody place down,' she says and stalks away.

It's obvious, now, where the path to the church was. I wipe a sheen of cold sweat from my forehead and hold Jack's hand tightly. I swallow uncomfortably and take a sip of water from the bottle I've brought with me.

The tiny church is cool, almost cold. I sit on a pew to try and pull myself together, while Jack strides about, pointing out features to Ava. I think she was humouring him, but now she's actually interested.

'It dates back to the twelfth century, but there was a pagan site here even before then. The whole church is in the shape of a cross. Take a look at the turret.'

'Oh! It's a hexagon,' she says, peering up into the rafters.

Someone has put vases full of roses next to the nave and their sweet, spicy scent fills the air. I try and keep my anxiety under control, but occasionally, particularly when I'm in unfamiliar places, it bubbles to the surface. I'd like to appear strong and unflappable for the girls, and sometimes I manage. The stained-glass windows are exquisite: Christ stands in a sea of white lilies, the bloodless marks where the nails were driven into his feet are tear-shaped.

'You always ruin everything,' hisses Stella. 'We're not little kids any more. You don't have to freak out when you can't see us for thirty fucking seconds.'

'Stella!' says Jack, pausing from his monologue. 'I don't want to hear you speak to your mum like that.'

Stella storms out of the church. I jump as the door cracks against the thousand-year-old stone frame. Jack follows her. Ava comes and curls into my side and I put my arm round her and tuck her soft blonde-haired head beneath my chin. Thank goodness for one sunny child who hasn't yet hit puberty.

STELLA

I'm standing by a stone angel when Dad comes out of the church. He has that look – his Dr Seuss expression. He really wants to bollock me, but he can't. He has to access his inner psychologist and work out how to 'connect' with a stroppy teenager, so I'll feel 'heard', but will be put in my place. Dad is quietly spoken, but that can actually be quite frightening. The angrier he gets, the softer his voice goes, until he snaps. It's only happened twice and it was terrifying. Both times it was about Mum. He's so uber-protective of her.

'Look,' I say, 'have you seen this headstone?'

Sometimes distraction can work, especially if you act like you're interested in all this historical shit. The headstone is an angel, a weird one, though. She's a young girl, really realistic, and she's got a stone star on her forehead. She's looking at the ground and pointing at the sky. The angel's about the same height as me. Perhaps it's the grave of a girl who died when she was my age. That makes me feel a bit strange, so I don't look at the inscription. She's covered in orange-and-white lichen. It's kind of cool, I guess, although the last place I want to be on a Sunday afternoon is a Norman bloody churchyard with my dad.

Dad puts his hands in his pockets and rocks backwards and forwards on his toes. He makes his face go all sympathetic.

'Go easy on your mum, sweetheart. She only acts like that because she cares about you.'

'She's just nuts,' I say.

He sighs, and looks up at the sky. It's gone an even darker grey. Why isn't there a cafe here? It's going to tip down, and I want a hot chocolate.

'She gets anxious at times, you know that. It's how she is.'

'Yeah,' I say. 'The accident.' Like I haven't heard it all before.

'It's not only that,' he says sharply.

'No?' I say.

Out of the corner of my eye, I see Ava coming towards us. I start counting: one, two, three, four . . . Mum bursts out of the church. It's probably a record. She won't let Ava out of her sight for a second now. The next couple of days are going to be a nightmare.

'Well, what then?' I ask. I want him to hurry up before Ava gets here.

'I don't know,' he says. I look at him sharply. Dad never says he doesn't know anything. He takes a breath. 'Something else. She won't talk about it.'

Mum wanders over to a headstone with carved flowers round it and acts likes she finds it fascinating.

'Then how do you know?' I say.

Ava leaps towards Dad and he catches her and spins her round, as if she weighs nothing instead of being a big lump of a girl, and she does that ballet-thing I detest, where she kicks her legs out and points her toes, like she's in *Sleeping* bloody *Beauty* and Dad is the handsome prince and she's in some pink frilly fucking tutu, instead of jeggings and Togz. She isn't really a lump. She's got those skinny-muscly dancers' legs. He puts her down and they hold hands. Dad doesn't hold my hand any more. Not that I want him to.

'Anyhow,' he says, turning back to me, 'while you're both here, there's something I want to tell you. It's a secret. Please don't say anything to your mum.'

Ava immediately jumps up and down with excitement.

'It's our fifteenth wedding anniversary in August. I'm going to hold a surprise party to celebrate. It'll be small – friends and family. Maybe in the garden. We'll get a marquee.'

He looks pleased with himself. By 'family' he means, Grossvater and Oma. No one from Mum's side.

'Yessss!' stage-whispers Ava. 'Will we have a giant cake? Can we have new dresses?'

'Yes and yes,' he says, and raises one eyebrow at me, because he knows there's no way on God's green earth I'll wear some fancy fucking dress.

The heavens literally open at that point. Mum pulls her hood up and comes running over to us, calling, 'Shall we go somewhere and have a hot chocolate?'

'Mum, we're in the middle of fucking nowhere.'

'A pub then,' she says cheerily and smiles at me, pretending I haven't sworn at her. 'I'll find one.'

And the thing is, I know she will.

LIZZIE

'Do you think we'll manage them all?'

The metal frame of their thirty-year-old backpack creaked as Paul adjusted the straps. She ran through their names in her mind: Pavey Ark, Thunacar Knott, Pike of Stickle, Loft Crag, Harrison Stickle – the five Langdale Pikes. If they even managed a couple of these hills, they'd be doing well.

'You never know. He might fall asleep. Yes, I'm talking about you, Pumpkin,' said Lizzie, taking Dylan's podgy hand and smiling up at her son.

He leaned over the top of the backpack, giving a gummy grin, drooling and kicking his legs with excitement.

'Might be a bit cold for the lad,' said Paul, looking at the darkening sky.

'Don't fuss. He's wrapped up warm,' Lizzie said. 'We'll see how we get on.'

They'd taken the path directly behind the back of the Sticklebarn pub, where Paul worked part-time at the weekends, past the gold blaze of larches in Raven Crag, and now they were heading along the ridge, with Dungeon Ghyll roaring below them.

'Bloody hell, he's quite a weight now, isn't he?' said Paul. 'He must have put on a few pounds since last week. Or is it all the other nonsense you've stuffed down behind him?'

'The "other nonsense" is our lunch and the waterproofs, and I've got them in my rucksack. You're such a lightweight.'

Lizzie inhaled deeply. The air smelt of peat and ice, sheep and moss. It was good to be out of the cottage. It came with Paul's other job as a ranger, and they were bloody lucky to have it, but it was cold. The windows were small, built in the 1600s when glass was costly, and it was gloomy. She took Dylan out in the backpack every day – sometimes they climbed up one of the pikes, or hiked across the Fell to meet Paul – but her son was growing heavy and she couldn't carry him as far any more. And although she loved living here, a stone's throw from the Cumbrian Way, and near enough to her parents and Paul's to get help if they needed it, she was still adjusting. Not that long ago, both of them had been students at Leeds University. Sometimes the quiet and the loneliness of being with a small baby every day got to her. She didn't want to admit it to Paul, but it was one of the reasons why she was looking forward to starting her new job. She was determined to finish her degree, though – but that too was a struggle, trying to write her final dissertation and revise for her exams, every time Dylan napped.

'Busman's holiday for you,' Lizzie said, 'spending your Sunday out here.'

Paul was repairing part of the path at the top of Loft Crag and he was up and down the ridge several times a week.

'Aye, but it's a treat to be out here with my wife,' he said, giving her one of his long, slow smiles.

They still felt self-conscious and delighted about calling each other Husband and Wife.

'Trust you to be up the duff on your wedding day,' her sister, Julia, had said, mocking her affectionately, but even though it had all happened much faster than they'd planned, and they were constantly worried about money, Lizzie had never been happier.

The tops of the hills were shrouded in mist and there was a dampness in the air, as if it might rain. The grass was interwoven with dead blond stalks, the lower slopes swathed with bracken the colour of rust and dotted with gorse, sprinkled with brilliant-yellow blossom.

'How's the pumpkin?'

Dylan had fallen asleep, one of his fat cheeks resting against the frame, a little bubble of spit balanced between his lips. He looked like a chubby cherub. Lizzie took the opportunity to put his gloves back on – Dylan always pulled them off – and tuck a blanket around him. He was already in an all-in-one with a woolly hat, but he could cool down quickly. Lizzie teased Paul about his caution when it came to hiking with their baby son, but she knew how fast the weather could change out here, and how easy it would be to get lost.

'Out for the count. Let's have a cup of tea at the top of the Pike; we can always cut back down Thorn Crag, if we need to,' she said, and Paul nodded, glancing up at the clouds again.

She loved the way it was like another world up here, bare granite poking through the thin skin of soil. On a clear day you could see ridge after ridge of mountains, and all the way to Scarborough Bay. Paul sat down carefully next to the cairn at the top, so he wouldn't wake Dylan, and Lizzie poured them tea from her flask and opened a packet of Tunnock's.

'Are you worried?'

'Aye,' he sighed. 'But I should be asking you that.'

'I'll be all right,' she said.

'Tough as old boots, you are,' he said, smiling at her. 'I wish you didn't have to go.'

'Me too,' she said. 'I'll miss this.' She nodded at the thick mist, swirling round the summit.

They didn't have enough to live on – Paul was working two part-time jobs, as a ranger and a bar-keeper for the National Trust, and was volunteering as often as he could, while they waited for a full-time position to come up. There was nothing here that Lizzie could do, particularly with an unfinished degree; most of the casual work was seasonal, so there wouldn't be anything until the spring when the tourists came back. She was about to start a job in Ikea in Leeds, but it was too far to commute, so it meant she'd be away from home for three days a week, and Paul and his mum would have to look after Dylan between them.

'I'll miss you,' said Paul.

'I'll miss both of you,' she said, kissing him. 'But it's not for long. I'll be home before you know it.'

'What time's the bus?'

'You've a brain like a sieve,' she said. 'I've told you a million times. Thirteen minutes past six. I couldn't get one early enough on Monday morning.'

'Aye, you did tell me, right enough.'

'Let's not spoil today, eh?'

For a few moments the mist cleared, and a small patch of blue sky appeared.

'Not bad for October,' said Lizzie, pulling Paul to his feet.

'Race you to the top of Harrison Stickle,' he said, grinning at his wife.

EMMA

Katie's in a state when she arrives at work.

'Nate's off sick, and today's the first delivery.' She stands in the doorway, her hands on her ample hips, her frizzy curls escaping from beneath a scarf patterned with sunflowers. Her fluorescent-pink Crocs are covered in Disney princess shoe-charms. 'He's texted to say he has flu,' she spits out, as if Nate's malingering.

Although she looks as if she might explode with rage, I know she's trying not to show that she's nervous. And it is a big deal – we're starting a new contract with the National Trust today. The guys have been baking since 4.30 a.m. yesterday.

'I'll do it,' I say. 'I'm insured to drive the van.'

I wipe my hands on a tea towel and start taking off my apron.

'Really? You're an angel, Emma.'

'It's all loaded, you're set to go,' says Harry, tossing me the keys. 'Want me to . . .?' he nods at the boxes of dough at my station, ready to be weighed and put in bannetons to prove.

'Thanks, lovely,' I say.

Harry is thin as a whippet, but he's got the strongest hands of anyone I know and he's the best baker Katie has. My sourdough will be in good shape.

I shiver as I leave the warmth of the ovens. It's 5.30 a.m. and it's not quite light. There's a thin band of cream silhouetting the cranes that hover over the half-built office blocks in the city centre. I head along the river, below an arc of houses that will be bright as jewels when the sun comes up. I hate driving when it's busy, but at this time of day the roads are nearly empty. I switch the station from Ujima to Radio 2. The van still smells faintly of Nate, of rolling tobacco and that distinctive odour of young man – testosterone and fresh sweat; the passenger seat is littered with Pukka Pie wrappers and takeaway coffee cups. I swerve over to a bin and chuck the lot in.

My heart feels too large for my chest; my pulse is erratic. It's as if there's something in my throat and it catches my breath. It's always like this after a panic attack: it takes me a couple of days to return to my normal self. At least I know what it is and how to deal with it, I think, as I count my breath in and exhale for two, three, four, five – as my therapist taught me – and don't panic even more, believing I'm having a heart attack. 'Don't let it control you,' he'd said.

Now, without Nate's rubbish in the van, I inhale the smell of freshly baked bread, hot and yeasty, and once I've taken a few deep breaths, I sing along to 'Rumour Has It'. I drive back the way I came this morning – Jack keeps suggesting I cycle to work, and I can see why: there's a path most of the way along the Avon and, at this time of the day, it's beautiful; the river is still, and seagulls fall above it, like flecks of confetti. But there's hardly anyone else around and there's no escape off that path, save into the sludge-coloured water. The thought of it, narrow and dark and fenced in, makes me hyperventilate again. I wind the window down and pass the turning to Long Ashton, where we live. I think of Jack and my two girls, still sleeping, tucked up in bed, and I draw comfort in knowing they're safe.

Tyntesfield is a Gothic mansion with a private chapel – another of Jack's favourites – but perhaps because it's so close to our house, we haven't been for a while. I'd forgotten how long the driveway is. It plunges steeply downhill; the rising sun gilds the trees that flank it, so that the leaves look as if they've been cast in bronze. It's going to be a beautiful day.

The main cafe is in a converted cowshed, and I unload the trays of sourdough loaves, and a selection of Katie's signature cakes: chocolate-orange brownies, marmalade-and-coconut polenta, Amaretto-and-raspberry Bakewell tart and gin-and-tonic sponge. Katie loves her cocktails, so there's always something booze-soaked on the menu.

'Do you mind dropping the rest of it off at the Pavilion?' asks the woman who's helping me.

I wonder why she sounds apologetic, and then I remember. There's another tiny cafe but it's at the far end of the estate, past the house and down by a walled vegetable garden. It's at least a mile or two away.

'No problem,' I say, smiling at her.

'Thanks, love. Do you know your way?'

'I think so,' I say. 'Back the way I came and then follow the estate road round?'

She nods and laughs as my stomach rumbles. 'Make sure they give you a cup of tea and a slice of toast when you get there.'

The road swings behind an ornamental rose garden and the mansion, before cutting through a wood. I notice a couple of cottages tucked away – presumably they were once for the workers but now, no doubt, the National Trust has rented them out as holiday homes at extortionate rates. The back of the Pavilion cafe looks out over fields full of cows, and I remember the ha-ha running in front of the mansion, and how Ava and I would leap backwards and forwards over it, shouting 'Ha-ha! Ha-HA!' until we were laughing properly. It must have been two or three years since we were last here. Even then, Stella would never have deigned to join in.

———

I sip my complimentary cup of tea and stand in front of the Pavilion cafe, enjoying the early-morning sunshine. *Kate's*, the bakery where I work, is in a tunnel under the train station and there's no natural light, so on my breaks I sit outside, even if it's raining, and watch people rushing into Temple Meads, their faces furrowed with tension, dragging suitcases behind them. The traffic and the trains are loud, and the cafe at the front of the bakery is always packed. I like being surrounded by people – it feels safe – but sometimes it's good to stop, to pause.

A robin sings surprisingly loudly from behind my shoulder, and black calves jostle at a water trough. I take a last sip of my tea and think about the thick slab of buttered sourdough toast waiting for me back at the bakery. Caleb, our chef, will fry me up some bacon, if I'm lucky. I'm about to leave, when I realize I'm not alone. The two young men prepping for the day are still inside, but there's someone else out here.

I saw a shadow pass across the windows of the orangery, I'm sure of it. I feel the muscles around my shoulder blades lock. I take a couple of steps forward. It's too early for visitors to be allowed in or for anyone to have started work in the gardens – it's barely light. The orangery is cloudy with condensation, the lemon trees inside are indistinct shapes against the glass. Perhaps I imagined it. I realize I'm holding my breath and I let it out in a whoosh. My mouth tastes of tea. I set my china mug down on a bench and walk a little way along the path. It's nothing to be concerned about, I tell myself. I just want to check I'm not seeing things.

I'm safe, I am safe, it's safe here, I repeat to myself.

I shrug my shoulders, releasing the tension, and feel the knots in my back grate against one another.

I'm about to go when I see him. He's in the cut-flower garden, walking slowly past the beds, which are ablaze with dahlias. *No one I need to worry about, only a man looking at a peony.* But my guts feel as if they're being ripped out. I struggle to inhale. I know this man, I'm sure of it. He's above average height with square shoulders; he's broad, craggy. I can almost feel his hands against my skin. He half-turns and bends towards a dahlia – it's a ball of spikes, pale pink and sea-green, like a sea urchin – and a shaft of sunlight catches his face and I have to shut my eyes because I think I'm going to fall to my knees.

It's Paul – Paul Bradshaw. I can't be sure – he's several metres away, and now he's hidden by a trellis heavy with clematis – but my body knows. I'm certain it's him. I stand for a moment longer and watch as he walks into the shadows. *It can't be*, I think. The last time I saw him was sixteen, nearly seventeen years ago. He might have changed. He must have changed. I know I have. I'm imagining things; a kind of hallucination brought on by my panic attack, because why on earth would Paul Bradshaw be here, outside a Gothic mansion on the outskirts of Bristol?

Now he's barely discernible in the long shadows cast by the low sun and it takes all my willpower not to run after him. Not to call his name and take his face between my palms and look into his eyes once more . . . I suddenly think of Lizzie Bradshaw too, with her wild, auburn curls blowing in a gust of wind, laughing and waving like the carefree girl she once was. I close my eyes and push away the memory because guilt sears through me, as livid and painful as if it had happened yesterday. When I open my eyes, the man has disappeared. I run back to the van, forgetting to give the guys in the cafe my empty mug, shove the plastic trays back in the van and drive away, as fast as I can on this narrow road, with its sharp bends and pools of light and dark that momentarily blind me.

LIZZIE

Lizzie took out her textbooks and notes. The bus was almost empty and she could spread out her work on the seat next to her. She was writing a dissertation on *Renewable Energy? The Environmental Impact and Sustainability of Electricity Generated by Nuclear-Power Stations, using the proposed Moorside power plant as a case study.* It was hard trying to finish the course without the support of the other students and her lecturers, but she was determined to get a good mark. She had a provisional place at Lancaster University to do a Masters in Environmental Science. She hoped she could finish her degree and save up enough money to be able to start in a year. And focusing on her coursework took her mind off leaving her new husband and six-month-old baby.

It was dark outside. If she leaned her head against the window, she could just make out the stone walls that followed the line of the road and bisected the fields beyond. Paul had crushed her in his arms before she left, and then she'd picked up Dylan and cuddled him. The baby had been excited, waving his fists and kicking his legs at her.

'Hey, look, his bottom teeth have come through!' she'd said, showing Paul the little white serrated edges.

'Thank God for that – I might get some sleep, if he's stopped teething.'

'Only eighteen more to go,' she'd said. 'Don't let your mum put whiskey on his gums.'

'As if! I'm going to need it.'

She'd taken a last look round their cottage. There were some rowan berries and dried sedges in a jam jar on the table; a burnt-orange throw over the lumpy sofa, a bookcase by the fireplace made out of scaffolding planks and bricks, and a misshapen oak basket that Julia had made them on a course she'd done, which was filled with charity-shop toys. It was as homely as she could make it.

She'd given Dylan a last kiss on his soft cheek and wrinkled up her nose.

'Think he needs a nappy change,' she'd laughed, handing the baby to Paul and giving her husband one more kiss goodbye.

Were they doing the right thing? Dylan was still so little. Her eyes welled up with tears. She rubbed them away. 'Beggars can't be choosers,' her mother – ever the pragmatist – had said, when she'd talked about it with her.

Dylan would be fine. Paul was brilliant with him, and his mum would pop over when she could. And she would be home again on Wednesday night. *It will fly by*, Lizzie told herself and turned back to her textbooks.

It was late by the time she'd got to Leeds, changed buses and reached Belle Isle. It hadn't looked too bad on the map – the suburb was only a short bus journey away from Ikea and it wasn't far from Middleton Park, so at least she'd have some open space to walk through, if she had any time off – but when she arrived, the dark streets, with gangs of youths loitering on the corners, gave her the creeps. Still, Leeds was so expensive, if she was going to save any money at all, then subletting a room here was the only way she was going to manage. She kept her head down, thankful that she was good with maps and had memorized the hand-drawn one Miriam had done for her and she didn't have to scrutinize it on the way. It would have made her stand out.

'Hey, you!' said Miriam, opening the door. 'You got here okay!'

Lizzie did a double-take. 'Wow!'

Miriam grinned and pulled her inside. 'Do you like it?'

'You look fantastic,' she said, trying to sound enthusiastic. She'd never really given a toss about appearances.

The hall light was stark; there was no shade. Miriam twisted beneath it, sending shadows spilling across the once-white walls to show off her new hairstyle. Her dull brown and limp hair was as shiny as silk, and bright blonde. Miriam had a heart-shaped face with a sprinkling of freckles and grey eyes, the same colour as Lizzie's, but hers were larger and further apart and she didn't have to wear glasses, either. She and Lizzie had always been the same height and build when they were growing up, but recently Miriam had grown curvier. When she hugged her, Lizzie felt hard and bony in her friend's embrace.

'Come on,' she said, tugging, Lizzie's hand. 'Girls, Lizzie; Lizzie, girls,' and she waved a hand at the four young women watching TV in the dark in the lounge, the blue light of the screen flickering over their faces.

They barely looked up. Miriam had told her that three of them were student nurses and the other one – Gillian, she remembered her name now – worked at Toys R Us.

'Probably tired,' Lizzie said quietly.

'Just rude,' Miriam whispered, making a face behind their backs.

As she followed Miriam up the stairs, she did a quick count – four bedrooms, six women. At least she was only here for three nights a week.

'Never knowingly separated from your backpack,' Miriam teased her as she unlocked the door to her room.

'You know me,' said Lizzie, sliding the bag off her shoulders with relief. They'd been best friends for years. Lizzie had grown up on the Bolton Abbey estate and Miriam had lived in one of the tithe cottages with her mum and her sister. They'd spent their weekends rambling around the countryside – although that had turned into drinking Thunderbird in one of the empty car parks with the local lads, in their late teens.

Lizzie's dad was the head ranger on the estate and her mum was a cook in the restaurant. As soon as she was old enough she'd started working there, too – selling ice cream out of a van, before graduating to waitressing. Miriam had joined her on Saturdays and in the summer holidays. Lizzie had been relieved when she'd turned sixteen and had finally been able to join her dad's team. By the time she was eighteen she could fell a tree with a chainsaw more efficiently than any of the lads. When Lizzie went to university, Miriam had stayed in Bolton Abbey, working full-time in the restaurant with Beth, Lizzie's mum.

'This is yours,' Miriam said, pointing to a mattress on the floor. 'Sorry. It's all I could get off the landlord. The bedside table is yours, too, and this bit of the wardrobe.' She opened the door to indicate a narrow gap at the end of the rail and two bare shelves.

'It'll be like camping,' Lizzie said. 'I've brought my sleeping bag.'

'Yeah, don't leave your walking shoes lying around, okay? I know how bad they smell.'

'They do not!' said Lizzie.

'Remember that time we camped in your garden and we used a sheet for the tent?'

'Yeah and the tent poles were the hazel sticks holding up Dad's runner beans? He was furious.'

'The tent *and* the beans collapsed,' said Miriam with a grin.

'What's with all the new clothes?' Lizzie nodded towards the wardrobe.

'I can wear what I like at work, as long as it's black,' Miriam shrugged. 'And it's not like I need my North Face gear at the moment, is it?' Miriam had recently started working in the Slug and Lettuce in Leeds city centre as an assistant manager. She eyed the space she'd left for Lizzie. 'You won't need much room, will you? Just somewhere to hang up that hideous uniform of yours,' she smirked. 'By the way, Gillian is a right cow; you want to keep on her good side. She won't let you use as much as a teabag. There's sticky labels in the kitchen to put on your food. What else do I need to tell you? Payphone's in the hall, and you chip in for the utilities – a sixth of all the bills.'

Lizzie was going to protest – she was here for less than half the week – but decided not to. Miriam was doing her a favour, letting her share her room.

'Here's a set of keys. Come down when you're ready. You can borrow our "communal" milk to make a cup of tea,' she said, miming quotation marks. 'Just don't tell Gillian,' she added, winking. She turned to go and then spun back round and squeezed Lizzie's arm, her eyes wide, the lashes longer and blacker than they'd been last time Lizzie had seen her. 'It's so good to have you here,' she said breathily. 'It's going to be like old times – we can have a proper catch-up. I want to know how my godson is getting on,' she said.

'Yeah, sure,' Lizzie nodded and swallowed, her throat dry.

She wasn't used to feeling awkward with Miriam. But it had been odd, coming home from university in the holidays and finding Miriam there; she spent more time with her mum, and seemed to get on better with her, than Lizzie did. Bringing Paul with her was even stranger, like she needed Miriam's approval as well as her parents'; it had felt as if Lizzie had been the visitor and it was Miriam's house. Not that she needed to worry – Paul and Miriam got on like a house on fire, and Miriam adored Dylan. She'd still been living in Bolton Abbey when Lizzie and Paul had last visited with their son – when was that? Barely a month ago, but they'd hardly seen her, as she'd been working double-shifts in the restaurant over the bank-holiday weekend. Maybe now Miriam had finally left Bolton Abbey, their friendship would get back on track, she thought.

It didn't take her long to unpack – she'd only brought one new outfit and her Ikea uniform: which was a horrid yellow and blue. She hung it next to Miriam's black pencil skirts and fitted blouses. Her eyes filled with tears. She missed Paul and Dylan so much already.

EMMA

Harry is folding malted sourdough, the mixture squeezing between his fingers, which are bright with thick silver rings. Muscles, thin as climbing rope, jump in his forearms. He has tattoos that run like sleeves, from his wrist bones to his shoulder blades. You can see them curving – roses and water lilies and the soft brush of feathers – round his scapula when he wears a vest. I'm making focaccia for the weekend, pressing garlic cloves into the silken dough. I scatter rosemary leaves, the smell clean and sharp in my nostrils, sea salt and shavings of lemon zest over the bread, before I finish it off with some olive oil, the colour of old gold. The salty citrus scent reminds me of our last holiday to Corsica. I think we'll manage another two, maybe three holidays as a family before Stella opts out. The thought makes me feel as if I've tried to swallow an ice cube and it's got stuck. I finish the last batch and slide the trays into the oven.

There's a lull in the early morning, after the commuters have left and before the mums and babies and the railway staff arrive for their elevenses. I make myself a cup of tea and swipe a broken blondie from the back counter. I sit on the stone steps outside and tip my head up to the sun; letting the breeze cool my skin. I can feel sweat trickling down my back; stray hairs are stuck to the nape of my neck. I love the warmth of the bakery.

Harry joins me, holding a mug of black coffee.

'You okay?' he asks, as he takes out his Rizlas and lighter.

'Yes, why?' I ask, looking at the wrought-iron staircase up to the station, which is silhouetted against the pale blue of the sky.

'Just been a bit quiet, is all,' he says, licking the paper and tweezing a flake of tobacco from his lips.

'Katie's loud enough for several of us,' I say, and he snorts in agreement.

'Tell me about it. You know when she's in the building.'

I'm not, though. I'm not all right. I can't get the image of the man in the garden out of my head. Katie has sorted out a rota to cover Nate, so I haven't been back to Tyntesfield, but the thought that it could have been Paul Bradshaw nags at me. I don't understand why he would be here, though; it's the last place I'd expect to find Paul. I can't help wondering if I'm going mad. I mean, he's always at the back of my mind, somewhere, but I'm better when I don't dwell on him. My therapist taught me some CBT techniques that help with, as he put it, 'unwanted thoughts'.

'I brought a baby coffee-tree in for Ava,' Harry says, blowing a thin stream of smoke out of the corner of his mouth. 'You know, for her project.'

'That's sweet of you, thanks.'

Harry keeps coffee-plants in his bedroom and does a double-shift on Fridays at the coffee-roasters that supplies *Kate's*. When I told him Ava was doing crop lifecycles in Geography, he got excited and texted me a whole load of links to 'understorey cropping systems' – something to do with growing coffee in rainforests without chopping down the trees. Ava thought it was cool that toucans could eat the fruit and poop out the beans.

I bite into the blondie and feel the chunks of white chocolate melt and ooze over my tongue in a glorious burst of sweetness. Harry never eats the cakes we sell, which is probably why he's so skinny.

'Has Katie put me down for another delivery run?' I ask as casually as I can.

A cloud of pigeons wheel overhead and alight at our feet, scavenging for crumbs.

'She's hoping Nate will be back next week. Keeps saying he's got man-flu, like he's not really ill. You know what she's like.'

'It would be good if she planned ahead,' I say, furrowing my brow. Jack hates it when I do that. He smooths my forehead with his thumbs when he catches me. I have deep lines between my eyebrows; at a certain age, you get the face you deserve. 'I'll do Monday if he's not back.'

Harry nods, but as I finish my tea and get up to tidy my station before I leave for the day, I think, *It's Thursday and I can't wait that long.*

Not three whole days. And Nate will probably be better. But I could go to Tyntesfield after work and still be able to pick up the girls. If I'm quick.

I change out of my chef's black trousers and floury T-shirt into a wrap-dress and sandals. I let my hair down – it's long, blonde and falls in soft waves; with a pair of tortoiseshell-framed sunglasses, red lipstick and a cream scarf, I hope I'm unrecognizable as the woman who dropped off the bread at the beginning of the week. I always carry a spare change of clothes. Just in case. When I arrive at Tyntesfield, I head to the reception desk. I lean in and ask quietly if they have a new member of staff by any chance, a man called Paul Bradshaw? I'm assuming he does work here, because the person I saw was there far too early to have been a visitor. But then, I suppose, if you lived nearby you could get in anywhere at any time. Take a shortcut through the woods, for instance. I realize too late that the elderly man I've asked is a volunteer. He looks flustered.

'Do you know where he might work?' he booms.

I shake my head. I'm at a loss to know what Paul could be doing. 'On the estate, somewhere?' I say. His dad was – perhaps still is – a sheep farmer. 'Maybe with the cows?'

'Oh, we don't own them, my dear,' he says. 'We rent out those fields.'

I look round and catch the eye of a young woman selling tickets. My heart is beating hard and my palms are slick with sweat.

'Paul Bradshaw?' she says when she finishes handing out leaflets to a mum with a toddler and a baby in a buggy. 'Yes, he started a little while ago. Easter, I think it was. Can I help?'

I try and appear calm.

'He's . . . he's a friend,' I say.

'Do you want me to pass on a message?' she prompts.

She's only trying to be helpful, but I hadn't thought this far. I shake my head too vigorously.

'I don't want to disturb him. I might try and catch him later. Where does he work?'

'He's normally in the Kitchen Garden,' she says.

She's looking at me sceptically, as if weighing up why a married woman, clearly not dressed for a walk, is asking about a good-looking man in his mid-thirties. I can feel the blush blooming beneath my collar bone and spreading up my throat.

'Thank you,' I say.

I mean to leave, I really do; it's not safe for me to be here, asking these kinds of questions. Instead, I hand the woman behind the desk my Family National Trust pass. She scans the barcode and gives it back to me, not making eye contact. She's probably seen on the computer screen that I have two girls and a husband. I wonder if Paul is single. Perhaps it's the reason he moved here? I imagine Paul, hemmed in by those high stone walls in the vegetable plot. He's a man used to space and freedom. Surely he would hate it? So why is he here? It must be for a woman. And I stop myself, just in time, from thinking of the real reason why I am here, pursuing a ghost from the past.

The walk to the Kitchen Garden is long. I suppose the people who once lived in this mansion didn't want to see where their food came from, wishing it to appear magically on the table: lemon trees wheeled to the side of the dining room, pineapples conjured as centrepieces, without a whiff of the muck they were grown in. It's hot and I start to sweat. My thighs rub and small stones catch in my sandals. I should have brought a sunhat. I mentally add it to the list of items that need to be in my Just in Case bag in the car. The bobble that was holding my hair up is round my wrist. I take the elastic between two fingers, pull it away and let it snap back. I do this several times as I walk past the line of ornamental shrubs, pruned into spheres, like children's drawings of trees. The pain makes me flinch and peels the skin off my wrist, but it takes my mind off my thoughts. Another of the things my therapist taught me.

I hesitate when I reach the walled garden, but I can't bring myself to go in. Instead I buy a cup of tea and a piece of lavender shortbread from the Pavilion cafe and sit on the stone steps of the orangery in a small patch of shade. I let the chill seep into my bare skin and I take deep breaths, inhaling the honeyed scent of the lemon blossom. I've got to be brave, I tell myself. Besides, I haven't got much time before I need to pick up the girls. I force myself to walk through the cut-flower garden, where I saw Paul last week. In front of me are a couple of greenhouses, and to my right are long, thin outhouses that run along the edge of the walled vegetable plot.

There's someone working in the furthest greenhouse. I stand outside the nearest one, the taste of butter and lavender still in my mouth, inhaling the heady tide of citrus scent from the pelargonium blooming behind the glass. He's a dark and indistinct shape. There must be other gardeners here; it might not be him. I pull my scarf over my hair and duck my head. I walk quickly past and slip into a stone archway. I sit on a bench carved into the wall, in the shadows, half-hidden by a tree fern. I know it's him. I recognize the breadth of his back. He turns towards me and now I can see what he's doing. He's picking chillies. The way he moves is so familiar I can barely breathe. Slow, methodical, careful, and then a sudden flash of speed.

I remember him laying granite slabs in the Lake District, his hair standing on end in the wind, grinning like a lunatic, as he signalled the helicopter to make the drop. Then biting into the earth with his shovel, edging the stone into place; little by little, a path appearing at the top of a mountain. That is what I remember most about him: his strength, his joy, his patience. I squeeze my eyes tightly shut and snap the band at my wrist. But more memories come flooding back: of him coming home, glowing with satisfaction because he'd laid another metre of path that thousands of walkers would follow, his face gleaming with rain and sweat. I remember him kissing Lizzie, almost crushing her in his embrace; the way he cradled his baby son in his hands, tucking him into the crook of his elbow; how he smiled, slow and sure, his eyes crinkling at the corners. He was so alive, like a stag or an eagle, in his element in that wild windswept country. So what has happened that he should end up here, his shoulders stooped, picking minuscule chillies in hands more used to hefting pickaxes and hewing granite? And is it, I can hardly bring myself to voice this fear – is it my fault?

I want to touch one of those hands again. Slide my fingers between his. I immediately think of Lizzie and I push the thought away. I make myself get up, turn away. I have to fetch the girls. I can't be late. And I cannot let him see me. I trudge back up the hill, across the ha-ha, past the mansion and those bloody pollarded trees. I'm limping; blisters are forming on my heels and I'm trying not to cry. The main thing is to focus on the positives. How you think about an event determines how you feel, my therapist taught me. So what can I say about this?

These are the facts: Paul Bradshaw works here. I'm not mad, I wasn't imagining things. And now I know it was him, I must never, ever come back again.

STELLA

Me and Ava are sitting on a low wall outside school, waiting for Mum to pick us up. Well, I'm sitting on it. Ava is using it as a barre and doing stupid pirouettes and turning her feet out at weird angles. It's embarrassing to have to wait for your mum at my age, and be in charge of an annoying little sister. I keep telling Mum we should get the bus, but she says she likes picking us up. She finishes work at the bakery in the early afternoon, so she's got the time, not like most of the other mums, who work until five or later. She says it's why she took the job, even though she starts work 'horrendously early'.

At least it's sunny. I take out my copy of *Jane Eyre* and start to read it. We're studying it in English, which is brilliant, because it's my favourite book. I must have read it a billion times. I check my phone. It's not like Mum to be late. She's normally waiting for us; she's got this thing about it. All the clocks in our house are five minutes fast, so that Mum will arrive on time. If she goes anywhere with us, though, she never is, because we know the clocks are wrong. It used to stress me out when she got stressed, but now I don't care. She should grow up and chill out.

Ava's stopped humming Tchaikovsky, or whatever it is, and says, 'Has Dad said anything to you about the party?'

'What party?' I say, not looking up from my book.

'The secret anniversary party,' she says, doing a little plié and a bendy thing with her arm.

'Nope.'

'Do you know when we're going to get our new dresses? I can't wait!'

She starts humming again. I should leave it, but I can't resist.

'Why? Will yours be pink?'

'With sparkles!'

I make a disgusted sound.

'Maybe dark pink?' she says, and I feel bad when I hear the uncertainty in her voice. 'Dad might let you wear jeans,' she says kindly.

'I doubt it.'

'You can just get, like, posh jeans. Or a jumpsuit?'

I make a face. 'Ava, shut up about it, will you?'

'Mum's pretty late, isn't she?' she says, looking at her watch and sitting down next to me.

'She's probably stuck in traffic.' I get out my phone and check, in case there are any messages.

'Should we ring her?'

I want to tell Ava to be quiet, she's being ridiculous, but Mum has never been this late before to pick us up. In fact she's never been late, ever. I ring her but it goes straight to voicemail.

'She must be driving,' I say, trying not to sound worried.

Ava snuggles into me. I'm sure I wasn't this clingy at eleven. I push her away and go back to my book. I can't see the words, though, they dance about on the page. I ring again.

'Shall we call Dad?'

'No, he'd be annoyed. Anyway, he's doing some presentation thing today. He wouldn't be able to get us. Let's catch the bus.'

We're right by the bus stop. Mum always said we could wait inside the shelter if it was raining, but we've never had to.

'What if she comes, though?' asks Ava. 'While we're on the bus?' Her voice is going all anxious and high-pitched.

'Well, she should have been here to pick us up. Anyway, the bus will take ages to come. She might arrive while we're waiting.'

'But what if she doesn't?'

I look at the bus times and my brain feels fuzzy. The school bus has already left and the regular buses don't go to Long Ashton. We're going to have to change. I don't know which one we need, or where we're supposed to get off. I hesitate. Perhaps we should ring Dad. But he would be angry. He told me his presentation was important: it's a pitch to get a new client. I wonder about asking one of the people waiting, but there's only some older boys, mucking about, and I know they'll make fun of us and I'll go bright red. Ava is hopping from one leg to the other with worry, her face all crumpled up.

I google it and get a map showing which bus, when it arrives and where we need to change. I send the directions to myself and slump down on one of the seats. It's hot under the shelter, so I get up again and push Ava out ahead of me.

'There's a bus in thirteen minutes.'

'Will you text Mum and tell her?'

I sigh. It's going to take us an hour to get home. I'm starving – normally we'd be back by now, having peanut-butter and jam sandwiches with the bread Mum's brought from the bakery. On Saturdays she brings home a load of leftover cakes. I suppose I should tell her. She'll go mental if she turns up and we're not here. It's kind of ironic – I'm annoyed at her for not being here, but I wanted to get the bus. The school bus, though, not the one for old ladies and weirdos.

A couple of minutes later her car screeches to a halt in front of us and she gets out, nearly hitting another car with the door, and starts shouting and gesticulating wildly. Ava runs over and flings herself at our mother.

'Are you all right, Mum?'

'I'm fine, love. I'm so sorry – the traffic was terrible. I got stuck and no one moved for ages.'

I give a one-shouldered shrug and slouch into the car. The boys are all leaning forward, staring at us curiously and imitating Mum. She's still going on about it – the roadworks and the queue, how it only *inched* forward, how terrible she feels – when I interrupt.

'Have you got anything to eat?'

'No, sorry, love. You can have an apple when you get home.'

'An apple?'

'Or a banana.'

I lean back in disgust and fold my arms over my chest. It's only when we pull into our drive that I realize we've had an uneventful journey. There were no roadworks or traffic jams. It's not like you can really take another route from our house to school. And it's also odd, when I open the door, that the house smells different from normal. It doesn't smell of bread. There's always fresh bread here.

I switch off the alarm system and go upstairs. Dad designed our house so it's upside down – it's so that we have the view from the sitting room and the kitchen, and something to do with energy-saving. I take an apple, but then I can't be bothered with all that crunching and I put it back in the fruit bowl. Mum immediately moves our bags from where we've dumped them by the front door. Honestly, my parents are both OCD. She notices me glancing at the calendar.

'Can you have a quick check, Stella? Make sure it's up-to-date.'

'I'm sure it's fine,' I say, not bothering.

Mum puts all our appointments in one calendar – Ava's are in pink, of course; Dad's are blue; mine, green; and hers are yellow. There's also a section for things we're meant to do together, but there's a lot fewer of them. Mum puts everything in the calendar – every single one of Ava's ballet and swimming and piano lessons, even though they're at the same time every week, and the days she works – 5 a.m.–2 p.m. Tuesday to Saturday, 4.30 start on a Friday – like we need those in a diary. She does it on her iPhone and she prints a new sheet out each week, so we can all tell where we are, even if, like Ava, you haven't got a mobile or, like me, you don't give a fuck.

I trudge downstairs. I could have done half my homework by now. In my bedroom I take out my journal. I bought it with my pocket money. It's moleskin with thick, cream pages and, best of all, a padlock with a tiny gold key. I smooth the paper with the tips of my fingers. I haven't written anything in it. My life is bland. But Ms Heron, my English teacher, says we should write one sentence a day. Everyone has time for that. Everyone can say something exciting about their day in one sentence. I'm not sure about that. I bite the ragged bits of skin round my nails while I try and think what to write.

My thoughts stray back to Mum. She's always been anxious and jumpy, although she has a really nice, easy life and she's got nothing to be worried about. I mean, it's not like she works in a factory in Bangladesh, trying to feed five kids on sweatshop wages. I don't suppose you earn much money baking bread for a living, and I doubt Mum could do anything else: she hasn't got any qualifications. But we're properly middle-class, thanks to Dad. Mum hadn't had a panic attack for ages, until the one last week. She's never, ever been late to pick us up from school. Dad says it's because of her mum, her dad and her sister, Julia. She would have been our aunt. They were killed in a car crash when Mum was seventeen. She hasn't got any other relatives, and she says she kind of fell off the rails. I think she means she stopped going to school.

'Things were tough for her,' he said to me, in one of his lectures. 'We're all she has, that's why she worries.'

Yeah, right. I wonder what the other thing is. The one he 'allegedly' doesn't know about.

I turn my journal over and flip it upside down. On the back page I write the date last Sunday and what happened outside the church, and then today's date and '50 minutes late to pick us up from school'. At least I've written something, even if it is about Mum.

LIZZIE

Could be worse, Lizzie thought, looking round at the acres of blond-wood tables, subdivided by wooden planters topped with plastic grass, and Maskros lampshades, like giant dandelion clocks, overheard. There was no natural light, and the wall entirely covered in a photograph of snow-clad mountains seemed like a peculiar irony. But at least she got free meals and there was a staffroom she could retreat to and read her textbooks on her breaks.

She called Paul as she was leaving.

'Hey, you. Long day. You just finishing?'

'Yeah. The supervisor was so impressed he offered me double-shifts.'

'Bet they don't get many environmental scientists working in the caff. Don't overdo it. You don't want to knacker yourself and end up with one of your migraines. We'll manage, whatever happens.'

'What else am I going to do? I can rest on the bus on the way home.'

'Well, take it easy.'

'How's the pumpkin?'

'Sleeping, at last. I couldn't get him down for his nap. But we did okay. Went to the park.'

'Bloody hell, Paul, he's only six months old.'

'Yeah, he loved the swings, and I sat him on my knee and took him down the slide. We miss you.'

'I miss you, too.'

Christ, she thought, *bloody hormones.* Her eyes had filled up with tears, simply talking to her husband. Using her staff discount, she bought Dryck Blåbär, Knäckebröd Råg and Bost Blåmögel from the Ikea Food Market: some sort of blueberry drink, crackers and cheese, to eat at Miriam's.

Lizzie stuck her head around the sitting-room door when she got in.

'Hey, babe, did you get more milk?' asked Gillian, the girl from Toys R Us, who was painting her nails. She was small and waif-like, with black hair cut in a pixie style and a surprisingly deep voice.

Miriam was sitting cross-legged on the floor, straightening her newly bleached blonde hair. She smiled up at Lizzie and rolled her eyes.

'Sorry, I forgot.'

'We're all desperate for a cuppa. You couldn't nip out to the newsagent's and get another pint? Anyone need anything else?'

The other girls looked up, as if registering Lizzie's presence for the first time.

'Yeah, some Dairy Milk,' said one of the nurses.

'Packet of Marlboro Lights.'

'And some Quavers,' added Gillian.

Lizzie was tired and hungry. Her legs ached from standing all day, and the last thing she wanted to do was go back out into the dark streets on a shopping trip. She bit her tongue. Better to try and get on with Gillian, though, she thought, remembering what Miriam had said.

'All right. Where's the newsagent's?'

'Left, left and right. We'll settle up when you get back,' said Gillian, as if she didn't quite trust Lizzie not to abscond with their crisp-money.

'Don't mind her,' whispered Miriam, who suddenly appeared behind her in the hall. 'Hey, when you get back, do you want a glass of wine? The Slug chucks out all the half-empty bottles and I've been bringing them home. Got a Zinfandel in the fridge, if you fancy it?'

Lizzie shook her head.

'Oh, yeah,' said Miriam, her voice rougher, 'forgot you only drink beer.'

'Sorry, I'm just tired. I'll get a bottle when I'm out and we can have a catch-up. I feel like I've hardly seen you.' She tried not to sound hurt. Miriam seemed to have forgotten all the lost Sunday afternoons they'd spent in the car park, with their Thunderbird and their stubbies.

'Our shifts clash a bit,' said Miriam. 'Archers and ginger beer then? I've got some of that, too.'

'Look at you, getting all sophisticated with your cocktails.'

'Not as good as Paul's G&Ts,' said Miriam, sounding wistful. 'Remember that time I came to visit and we hung out in the Sticklebarn all day and he kept bringing us free drinks?'

The only time you came to visit me in Elterwater, thought Lizzie, but she smiled and said, 'Dylan slept the entire time – it was a bloody miracle. And I beat you at Scrabble.'

'There's no need to be smug, just cos you've got a degree now.'

'You going, or what?' shouted Gillian from the sitting room.

Lizzie swore under her breath. She'd known girls like Gillian at school: hard as their manicured nails, with brittle good looks that would have fled by the time they were thirty. They'd looked down on her then, too; she'd never cared about her appearance and she was happiest outside. Back then, Miriam had always stuck up for her. She glanced at her friend, but Miriam said nothing.

'Do you want to come with me?'

Miriam shook her head. 'Got to finish getting ready. I've got an early tomorrow.'

Miriam was wearing a black shirt-dress, tightly belted, which showed off her hips and waist: a perfect hourglass figure. She had a new shade of red lipstick and her dyed lashes made her pale, grey eyes look even larger. It was hard to believe this was the girl who, not so long ago, had raced her to the top of Simon's Seat, her short hair tousled by the wind, screaming with laughter. Back then, they'd looked so alike, people often thought they were sisters.

Peas in a pod, her dad used to joke, both as tomboyish as each other.

'See you later, yeah?' said Miriam.

Lizzie nodded and let herself out. Her friend was even starting to sound different; she was losing her soft West Yorkshire burr.

At the second left turn there was a large concrete block of flats. A couple of boys around thirteen, but already taller than her, were hanging about on the street corner, and there was another group of young men in the centre of the housing estate, smoking and swigging from cans. She could hear the wind, boxed in by the flats, moaning round the corners. Chocolate wrappers and newspapers rustled across the ground, and a Staffordshire terrier tied to a bench with rope growled at her through bared teeth.

She ducked quickly into the newsagent's.

'That dog gives me the heebie-jeebies,' said a voice in a strong Bradford accent.

A tall Asian man was standing behind the counter, smiling at her.

'What can I get you, love?'

'Crisps, chocolate, cigarettes and milk,' she said.

'Life's essentials,' he said as he walked round the small well-stocked shop, showing her where everything was. 'I've not seen you here before. Are you new, love?'

'Yes,' she said, smiling back. He had very white teeth and short black hair, a freckle in his nose where some of her friends had studs.

'Welcome to Belle Isle,' he said, holding out his hand. 'I'm Arjun Kumar.'

She stared at him quizzically – she hadn't thought anyone round here would be friendly; certainly no one had said a kind word to her since she'd arrived.

'We're new, too,' he said, putting her purchases in a thin blue plastic bag. 'Moved here from Cleckheaton a couple of months ago. Me and the lad.'

She hadn't noticed the boy until he ruffled the child's hair. He'd been sitting so still and so quietly, and he was mostly hidden behind the counter. Arjun had set up a small desk for him, and he was colouring in a picture of Spider-Man and eating green grapes out of a paper bag. She smiled at the child and gave a little wave.

'My wife passed away,' Arjun said. His Adam's apple bobbed in his thin throat as he swallowed.

'I'm so sorry,' she said.

He was young to have lost his wife, she thought. Arjun turned away and started tidying shelves. It can't have been that long ago; his grief still seemed so raw.

'What's your name?' Lizzie asked the child, crouching down next to him. Seeing the little boy with his thick blue-black hair and large, brown eyes, round as Smarties, made her long for her own son.

'Dev. I'm six and two-thirds,' he said.

'I'm teaching him fractions,' said Arjun, managing a smile again. As she opened the door, setting off the bell jangling overhead, he added, 'Don't walk through the estate on your own. Goodnight, love.'

EMMA

I'm laying the table when Jack comes in. Both girls are in their bedrooms, although not yet in bed.

'How did it go?' I ask.

Because of his presentation, my husband is home later than usual.

'I think it went very well,' he says, smiling.

That's Jack-speak for 'bloody brilliantly'. He kisses me on the cheek and I can't help thinking about Paul, the way he would crush Lizzie in his arms. I imagine how his lips would have felt, soft and yet cold from being outdoors, and the way his stubble would have grated against her smooth skin. Jack is never less than perfectly shaved and he's warm from being in the car.

'What's wrong?' he says, spinning me round and looking into my eyes.

His are dark grey; in some lights and in some moods they look blue, at other times, almost black. There's a piercing intensity about Jack's stares, and little escapes him.

I sigh and push Paul to the back of my mind. 'I was late to pick up the girls.'

'Oh. That must have been hard for you.'

Sometimes I'd rather Jack didn't talk to me as if he were a psychologist. He might have studied psychology originally, but he works in HR, and I'm his wife!

'It's fine,' I say. 'The traffic was bad, and the girls were okay.'

I swallow. I was mortified that I'd mistimed the journey to Tyntesfield and got stuck in rush-hour traffic on the way home, leaving my girls to sit by the side of the road . . . I take a breath.

Concentrate on the facts: they were okay; nothing happened to them. It'll never happen again.

My eyes slide away from Jack's.

'I've brought you a present,' he says, smiling.

He takes a slim moss-green box, bound with gold thread, out of his briefcase. Inside, there's a tiny bottle wrapped in tissue-paper. It says 'Stress-Fix' on the label and I can't help laughing. He takes it from me.

'This is what you're meant to do with it,' he says. He puts a few drops of oil on his palms and rubs them together. 'Close your eyes.' I obey. He holds his hands in front of my face, his forearms pressing down on my shoulders. 'Take three deep breaths. Inhale. Exhale. That's it.'

The smell is divine – lavender, and something else I can't put my finger on. When I've taken my third breath, he runs his fingers round the nape of my neck and slips his hands beneath the top of my dress. His thumbs, slippery with oil, slide across my skin as he kneads my shoulders. I feel my muscles liquefy.

'Hmm.' He puts his arms round me and kisses me properly.

'Thank you. That's exactly what I needed,' I tell him, marvelling that he found the time, alongside his presentation, to find me the perfect gift. 'You always buy such wonderful presents,' I add, nuzzling his neck.

The girls are supposed to go to sleep before me – in practice; because I have to be up by 4.15, I go to bed while they're still procrastinating, and leave Jack to police them. Thankfully I fall asleep straight away, even though I can hear him arguing with them. Those sounds – their voices, their footsteps – are familiar. Safe. And then I'm suddenly wide awake, my whole body rigid. I try and work out what has woken me. I look at the clock by my bed and lie completely still, listening. Water is running; there's a chink of light beneath the bathroom door. It must have been the latch. I allow myself to sink into the mattress. I let my heart rate return to normal. Some nights are worse than others, but I can't remember a night when I haven't woken up, startled by a fox cry or a car door; Jack moving about downstairs; a sudden squall of rain at the window.

A few minutes later he slides into bed and folds himself around me. He's warm and still slightly damp from the shower. He cups my breasts in his hands and nibbles my earlobe.

'I love you,' he says.

'I love you, too.'

I turn towards him and run my hand down his chest. I can feel the definition in his stomach muscles. He seems too lean, his skin too loose, as I remember what it was like to lie beneath another man, one who was broader, his dark hair coarse beneath my fingertips, his back strong and thick from carrying slabs of stone and hiking up mountains. I dig my nails into my husband's shoulder blades and try my hardest not to think of Paul Bradshaw.

EMMA

On Fridays, we go to the pub. It's a family tradition. It started just after Stella was born and we couldn't afford to get a babysitter – Jack was still re-training then – and it made us feel like normal human beings, able to have a pint and a meal that I hadn't burnt. We've also always tried to dress up a bit, make an effort. It's a time for Jack to catch up with the kids, too, now. But today he wants us to eat at home, on the balcony. He sends another text.

Can you pick up some tapas and fizz? We need to celebrate! xJ

Jack must have been signed up by the business he was pitching to last week. I buy a loaf of sourdough, some filled croissants and sausage rolls and a selection of cakes from *Kate's* before they sell out, and swing by M&S for posh nibbles and Prosecco, before I pick up the girls.

Our sitting room, dining area and kitchen are all one huge open-plan space, with a terrace overlooking the garden and valley below, the river meandering through the fields. As the crow flies, the woods surrounding Tyntesfield are straight ahead. I'm distracted by the view. I put the thought of Paul out of my mind, as I've been trying to do all week. On a Friday, Ava has piano lessons, and as I whisk up a salad dressing with walnut oil and balsamic vinegar, Mozart fills the room. I slide open the French doors so that the outside and the inside become one. The late-afternoon sunlight has gilded the roses; their perfume drifts up and seems to weave in with the notes. I throw a white cloth over the table on the terrace, and set out champagne glasses. For a moment I see my hand as if it belongs to someone else, and I think of what Lizzie would have been doing on a Friday. She'd have been appalled if she'd seen our bags of baby leaves, packed with some kind of noxious gas and air freighted in from Kenya, the leaves as glossy as if they have never seen a speck of soil. She'd have been in the pub with Paul, a pint of Stickleback in her hand, sharing a plate of cheesy nachos, her cheeks rosy after the two-mile walk from their cottage.

'That's beautiful, Ava,' I tell her, when she finally masters the rondo, and she and her young tutor grin at me.

Of course Ava could go to lessons at the school – it would be much cheaper – but I'd rather she was here with me. Where I can watch over her.

'*Eine kleine Nachtmusik*,' says Jack, as he comes in. He kisses her and says, 'Keep practising your finger exercises – your hard work is paying off, sweetheart.'

He's read some study about kids doing better if you praise them for effort, rather than achievement; he keeps reminding me, but I never remember to say anything other than 'Brilliant!'

'Thank you for doing this, darling,' he says, hugging me and nodding at the spread I've laid out.

The thickly sliced bread and the butter, pearling with condensation, are for me and the children; but I've also bought the kinds of things that Jack likes to eat: anchovies glistening with oil, salami and prosciutto, pickled herring scattered with fronds of dill. There's also grilled artichokes and olives stuffed with slivers of almond, a couscous salad with pomegranate seeds, and wedges of Manchego dusted with rosemary.

'So you got the job?' I ask, and he grins.

'It's a big one. An energy company,' he says.

After the tutor leaves, Ava comes skidding across the wooden floor and Jack picks her up and spins her round effortlessly, as if she were one of his kettlebells.

'Where's Stella?'

'In her room. Doing her homework.'

'Stella!' he shouts down the stairs to where our bedrooms are. He glances back at the table and frowns. 'Those forks are from a different set,' he says, 'I keep telling you not to mix them up.'

I watch as he removes them and replaces them with ones that match — it winds him up that I just bung them all in the drawer together — and then he tweaks every place setting until the cutlery is perfectly aligned. I try not to get annoyed by Jack's foibles. After all, the positive side of living with someone who is so precise is that he is the kind of man who would never forget to check that the doors are locked at night. I'm about to open the Prosecco, but Jack pulls a bottle of champagne out of his bag.

I raise my eyebrows at him. 'Must be a big contract.'

He grins at me and eases the cork from the bottle. When I first met Jack he was re-training to be a 'business psychologist'. Essentially he helps companies structure or restructure their staff, with a side order of happiness and well-being. At first he worked with start-ups and small local firms, and so now, just over a decade later, to win a contract as a consultant to such a large organization is a big deal. He pours us both a glass of champagne and I give Ava sparkling apple juice in a flute.

'Can I have one?' says Stella, slouching into the room. She's ignored my request to change into something nice and is wearing jeans and a T-shirt.

'Why not?' says Jack and she looks surprised, as if she'd been trying to pick a fight.

We chink our glasses and Jack says, 'I've got a present for you.'

'What have I done to deserve another present?' I kiss him on the cheek and Stella rolls her eyes.

I have a sudden twinge of anxiety. It's not my birthday. Have I missed our anniversary? No, it's in August. I've put it in the calendar already.

He looks excited. 'Wait here,' he tells us.

'Do you think he's got me something?' whispers Ava.

'I don't know. But I bought those peanut-butter brownies you and Stella love,' I say.

Jack surprises us by appearing from the other direction. Our house is built on the top of a steep hill and he's climbed a set of wooden steps from the ground floor up to the balcony where we're sitting. He sets down the bike he was carrying. It's a cream Pendleton, with a biscuit-coloured leather seat and a wicker basket at the front.

'It's gorgeous.'

I must look puzzled because he says, 'You're always saying you want to get fit. And I thought this might help.'

'Knew there'd be a reason,' Stella says, downing her champagne in one draught. 'It's actually because he thinks you're fat.'

'Stella!'

'You're mother is stunning,' says Jack, just about controlling his temper.

I smile at him. 'Thank you. I love it.'

And I do. Normally I'd be irritated but try to hide it. Jack has been attempting to get me to exercise for ages, and although he always says he loves my curves, I'm sure he'd rather I was slimmer. I swallow the guilt that burns the back of my throat and feel a blush flare across my neck. Because, as if my mind has made the decision for me, without me even realizing, when I look at this elegant bike I know exactly how useful it's going to be.

STELLA

Mum is late home from work. Nearly two hours late. It's Saturday afternoon, so I don't suppose it matters because I don't need looking after and Ava is with Dad. But still, it is weird. I can't remember my unspontaneous mother ever doing anything without notifying us in triplicate. Dad took Ava to ballet this morning and then he texted to say they were going to Cabot Circus to look for dresses.

Ssssh! x Dad, he added.

I groan inwardly. The anniversary party isn't for weeks. At least he didn't make me join them. They're not home, either. At first I was pleased to have the house to myself. There was no one here to force me to have breakfast or to tell me off for eating peanut-butter and jam sandwiches for lunch. I'm writing an English essay, sitting on the terrace without having to answer stupid questions or listen to anyone plonking on the piano.

I'm a bit stuck with my essay, though, so I go inside and put *Vampire Diaries* on. I balance my laptop on my knee and look at what I've written. You have to pick a theme from *Jane Eyre* and then discuss it. I've chosen 'personal discovery'.

'*Jane Eyre*,' I wrote, 'is a *Bildungsroman*, a type of novel where the heroine, Jane, goes from being a child to an adult. Through her experiences and her suffering, she realizes who she is and what her true identity is.'

I give the example where St John begs her to marry him and she's about to say yes, but then she says no. She says, *If I were to marry you, you would kill me.*

She means it symbolically, obviously. He's not going to murder her. But it's the bit in the novel where she has the strength to stand up for who she really is, and realizes that a marriage without love would actually be deadly.

I wonder if anyone will fall to their knees and beg me to marry them. Probably not. St John isn't angry, though, like you'd expect, if you'd just been turned down. He says, *I know where your heart turns and to what it clings.*

By the end of the novel, Jane knows who she truly loves, although it's a bit blurry in the second-to-last chapter, when she and Rochester finally get together and she says it's like they're the same person:

> *I am my husband's life as fully as he is mine. No woman was ever nearer to her mate than I am: ever more absolutely bone of his bone and flesh of his flesh.*

It's pretty sappy and not exactly feminist.

Will anyone love me like that? And will I have worked out who I am by then? I sigh. How can I tell who I am when I constantly have to do stuff I don't want to do? Like tomorrow. Dad's planning to take us to Ashton Court because there's an open day, so you can actually get inside the mansion and look around. As if that's what we want to do with our Sunday. I think I hear a car, so I pause *Vampire Diaries* and look out of the front window. It's not Mum, though, hers is still parked on the drive. There's no sign of her. Now I really can't concentrate. I check my phone but there are no more texts. I send Kaylee a quick message to say let's meet up later. I can't believe Mum would have biked to work. She hasn't ridden a bike in years and she's so scared of the dark, she'd never cycle at

4.30 a.m. I'm wondering whether to make myself a bowl of granola or to ring Dad to see if he knows where Mum is, when I spot her. She's pushing her bike up the hill.

I step away from the window, so she can't see me watching. I sit on the breakfast bar and eat granola straight from the packet. When she comes in, she looks different.

'Did you cycle to work?' I ask.

She shakes her head. 'Baby-steps. I can't remember the last time I rode a bike. No, I drove in, but then I took the bike for a spin when I got back.'

'A spin?'

'Along Festival Way. It's nice and flat. I'm pretty wobbly.'

Mum is wearing a tunic and leggings with Ash trainers, and she actually looks kind of cool. Normally she comes back from work in her ratty chef's trousers and rank Crocs, covered in flour. But she's wearing a silk scarf. And red lipstick. She puts my dirty cups and plates in the dishwasher without giving me a lecture. She's glowing. I don't mean in that old-fashioned perspiration way that ladies are meant to. Obviously she's a bit sweaty. I mean, she looks . . . agitated. It's like she's got electricity running through her. No one looks like that just because they've gone for a ride along a concrete path on an old person's bike. Something must have happened to make her even more of a nutcase than she already is. I have a weird sensation like a chill and a thrill at the same time.

'You're studying *Jane Eyre* in English?' she says, noticing my books spread out across the sofa. 'That's wonderful – it's your favourite novel, isn't it? Or does it ruin it, if you have to write essays about it?'

'It's okay,' I shrug.

'I loved that book when I was younger, too. Although I preferred *The Tenant of Wildfell Hall.*'

I roll my eyes. Mum's favourite novel is *Me Before You*, so this is a blatant lie.

'Do you need any help with your essay? I could read it for you, if you'd like?'

'I'll probably show Dad later. He's good at proofreading,' I say.

I slide off the counter and slip past Mum before she makes herself look even more ridiculous, or says anything about watching TV in the middle of the day. I go downstairs to my bedroom and get out my diary from where I've hidden it in the wardrobe under my jumpers.

I write, 'My mother has a secret.'

EMMA

How can I find out why he's here? The question nags at me all the time. I can't not think about him. It's beyond any of the counselling and the CBT sessions I've had, and the strength of will that is the one thing I have exercised since I last saw Paul Bradshaw. The bike has given me the excuse I need. Jack will be delighted I'm using it. And it means I won't be late for the girls. I quell the guilt I feel when I think about Jack – but I'm not doing anything wrong really, just going for a bike ride. I've got it all worked out. I did a trial run on Saturday.

Today is Monday and there are no customers in *Kate's*. It's the day when Harry and I can get ahead with the baking for the coming week. The chefs, Caleb and Toby, come in a little later; Katie's already here, talking constantly although she's meant to be organizing the rotas and ordering the produce for the week.

'Oooh,' she says, picking up one of the crates the grocers have dropped off. 'Strawberries.' She eats a couple so fast, it's as if she's inhaled them.

'Steady,' laughs Harry.

'So what shall we do with these, then?'

She sounds delighted with the challenge. The grocer drops off seasonal fruit and vegetables every week.

'Strawberry Bakewell tart?' I say, bending over the crate.

The smell is mouth-watering and I immediately think of Wimbledon and tennis whites, which is ridiculous because I've never been and can't play.

'Strawberry polenta cake with Limoncello drizzle,' says Katie.

'Nice one,' says Harry, turning back to the vats of sourdough leaven he's feeding.

'As long as there's alcohol in there somewhere,' I say, picking up the crate and taking it over to my station to start hulling the berries. Katie is so much more imaginative than I am.

By the time I've helped Harry prepare all the bread for the following day and made six kinds of cake, including Katie's special, as well as croissants, Danish pastries and pain-au-chocolat, my calves and feet are aching, and the calluses on my hands are throbbing. I've managed to finish early, though.

I park near the girls' school and take my bike out of the boot. It's an easy ride, even for me, through Backwell Common. There are few cars on this country lane, and I imagine being a girl again. There's a gentle breeze that cools the nape of my neck and stirs the heavy waves of my hair. My hands, gripping the chrome handlebars, are stained pink with strawberry juice and, though I've changed into clean clothes, I can still smell vanilla from the crème pâtissière.

The best bit about this route is that I can cycle directly into the bottom end of the estate, right by the old walled gardens. As soon as I chain up my bike behind the Pavilion cafe and wipe the sweat from my forehead, the anxiety returns. It's so familiar that I only register the tension seizing up my shoulder blades and the tremor in my fingertips because of the contrast with how I felt when I was on my bike.

I can't let Paul see me, but I have to find out why he's here. And, somehow, I need to work out where he lives. I wonder if I'm doing this for Lizzie or for me? I can't think about her, though. Today I'm braver. I go straight into the walled garden. Right away I can see he's not here. I saunter round the paths, pretending to admire the trellises of sweet peas and blood-red runner beans, the cherries and peaches trained against the sun-warmed bricks, whilst I think what to do. Dragonflies zigzag like green-gold splinters above the old well in the centre. I walk past a miniature forest of purple-sprouting broccoli and I come to a complete stop, as if my feet will no longer carry me.

It's a memory so vivid it seems to burn my retinas. Lizzie's parents – Beth and Adam – used to grow purple-sprouting broccoli in their vegetable garden, too. They lived on the estate at Bolton Abbey. Paul and Lizzie had come to visit with their newborn baby that summer, sixteen years ago. It was unusually warm for Yorkshire. We were all sitting outside, drinking mugs of tea, and her son had fallen asleep. Lizzie's mum said he'd get sunburn. Lizzie laughed and told her not to fuss; she put him in the broccoli patch. He slept for such a long time swaddled in a white cloth blanket, like a fairy child. The hum of our voices, and the cool green shade of the broccoli, must have made him feel safe. He was so tiny; I think he was about a month old. I remember sticking my arm through the plants and letting one of his hands curl around my finger.

The last time I saw Lizzie's son he was six months old. There hasn't been a day since then that I haven't thought about him and wondered what he's like now. The ache in my heart is so large, I don't know if it will ever heal. I loved that little baby so much. I wanted a boy, too. Of course I love Stella and Ava, but I wanted us to try again. *Third time lucky*, I'd thought. Jack said no. He said we couldn't afford another child. He was too exhausted. Where would we put him? By that time we'd moved into the house in Long Ashton that Jack had designed with the help of a local architect. There was no room in the plan for another child. Perhaps he might feel differently now that the girls are bigger, though? I'm in my mid-thirties. I'm not too old yet.

I should go, I think. I make myself move, but instead of heading back towards my bike, I walk straight on. I'll look in the outhouses and the greenhouses and then I'll leave, I tell myself. One last quick check. I feel a kind of despair as I think about my life: how pathetic I am, coming here in search of a man and a child I haven't seen for years, yet knowing I will feel compelled to return, day after day, even though this is not only the route to insanity, it's a path that heads directly towards a danger I've managed to avoid for so many years. That baby boy is almost seventeen years old now. Would I recognize him? The thought that I wouldn't – that I might walk right past him – fills me with a mixture of shame and self-loathing.

The outhouses run along the edge of the walls of the garden and you access them through an archway. I look inside one and it's like a throwback to the Victorian era. There are wooden-handled spades and forks lined up against the wall, worn smooth from use, and towering stacks of terracotta pots. Something brushes my arm and I jump and give a little scream. There's someone standing behind me. I whip round, my heart racing.

The man steps back, holds his hands up. My over-the-top reaction has alarmed him. It's Paul.

He's staring at me, his eyes wide in shock, his mouth slack.

I back away, out of the dim light of the building, ready to flee. He follows me, stretching out his arms. I can't let him touch me. This was a mistake. I could lose everything and everyone I love, if he recognizes who I really am. The bright sunlight in the flower garden is harsh. I slide my sunglasses back on, and pull my scarf more tightly around my throat. I hold my breath.

The sunshine illuminates his dark eyes, turns them tawny. We're so close I can see how he's changed. Crow's feet have appeared around his eyes, and the skin beneath them is paler, puffier. There are deep furrows across his forehead and between his eyebrows. Where he once had dimples, there are lines. The youthfulness of his looks has gone; his face has hardened. It's tougher, sharper. Sadder. I struggle for breath.

The hopefulness in his expression turns to disappointment and resignation.

'I'm sorry I startled you. I thought you were someone I knew,' he says.

He turns away and walks quickly back past the outhouse and through the archway, disappearing into the vegetable plot.

I stand still for a moment, struggling to get my breathing under control. *Inhale for six, exhale for eight.*

Relief floods through me, followed swiftly by a wave of pain. I'm aware of the heat of the sun on my fair hair, high notes of rose and the sweet scent of mock-orange blossom, the call of a bird. It's been so many years . . . Could he possibly have thought I was Lizzie? There might be some lingering similarity between me and Lizzie, some small thing that still seemed familiar. But Lizzie had short, curly auburn hair and I'm more voluptuous than she was. She was a hill-walker, always out on the Langdale Pikes with Paul. And she was so young. She was only twenty-two when it happened. She didn't have the luxury of time to get fat, to grow old, to see her son grow up.

STELLA

When we're let out of school, Mum's car is already in the car park, as usual. I'm so busy messaging Kaylee – moaning about having to go to ballet with Ava – that I don't realize until I'm right outside the car, and I'm about to shout at Mum that she hasn't bloody opened the doors, that's she's not actually in it. I look around. Ava waves at me and comes running over, but her face scrunches up when she arrives.

'Where is she? I'm going to be late.'

She's picked up on Mum's anxiety about being on time – and she hates missing a millisecond of ballet.

'No, you won't,' I say.

I've just caught sight of Mum. She's red in the face, cycling as fast as she can, which isn't very fast. Her cream silk scarf matches the cream of the bike, and if she weren't so chubby, she might look okay.

'I don't want to eat any more cake from *Kate's*,' I announce, as she pulls over. 'Stop bringing it home.'

Mum is so out of breath, she can barely speak.

She ignores me and kisses Ava. 'Sorry, girls, I mistimed that. I'm still not that fit,' she says.

There's a lot of faffing about as she tries to put one of the seats down in the car and get the bike in the boot. Ava hops around in agitation. I slide in when she's done. It looks like she's taking Dad's fitness edict seriously.

'How was school?'

I shrug.

'Will we get there on time?' Ava whines from the back.

'We will, sweetheart, we'll just make it,' says Mum, but her smile looks a bit cracked, like even her lips are tense. She glances at me and then back at the road. 'I should definitely eat less cake,' she says, 'but you have a lovely figure and you're still growing.'

I bristle. I mean, I could have developed a gluten intolerance.

'So you do think I'm fat.'

'Of course I don't! You're beautiful. And we only have cake once a week as a treat.'

'You don't.'

'Well, that's true. It's so tempting, being surrounded by it! You'd think I'd be sick of it.'

'And all that bread! You bring it home every day. Dad says we shouldn't eat it. It makes your blood-sugar rocket and it gets turned into cellulite.'

'I don't know how he lives without bread,' says Mum. 'No more cheese toasties.'

I suppose she does have a point. Mum pulls up outside the studio and I climb out and slam the door. It's really annoying that she won't let me go home on my own. The only way I get out of it is if Kaylee's dad picks us up instead. Mum trusts him, for some reason. Ava has ballet twice a week, but at least I don't have to go to her Saturday lesson, too.

'You know, when I'm sixteen I'm never going to your stupid ballet lessons ever again.'

'Don't you like watching me?' asks Ava.

'I don't watch you,' I say. 'I do my homework.'

Ava starts crying. God, she is such a baby. I go in and sit in the cafe and get out my Italian. I can't believe I've got exams soon and I don't know any of this stuff. I send Kaylee another message. A few minutes later Mum comes over with a pot of tea for us.

Normally she gets me a hot chocolate, but she must think I'm
on a diet now.

'Is everything okay?'

'Yup.'

'I'm sorry you have to come along, but I can't be in two places
at once. So, can you please stop upsetting your sister?'

Even when she's trying to tell me off, like now, Mum is gentle,
as if she can't quite believe I'd ever do anything mean. I take out
my list of verbs to learn. I do feel a bit bad, actually.

'And,' she says, reaching over to smooth a strand of hair out of
my face, 'if you hadn't dropped all your clubs, you'd be busy, too.'

'Not all of them. And I am busy! Just the twelve GCSEs, or had
you forgotten? And I could get the bus!'

'It's not getting the bus that I mind, it's—'

'The thought of leaving me alone in the house. Yeah, you've
told me like a million times. Dad says the accident has made you
over-protective of us.'

She ignores that bit.

'I know exams are stressful, love, but try not to take it to heart.
They're—'

'"Only" mocks, I know. But I actually want to get some
qualifications and do something with my life.'

I look sideways at Mum but she doesn't say anything. I wonder
if I've hurt her feelings. There's no fucking way I want to end up
baking bread for a living, and earning the minimum wage.

'Can I help you?' she asks, pointing to my homework.

'I doubt it. You don't know Italian.'

'I'm sure I could have a go at reading it out, if you need me to
test you.'

'It's a bit more complicated than that,' I say, and she sighs.

The cafe we're in overlooks one of the dance studios, and
normally Mum sits and watches Ava the entire time, but she seems

distracted, or maybe she's annoyed with me. I glance down. Ava is wearing a pink leotard and a sort of floaty skirt, like all the other girls in her class. They're in a line at the barre doing their warm-up exercises. I can't tell if Ava is special, if she's going to turn into some prima ballerina. All the girls are skinny and flat-chested with long, elegant limbs. They make me feel huge. How does it happen? One minute you're a kid running around, and then you turn thirteen and all this podge appears and you're too tired to do any running and, even if you did, the boys would laugh because now you jiggle whenever you move. I slump further into my chair and pull my hoodie down, so it covers my bottom.

Mum has a sort of glazed look on her face, as if she's somewhere else entirely. She's letting her tea get cold.

'Where did you go for your bike ride?' I say, to try and make up for being mean earlier.

She turns towards me slowly and I get this cold feeling, because it's like she doesn't recognize me.

'Oh,' she says, her expression warming, 'I went along Festival Way again. Not far. And then back to the school.'

She drifts away. I glance at her wrist. It's red and raw. The elastic band she normally wears isn't there, but she must have been using it a lot. There's an angry welt on her forearm, too. She says it's because she's clumsy, but she only burns herself at work when she's having a bad day. I bite the skin round my fingernails. I want to ask her if she's okay, but the words won't come out.

I close my eyes but instead of conjugating Italian verbs, I imagine the sentence I'm going to write, just like Ms Heron says to do. *Compose it in your mind first*, she says, *then set it down on paper*.

My sentence is going to be about my mother, and I'm going to remember it and write it in my journal when I get home.

LIZZIE

Commuting to Leeds was more tiring than she'd expected. There was the wrench of leaving Elterwater, and Dylan and Paul; the long bus journey through the night; and then getting a second bus out to Belle Isle, her heart sinking as she drew closer to the maze of streets and red-brick houses, her ache for her son growing larger. The job was exhausting, she spent hours on her feet, the artificial lights made her head throb – and then there was Miriam. Lizzie had thought they'd connect, like they had when they were at school, but Miriam seemed subtly different.

'I can't wait to go back home,' she'd sighed, pouring a glass of Pinot Grigio for them both, from the dregs that a customer had left behind.

It had been their last evening together before Lizzie had caught the bus back to the Lakes the previous week.

'I don't know how you do it, being so far away from your family. Beth's keeping an eye out for a management position for me at Bolton Abbey,' Miriam had continued.

Beth, Lizzie had thought. *Not 'your mum'.*

'You should come and visit,' she'd said, trying not to sound annoyed. Miriam constantly rowed with her own mother, but still, it made Lizzie feel uncomfortable to hear her friend talk about *her* mum as if she got on better with her than she did. 'Come and see your godson. He's growing so fast! You'd hardly—'

'I meant Beth and Adam,' Miriam had said. 'If you and Paul had stayed in the village, they could have helped you. You wouldn't have had to work in Leeds and leave your baby and husband, like you're doing. Me, I've got no choice. I don't have anyone to look out for me. But if I was married, I wouldn't be traipsing off to Leeds, leaving my man behind.'

'Paul and Dylan are my family. And it's not like I've got a choice.'

'Course you've got a choice,' Miriam had said, sipping her wine and staring at her over the rim of the glass. 'There's always a choice.'

Lizzie hadn't replied – she hadn't known what to say or where this new sharpness came from. Miriam drank a lot more, too. Although they'd had the odd bender when they were teenagers, this was different – this was wine every night after she got back from work. And sometimes Lizzie caught Miriam looking at her in a strange way. She couldn't really describe it: it felt cold, speculative almost.

She remembered what Julia had said the last time she'd brought Paul and Dylan back to Bolton Abbey: *She's dead jealous of you, you know.*

Lizzie and Julia had been lying on a picnic rug in the garden, soaking up the late-summer sunshine. Dylan was almost five months old, and he was balancing on Miriam's lap, sucking his fist and gurgling in her ear. She and Paul were sitting on rickety wooden chairs, their feet on the garden wall, looking out over the valley, their backs to Lizzie and Julia. Their shoulders were shaking with laughter, and Miriam had kissed Dylan's head and clinked her mug of tea against Paul's.

Julia had given Lizzie a knowing look.

'They get on well,' Lizzie had said, but her voice had come out all wrong, as if she was on the defensive; as if the way Miriam had just looked at her husband had been with adoration, and not friendliness.

Why would Miriam be jealous of her, with her skinny hips and sleepless nights, her horrendous commute to Leeds and her cold little cottage? Miriam was doing well; men loved her new, curvier figure, and she was making friends, having fun.

Lizzie had just finished her second double-shift and she was shattered. The girls in the house in Belle Isle were huddled round the TV as usual when she got in, but Miriam wasn't with them. Lizzie clattered upstairs and dropped her rucksack on her mattress. Miriam wasn't in her room, either. Lizzie picked up the book on her friend's bedside table. It was *The Horse Whisperer*. She snorted to herself. They'd first bonded in school over *Anne of Green Gables*, and Lizzie thought Miriam still read the same kind of things she did. But maybe not – she'd recently got into Barbara Kingsolver and Margaret Atwood and they didn't seem like the kind of authors Miriam would be into. And she didn't think she could tease Miriam about liking a grown-up version of *Black Beauty*, either.

'Where's Miriam?' she asked, entering the living room.

One of the student nurses shrugged. The other one said, 'Not seen her. Maybe she's changed her shift?'

Gillian swung her little face towards her, looking like a cross ten-year-old.

'Have you been using my Nescaf?'

'Yeah. Sorry. I was going to get some more tonight.'

'Don't tell me – you forgot.'

'I'll go to Kumar's now. I'll pick up some crisps and chocolates, too.'

'And teabags,' muttered Gillian.

'Can you let Miriam know where I am, if she comes back? It's not like her not to tell me where she is,' Lizzie said, but her housemates were already absorbed in their TV programme.

It would be nice to see a friendly face, too, she thought. Since starting work here, she'd visited the newsagent's nearly every day she'd been in Leeds. Arjun was always cheerful, and although they only usually chatted for a couple of minutes, it helped ease her loneliness a little. She missed having Paul to talk to about her day. Dev always seemed to be up, too – no one to look after him, she guessed – and seeing the child made her feel connected, even in a small way, to her own son.

As she walked down the street towards the flats, she felt as if she were in a tunnel that was gradually narrowing. The periphery of her vision began to blur and warp; flashes of purple and green streaked across her retina every time she moved her head. The first needles of pain sliced through her forehead. It was the start of a migraine. She wondered whether to give up on her errand, but she was almost at the newsagent's. She gritted her teeth; she could get her shopping and be back at the house in a few minutes, and then she'd be able to take painkillers and lie down in Miriam's room.

Her footsteps echoed hollowly when she reached the flats. The same gang of youths was perched on the back of a bench in the centre of the square, drinking Special Brew. One of them threw a can in her direction, and the last dregs of lager arced in the air, glinting in the orange of the street lamps. He shouted something, too, but there was a rushing in her ears and she couldn't make out the words. The pain pulsed through her molars. She almost fell into the shop.

'Hi,' said Arjun. 'Back from the Lakes already? That went quick, hardly seems two minutes since you were here.'

She stood still for a moment, her head spinning, trying to get her bearings, trying to remember why she was here. Everything in the shop seemed to be neon-bright, screaming 'Special Offers!' at her, the colours clashing.

Why had she come here? Coffee, that's what she needed. But the thought of the dried granules, smelling dusty and acrid, made her feel as if she was going to be sick.

'Are you all right?' asked Arjun, coming round the counter.

'I'm okay, I just want some . . .'

Painkillers was all she could think about. She took a step towards the shelves. The packet was red, wasn't it? What the hell was it called? She swayed, the nausea growing stronger.

Arjun took hold of her elbow. 'Lizzie, you don't look well.'

'It's a migraine.'

'Ah,' he said. 'My wife used to get them. Debilitating, that's what they are. Do you want to lie down for a minute? The stockroom isn't right glamorous, but it's dark.'

She tried to nod and the pain soared through her jaw, pressed against her scalp, sang down her spine.

'This way,' he said, steering her round the counter.

He said something in another language and Lizzie thought he'd made a mistake, assuming she could understand, but then she realized Arjun must be talking to his son.

In the light that spilled through the doorway, she saw that she was in a small room filled with racks of shelves, stacked with boxes and cans shrink-wrapped in plastic. In the corner was a camp bed.

'Dev sometimes sleeps here, if I've got no one to look after him,' murmured Arjun. 'I'll bring you some water and ibuprofen.'

She climbed onto the low bed and lay back, holding herself rigid.

Arjun appeared with a glass of cold water and popped two tablets out of a blister pack into her palm.

'It's the strongest I've got. My wife always used to take sumatriptan, but you need a prescription.'

'Do you like my duvet covers?'

'Shush, Dev, Lizzie's got a really bad headache.'

The bell over the door rang and Arjun quickly returned to the shop.

'Spider-Man is my favourite superhero for a duvet,' she whispered.

Dev crouched next to her, looking at her from under his lashes. The sheets smelt of a floral fabric conditioner, and of the child himself.

'Thank you for letting me lie down in your bed.'

'Are you going to die like Mummy did?'

'No, Dev,' she said, taking his small hand in hers. 'I'll be well again really soon.'

She closed her eyes. Colours pulsed and flared through the darkness, and she felt as if there was a vice tightening across her skull. She was so tired, it was a relief to let her muscles relax. The nausea started to subside, now that she was lying down. Dev's hot little hand slid from hers.

She wasn't sure how long she'd been there, whether it was only seconds or minutes, but she heard raised voices coming from the shop. She propped herself up on her elbows. The movement made her feel sick again. An irate customer, perhaps. She turned her head slowly, but she couldn't see Dev. How horrible for Arjun to have to deal with people who spoke to him like that; it was such a rough neighbourhood. The rushing in her ears was still muffling her hearing; she could tell the speaker was angry, but she couldn't make out individual words. She sat up and swung her legs round, pausing for a moment to let her head stop spinning. The least she could do, to repay Arjun for his kindness, would be to distract Dev, so he wouldn't have to listen to this.

That was when she noticed the boy. He was standing behind the door, which was ajar. She whispered his name, but her voice was hoarse and he didn't respond. As if she'd reached the top of a mountain and her ears had popped, she heard a man say, 'This is your final warning, mate.'

Why do men do that? she wondered. *Say 'mate' when they're not being friendly. What's he warning Arjun about?*

EMMA

I'm getting a little fitter. At least it's not such a struggle any more. I've been going for a short ride every day after work. It helps that it's been sunny. I can tell I'm going to be a fair-weather cyclist. Although I haven't been back to see Paul, I haven't been able to stop thinking about him. It's mainly his hands I imagine: their strength, how it would feel if he traced a line from my wrist to the crook of my elbow, his fingertips grazing the soft, secret flesh of my forearm . . .

Today is my day off and I've decided I've got to speak to him. It's stupid, and possibly dangerous. But he didn't seem to remember me and I have to find out what's happened to Lizzie's son. I owe it to her! It won't assuage the guilt I feel, but I'm going to risk it.

I ring the National Trust estate office before I set off, to check he's working today, and then I pack a bag to sit in the basket of my new bike. Jack thinks I take things that'll cover every eventuality, but I don't. I only take what's necessary. When I'm with my family, I bring what will keep them safe. But suppose you're on your own, like I am now, and something happened to you, and you couldn't get back, what would you need? What would be important to you? When you think about it like that, it's surprisingly little.

A credit card and a passport; a driving licence. Mini first-aid and wash kits. A decent moisturizer, lipstick and lip balm. It's surprisingly freeing because, of course, you can't take what is most important to you: your family and friends. I have photos, though, printed out, not just on a phone. Mobiles are easily lost, aren't they? And two recipes, the ones I think I couldn't live without. But all of it, when it comes down to it, is dispensable. Almost everything is.

I go to the Pavilion cafe and order an Earl Grey and a scone with cream and strawberry jam. The jam is home-made and the scone is still warm, steaming gently as I cut it open. The glorious sunshine we've been having is continuing, and I close my eyes and tilt my head back to soak up the warmth. The receptionist even told me what time she thought Paul's break would be, so I know I've got ten minutes before I can pretend to bump into him again. I'm sure she shouldn't give out so much information over the phone. I must speak to Katie, make sure she doesn't say anything personal about me to strangers. My thoughts drift from Katie to strawberries: there'll be more next week, she says, and I need to think of something creative to do with them. I'm too jittery to come up with anything, though.

A shadow falls across my face and I snap to attention, immediately alert.

'I've startled you again,' he says, 'Sorry. I'm Paul, one of the gardeners here.'

He holds out his hand to shake mine. Still the same old Paul, easy to be with, able to talk to anyone. He holds my hand fractionally too long and I don't want him to let go.

'Emma Taylor,' I say. 'Will you have a seat?'

'Thanks – if you're sure I'm not disturbing you. I'm on my break. I saw you and wanted to apologize properly. I must have seemed like a right idiot the other day.'

He looks around and waves at one of the waiters. 'Pete, any chance of a cup of tea, mate?'

'You can have some of mine. I've got plenty. It's Earl Grey.'

He wrinkles his nose. 'Bit flowery for my taste.'

I laugh. He really hasn't changed. And then I freeze, because here I am with Paul Bradshaw! I hold my cup inelegantly in two hands, so that he won't see the tremor in my fingers. I hope to God he still doesn't recognize me. This is so reckless, but I can't help myself. I just need to find out a few things and then I will never come here again, I promise myself.

'I've seen you a couple of times,' he says. 'Do you come here often?' He throws his head back and roars with laughter. 'That sounded like a dodgy chat-up line. And I'm not. Trying to chat you up, that is.'

'I live close by,' I say and I blush – a blush that flames across my cheeks and flares over my chest. 'I've just started cycling. Trying to get a bit fitter. And it's beautiful here.'

We both glance at my scone, oozing cream. I feel as if the layer of fat I've been building up since my twenties is protecting me, hiding me. He too has filled out – he's thicker, broader, but in a good way. Age suits him.

I feel my wedding band bite into the flesh of my finger.

If Jack knew I was here, I would say, *He's an old friend from back home. I bumped into him. We're having tea.*

It's a lie that, like the best ones, has a kernel of truth at its core.

Paul smiles and says, 'Aye, it is beautiful. And it helps to have the cafe to aim for. I've got used to having a biscuit or three on my tea breaks. Pete gives me the broken ones, don't you, mate?' he adds, as the young waiter hands him a mug.

'Have you worked here long?' I ask.

I have to be careful – he can't find out what I already know about him.

'Since Easter. I was a ranger in the Lake District before.'

'Oh!' So he'd stayed in Langdale all this time.

He's still smiling at me and I clasp my hands together in my lap to stop myself from taking his in mine.

'Too remote,' he says, taking a slurp of his tea. 'I loved it, but I've a lad – he's a teenager now – and it was a bit isolated for him.

I've been trying to get a relocation for years; there's not that many jobs like mine in the National Trust.'

'Would you like a scone?' I ask. 'I'm not going to eat both of them.'

'Aye, that would be nice. Thanks. Anyhow, this one came up, but the timing was a bugger. The lad's in the first year of his A-levels. Still, beggars can't be choosers. At least I don't have to be a bloody taxi driver any more, driving for miles to get him to his mate's house. Not that I minded, but he needs a bit of freedom. He can catch the bus himself now. Twenty minutes and he's in the big city.'

'So you live in Wraxall?' I ask, keeping my head down and concentrating on cutting the scone in half.

'No,' he shakes his head. 'It's one of the perks of working on the estate – me and the lad live onsite.'

I pass him his scone on my saucer, and I brush his arm accidentally as I do so. A shiver courses down my spine, like a small, electric pulse, and I blush furiously again, because I've done his scone just as he likes it, without asking him – butter and jam, no cream. I remember he preferred the ones with sultanas in, and Lizzie always liked them plain. I've got to be more careful.

'Thanks,' he says. 'I can't stand cream. Good thing you took it all!' He grins. 'So what about you? You got kids?'

I want him to say his son's name. I want to see what he looks like now. But asking straight out would sound creepy, stalkerish. If I give him a photo of my youngest daughter, perhaps he'll show me a picture of Dylan. I take out the little wallet of photos I always carry.

'Two girls – Ava, she's eleven.' I hand it to him. 'That's Jack, my husband.'

He nods and smiles at my beautiful, sunny, blonde-haired daughter and my handsome husband. He starts to turn the page. I realize I've made a mistake and I make a tiny, involuntary movement, as if I'm going to snatch it back. It's too late.

Instead I say, 'That's Stella, my oldest. She's fourteen.'

He freezes for a moment. He rubs his hand over his face. His fingers are ingrained with soil: he's not the kind of man for gardening gloves. He sets the photo down and bows his head. I know what he's going to tell me. I want to put an arm around his broad shoulders, to comfort him in advance for the loss he's about to describe. I pick up my scone instead, to keep my hands busy. Stella has Jack's sharp features, her hair is long and straight and she has pale-grey eyes. Like mine. And like Lizzie's. I shouldn't have given him the whole wallet of pictures. I'm taking too many risks.

'There's something about you that reminds me of my wife. My ex-wife,' he says. 'And your daughter is the spit of her. That's what I wanted to say – why I behaved so oddly last week. You see, she disappeared. I never found out what happened to her.'

I stop with my scone halfway to my mouth. I set it back down and shape my features into a concerned expression. I'm so agitated, it's not hard.

'That's terrible,' I say. 'When did she go missing?'

'Sixteen years ago – almost seventeen.' He smiles ruefully.

'And the police . . .?'

He shakes his head. 'Useless buggers.'

I rub my arms. I've come out in goosebumps, in spite of the heat. I notice Paul can't help glancing at my bare skin. Lizzie had a tattoo on her left bicep. It was of her son's name and the date he was born.

'Sorry,' he says. 'It's still so close to the surface, even after all this time. There was no—'

'Closure?' I say.

'There was no body, you see. I couldn't move on. The police as much as said she'd left me. Said it happens all the time. Partly my fault; I'd had a brief fling just before she disappeared. Stupid. I loved her.' He makes a face and I blush. He swallows painfully and continues, 'But I just didn't think – I mean, we were happy, we'd just had a baby . . .'

But not that happy, or you'd have been faithful to your wife, I think.

'Bloody hell, listen to me, telling you all this stuff. I don't—'

'You keep it in,' I say sympathetically.

'Aye.' He looks at me sharply.

I can't let him scrutinize me too closely. I duck my head and put my sunglasses back on.

'I'm sorry. I should go,' I say.

'Aye, me too. I've a heap of weeding to do. It's a bloody back-breaking job.' He stands and stretches. The joints in his spine pop. 'But someone's got to do it.'

Last chance, I think. *This is my last chance.*

'What's he called?' I ask, as nonchalantly as I can.

I want to hear him say it out loud. I have to be sure. It's sixteen years since I heard Paul Bradshaw say his name.

'Whose? My son's?' he says.

I nod.

'It's Dylan.'

'Dylan,' I repeat. 'Gaelic for faithful, loyal. How perfect!'

'Aye. Most people go on about the singer,' he says. His smile is wide. He sticks out his hand. 'It was nice talking to you, Emma.'

I walk as fast as I can to my bike. I've done what I set out to do: I know that he and Lizzie's son live close by and they are safe and well.

That has to be enough, I tell myself fiercely.

But by the time I've reached my bike, I can't see, my eyes are full of tears. Part of me is relieved that he still didn't know who I was, and part of me is saddened that he did not. I want to rage and scream and beat his chest with my fists. But I have to be strong. I repeat this mantra to myself as I cycle and cry, all the way back to our beautiful, empty house.

———

One of the many things my therapist told me is that keeping a diary of everything you're grateful for can help. I've never actually done it, but occasionally I make a list and run it like a loop in my mind. Sometimes it helps. Sometimes it doesn't.

This afternoon I cook a meal that I know Jack will like, to try and stem the tidal wave of guilt that threatens to overwhelm me, because I know I won't tell him about meeting Paul. As I do, I count my blessings:

1 I'm still alive.
2 Jack. My kind and caring husband, who was there when I needed him.
3 My beautiful girls.
4 I have a job that allows me to be around for my daughters.
5 We live in a gorgeous house.

I chop up parsley, basil and thyme, crush garlic, grind pink peppercorns and knead them into butter. *I'm alive.* I rub the herb butter into chicken breasts, pushing it across the skin with my thumbs. *My husband.* I sprinkle sea salt over the top. *Two girls I love more than life itself.* I rinse spinach, and drizzle oil over vine tomatoes, lay them in a roasting tray. *A good job.* I grate cauliflower to make carb-free rice, although I know my daughters will hate it and I'll have to cook pasta and fry up some sausages, too. *We live in this amazing house that Jack built.*

I go into the garden and pick roses – white and red – and intersperse them with lavender and purple sage and arrange them in a vase on the table. *Still alive.* I put some Chablis and some low-carb beer in the fridge to chill. *Alive.*

Jack and I met not long after the accident. I was drifting. Drinking. I was working in a deli, serving coffee, slicing Parma ham. They made the most extraordinary cakes, and that was where I learned how to bake. But at first I didn't have any direction and I was just going through the motions. Watching the milk foam, the coffee percolate through the machine. Letting my life trickle away. A man used to come in now and again, and then increasingly often. He always smiled. He always said hello. He was unfailingly polite. And, after a while, I'd smile before he spoke. I'd ask him how he was. He was older than me, with strikingly intense eyes, and hair in a buzz-cut. He was good-looking, but there was something about him that immediately put me at ease. It was how he spoke, I think.

Jack has the most wonderful voice: there's a rich timbre to it, a depth, a gentleness and a strength. You could imagine listening to that voice for ever, with its soft sibilance and hidden power. But the thing about Jack is that he's a good listener. When he focuses his attention on you, it's as if you are the only person who exists in the world. He finally asked me out, in such a diffident way I didn't quite realize that's what he was doing. He had tickets, he said, for a gig, on some boat in the harbour, and his friend had got flu. I'd be doing him a great service if I came with him and stopped him looking as if he had no mates.

It was a country-blues band and I'd never heard music like it, or even stepped on board a boat, let alone one that sold forty-three different kinds of cider and had a stage for rock music. Standing at the prow of the boat, between sets, looking out over the black water threaded with lights, drinking sparkling perry with a man almost twenty years older than me who seemed to hang upon my every word was the most romantic thing that had ever happened to me. I was twenty-two years old.

Jack, when he's with me, helps me forget my past. For a little while, at least.

By the time Stella, Ava, Jack and I sit down to eat, I'm calmer. I smile and serve our meal and don't rise to the 'Yuck' and 'I'm not eating that' from the girls, but simply pass them pasta and pesto and chipolata sausages.

'Thank you,' says Jack and reaches over to take my hand. 'This is perfect.'

After we've eaten, I clear up and Jack goes outside. I watch him out of the corner of my eye as I walk from table to sink and back again. He strolls through the garden, inspecting it carefully, his hands in his pockets. A little later, I pour myself another glass of Chablis and sit on the balcony. It's starting to grow cool. Jack prunes the roses and trims the box hedges. The snip of his shears and the evening song of the birds are soothing. He loves this garden, its neatness, its order. I think it helps him unwind. And I like to sit here and look at it. He glances up. I don't think he can see me refilling my wine glass, from his position on the lawn. He smiles at me and I smile back, because I love him, I really do.

LIZZIE

Lizzie stood up and began walking slowly towards Dev, who was standing in front of the door to the shop. She winced, her eyes half-shut against the pain of the migraine. It was one of those doors that could swing forwards or backwards, opening into the shop or the storeroom, and it hadn't quite closed after Arjun had left them. Dev's shock of hair was haloed by the light seeping in from the brightly lit newsagent's. She felt disoriented, as if she were on the deck of a boat and she might slide into the sea at any moment.

'Been here twice already. Stubborn bastard is still refusing. Doesn't know what's good for him.'

Her heart lurched. The voice, harsh and abrasive, sounded as if it belonged to a big man. A big, uneducated man, thought Lizzie. And he was talking to someone else, so there must be at least two of them.

'Everyone does it, Kumar,' he continued. 'We keep you safe. Think of it like an insurance policy.'

'I have insurance. Proper insurance,' said Arjun. 'Now please leave. I'm going to call the police.'

'Proper insurance, he says. Is that so? Pays out, does it? Against little accidents?'

There was a crash and the sound of glass shattering. Fuchsia and scarlet exploded behind her eyes and she was stopped dead by the pain pounding through her forehead, pulsing down her spine.

Dev whimpered. Lizzie clenched her jaw and reached out to him, her heart racing.

'Or like this?' roared the man, and there was another almighty crash, more glass splintering, the crack of cans tumbling onto the floor.

Dev shrank back and Lizzie tightened her arms around him. She crouched down until she was at his level and put her finger to her lips. Dev's eyes were wide, his ribs flaring as his breathing increased. Whoever these men were, they were dangerous and she couldn't let them find the child.

Through the gap she could see the man had overturned the shelves running all the way down the middle of the shop. The floor was covered with broken bottles – ketchup and brown sauce, chicken korma and pools of cider, still fizzing. He was at the far end of the shop, and now he turned and strode back to Arjun. He was well over six foot, with broad shoulders and a solid beer gut, meaty hands and a shaven head. There was a blurred tattoo like a smear down one side of his face. His eyes were sunk into the flesh of his cheeks. He was wearing black combat trousers and a ribbed jumper, as if he was a builder dressed in army surplus. She felt fear flood through her.

'Last chance, Kumar,' the man said, as he drew closer, his breath laboured.

Someone else was talking now, not Arjun or the other man, but someone who was so quietly spoken she could barely hear his words. Her bag had fallen down the far side of the camp bed. She picked it up and felt inside it for her mobile, hoping she wasn't making too much noise. When she finally found her phone, she pressed mute and started to key in the numbers.

'Well now,' said the quiet man, who seemed to be standing on the other side of the door, 'I think we've taken up a little too much of Mr Kumar's time.'

She could barely comprehend what was happening: the mismatch between this man and the violence of his companion was so extreme. His voice was soft, gentle, warm even, almost humble. *Thank God*, Lizzie thought – whoever they were, whatever they wanted, they were about to leave.

'Now, Mr Kumar, I don't like my people to be unhappy, but equally, we cannot let this slide, can we? This is what you owe me, I believe, with interest added. If you'd be so kind, we'll be on our way, and you can continue to do what you do best: serve our community. Once you've cleaned up your shop, naturally.'

'Please leave,' Arjun repeated. There was a tremor in his voice, although he struggled to sound dignified. 'I will call the police.'

Lizzie couldn't see Arjun, but it sounded as if he was standing to one side of the door, behind the cash register. But Arjun must have picked up his phone, because the man leaned right across the counter and there was a dull thud as his fist connected with his face. Dev cried out. Lizzie dropped her mobile and reached for the child.

'No? Well, perhaps this will persuade you.'

The man's arm shot through the gap in the door and seized Dev. He pulled the boy into the shop.

Her whole body froze, paralysed by fear.

Arjun was shouting, almost drowning out the sound of Dev's screams. The door swung backwards and forwards and, for a brief moment, she glimpsed him – he was holding the child by the throat, and then he moved out of her sight.

'Don't touch my boy! Don't touch him. Take the money, take it all!' It was Arjun's voice, high-pitched with fear.

As the door swung open a little way, she saw the massive man hurl himself towards Arjun and she heard grunts and the sound of them wrestling. Through the thin gap she could see the back of Dev's head, his thick shock of hair, a sliver of narrow shoulder. And then the quietly spoken man stepped forward and she saw a triangle of white shirt, the edge of a navy suit jacket; he raised his arm and his gold cufflinks glittered. There was something in his hand, something long and thin that flashed in the shop's strip-lighting. A knife. The blade, a blur of silver, sliced through the air towards the child's face. The door came to rest and she could no longer see what was happening. There was a terrible, high-pitched scream that went on and on. Arjun was bellowing, his words incomprehensible, like an animal being slaughtered. As if the paralysis had finally worn off, Lizzie fell forward, crashing through the door and falling into the shop. But it was too late. She was too late.

STELLA

Once a fortnight I get out of trailing around after my super-athletic, freakishly talented sister, who's gone swimming today. It's Book Club. Ms Heron takes it, but she doesn't act like my English teacher when she does. She's all kind of informal, like she's one of us. Not many people go to Book Club – none of the cool kids, anyhow, and that's good, because otherwise I'd be too shy to say anything.

"Today's book is *The Golden Bowl* by Henry James,' says Ms Heron. 'It's pretty long. Did anyone manage to get halfway through?'

Everyone apart from me shakes their head. Ms Heron smiles at me. Not much gets past her.

'I watched the film,' says Kaylee, and the others laugh.

'It's so-o-o hard to read,' says Theo. 'Every sentence is really complicated and you get to the end of one, two pages later, and you're like: what was that all about?'

'Uma Thurman's really hot in the movie and none of her sentences are hard to understand,' says Cian.

Nuala rolls her eyes at me. The door opens and a boy comes in. I've never seen him before. Kaylee elbows me in the ribs.

'Can I help?' asks Ms Heron.

'Is this Book Club?'

'Yes.'

'I want to join.' He glances at the rest of us from under his fringe.

I hate it when other people want to come to Book Club. I know everyone here really well – even if I don't like them all that much – and it upsets the balance when there's someone new. For a while I get all tongue-tied, and then they always leave after a couple of sessions anyway, when they realize you actually have to read the books.

'Of course. Have a seat. What's your name?'

'Adam,' he says.

There's something about the way he walks that's different. He doesn't slouch like the other boys in my year. He actually strides, like he owns the room. He sits in the empty space between me and Khadiija.

'We're talking about *The Golden Bowl*.'

'I haven't read it. I'm happy to listen, though.'

Typical, I think – but, to be fair, the only other person I know who's read it is my dad. Kaylee nudges me again and writes something in her exercise book.

He's new.

That explains it then, why I haven't seen him before and his – his *insouciance*. He hasn't had any crap knocked into him yet.

'Anyone want to say what it's about?' asks Ms Heron.

'It's about a prince who's poor and he marries a young, wealthy American girl for her money,' says Fee. 'But the whole time he's having an affair with a woman his own age.'

'He's a total bas— rotten young man,' says Theo.

'It's actually about love,' I say. 'There's this bit in it that kind of sums up the whole thing.' I open my copy of the book and read:

My idea is this, that when you only love a little you're naturally not jealous – or are only jealous also a little, so that it doesn't matter. But when you love in a deeper and intenser way, then you're in the very same proportion jealous; your jealousy has intensity and, no doubt, ferocity.

I look up and see the new boy, Adam, leaning right round to listen to me. I blush and snap the book shut. I wish I'd never opened my mouth. He's good-looking, which kind of makes it worse. He's got blondy-brown hair, a bit straggly, like a cut that's grown out, and sort of mud-coloured eyes, like they can't make up their mind whether they're blue or brown.

'It's also about betrayal,' says Ms Heron.

'And sex,' says Cian, and everyone giggles.

It's not one of our better Book Club sessions, since no one apart from me and Ms Heron's read much of it, and I don't want to say another word, although I have a whole heap of questions. I can't help being distracted by the new boy. And it's totally embarrassing how much Kaylee stares.

When it's time to go, Ms Heron says, 'Who'd like to choose the next book?'

'*Oryx and Crake* by Margaret Atwood,' Adam says.

I look at him in astonishment. I'd never dare to be like that. Like, he doesn't know us, he's never actually been to Book Club before, and yet he wants to choose the next book.

'It's set in the future. It's about a guy called *MaddAddam*.' He points to his chest and the others laugh.

'Good choice,' says Ms Heron, smiling at him. 'We'll have lots to talk about, with that one.'

I spend ages sorting out my stuff and Kaylee minces about the room.

'Come on, you're taking for ever.'

'You just want to walk behind that guy and admire his arse.'

'Totally!'

We're too late, though, which is exactly what I wanted. He disturbs me. I don't know why. I mime texting with my thumb to Kaylee and get in the car with Mum and Ava. My sister's hair is wet and slicked back, like she's a young Shakira, and the whole car smells of chlorine. The bike's in the boot, so I guess Mum's keeping up the cycling. She's still a chubster, though. I glance at her as we set off, trying to gauge how she is today. No new burns. Her wrist isn't so red. But she's somewhere else. She's driving like a robot and her eyes are far away. I pull the hood of my sweatshirt up and sink down in the seat. Sometimes I think she's like a barometer: whatever her internal weather is will be how our family ends up feeling. What is she today: cloudy with the threat of squalls?

Mum pulls into the car park at the farm shop.

'We need some milk. And cheese. Would you get it, love?'

She passes me her wallet. I don't make a fuss, like I normally would, because I've had an idea.

'Can I have some Hula Hoops? And a Snickers bar?' asks Ava.

'Go on then. Just don't tell your dad. You can get something for yourself as well,' she says to me.

I throw a bag of toffee popcorn into the basket and then go to the back of the shop where the fruit and veg are stacked. Mum isn't looking, but she couldn't see me here even if she were. I open her wallet, as if I'm looking for the right change, but instead I pull out a bundle of receipts. I go through them one by one. I'm not really sure what I'm looking for. It's just that I don't believe in Mum's bike rides. There are all the usual ones: things she buys with her staff discount at *Kate's*, M&S, Ava's next lot of ballet lessons – but then there are a whole load of receipts from the same place. The Pavilion cafe at Tyntesfield. They're all for cups of tea and cakes. No wonder she isn't losing any weight. I push them back into her wallet and go and pay.

Why is Mum going to Tyntesfield by herself? It's the sort of place Dad would visit – Gothic Revival architecture really rocks his boat – but he'd never go to the cafe on his own. Anyway, he's too busy. Maybe it's the destination for her bike rides, and she wants a bit of a sit down before she cycles back. That would be so like Mum.

'Thanks, love,' she says when I get in, like I've just completed some Herculean task.

'You've been out on your bike today then?'

'Yes – it's getting much easier. Your dad was right. I just had to stick with it.'

'Do you go somewhere?'

'No,' she laughs. 'I still cycle up and down Festival Way. I'm so boring.'

'You're not boring, Mum,' Ava says.

She just lied to me and, if I hadn't seen those receipts, I'd never have known. It's what my drama teacher would call 'a flawless performance'. *Why would you lie about going to a cafe?* I wonder. But it's not until we get out of the car that I have a cold feeling in my stomach. If she lied about such a little thing so convincingly, what else is she lying about?

When Dad comes home, I say, 'Why is *The Golden Bowl* called *The Golden Bowl*?'

He ruffles Ava's hair and kisses Mum, but he doesn't touch me. He knows I don't like it.

'Well,' he says, shrugging off his jacket and rolling up his shirt sleeves, 'it's a quotation from the Bible: "or the golden bowl be broken . . . then shall the dust return to the earth as it was".'

'Yeah, but what does it mean? In the novel.'

'It was Book Club today, wasn't it?' he says, glancing at our schedules. 'It's ages since I read it. Wasn't the bowl meant to be a wedding gift?'

I nod. Dad gets out a packet of kale and some salmon fillets from the fridge. I hate it when he cooks. Ava is pulling a face behind his back, and Mum is whispering to her to stop it and trying not to laugh.

'Well, what do you think?'

I groan. It's so annoying when he does that. I stomp downstairs. Obviously it's some kind of metaphor, the crack in the bowl symbolizing the crack in their marriage, or something. But that's not what I really wanted to know. I actually want to know what my mum's secret is. I get out my journal. I'm going to follow her, I decide. I need to be able to get to Tyntesfield after she leaves work and before she picks me up from school. But then the school would tell her, if I bunked off early. And how would I get there? I groan again and throw myself on the bed.

I could go on Saturday, I think. I rule out asking Dad to take me, although he'd jump at the chance. I send Kaylee a message. She spends the weekends with her dad and she's got him wrapped round her little finger.

EMMA

I pour myself a glass of wine and go downstairs. Our bathroom is huge – Lizzie's entire sitting room could have fitted in here. I run water and add scented oil and bubble bath. Although it's still light outside, I have to be up early for work. I leave the curtains and the windows in the bedroom open. The beauty of Jack's design is that the sitting room has superb views and we can walk directly into the garden from our bedroom. Jack is right outside, mowing the lawn. The sweet scent of cut grass permeates the room and stops me thinking about the smell of wood smoke that trickled into Lizzie's house from the draughty chimney.

These are the things that help me now: alcohol and hot baths. They prevent me dwelling on the past, on memories I'd rather forget. After the accident, I drank far too much to blot it all out. Jack helped me get my drinking back in control, and now I try not to have more than two glasses in a row. If it weren't for Jack, I'm sure that would slide to three or four large ones a night. I let myself sink beneath the surface and the hum of the lawnmower fades.

As I'm climbing out of the bath, I catch sight of myself in the mirror. I examine myself critically, as if assessing another person, a stranger. The skin on my face is flawless – I had all my freckles removed and I've had considerable work done. Even now, I occasionally glimpse myself in a shop window or a mirror in a department store and it takes a moment to realize that the woman in the reflection is me. I spend a considerable portion of my wages on my hair – some people say it's like a second mortgage, don't they? My hair is blonde, with a smooth wave in it. I get my roots done every couple of months and have a relaxing treatment twice a year. I'm less happy with my body. I'm much bigger than I used to be, although I suppose it's not a bad thing. It's like a disguise. Being heavier has altered everything about me physically – how I walk, how I stand, the shape of my jawline, the roundness of my cheeks, the slope of my shoulders. After the accident, I let myself go, and then pregnancy pretty much ruins your body – there's the weight gain, of course, but also sagginess, the silvery sheen of stretch marks, bigger, distinctly less pert breasts. Still, that's what a good bra is for.

I open one of the drawers in our walk-in wardrobe. It's full of beautiful underwear. Every time Jack goes away for work, he comes back with a set. I don't wear it most of the time: it's gorgeous, but uncomfortable. The silken fabric whispers between my fingers. I select a cream bra and pants, edged with lace. In the twilight they have a pearlescent glow. As I put them on, I think of Paul, stretching before he went back to work, the way his T-shirt rode up, how the sunlight illuminated his eyes, the dimple that had become a line in his cheek, which I wanted to trace with my finger.

I put my eye-mask on, to help me sleep and block out thought.

There's a single moment when I lie, rigid with tension, every muscle locked, my heart pounding, and then I remember where I am and who I'm with, and I relax again. Jack must have woken me. He caresses my stomach, his fingers gliding across my skin, still slick with bath oil, and I hear his intake of breath as he feels the grosgrain ribbon and the tiny, heart-shaped space in the lace.

I turn towards him and reach up to take off the eye-mask, but he whispers, 'Don't. Leave it.'

I arch my back as he enters me.

'You know,' I say, my hands curling round his shoulders and running down his biceps, 'we could try for a son. Third time lucky,' I whisper into the dark.

He stops moving and I think he's going to withdraw. I want to take the mask off and see his face, but maybe it's better like this. His kiss on my lips is unexpected and butterfly-light. I feel it tiptoe down my spine.

'I'm too old for all that . . .' he says, 'nappies and getting up in the night. I'd be heading towards retirement by the time he's ten. And we have two beautiful girls. We're lucky. Why risk it?'

I wonder if that is what he really feels; if he's accidentally hit on the words that will set off small explosions in my mind – trigger-phrases like risk and safety, danger and security, love and loss, and the other ones that I never say: Paul. Lizzie. Dylan.

'You're right,' I say, 'we're so lucky.'

He pushes the stiff silk of my bra down and takes my nipple in his mouth. The smell of the newly mown lawn is sharp. I'm a little afraid of not being able to see, but Jack's arms are around me, and now I'm glad of the mask because its soft fabric soaks up my tears.

STELLA

'Why are we following your mum?' whispers Kaylee. 'Shush!' I say.

We're in the back of her dad's car driving to Tyntesfield. Ted's whistling. Normally he doesn't know what to do with Kaylee on a Saturday; he drives us to Cabot Circus and hangs about awkwardly at the back of Next, or sits in Costa while she drags me round Primark.

'Did you know, the Tyntesfield estate has been owned by the Tynte baronets since the 1500s?' he says, glancing at us in the rear-view mirror.

Kaylee rolls her eyes. 'You just googled that.'

We've told her dad that we're doing a history project and we need to go round a mansion.

'Okay, how about this then? *Sherlock* was filmed here. The one with Benedict Cumberbatch in. That's cool, right?'

I smile at him. He really tries hard with Kaylee, and she's mean to him.

'Yeah, we saw them filming it,' I say.

I'm pretty sure my mum won't be in the house, though. I mean, I've looked at the estate on Google Earth and there's no way she'd get up that hill to the entrance on her bike. She has no interest in Gothic, revivals or otherwise. The receipts were for the Pavilion cafe – which is at the bottom end, plus she could easily cycle there. And I sure as hell don't want to be dragged round a mansion by an over-excited single parent downloading bollocks about the Victorians on 4G.

'The thing is, Ted, our project is more about, you know, how they grew their own food.'

'Oh, I see. You want to go to the far end then, where the Kitchen Garden is.'

I smile at him again and Kaylee elbows me. 'You haven't answered my question,' she hisses.

'Laters,' I say, and look out the window.

I check my watch. I hope we haven't missed her. If she's coming, she would be here now. I walk faster and take Kaylee's arm, hurrying her along. We run down the hill past the tennis courts and to the boating pond that's now a lake of concrete with a pathetic, broken wooden boat stuck in the middle. I glance back. Ted is on the path above us.

'I just want to see why she keeps coming here,' I say. 'But I don't want her to see us. Okay?'

'You're not in bloody MI5, you know, Miss Moneypenny.' Kaylee tosses her long, dark hair out of the way. Her mum's Greek and she's inherited her large hazel eyes and skin, which is the colour of a cappuccino. And her temper. 'I don't get why you want to know. Your mum goes to a cafe. What's the big deal?'

I open my mouth to reply, but I can't think what to say. She's right. It doesn't seem so weird, when she says it like that. But Mum always complains about having too much to do, what with ferrying the prima donna to all her classes, and attempting to keep the house immaculate for Dad, and getting up so frigging early for work. I shrug.

We reach these old stone archways, with tree ferns and other shit growing round them, and go past some greenhouses. Ted's shouting at us because we've shot right past the vegetable garden, but Kaylee's spotted the Orchard playground in front of the cafe and she's sprinting there like she's a five-year-old. Mum clearly isn't here, so I join her, jumping from one upturned apple box to another and balancing on ropes. A couple of mothers scowl at us, worried we'll scare their toddlers into falling off the giant wooden snail.

I'm balancing on the tractor when I see her. She's in the orangery. I get down quickly and grab hold of Kaylee.

'Can you get rid of your dad? Just for a couple of minutes.'

'Where is she?' asks Kaylee.

I tilt my chin in the vague direction. 'Don't look!'

'Dad? Dad!'

Ted's given up educating us, and he's checking his emails.

'Can we have a Coke? And some cake?'

'Nice one,' I say, as he heads into the cafe.

As soon as he's gone, we run towards the orangery and duck behind a hedge. Mum is sitting inside on a stone bench. I can barely see her, because she has her back to us and she's surrounded by lemon trees. At first I think she's alone, but then I notice the man. He's sitting next to her. They're both holding mugs of tea and they're leaning towards each other. They're almost touching. It's like they want to, but they can't, because of the tea. I feel kind of strange, watching my mum when she doesn't know I'm there. I can't see him properly, though. Maybe he's one of our family friends, the old people who come round for dinner and bore us and will probably turn up for the big anniversary party.

I nudge Kaylee and we creep round the side. She does an annoying exaggerated tiptoe thing. We crouch next to a flowerbed and can just about see through the window.

'He's a bit of a looker, isn't he? I mean for an old guy.'

I worry about Kaylee sometimes. She's got a thing for older men and she's obsessed with sex. The man is about my mum's age, and Kaylee's right: he is good-looking, with dark, messy hair and eyes. He's all in brown and there's a logo on his chest, so maybe he works here.

'So who is he? Do you think they're doing it?'

'Don't be dumb,' I say.

It had occurred to me, but the guy has his elbows on his knees and is hanging his head, and my mum is looking so sad. If they were having an affair, they'd be happy, wouldn't they?

'You going to talk to her?'

'We should go back. Your dad'll be wondering where we are.'

'You've missed the point, as usual. We'll go and find him, because he's got Coke. Anyway, are you happy now, Sherlock?'

I don't have to answer, because Kaylee's seen her dad with big wedges of chocolate-fudge cake and she races over to him. I think about what my mum was doing there and who the man is, all the way back home. At least I've got something more substantial to write in my journal.

Mum is already back when Ted drops me off. She's got that same sheen about her, like she does after her other bike rides. As if she's crackling with energy, but it's not *joyful*. I feel myself starting to get nervous and prickly, too, so I go downstairs, intending to get my diary out. When I open the door to my bedroom, Ava sits up.

She'd been lying on my bed and her face is streaked with tears.

'You abandoned me,' she says, over-dramatically.

'What? I went out with Kaylee and her dad. You were at ballet.'

'Yeah, and then Dad left me in the house all by myself and went in the shed.'

Dad has an office at the bottom of our garden. It's like, state-of-the-art, with its own Wi-Fi and AVG system, but he still calls it his 'shed'. When he's there, he sets the alarm for the main house. Ava hates it, because she'll trigger the alarm if she goes outside and she doesn't like switching if off her by herself, and she thinks it's childish to ring Dad when he's only in the garden.

'I was trying to do my Citizenship project and you weren't here to help me.'

'Well, ask Mum. She's home now.'

'I can't.'

She pushes her homework across to me. I glance down at it, intending to tell Ava to get out of my room and leave me alone, but then I see why. The pamphlet says, *Write about where you come from. Who are your relatives? Where were they from?*

'You could do Dad's,' I say.

She nods and points to the page she's filled in, next to the blank template for a family tree. She's written:

My dad is called Jack Taylor. He lived in lots of places when he was little but then his family moved to Belfast but he doesn't have an Irish accent. His dad is from the Black Forest in Germany like the cake and his mum is from Ireland. We call them Grossvater and Oma. He doesn't have any sisters or brothers.

'You just have to write what happened. No one will ask you any more questions then.'

We both know she can't ask Mum, because she'll get upset and she'll be sad for days.

'I'll stay with you while you do it,' I add.

When Ava isn't looking, I get out my journal and sit at my desk and think what to say about seeing Mum today. Ava lies on my bed. She shows me what's she's written:

My mum is called Emma. She lived in Bath when she was a little girl and then she moved to Bristol. When she was seventeen her mum, dad and sister were killed on the motorway in a car crash. My mum was on her own until she met my dad and had me and my sister. She doesn't have any other relatives.

'That's really good, Ava. Maybe you could say what her name was before she got married. You know, her maiden name?'

'I don't know what it was.'

'Emma James.'

'No cousins, or aunts or uncles,' she says moodily. 'What's the point of doing a family tree? And how do I know where *I* come from? Or who I am?'

She throws herself back on the bed. She's about to start crying again, so I say, 'But you do know! You're a quarter Irish, a quarter German and half from Bath.'

'I'm half a bath.' She snorts with laughter and my little sister is back to being her sunny self again.

LIZZIE

Dev was screaming. He had his hands over his eyes and his face was covered with blood and something else. Arjun was kneeling by his son, sobbing, holding the boy.

'Help him!' he shouted at Lizzie.

She didn't know what to do. They needed to stop the bleeding. An ambulance. She fumbled for the light switch in the stockroom and picked up her mobile. The screen had cracked, but when she lifted it to her ear, it had already connected and she could hear a voice saying over and over again, 'How may I help you? Hello? Hello? Which service do you require? Hello?'

'Ambulance. Police,' she shouted. 'I don't know what to do. He's bleeding.'

'Tell me who is hurt and what happened,' the call handler said.

'I can't tell how bad it is. He's bleeding . . .'

'Who is bleeding?'

'A child. His face—'

Is the child breathing?'

'Yes.'

'Where are you? Tell me where you are,' the dispatcher said.

'The newsagent's. Kumar's. Belle Isle. I don't have an address. It's, you know, near an estate. I don't know – I don't know where exactly. What do I do?'

Arjun had ripped his shirt off and was holding it to the boy's face.

Dev was screaming, 'Daddy, Daddy, Daddy!'

She couldn't hear what the man was saying and then his voice returned, louder this time: 'Found it. The ambulance is on its way. Who is injured?'

'A boy. He's six.'

'What is the nature of the injury? What happened?'

'What happened?' the dispatcher repeated.

Arjun was weeping, his hands covered in blood.

'Try and tell me what the injury is.'

'He stabbed him. In the eye,' she said.

Arjun howled with pain.

'Okay, do not apply pressure. Put something sterile over his eye, a clean cloth. The ambulance will be there in four minutes,' he said.

'A clean cloth.' She found she was saying it over and over again.

'That's right. A handkerchief. A bandage. Remember, even though he's bleeding, do not apply pressure.' The man's voice was calm, soothing.

'First-aid kit,' said Arjun.

It was under the counter, below the smashed till. She put the phone on speaker, tore the kit open, ripped the packet with her teeth.

'Okay, ready?'

Arjun nodded, dropped the shirt and gripped the screaming child's hands. Lizzie thought she was going to faint. Her vision blurred. Her knees crumpled. She took a deep breath, placed the bandage against the child's face and held it there gently. Arjun crushed the boy to his chest.

Dev was screaming, 'I can't see, I can't see, I can't see!'

Sirens wailed, the volume ear-splitting, drowning out Dev's cries; the lights, red and blue light, pulsed across the ceiling. When the paramedics burst through the door, they had to prise both of them away from the boy. Within a couple of minutes, they'd put Dev on a stretcher and secured him in the ambulance, with his father next to him.

Lizzie was left behind, standing in a pool of tomato sauce, shards of glass crunching beneath her feet. She looked down at her hands. They were covered in blood. She was shaking.

'You're going into shock,' someone said, taking hold of her arm. 'Let's get you to hospital.'

The child's screams were still ringing in her head.

'Is he going to be okay?' she asked the police officer, who was steering her out of the newsagent's.

'They'll do everything they can,' he said, helping her inside the ambulance car.

EMMA

I haven't been able to stop myself. Most days, after work, I cycle over there and, when I arrive, he goes on his break and we have a cup of tea together. I chat about work and the girls, but I don't mention Jack. I suppose that's not a surprise. Paul hasn't said anything about Lizzie since that first time, which is a relief. It's too painful to think about her and the life she might have had; it's hard enough being with Paul, as it is. He reminds me of the past, and I need to focus on the present.

I want to know about Dylan. I tell myself that's why I'm here, why I'm taking such a terrible risk. The last time I saw him, I kissed him on top of his head. His fontanelle hadn't closed over yet, and I could feel the softness beneath my lips. He'd started teething and he was dribbling. He waved his fists at me and gave me a gummy grin. I didn't realize then that I would never see Lizzie's son again.

I want to know what he's like. What he looks like. Would I recognize him if I saw him now? And will he ever forgive me for what I did? I want him to know how much he was loved, how much I still love him, how often I've thought of him. On my worst days, I've imagined him in that cold and draughty cottage and tortured myself with how he must have felt, growing up without a mother's love. What would a child become, if he'd been abandoned practically from birth? And how much of what happened is my fault, the decisions I made?

I've found out exactly where he and Paul live – the cottage on the edge of the wood overlooking the estate. It's not far from the Pavilion cafe.

I can't ask Paul much about his son, though. It might look odd. He pauses sometimes and glances at me out of the corner of his eye and looks away. Is he beginning to remember me now, but doesn't want to say, because . . . well, that would be difficult, wouldn't it? And when he does, it'll be over. So first I need to find out as much as I can. But it doesn't mean I don't think about Paul every day, that I don't imagine peeling off his clothes, that I don't fantasize about what it would be like to rest my head against his bare shoulder and run my hands down his chest; that when I'm with him, sometimes I can't look him in the eye in case he sees the rawness of my old desire resurfacing.

I've had to plan what I'm doing today quite carefully. The disadvantage of my schedules – printing them out and making sure Stella and Jack have them updated on their phones – is that everyone in my family knows where I am at all times. Well, most of the time. I miss some of my appointments off the calendar.

Today I create a new one showing that I'm working, when really it's my day off. I get up at the usual time but, instead of going to the bakery, I park in Failand. I set off through the wood, towards the cottage where Paul and Dylan live. The sun is rising and beams of clear honey-coloured light slant through the oak trees. The path is grassy and gleams with dew. There's a grating noise and I jump. It's just rooks, though. I'm nervous about being here on my own in the early morning when there's no one else around, but I twist the elastic band round my wrist and force myself to keep going. I imagine Paul walking through these woods. I wonder if he's brought Gil with him, his border collie.

It's safe, I tell myself, *this is safe.*

It's so far removed from the places I have nightmares about that gradually my fists uncurl and I release the tension in my shoulders.

And as I relax, my thoughts return to Paul, as they do all the time I'm not with him. I need to know how Dylan is. I need to see him again. But my body aches for Paul's. My fingertips prickle, as if, as I walk, I can feel his lips grazing my skin. I touch my own lips and they feel swollen, as if he's kissed me too hard and his stubble has bruised my flesh. I flush, ashamed of myself: it's a betrayal of Jack even to think about another man like this.

I reach a narrow track, just about wide enough for a car, and follow it until I see Paul's house. The cottage has its back to the wood and faces towards the fields and the vegetable gardens where Paul works, across the gentle slope of Backwell Common and down to the River Yeo below. The fields are a lush green, glazed gold in the early-morning light. The garden is overgrown, dense with honeysuckle and white roses; small birds are already crowded round the feeders. The front garden is a riot of artichokes, the buds ready to burst open like giant purple thistles, and towering hollyhocks. I curl up on some tree roots, hidden by a hazel, and I wait.

I've brought a flask of coffee. I never normally drink it because it makes my heart race even more than it usually does. Today, though, I want to be alert. The coffee is good: it's from *Kate's*. But when I pour myself a cup, the smell transports me to the Lakes. Three days a week Paul used to work a double-shift, finishing his ranger duties early and then heading over to the Stickleback, a pub owned by the National Trust. I remember him prepping in the kitchens at the back, grinding beans and chopping limes, before going behind the bar. I'm sure his cheeky grin and easy banter were why they did so well when he was working. Lizzie used to come over in the late afternoon with Dylan in the backpack and sit by the fire, playing Scrabble while her baby slept, and Paul would bring her a Stickleback gin and tonic on the house.

The coffee keeps me sharp, focused. I'm waiting to see Dylan as he leaves for school. Once I know what he looks like – and I find out from Paul which school he's at – I can follow him. Maybe even get up the courage to speak to him. The old fear envelops me again, of all that I stand to lose: my husband, Jack, my girls, even Paul and Dylan, all over again. The danger is real; it's not just in my head. I've been so careful all my adult life; I mustn't screw up now. What if someone sees me? What if my plan fails and I'm caught? My mind spins round and round: how would I explain this away, if Jack somehow found out what I was doing? I twist the band tightly round my wrist again, let it snap. The pain brings me back to the present.

I jump as I hear the click of the front door. It's too early for Dylan, surely? My heart starts to pound. It's Paul. He whistles, and Gil comes bounding out. He was a youngster when I last saw him and he's filled out since then. I'm holding my breath. I let it out slowly. All sorts of possibilities are running through my mind. If Paul takes Gil for a walk, Dylan will be on his own in the house. If I look through the window, I might see a photo of his son. But what if Dylan is up already, having his breakfast? I'm being ridiculous. I need to sit and wait patiently for him to emerge. When I close my eyes, though, I see Dylan sleeping; in my imagination, I'm standing over him and he turns towards me so that I can see his face, and I hold out my arms to him . . . I can't imagine what he looks like, though.

There's a woof, and Gil is leaping up at me, barking and whining, wagging his tail and licking my face. I hug the dog's solid body to mine and stroke his soft ears. I've missed him, too.

'Emma?' Paul is in front of me. He looks confused. 'What are you doing here?'

'I . . . I was walking,' I say.

Paul looks from the dog to my spilt drink and overturned flask.

What am I going to say? Why would I – a woman he barely knows – be sitting outside his house in the middle of a wood, drinking coffee at 6.30 in the morning? I feel the heat rising from my chest, spreading across my face, prickling through my scalp. I stand up and open my mouth to speak. But there's no need, because Paul's face suddenly creases into one of his big, slow smiles. He stretches out his hand and pulls me towards him.

'What a nice surprise,' he says softly, and then he's kissing me.

I don't even hesitate for a moment. It's as if it's a reflex. I kiss him back. It's long and passionate, his lips are hot and it's as if I can taste the sharpness of juniper on my tongue.

'Come with me,' he says, taking my hand, and he leads me towards his cottage.

At the front door, I hesitate. What if he recognizes me when we're in bed together? I might let my guard down. Perhaps the way I make love is so distinctive, he'll remember who I really am. I want him, though. I'm trembling. And I have to find out about Dylan.

I can hardly speak, my tongue feels so swollen. 'What about your son?'

'Dylan's not here,' he says. 'He went to a club last night and stayed over with a friend.'

I'm disappointed, of course, but it's as if my body is on autopilot. I follow Paul up the crooked staircase, into his bedroom. Like the one in the Langdale Pikes, it's under the eaves and he can barely stand upright. The room is dark; the early-morning light filters through the Virginia creeper that spreads across the narrow windows, so it feels as if we are underwater. He takes off my coat and undoes the buttons of my shirt, one by one. And it seems both familiar and unfamiliar, as if I've done this before in a dream. For a moment I think about stopping him, about running out of this room, this house, this wood. I think about Jack and what a terrible thing I'm about to do to him, and then I shut my eyes and push the thought of my husband away.

And afterwards – afterwards, I lie in Paul's arms and I can't stop crying. It's as if I've come home after being away for a long time.

STELLA

'Did you find out who that guy was?' asks Kaylee as we head out of school.

I shake my head.

'What are you going to do now, Miss Moneypenny?'

I shrug.

'Want to come to Cabot Circus? Dad's taking me.'

'I'll ask my mum,' I say, knowing Mum will say no and that I need to go home with her. I hate being told what I can or can't do, but it's a good excuse, when I really don't like shopping and I haven't got any money anyhow. I wouldn't mind going to Waterstones, but Kaylee thinks that's boring. There's a group of sixth-formers hanging around at the school gate and I notice one of them is standing a little to one side. He's looking at us. It's Adam. I can feel myself going hot and prickly.

Kaylee nudges me.

'Don't stare,' I mutter.

She gets out her lipgloss and starts applying it. It smells sickly, like blackcurrants.

'My dad's here,' I say in surprise. I've just spotted him leaning against the car. He waves at me and climbs in. 'Gotta go. Talk later, yeah?'

She nods and tosses her hair, for the benefit of the boys.

'Where's Mum?' I ask Dad.

'Ava has extra ballet practice – she's got a performance coming up soon. I said I'd pick you up.'

'I can go on the bus,' I say sulkily.

'Yes, but I need your help,' he grins at me.

'Oh yeah? You're not going to make me buy a dress for this frigging anniversary party, are you?'

'Heaven forfend.'

'Then what—'

'You'll see,' he says, with that smug look I can't stand.

'I've got homework,' I say, trailing after him, once he's parked. 'And revision.'

'You can do it where we're going. I'll test you, if you like.'

'No bloody way. I need a computer, not an old person.'

'I've got my laptop with me. And a dongle, so you'll have Wi-Fi.'

His smile doesn't reach his eyes, so I know I've pushed him as far as it's safe to, without a minor explosion.

We walk through Castle Park. It's kind of pleasant. There are people sitting out in the late-afternoon sunshine eating ice cream, and swans drifting down the river. We go into St Nicholas Market and Dad asks me what I want to drink.

'Coffee,' I say and, to my surprise, he gives a curt nod. He doesn't approve of minors having coffee, but then he thinks Coke is the devil's drink.

I sit where he's told me to, at a table opposite a flower stall with bunches of early sunflowers and sunset-orange roses. They make me think of *The Golden Bowl* again, but there's no point asking Dad about it. He comes back with my Americano and three slices of cake. I look at him in surprise.

'We've got to choose,' he says. 'I'm ordering a cake for the anniversary party from here, and I don't know which one your mum would like best.'

'Are you having some?' I ask suspiciously, picking up a fork. Dad never eats carbs, so sugar is definitely not on the menu. Surely he's not going to let me eat all this by myself?

'Of course.' He points with his fork. 'Black Forest gateau, coffee-and-bourbon, orange-and-polenta.'

I raise my eyebrows. 'Not very traditional. I thought you'd go for fruit. You know, the boring one with tiers, like you have at a wedding.'

'I know what you meant. I don't think that's your mum's idea of a cake, either.'

I try a bit of each one as I work out how to tell him. I'm not good at being tactful, but I might as well make the most of the free cake and caffeine. I can't think how to say it kindly, though, so I end up just blurting it out.

'You know there's no way on God's green earth that Mum would want a surprise party. She hates surprises. She'll freak out.'

'Hmm. But sometimes the things you don't want are what you actually need.'

I snort and take another mouthful of cake, so I can't tell him what a crap philosophy that is.

'Look, I don't expect you to understand this, but I love your mum dearly. I want her to know how much I – we – love her. It's an achievement and something to celebrate, when you've been married for fifteen years.'

How hard is it to get married and stay married? What does he want – a fucking medal? I bet they only got married because she was pregnant with me. It doesn't take a genius to do the maths.

It suddenly occurs to me that maybe he was married before. He's never said he was but . . . well, he is a lot older than Mum and he doesn't like being bad at things. When I ask, though, he shakes his head.

'I had a couple of serious relationships, but they didn't work out. Until your mum came along. She's my ideal woman.'

I make a face. Too much information. I wait until I've eaten half of all three cakes and then I say, 'Mum won't like any of these. I mean, she'll eat them, sure, because she always eats cake and she likes pleasing you. But if you want to give her something special, these aren't them.'

He looks taken aback. 'But . . .'

'She doesn't like alcohol in cakes. That's Katie's thing. And she isn't into gluten-free or, you know, polenta. She doesn't think it's right for cake. Anyway, it's what poor people eat.' My dad winces, in spite of his best Dr Seuss face. 'In developing countries like Mexico, I mean. You have to be middle-class to afford it here.' That didn't help. When you get stuck, stick to the facts – that's what Dad always tells me. 'She'd like a Victoria sponge with lots of cream and some fruit. Raspberries and jam. Something simple.'

He looks disappointed. I can see he wanted a statement of a cake. Like his love.

'I'm sure they'll be able to make it look fancy,' I say as I get out my revision notes, and Dad looks a bit more cheerful.

'Perhaps they can decorate it with real flowers,' he says, noticing the little stall behind us.

'Seeing as you're here, maybe you can help me. But just keep to the answers on the papers, not what you think they ought to be,' I say, handing him Religious Studies.

LIZZIE

'I don't understand. I don't understand what happened. He sounded so nice. Refined.' She started crying. 'I need to talk to my husband.'

'I spoke to him earlier.'

'What? How do you know—'

'He phoned, wanting a chat. One of my officers answered your mobile and passed him on to me. I told him you'd seen a crime, but you were unharmed,' said the detective. He'd introduced himself earlier as DI Simon Duffield. 'I need you to finish this statement, love, while it's all fresh in your mind. Then one of the officers will take you home.'

The two officers who'd escorted her to the hospital had brought her here, to Millgarth, the HQ for Leeds Met. It was like some red-brick Orwellian building, with slit windows and concrete staircases on the outside, sandwiched between the A61 roundabout and Leeds City bus station. She wished she was on one of those buses right now, heading back to Elterwater, to Paul and Dylan.

'Can I get you anything? Cup of tea?' asked the female officer who was sitting in with them.

'Coffee, please,' she said, wiping her eyes. 'Milk and two sugars. I need the caffeine.'

It was one-thirty in the morning and the adrenaline was wearing off. She felt completely beat and, at the same time, wired. The hospital staff had given her medication for her migraine, so at least the pain had gone.

The woman – she'd introduced herself, but Lizzie couldn't remember her name – spoke to someone outside the interview room and returned to her seat at the desk.

DI Simon Duffield resumed recording the interview.

'So you said the two men wanted money from Mr Kumar. Did they say why?'

Simon had thick eyebrows. He looked up at her from under them. He was in his fifties, with short, dark hair and a square chin. His stubble almost hid the three moles that ran in a line along his right jaw.

'Insurance, they said. But they can't have been there for that, can they? Were they blackmailing him?'

'You described the man who destroyed Mr Kumar's shop and punched him in the face. What about the other one? The one you said stabbed Mr Kumar's son?'

'Will he be okay?'

'Dev's in a stable condition, according to the hospital staff,' said Simon.

'What about his eye?' Lizzie whispered.

'We don't know yet. I'm afraid he might lose the sight in that eye, and it's possible he could have brain damage. It depends whether the knife pierced his brain, or if the bleeding caused internal damage. We have to wait and hope for the best. So can you describe the man, love, the one who injured Dev Kumar?'

Another officer brought in a coffee and a plate of biscuits and set it down in front of her. She took a sip and shut her eyes. She tried to focus on him, on the man, and block out what he'd done to the child.

It was such a fleeting glimpse, through the crack in the door . . . With her eyes still closed, she said, 'He had light-brown hair. Thin. Small. He was white. Like someone you'd pass on the street and you'd never notice. Nondescript, you know?'

She opened her eyes and looked into Simon's kind ones.

'Can you think of anything else? Anything distinctive about him?'

'The really odd thing about him was what he was wearing. I'm sure it was a suit. As if he really was an insurance salesman. I don't think I've seen anyone in a suit in Belle Isle. He had gold cufflinks.'

The female officer and Simon exchanged glances. He pushed a photo across the table to her.

'I'm showing Ms Elizabeth Bradshaw a photograph of six suspects in a police line-up. Item reference CXZ2358. Lizzie, do you recognize any of the men in the photo?'

She looked at it, assuming she wasn't going to be able to pick him. But as she scanned the row, it was as if she could see his face in slow motion, the half-turn towards her, the way he seized Dev's throat with those spidery fingers, the one brief moment when he glanced up and it felt as if he'd looked right at her. She shuddered.

'This man.'

He was shorter than the others, his hair trimmed into a neat cut and he was looking nonchalantly to one side. Duffield pushed another photograph across the table and explained what it was, for the benefit of the tape recorder. It was a mugshot. The man was five foot six, in his late forties, perhaps early fifties. He looked as if he should be working in a bank. His features were bland, his face relaxed and set in an almost pleasant, composed expression. Apart from his eyes. She recoiled.

Lizzie prided herself on her scientific training, on being rational, logical, practical. But none of her ideas about herself and the world, or the education she'd received so far, could prepare her or explain the effect this man had on her. His eyes, staring out at her from the photograph, looked – she searched for another word to describe them and failed – he looked evil. There was a blankness to him, as if the normal human emotions that you took for granted in everyone you met had been excised. It was the kind of stare you might see in a wolf or a shark; a creature who did not care how kind you were, what your story was, the dreams you had for your child.

'Yes. It's him. This is the man I saw.'

'Are you sure?'

'Yes.'

'Jon Lilley,' said Simon. 'He's a well-known racketeer. He extorts local businesses right across Belle Isle, Morley, Churwell, Beeston, Robin Hood . . . you get the picture. They pay him, or his men trash the place. Or worse. Mr Kumar hadn't been in the neighbourhood long, had he?'

She shook her head.

'We've been following Lilley for years. There have been almost no sightings of him. We can only assume that since the initial threats against Mr Kumar hadn't worked, he thought he'd deal with the situation himself.' Simon leaned across the table. 'Jon Lilley is an extremely dangerous individual. He's been responsible for five murders, eight mutilations – nine, if you include Dev Kumar – forty-seven incidences of GBH and numerous savage beatings. We have two witnesses: you and Mr Kumar.'

She realized she was holding her breath. Simon seemed almost excited.

'With your help, your testimonials, we can finally convict him and get him locked up for the rest of his life.'

She exhaled. She glanced at the female police officer, but the woman would not meet her eye. Lizzie looked down at her hands, which were clasped in her lap, and twisted her new wedding ring.

Simon stretched even further across the table. 'What if it had been your son? What if it was Dylan in that shop?'

She thought of Dev and her eyes filled with tears. She should have protected that child. She couldn't bear to imagine anything like this happening to Dylan.

'I'll do whatever you need me to,' she said.

EMMA

It's just Harry and me. We've got two hours before the bakery opens to the public. Harry turns on the enormous ovens so they'll warm up. The loaves that we made yesterday are all stacked on trolleys in their bannetons, waiting to be baked. He's feeding the sourdough leaven, and a pungent, yeasty odour bubbles from the buckets it's kept in.

Paul's last words to me before I left were, 'Meet me. Meet me again.'

I roll dough through the pastry brake and then lay a plaque of butter on top. It's about the size of a sheet of A5, but half an inch thick. I've given up thinking that it's a lot of butter. I fold the dough to encase the slab and feed it through the giant rollers of the pastry brake again. I'll need to laminate it one more time, interleaving the pastry with the butter, and then I'll be able to start shaping it into croissants. The work is methodical and my hands know what to do by heart. Today, though, I'm all fingers and thumbs, yellow globules of fat squeezing through the dough where it tears, the mix catching in the rollers.

'You all right, mate?' asks Harry.

'Yeah, just the heat,' I say, 'and, you know, dealing with a moody teenager.'

'Sorry, can't help with that,' he says cheerfully and turns on a beater that's the height of a small child, drowning out any further conversation.

It would be wrong to see Paul again. I know that. Jack would be devastated if he found out. And my girls . . . the shame I'd feel if they knew, it doesn't bear thinking about. I cut the dough into triangles and begin to roll one, so that it grows thinner. As I think about Paul, my heart beats a little faster, pinpricks of sweat break out on my palms; a flush blooms on my cheeks. My hands are slick with oil and the pastry feels silky against my fingers. I start to fold it and tuck it: it's like origami for bakers. I remember that our limbs felt cool in the early morning and then, as we fell into his still-warm bed, his chest, pressed against mine, was so hot I felt as if I was burning. I bend the pastry into a crescent and slide it onto a tray.

I still don't know what Dylan looks like or how to find him. I have to go back and see Paul. I have no choice. I have to see him again. And although it's stupid and irresponsible and dangerous, I can't walk away. Not yet.

Just one last time, I tell myself.

I put the tray of croissants in our walk-in fridge and I stay there, standing still, for a single moment, letting the chill air flow around my entire body. This time I'll ask to see a photo of Dylan.

I go after work. I wear a sunhat with a cream ribbon round the brim and a wrap-dress with mint-green hearts on a dusky-pink background. I stroll amongst the dahlias and brush past Japanese anemones; the touch of the petals sends whispers down my spine. My thighs rub together as I walk, and I imagine Paul tracing a line down the inside of my leg with his thumb . . . I feel desire pool in the pit of my stomach, hot and sharp. In spite of scrubbing my hands before I left, there's still dough embedded in the cuticles of my fingernails and, when I move, my hair releases the smell of salted caramel. Paul comes striding towards me, and as I turn towards him, excitement floods through me like a draught of neat whiskey and I wonder if it's obvious to the other visitors. He says nothing, only smiles and takes my hand. He leads me towards the walled garden, but when we reach the archway, he opens one of the outhouses and then locks the door behind us.

Inside, it's cooler. The long, thin windows are set high in the crumbling brick wall. Dust-motes float in the dim air. As my eyes adjust, I can make out rows of forks and spades, wooden shelves stacked with rolls of twine and slate plant labels. There's the smell of earth and the sickly scent of sweet peas. For a moment, we simply look at each other.

Does he know? I wonder. *Has my body given me away?*

He takes the end of my scarf and gently pulls it free. The silk whispers across my skin. He strokes the top of my breasts; his fingers are rough; I can feel the calluses on his palms. He undoes the tie on my dress and lets it fall open. I look different: pregnancy, breast-feeding, the passing of the years, they've all taken their toll. I have curves and folds and the silver-streak of stretch marks. I turn my back to him to hide myself from his gaze and I lean against the potting bench, laid out with autumn bulbs, and he slides his hands along my thighs, pulls down my pants and eases himself into me. He lifts my hair up and a cool breeze whispers across the nape of my neck. He winds my hair around his hand until he's holding it tight.

That's new, I think, and then, *Did he do that with her?*

I bite my knuckles so that I won't make a sound.

STELLA

I've been reading *Oryx and Crake* and wondering about the boy who chose it. I had an idea and searched for him on Instagram. I was right. His user name is **MaddAddam.** At least, I think it's him. The photo's of a green eye in a blue face. His profile reads:

> *Adam named the living animals, MaddAddam names the dead ones. Do you want to play?*

Mum is helping Ava tie her new ballet shoes.

'When can I get shoes with blocks in them?' she whines.

'Your toes aren't strong enough yet,' says Mum, crouching on the floor to pull the satin ribbons tighter.

'But I am really strong! I do all the exercises every day.'

'I know, sweetheart, but you're only eleven. You need to wait until you're a little older.'

'But when?'

Oh my God, she is insufferable! I look up from MaddAddam's photos and say, 'You shouldn't be *en pointe* anyway! It makes girls look really fragile, like their legs might snap, and they have to hang off the boys' arms and not stand up for themselves. It's so unfeminist!'

'Mum! Tell her! She's always mean to me.'

'I am not!'

'Stella,' says Mum calmly, 'that's not a particularly helpful opinion at this moment in time.'

'Jesus,' I say, 'you sound like you're on the fucking *Today* programme.'

I look back at Adam's photos. What kind of person is he? *Oryx and Crake* is set in a post-apocalyptic dystopian future. The two main characters, Crake and Jimmy, get high and watch child porn and live executions. There's a lot of biology. Crake creates some genetically engineered creatures that are humanoid, but blue. All the males have sex with all the females. Crake hires Oryx as the Crakers' teacher and his prostitute. I look through MaddAddam's photos on Instagram. They're all of nature: a fox, a spider's web with dew on it, a bird with its beak open and a little puff of frozen breath. If it is the Adam from school, is he also into gene-splicing and gratuitous sex?

I feel embarrassed already. I don't know what I can say about this book. I can't wait to drop biology after my GCSEs. I've got a lot of time to read at the moment, because I'm now sitting in on two of Ava's ballet classes as well as her swimming lesson. Ava's finally stopped moaning and is in the studio in a line with three other girls. They're all holding hands and doing something twiddly with their feet. They're performing *Swan Lake*, and it's weird reading about naked blue men waving their penises about, to Tchaikovsky. Mum is humming along to the waltz and that's even more annoying than hearing the actual music. I plug my headphones in and turn up Kiss FM.

I sneak a sidelong glance at Mum. She's leaning forward and watching Ava, but it feels as if she's somewhere else. Again. I mean, she's right here, obviously, but her mind isn't. She still rides her bike after work. Dad says we're due for a cold snap soon and that'll be the end of our summer. He's worried about the party, I can tell, but it's not for frigging ages. I wonder if Mum'll keep cycling when the weather's bad.

'Can I get some crisps?' I ask.

Mum hands me her wallet. At the counter, I check to make sure she's not looking and then I take out her receipts and go through them. There aren't any for the Pavilion cafe. So where is she going? What is she doing? She seems calmer. She doesn't jump so much at every little thing, and she hums all the fucking time. Her wrist is healing. Her skin is glowing. What is going on?

I think of a line from Adam's book:

These things sneak up on him for no reason, these flashes of irrational happiness. It's probably a vitamin deficiency.

EMMA

I've updated the schedule and printed new copies, which I've pinned to the fridge with magnets. It gives me a feeling of satisfaction, to see where everyone will be and to know they're safe. It's so busy at the moment, though, what with the new National Trust orders for *Kate's* and Ava's extra ballet lessons. Jack is putting in long hours and is working in the evenings in his glorified shed. He's preparing a presentation for his new client, something about reorganizing the personnel structure for the entire business.

But there are things that I don't put in my schedule and that I never have. I keep them from Jack, too. Trips to my dermatologist, for instance. And all those hairdresser appointments. Of course, everyone goes to the hairdresser. Twice a year I have a trim and highlights and I make a big fuss about it, so that Jack knows he should compliment me when I get home. But I go much more frequently than that – I don't want anyone to know what my natural hair colour is. I used to have voice-coaching lessons, too, but that was years ago. Although I don't need them any more, I do worry whether my voice is sufficiently different. I thought I sounded convincing, but that was before I met someone who might remember me from my past . . . Now I look through the other appointments that I don't tell anyone else about, and check the new app on my phone that allows me to send private messages.

Today Paul said to meet him at the far end of Tyntesfield – by the birdcage. It's actually a little house on stilts, with a pitched roof.

It reminds me of the one in *Hansel and Gretel*. I sit on a bench in front of it and crush lavender between my fingers as I wait for him. The leaves are soft as velvet, and the scent is sweet and sharp at the same time. The sun-warmed wood feels hot through the thin fabric of my dress. I'm both excited and nervous, and beneath it all are my twin fears that Jack will somehow find out; that I will not see Dylan before it's too late.

Paul doesn't appear from the direction I'm expecting – round the front of the mansion – but suddenly emerges through a small door in the garden wall that's hidden by a giant magnolia. He's in his gardening clothes, brown cargo trousers and a polo shirt with an oak leaf on his breast pocket. His hair is unkempt, he has stubble on his chin and he smells of wood shavings.

'Where are we going?' I ask.

I'd been hoping for the cool of the cafe in the old cowshed. I wonder if I can drink a crisp glass of white and still cycle home.

'It's a surprise,' he says, grinning at me.

I don't like surprises. He disappears back through a gap in the wall. I hesitate and then I follow him. We're in a narrow passageway. There's an old brewery and stone steps that I imagine lead to cellars beneath the house. In front of us are the stable yard and the private chapel, but Paul pulls me through a door before we get there.

'The old servants' quarters,' he says, and takes my hand.

He leads me along the corridor: the walls are pale yellow with a chalky hue; there's the smell of beeswax, and the ceramic-tiled floors are cold beneath my sandals. We go up a small wooden staircase and along more corridors, until he stops and opens a green door. I step inside. The room is papered with sage-green wallpaper patterned with darker olive scrolls and peppered with scarlet fruit. A threadbare blood-red Persian carpet is laid across the uneven floorboards. There's a thin turret at one end of the room, with a stone windowseat. The windows are mullioned and polka-dotted with birds in daffodil-yellow stained glass. I look out and can see the gardens below us; a stone gargoyle in the shape of a griffin leers down from the lintel. Paul puts his arms around me, and I turn inside his embrace to face him.

'Luxury,' he says. 'Look, a bed.'

It's a small four-poster bed, the wooden posts carved with peacocks and pomegranates. The bedspread matches the wallpaper.

'Really?' I say. 'But . . .'

'It's okay,' he says, 'this part of the house isn't open to the public.'

He locks the door and starts to undress me. He's slower this time, releasing the clasp of my halter-neck before peeling it down and exposing my breasts. Was it like this before? I can't remember any more. We've made ourselves afresh, I think, as I run my hand down his chest and undo the top button of his trousers. I mentally push away the thought of Lizzie, and the guilt I always feel at this point. I stand on the bed and hold onto the wooden posts; the beak of a finch digs into my palm. Paul traces a line down my stomach with his tongue.

Later I'll look in his wallet and see if he has a photo of Dylan.

Later we lie intertwined; a sheen of perspiration coats our skin. I briefly worry about marking the aged damask we're lying on, but the thought of Dylan consumes me. I feel Paul's muscles start to tense. He's going to get up and go. What was I thinking? It's not as if we're in a hotel, where he'll nip to the en suite and I'll have a chance to go through his pockets. Yellow light from the stained-glass birds falls across our naked bodies.

'Do you have a photo of him with you?' I ask.

I'm aware of how odd it sounds; it's the first thing I've said since we've had sex.

'I'm always talking about my girls,' I say, with a half-laugh. 'I hardly know anything about Dylan.'

'I don't have one on me. And my mobile is so ancient I can barely use it to make phone calls, never mind store pictures,' he says.

Typical, I think, *that is so like Paul.*

The disappointment is crushing.

STELLA

It's the middle of the night. I lie for a moment, trying to work out what woke me. I can't hear anything, apart from my stupid sister snoring. I go upstairs. The house is in darkness. There's no one here. Something moves and I nearly scream. But it's only the long, gauzy curtains in front of the French doors. Someone has left them open. I go and stand in the gap and look at the valley below me, black woods and fields and the river glinting in the moonlight, all the houses with their lights out. I have a weird feeling, like I want to be able to reach out and grab something, but I don't know what it is and it might slide right past me anyway. I think about making a peanut-butter sandwich and going back to bed. Or maybe lying up here and watching TV for a bit. I go over to the screen and that's when I notice – Mum's car isn't there. I look at the digital display on the DVD player. It's 3.20. She's like clockwork: up at 4.15 and out the door by 4.30. Or so she tells me. I'm never awake that early. I have a shivery feeling.

It's hard to get up when it's time for school. Dad is frying bacon and eggs, and Ava is eating porridge and twirling her fingers in time to whatever tune is running through her head. Dad switches the radio over to Classic FM and they both smile at each other, like it's some joke I'm missing out on.

'Want some?' he asks.

I make a gagging sound. 'No fucking way.'

'There's no need to be unpleasant,' he says, glancing at the clock. 'You should eat something.'

I look in the bread bin but it's empty. She's even forgotten to bring home bread – and she works in a bloody bakery.

'Where's Mum?'

'At work,' he says, looking at me like I'm an imbecile.

I pour myself a glass of orange juice. I glance at the schedule, but it's exactly the same as it always is – work, work, ballet, ballet, swimming, piano.

'I've got Book Club tonight,' I say.

'Mum's picking you up.'

I make a face.

'Eat something.'

I grab a banana and go downstairs to finish getting ready. I have a queasy feeling. I look in Mum and Dad's room. He's made the bed neatly, folded back the quilt, heaped those fiddly cushions on the top. Only Mum's side is messy, her armchair and bedside table are piled high with clothes and books. But there's nothing here that can tell me what my mother's up to.

I check Dad is still upstairs and then I get out my diary and quickly write, 'My mum is hiding something from us.'

EMMA

I dream of Paul. He's lying with his back to me and I run my fingers down the curve of his spine. He turns towards me and smiles, takes my face between his hands. I move closer, slide my hands round his waist . . . When I wake, it's early, even earlier than I would normally get up. I can't wait until my next day off – I know this has got to stop but I can't, not until I've seen Dylan. Even then, I worry that I might not be able to give up seeing Paul. Everyone is still asleep. Ava is snoring. Outside it's cold and dark. There's a thin crescent moon. I don't want to walk through the wood to Paul's house on my own again. Instead I drive down back roads and tiny lanes. I park on a track, a little way away from Paul's cottage. I can see him before I start my shift.

He'll let me in; he'll think I'm here for sex. And, of course, I am. I fantasize about him all the time. But then I'll see Dylan before I leave. I'll walk around the sitting room and look at photos of the two of them; I'll sneak into his bedroom and watch him sleep. The thought of the bravado this will take brings me out in a cold sweat. But I have to do it. I grit my teeth and remember the last time I saw him. I know I can't explain to Dylan what really happened to Lizzie, but I have to try – for her sake. I want, at least once, to tell him how much she loved him and how much I have always loved him.

I walk up the path to Paul's front door. The hedge is thickly interwoven with jasmine; the flowers glow spectral white in the pale moonlight and the smell is intoxicating. I knock softly on the door. I wonder whether to throw pebbles up at Paul's window, but knowing my luck, I'd put a stone through the glass. I knock again, a little harder. What if Dylan wakes up and answers the door?

Be careful what you wish for . . .

There's a soft woof and a whine. Gil is on the other side. He rattles the door with his nose. I can almost feel him wagging his tail. A few minutes later, I hear the stairs creaking. Someone is coming. I can't tell if they're Paul's footsteps or not. The door opens a crack and Gil comes bounding out, panting with delight at seeing me. Paul's hair is on end and he's only wearing his boxer shorts. He gapes at me.

'Emma!' he whispers. 'What the fuck are you doing here? Do you know what time it is?'

I feel stupid and embarrassed. In my mind, Paul immediately enveloped me in a hug, pressing his warm, sleepy body against mine.

'I thought . . . I thought I could see you before my shift started.'

'Are you out of your mind? It's the middle of the fucking night. What if Dylan saw you?'

'Would that really be so bad?' I ask, stretching out my fingers to touch his chest. He bats me away as if I'm a child.

'Emma. He doesn't know anything about you. I haven't told him. I can't tell him. You're married, for fuck's sake!' He rubs his hand over his face, his stubble making a scratching sound. 'I'm not going to introduce you as my bloody girlfriend! What the hell would he think of me?'

I inhale sharply. He might as well have stuck a thin blade in between my ribs, the pain is so intense. Paul yanks Gil back and shuts the door. I stumble down the path, my sight blurring with tears. The jasmine smells sickly now; I think I might retch. I wipe my eyes and try and pull myself together. I can make it as far as the car and then I'll let myself cry. Paul's right: what was I thinking? That was an insane thing to do. I feel so stuck. I can't carry on deceiving Jack like this. I love him and he doesn't deserve it. But I can't stop seeing Paul, even though the guilt is overwhelming. I'm so close to Dylan, too, so close . . . Being with Paul is – stupid and dangerous; the rational part of my mind tells me. But that's not how my heart feels.

'Wait!'

It's Paul, running up the track towards me. He's put his boots and coat on, but nothing else. I nearly laugh and then find I'm crying.

'I'm sorry,' I say, when he reaches me. 'It was ridiculous to turn up like that. I don't know what I was thinking.'

'No, I'm sorry,' he says, cupping my face in his hands and stroking away the tears.

His coat falls open and I hold onto him as if I could keep him here with me for ever.

'What sort of man turns a beautiful woman away from his door? It's complicated though, isn't it?' And now he does hug me back. 'Of course I want you to meet my son. I wish you weren't with someone else. But—'

I kiss him to stop him talking. He undoes the buttons of my jeans and yanks them roughly down. We half-fall backwards onto the grassy bank. It's still dark; there's the glint of a star trapped between the oak boughs overhead. The grass is damp beneath my back. There's the smell of crushed bracken and wood-loam. And I can't help thinking how different it is, how different from sex with Jack. He would never make love in a wood – or an outhouse or a Gothic mansion, for that matter. Jack is tender and controlled; Paul is gentle and rough; his stubble scrapes my skin, he pushes into me hard. When I come, the stars and the branches blur and I feel dizzy, as if I'm falling, falling away from myself.

LIZZIE

She was assembling prawns on rye bread in the restaurant kitchen – most of what she had to do could hardly be classed as cooking: it was more like constructing, clearing and cleaning. Nearly everything arrived frozen, chilled or pre-cooked. It was tedious, but she tried to think about her dissertation, so she could make the most of the bus journey to and from Leeds to make notes or write up ideas. Usually she daydreamed of Dylan and felt guilty about being away from him.

The flesh-pink of the prawns and their rubbery feel made her nauseous. She set aside the open sandwiches and started chopping vegetables for a side salad. The knife was sharp and sliced easily through blood-red peppers; the blade glinted in the kitchen's stark lights. She put it down and took a breath, wiped her eyes. It was mid-November, nearly a month after it had happened, but the events of that October night replayed in her mind over and over again.

All she could think about was that she should have saved him. She should have held the boy tightly, stopped him going anywhere near the door. She could have phoned the police earlier. She shouldn't have fallen asleep. She should have got the child out of there. Why the hell hadn't she been braver? Thought faster? Protected the boy. It was her fault Dev was still in hospital; they didn't know if he'd recover any of the sight in his eye yet. Thank God Jon Lilley's knife hadn't pierced his brain, but the bleeding could have damaged his frontal cortex; DI Simon Duffield told her they were still waiting to find out whether the child would be blind as well as brain-damaged.

Simon had asked her to testify against Jon Lilley and had assured Lizzie that she'd be able to give her statement in court anonymously. He'd also strongly advised her not to discuss the case with anyone, not even Paul. She'd told Paul and Miriam she'd seen a mugging. Miriam was utterly fed up with her: she said Lizzie was keeping her awake with her nightmares. The feeling was mutual. Maybe, she thought, if Miriam had been there that night, she'd have told her everything and Miriam would have been sympathetic. But Miriam had dismissed seeing a mugging as 'nothing'. It happened all the time, and at least it hadn't been Lizzie whose wallet had been stolen, she'd said. Miriam hadn't turned up until the following day – she'd gone out with her sister and stayed at a friend's house. Lizzie had been hurt; she got on well with Miriam's sister, after all they'd grown up together, and she'd have liked to have been invited, too. And she knew it wasn't fair, but everything that Miriam said or did seemed so superficial – should she go brighter blonde, or maybe have a light perm to put a bit of curl in her hair; what the latest cocktail on the menu was, a cake recipe she wanted to try out because she'd seen it in an article in a magazine; oh, and she was thinking of getting a tattoo on her arm. Lizzie grimaced. It was all so fucking meaningless compared to what had happened to Dev.

Things weren't much better with Paul. She was distant, preoccupied, and after she told him about the mugging, he'd said it wasn't safe and she should give up her job in Leeds.

'We can manage. I'll get a full-time ranger job eventually, and both of us can take on bar shifts in spring when the tourists arrive.'

'But we need the money now, Paul,' she'd said.

And they did, but she also knew she wouldn't have enough to go back to university if she didn't return to her job. As it was, she'd almost nothing left to put towards her degree after she'd paid rent, bus fare, food and bills, not to mention the vast amount they were spending on nappies. She'd insisted on having cloth ones at first, but they rubbed sore patches on Dylan's chubby legs and gave him a rash. Who knew having a baby would be so bloody expensive?

'I promise I won't go anywhere near that estate. Bus station, Miriam's, Ikea – that'll be it.'

'You might get scurvy.'

'Don't fuss – Knäckebröd, cheese and Fläder – it's a totally balanced diet.'

'Sounds like something a pirate would eat,' Paul had said, kissing her on the forehead. 'Well, if you're sure. But for God's sake, be careful.'

But each week he'd continued to object: it wasn't safe, it was too far away, she was gone for too long, he didn't like the idea of her living in Belle Isle. She was starting to suspect there was something else wrong. It wasn't like Paul to be this anxious or bad-tempered with her. If she could only tell him what had happened, perhaps things would get better. Lizzie caught her supervisor's eye and picked up the knife again. She sighed and pushed the heap of chopped peppers to one side and started slicing through a crisp iceberg lettuce. It was probably just her. She'd have to try to act normally, stop thinking about Dev all the time, and then she and Paul – and Miriam – would all get along again.

The knife slipped. For a moment she was still, not sure how bad the damage was. It didn't hurt; the cut on her finger gaped, pink and shiny like raw chicken, but then the blood welled up, scarlet and bright under the artificial lights, and the pain began.

STELLA

'Today we're talking about Adam's choice: *Oryx and Crake* by Margaret Atwood,' says Ms Heron.

I've had this strange feeling all day, like I'm tense and nervous. I couldn't even eat my banana until first break. I can't look at Adam, although out of the corner of my eye I see he's smiling. Kaylee is staring at him adoringly. I stamp on her toe and she kicks my shin.

'It's sci-fi,' says Nuala shrugging. It obviously didn't float her boat.

Adam clears his throat. 'Margaret Atwood says it's not. She calls it "speculative fiction".'

'What the hell's that supposed to mean?' asks Theo.

The boys don't like Adam.

'It's going to be made into a TV series,' says Cian.

Adam ignores him. 'It means that everything in the book could happen right now. It's set in the future, but we've got the technology already,' he says.

'Yeah, right,' says Cian, 'to make blue humans that wave their dicks around.'

Adam grins. 'What about the pigoons? We could splice human genes into a pig and grow replacement organs, if we wanted.'

'Aren't pigs, like, really smart?' says Kaylee.

'Think how much smarter they'd be if they had human brain cells,' says Adam.

He sounds delighted and I shiver.

'Who's MaddAddam?' asks Theo.

'Crake,' I say. 'He was called Glenn and then he set up that Extinctathon game online, and Crake was his username until he started calling himself that in real life. "Adam named the living animals, MaddAddam names the dead ones—"'

'"Want to play?"' Adam finishes my sentence and smiles at me.

I duck my head. The book makes me uncomfortable. Adam makes me uncomfortable.

As Kaylee and I are walking down the corridor afterwards, Adam comes up behind us and says, 'A few of us are going to The Station. Want to come?'

I glance up at him to make sure he's really talking to us. Is he teasing? Kaylee elbows me in the ribs.

'I can't,' I say.

God, I feel stupid. I burst out of school and into the playground. Mum's car is parked outside the gates. My mouth has gone all dry, and my tongue won't work. I can't let her see me talking to a boy – she'll have endless questions.

'Another time maybe?' says Adam.

'I'll go,' says Kaylee.

'What? Without me?' I can't help saying, and I blush.

She tosses her hair and looks sideways at me. 'Nuala would be up for it, even if you aren't.'

'See you later then,' says Adam.

I mutter bye to both of them and walk quickly away. Waves of heat run through me. He was definitely talking to me, not Kaylee, even though I couldn't bring myself to look at him properly. And how could she go without me and make me feel stupid for not being able to? I watch as she links arms with Nuala, and they follow Adam towards the other kids waiting at the bus stop. She'll flirt with him. What if she ends up being his girlfriend? A small, cold crack appears in my chest. I slam the car door and, without speaking to either Mum or Ava, I get out my phone and send her a message.

'Tell me all about it later,' I type, and add hearts and smiley faces, although I feel like strangling her.

'What time shall I pick you up?' Ted looks at us in the rear-view mirror.

'I'll call you, yeah?'

'I might be busy.'

'Yeah, right.' Kaylee rolls her eyes and then grins at him.

Putty in her hands, I think. Ted pulls up illegally in the bus lay-by outside Primark and we get out and wave to him until he's driven off.

'Let's go in round the back,' says Kaylee, 'in case he sees us as he goes past.'

It's a one-way system here, so just at the point Ted will be on his way home, we'll be right outside a place we're not meant to be. Sometimes Kaylee can be clever. We dodge in and out of shoppers as we walk away from Primark. It's Saturday afternoon, and Ted and my parents think Kaylee and I are hanging out at Cabot Circus. Instead, we're going to go round the block before heading to The Station; apparently Adam will be there with some other sixth-formers.

I nod and say, 'So, tell me again. What did he say when you guys went out last Wednesday?'

'He said, "Bring your friend – what's her name?" and I said, You mean "Stella", and he says, "Yeah, bring her. The more, the merrier."' She smiles smugly at me. She wants to rub it in. She spent the evening with Adam and his friends and he doesn't even know my name.

But maybe that was Adam's way of getting Little Miss Pushy to ask me along? He wouldn't want to seem too keen.

'He wanted to know why you couldn't go out the other night, after school.'

'What did you tell him?' I ask.

'I said your mum is a nut-job and won't let you and Ava out of her sight.'

'Thanks for that,' I say grumpily. I've got what feels like jumping beans in my stomach. My breathing has gone shallow. I have that sensation I get sometimes, like: what if I can't take any more breaths? What if I literally can't breathe any more and I fall to my knees and choke on the pavement?

'Least he doesn't think it's because you're frigid,' she says, linking her arm through mine.

'What?'

'You know, a square. Yeah, thanks, Kaylee, you're an angel.'

I snort. 'That's the last fucking thing you are.'

She smiles at me and I think that we're back to being properly friends again, but then she says, 'Nuala's coming too. I had such an amazing time with her, I asked her along. You'll love her, she's so cool. I can't believe we haven't hung out before.'

I don't want to hang out with Nuala. Kaylee is a handful, but she's my friend. If Nuala's there, she and Kaylee might go off together and not speak to me. I only know Nuala from Book Club, and I've never wanted to know her better. I start slowing down. I've got so much homework to do. And it's not long until the exams. I have to know all my English literature books practically off by heart if I'm going to get a decent grade. There's no bloody way I'm going to end up like my mum.

'We're here. Stop fucking dithering,' says Kaylee, steering me inside.

It's an old fire station that's been converted into a place for the 'Youth'. There's an STD clinic and workshops and sports clubs, but also a cheap cafe and music in the evenings. I could get checked out for chlamydia while I have a Coke. It's opposite the police station, so if Dad knew I were here, he'd probably approve. I pause in the entrance.

'Look, you can do *Bake Off* classes.'

'I'll fucking shoot you in the head if you sign up to that.'

I was thinking that maybe I could make a cake for my mum, for the anniversary party. She'd probably like it if I made an effort. But the thought of my mum, and what she's doing and why she's lying to us, makes me feel sick again.

'You know . . .'

'For fuck's sake,' says Kaylee and drags me inside.

Adam's playing pool with a couple of his friends. I walk swiftly past. Kaylee gets Cokes for us and Nuala, who's there already, looking sophisticated. I take a sip of my drink. The ice makes my teeth hurt. Mum must be having an affair. There's no other explanation for it.

'You made an effort, then,' says Nuala, chinking her glass against mine.

Like Kaylee, she's wearing contoured make-up, so she'll look brilliant in photos. I wonder if she and Nuala have been messaging each other, because they're wearing identical ripped jeans and off-the shoulder T-shirts that reveal their smooth, dark honey-coloured skin, and they both have glossy hair that's somehow straight but with a heavy wave in it. Kaylee, even if she does drag me round the shops with her, has never tried to force me to wear anything other than the black Levis, Converse, Gap tees, plaid shirts and hoodies that are like a uniform to me. I glance at her, but she doesn't defend me.

'Just kidding,' says Nuala. 'You do retro-cool pretty well.'

I flush and slide onto the bench. The table is sticky with spilt drinks. The music is too loud. I wish I hadn't come. Nuala and Kaylee start taking selfies. They wave at me to join them, but I shake my head. I always look rubbish in photos. They move over to the window to get better light on their already flawless complexions.

'Hey, you came.'

I look up as a tall, dark shape looms over me. It's Adam.

'You going to let me sit down?'

'Oh. Sorry.'

I move further along the bench and look sideways at him. Up close, he's even better-looking than I remembered. He brushes his hair out of his eyes and, now that I can see them properly, they're kind of blue, with brown over the top.

I expect him to make some sarcastic comment about my mum letting me out to play, but he says, 'Sorry I made you read *Oryx and Crake*.'

'What? Why?'

'You didn't like it.'

I shrug. 'That's not the point of Book Club. If I only read books I liked, I'd be reading *Jane Eyre* over and over again.'

Oh, shit, I think, *that was such an uncool thing to say*, but then I realize – he could tell what I was thinking. And I barely said anything in Book Club.

'To be honest, I'm not that into novels. I prefer non-fiction, and that book was the closest thing I could find to the stuff I'm interested in,' he says.

I'm about to do my usual thing and say something sarcastic about him being into child porn and live executions, like Jimmy, but instead I say, 'That would be books about wildlife then.'

'Yeah. How did you figure that out?'

'MaddAddam. I saw your Instagram profile.'

'Right.' He's smiling at me. It's a long, slow smile that takes a while to spread across his face and reach his eyes. 'I thought I'd cultivate a whole new persona when I came to this school, but I see I've failed.' He doesn't look that bothered, though. 'I'm going to get a coffee. Want another Coke?'

'No,' I say, too forcefully. 'A coffee.' Thank God I can get one now, without looking like a complete tool. Kaylee is making faces at me, blowing pretend kisses, but I can tell she's mad. 'I'll come with you,' I say.

We sit at the bar with our coffees and for a few minutes I feel normal and grown-up and I don't dwell on my mum and my mocks. I stir three cubes of sugar in, and think of the lecture Dad would give me on obesity if he saw. I tell Adam about *The Road*, another dystopian futuristic novel, that's dark and disturbing and has a kind of boyish style that a person might like if they didn't usually read fiction. No gene-splicing, but some horrific cannibalism. He listens and doesn't say, 'They made it into a film.' I notice he's wearing almost the same clothes as me, except his jeans are by Howies, a trendy eco-company; they have the Welsh coastline stitched on the back pockets. I'm strangely pleased, and then I remember that boys don't like girls who dress like them.

'Did you take those photos yourself? The ones in your Instagram feed?'

'Yeah.'

He smiles again and gets out his phone and shows me a few of them. He's so close, his hair brushes against mine; I don't think he's noticed, he's engrossed in explaining his pictures, but I can feel Kaylee's rage like a force-field. He's involved in an urban-fox project, he says. And then she's right next to me, flicking her hair over her shoulder.

'My dad's going to be here in five minutes. You coming?'

'Thanks for the coffee,' I say to Adam and hop off the bar seat. Kaylee stalks away without waiting for me.

'What's your Instagram name?' he calls after me.

'Work it out,' I say with a smile.

I grab my coat and run after my so-called best friend. I catch up with her just as we reach Ted's car. He's pulled over illegally again, outside the police station, which is hardly a stellar move.

'Did you have a good time with Nuala?' I ask tentatively.

'Why don't you fuck off?' she says.

I sit and squirm in the car in silence while Kaylee expertly fends off Ted's questions, but eventually he gives up and I say in a tiny voice, 'Sorry I didn't spend much time talking to you.'

She squeezes my hand and says, 'Are you going on a date with him?'

'No. It's not like that.' I can feel myself going hot. 'We were just talking.'

I've never had a boyfriend before, so what do I know? I'm not even sure if Adam is interested in me. Kaylee gives me a look, like she's about ten years older than me. Does she know how I feel, or is she thinking she's got a chance with him? Guys always go for Kaylee. She's beautiful and sexy and bubbly. I'm not beautiful or sexy and I'm definitely not bubbly. I've got those clear-eyed, pale-faced looks that are right out of a nineteenth-century novel. You'd have to be Mr Rochester to find me remotely attractive. I turn away from her and bite the skin around my fingers.

LIZZIE

'Look, just quit. Leave what's-his-face a message.'

'Gregor.'

'Yeah. People must walk out on that kind of job all the time.'

'That kind of job is paying our bills,' Lizzie said, doing up her rucksack. 'Paul, what's the matter?'

'Nothing, I don't want you to go, that's all. I don't like you staying with Miriam.'

'What?' She turned to face him. 'Miriam's my friend. What is going on with you?'

Paul wouldn't meet her eye. He was holding Dylan on his lap, bouncing him slightly, and had his head bent over his son's. He kissed his hair.

'She came here,' he said eventually.

'What are you talking about?' She heaved the rucksack onto her shoulders. 'I'm going to be late for the bus.'

'Miriam,' he said, finally looking at her. 'That week when you saw the mugging. She came here.'

Lizzie frowned. She closed her eyes to block out the feel of Dev's blood, hot on her hands. How, at the end of that terrible night, shaking with exhaustion, she'd returned to the house in Belle Isle, only to find her room empty, her friend gone.

'She told me she met up with her sister.'

'She stayed over.'

Lizzie slid her bag off again and propped it by the door. 'Miriam came here and stayed over while I was in Leeds?'

Paul nodded. 'Nothing happened.'

'I should bloody well hope not. Why? Why was she here? And why did she lie about it?'

Paul looked miserable. He held Dylan against his chest and stretched one hand out to her. 'I'm sorry, Lizzie. I miss you when you're away.'

'Hang on a minute,' she said, backing away so that he couldn't touch her, as it suddenly sank in. 'You're saying that Miriam came here because . . . Had you arranged this with her?'

'No. She just turned up. And you know what she's like—'

'Paul, I have to get my bus. No, I don't know what Miriam's like any more. Just bloody tell me what's going on.'

'She kissed me. She started it. I . . . I kissed her back. But that's it.'

'What? You kissed my best friend? Why didn't you send her home?'

'I couldn't make her go all the way back to Leeds in the middle of the night.'

'I don't see why the hell not. Where did she sleep?'

Paul put Dylan over his shoulder and tapped his back as if to wind him, but he carried on mechanically patting him, even after Dylan had let out a satisfying burp. 'In our bed. I tried to tell you, Lizzie, I tried to say. I didn't want you to go—'

Lizzie put her hands over her ears. 'Don't bloody tell me this is my fault! I can't deal with this – with *you* – right now. I've got to go, I'm going to miss my bus.'

She hoisted her rucksack over her shoulders. She edged around Paul to say goodbye to Dylan. He beamed at her, a long string of sick trailing from his mouth and down her husband's broad back.

'Jesus, Paul!' she said, stroking her son's smooth, fat cheek.

She jogged down the dark lane towards the bus stop, her pack bumping against the small of her back, hot tears streaming down her cheeks. She cried most of the way to Leeds. She hadn't wanted to have sex after Dylan was born – she was too tired and sore – but she'd assumed that was normal and that Paul understood. After all, they had the rest of their lives together to make up for it.

When she reached Belle Isle, Miriam wasn't in. It was late and the others were all in their rooms and Lizzie wondered, as she paced up and down between her mattress and the bed, whether Miriam was, at that very moment, making her journey in reverse, to Paul and her baby son and their little cottage in Langdale. She'd kill them, she thought, she'd fucking kill them. How could they do this to her? And then she remembered what Julia had said to her that afternoon in Bolton Abbey: *She's dead jealous of you, you know*. So that was what her sister had meant – Miriam wasn't jealous of her, she was jealous of what she had: a husband, a child, a loving family.

She laid slices of Daim cake on plates and slid them into the fridge as the first customers started trickling into the restaurant for their free coffee. She'd leave, she decided. She'd do it today, so she didn't have to spend another minute in Miriam's house and risk seeing her so-called best friend. She'd barely slept the night before and her eyes were red from crying. She loved Paul, she loved him so much. Had it just been a kiss? She didn't know whether to believe him or not. She'd never imagined he'd betray her like this. And in their bed, too, with Dylan in the cot next to them! Had they had sex? She had a sudden image of Miriam, that long blonde hair tumbling down her naked back, Paul's hands fitting into the curve of her neat waist, the swell of her hips . . . She felt as if her heart would break.

Gregor came over. It was as if he could tell there was something wrong. She'd quit at the end of her shift, she thought. No point in annoying him now. Her supervisor was tall and dark-haired, with flaky red skin, dandruff in his eyebrows and a faint yellow tinge to his complexion, as if he never ventured out in daylight.

'Hey,' she said warily, continuing to plate up the cakes.

'How are you today?' he asked.

Gregor was from the Ukraine and had a clipped accent and an even brusquer manner. He'd been sympathetic last month, allowing Lizzie to take one day off sick after witnessing the 'mugging', but then he'd left her a message, saying that if she wasn't able to return to work the following week, he'd have to let her go.

'I'll do the apple cakes next,' she said, pointing the tip of her knife at the stack of desserts wrapped in plastic film.

'Yes, I can see. I came to tell you letter has arrived for you.'

'A letter?'

'Yes. Was hand-delivered. No stamp.'

'Who'd be writing to me here?'

He shrugged. 'Maybe detective you keep seeing?'

'No.' She shook her head. 'He always rings, or comes and picks me up straight from work.'

Gregor raised his eyebrows and Lizzie shuddered, thinking of flakes of his skin falling into the food.

She was about to peel off her latex gloves to take the letter from him, but he said, 'I left in staffroom for you. You have break in twenty-three minutes.'

'Thank you,' she said, swallowing her annoyance. It was typical of Gregor that he wouldn't even allow her the thirty seconds it would take to read the letter.

The staffroom was furnished with Norsborg sofas in Finnsta red, the seat cushions shiny from use, the arms frayed, leaking stuffing, dust balls gathering round their birch-veneered legs. There was a photograph of a beech wood on one entire wall that did nothing to alleviate Lizzie's claustrophobia. Gregor had left the letter on one of the sticky-surfaced Lack tables. She was sure that wasn't company policy: anyone could have opened it.

The envelope was cream, with a ridge embedded into the paper. On the front, it said: 'Ms Elizabeth Bradshaw, Ikea'. She wondered briefly if it was from Miriam. An apology, maybe? Or a declaration of war: *I love your husband. I'm going to have him.*

Inside there was a single sheet of paper, in matching stationery, thick and expensive-looking. Like the address on the envelope, it was typed, but in a font that made it look like beautiful, calligraphic handwriting:

Dear Ms Bradshaw,

We only had the pleasure of meeting fleetingly. I believe you were hiding in Mr Arjun Kumar's store cupboard. I cannot think why you might have been there; you don't strike me as a thief, nor as a young woman who might indulge in a sordid affair with an Asian man in such a public place whilst accompanied by a child.

My solicitor tells me that you witnessed an unpleasant encounter between Mr Kumar and myself. I do apologize, Lizzie, if I may be permitted to call you that – I believe it's the nickname your friends use. Further, he tells me that you are planning to act as a witness and to testify against me in court. The police, will, no doubt, have told you that you would be able to give your testimony anonymously, but, as you can see, my dear, I know who you are and where to find you.

It pains me to say this to such a beauty – and there is something Orphelian about your curls, although your hair is a little short for my taste – but if you give evidence against me, I will kill you.

I doubt you are a martyr, but should you decide to risk your own life, I can assure you that, as well as killing you, I will hunt down your family and I will kill them, and then I will find your friends and I will kill them too. I do hope, Lizzie, that you will reconsider, for I am nothing if not a man of my word.

> *Kind regards,*
> *Jon Lilley*

PS My dear Lizzie, should you doubt my veracity, ask Detective Inspector Simon Duffield to tell you about his three previous witnesses.

She sat down on one of the sofas, clutching the letter. She read it a second time, her heart constricting, phrases jumping out at her: *I will kill you . . . I will hunt down your family . . . I am nothing if not a man of my word.*

How did he know who she was? How had he found out? She looked round the staffroom as if he might be here, as if he might be spying on her right now. There were three cleaners at the other end, two on their phones, one napping on the sofa. None of them had even glanced at her as she'd walked in.

Paul had been right, even though he didn't know what had really happened: it wasn't safe. She'd seen what Lilley had done to Dev; Simon had reeled off a list of atrocities he'd committed and she was sure that he'd only scratched the surface. Her hands were clammy and her breathing sped up. *Her family.*

She considered phoning Paul, but even if she managed to get hold of him, he'd panic. He'd want to know why she'd lied to him in the first place. And he might be so caught up with his thoughts about Miriam that he wouldn't listen properly. She'd call Simon, she thought, and tell him she couldn't be a witness. He'd understand.

'Duffield,' he said, answering on the first ring.

'I've got a letter. It's from Jon Lilley. He says he's going to kill me. And then everyone I know.' She tried to keep her voice low so that the cleaners wouldn't hear, but by the end she'd become high-pitched and hysterical.

'Christ! Is it addressed to you personally?'

'Yes. You told me he didn't know who I was. You said I'd be safe!' She struggled for control.

'Where did he send it? To your house?'

'No. Here to me at work. It was hand-delivered. There's no stamp.'

'He'll have got someone else to drop it off; he wouldn't let himself get caught on CCTV,' said Simon, as much to himself as to Lizzie. 'Where are you now?' he asked, and the urgency in his voice made her heart race even faster.

'Still here. I'm in the staffroom at Ikea.'

'Leave, now. Don't speak to anyone, don't tell anyone you're going. Don't ring anybody, not even Paul. Meet me in the cafe in Next. I'll be there in ten minutes.'

She hung up. She felt even more frightened than before.

EMMA

The weather has changed and it's cold, as if the spell of warmth we've had is over and summer is finished before it's begun. Paul found us a tiny room off the scullery in the big house, and he brought blankets. We have to be quick, though; there are people walking past, their footsteps echoing on the old flagstones.

A boy, his voice high-pitched and indignant, says, 'When are we going? We've been in this room for ever.'

I get a fit of giggles halfway through when I hear a woman say, 'Oh! It's just like being in The White Company.'

Someone else replies, 'I know! I gave up the zoo for this.'

Paul stops. 'What the hell is she on about?'

'She gave up her membership, I guess,' I say, laughing. 'I don't suppose she actually owned one!'

He puts his hand over my mouth and then he kisses me again.

Afterwards we go to the Cowshed Restaurant and tuck ourselves into what was an old byre, complete with hay rack and manger, and sit in large armchairs. Paul goes to get us a pot of tea, and while I'm waiting I notice something in the shop that catches the light. It's going to be our fifteenth wedding anniversary in August: mine and Jack's, that is. One of the symbols is crystal, and the websites I've glanced at all say to give cut glass or a watch as a present. And if there's one thing I do know about Jack, it's that he likes to do things by the book.

I walk over to see what it is: it's a paperweight with a dandelion clock perfectly preserved inside. I hold it in my hand. It's smooth and heavy. It would be just right for my husband. I can imagine it sitting on his desk: a single, solitary *objet d'art* in the midst of that smooth expanse of wood. As I pay for it, I start to blush, a blush that grows stronger and deeper, flaring over my chest and making my ears burn.

I'm buying a present for my husband while I'm with my lover.

I hurry back to our nook, but I get there at the same time as Paul.

'Ah,' he says, catching me slide my tissue-paper-wrapped gift into my handbag, 'this place is lethal. I try not to look at the posh biscuits and beer on my way in.' His expression changes. 'You okay?'

I nod. 'I'm cold.'

'Cold?'

I'm wearing a summer dress and stupidly I didn't bring a jacket. Even though my face is bright red, my arms are covered in goosebumps and I shiver. Paul fetches a heather-coloured blanket and drapes it round my shoulders.

'You look like someone just walked over your grave,' he says.

I pour tea for both of us, as I wait for my shame to subside. Paul has been taking a longer break than he's meant to, so that he can see me after I've finished at the bakery and before I need to pick up the girls. He starts early or works late to make up for it. I'm sure he'd get into a lot of trouble if the Trust found out why – and that he's using keys to the house for illicit purposes. I suppose I should be more careful, too. I've never seen anyone I know here in the middle of the afternoon, but there's no reason why I wouldn't bump into a neighbour or another mother from school.

I'm about to tell Paul we should take precautions, when he says, 'You remind me of her.'

I inhale sharply.

'Who?'

'My wife. You don't look exactly like her, or like she might look now if . . .' He pauses, collects himself and then says, 'There's something about you, though, some quality – I can't work out what it is. Or maybe you just make me think of that period of time in my life . . . Sorry, it's probably the last thing you want to hear. Me going on about my missing missus,' he adds, trying to make light of it.

'It's okay.'

The light filtering into the cowshed is muted; it looks as if it's going to rain.

'Do you wear contact lenses?' he asks.

'Me? No. Never.'

'Lizzie wore glasses.' He gives a small half-laugh. 'She was as blind as a mole.' Because we're in a narrow stall, we have more privacy than you'd expect in a busy restaurant and he takes my hand. He caresses me with his thumb, his skin rough. 'It's the reason why it's so easy with you,' he says, softly. 'I've let down my guard, when I barely know you. I said some terrible things to you the other day. The thing is, I've hardly had any relationships with women since Lizzie. None that mattered. None that I knew would last. I didn't want—'

'To get hurt,' I finish for him.

'Or for Dylan to feel like he was going to be abandoned again.'

I wince. I want to protest, but I mustn't because, after all, what happened was not Lizzie's fault.

'Technically I'm still married,' he says, with a rueful smile. 'I mean, there was no body. She could still be alive. I've been in limbo – I couldn't believe she'd walk out on us, but the police seemed convinced she had.'

I'm still married, too. I feel hideous, doing this to Jack. I look up at Paul. His eyes are large and dark. How I've missed him. I *can't* leave him. Not yet.

'And I should never have – you know – cheated on her,' he adds.

For a moment the name *Miriam* hovers between us, unsaid, unspoken. I wonder if he'll say it out loud, I slide my hand from his and pick up my tea, so it doesn't look like an unkind gesture, and try and think of an appropriate response.

'It feels so easy with you, too. So right. Although I know it's wrong,' I say eventually.

'Yeah,' he says, sighing. 'But it's brought it all up again for me. I've been thinking about Lizzie's family.'

I freeze. I wrap the blanket more tightly around myself. I don't like the way this conversation is going.

'Oh,' I say, wondering how to change the subject.

'She had a sister. When Dylan was little we used to see her, but afterwards Julia blamed me. She said I should never have let Lizzie work in Leeds, especially after that mugging she saw. She was convinced something terrible had happened to her. And I got drunk one night and blurted out about . . . about the woman I'd had that fling with. Miriam. Julia never forgave me for that, either.'

I dig my nails into my palms. I must not cry. Or snap the elastic band on my wrist in front of him.

'Julia saw Dylan on her own – well, with Lizzie's mum – a few times, but then she and her husband emigrated to Australia and I never heard from them again. Since I met you, it got me thinking about her again. I was curious. I looked her up on Facebook.'

Husband? I think in surprise. She had a boyfriend when I last saw her, but I didn't realize she'd married him. I can't remember the number of times I've wanted to look up Julia too, but I never use social media. I clear my throat.

'And did you find her?'

'Yes.'

I swallow hard and put my cup down before I drop it.

'She's got privacy settings on her account, though, so I couldn't see any photos or information about her. I'd have to be her friend. But she's got two kids now. Girls. At least, I assume they're hers.

They were in her profile picture. Along with a sliver of sea and half a palm tree,' he said, smiling ruefully. 'Bondi Beach maybe.'

'And did you ask to be her friend?'

'Julia's? No, I hardly ever use Facebook and it would be . . . awkward. I should make an effort, though. Maybe I'll phone her. I'm sorry,' he says, leaning forward and wrapping his arms tightly around me, 'I've upset you.'

'It's okay,' I say again.

I desperately want to know how Julia is. I miss her and Lizzie's parents so much, too: Beth and Adam.

'Did you . . . did you keep in touch with Dylan's grandparents?' I ask, pulling away from him.

'To begin with,' he says. 'Beth was brilliant. She took some time off work and came to help out with Dylan when he was a baby.'

He stops and I have a horrible feeling, as if something is crawling inside my chest and scrabbling at my throat, trying to claw its way out.

'What happened?' I ask.

'They died,' he says. 'Beth had breast cancer. She'd been going to tell Lizzie – she was waiting for the right time, but then it was too late. And her dad, Adam, he had a freak chainsaw accident after his wife died. Personally, I think he was grief-stricken – lost his wife, his daughter, the other one had emigrated – I don't think he was paying attention. He didn't care any more.'

I take a juddering breath. Someone is trying to hack out my heart with a blunt penknife, but I cannot show Paul how much pain I'm in.

'I'm sorry,' I whisper.

'Me, too,' he says. 'Me, too.'

I try to remember my lessons: how you think about something determines how you feel about it. This situation can only hurt me if I let it do so. They have all been as good as dead to me for so long. And I have so much to be grateful for. Stella and Ava are everything to me. That's what I have to focus on, not the past. Right now, I remind myself, the main reason I'm here with Paul is to see Lizzie's son. I sit up and wipe my nose. *I will grieve later*, I think, clenching my hands into fists.

'Can we . . . can I . . .' I clench my hands into fists and force myself to say it. 'Can I meet Dylan? Please.'

He turns away from me and I think he's going to get angry, or leave or tell me how ridiculous I sound, like some kind of teen-stalker, but when he speaks, his voice is gentle.

'I'd like nothing more than for you to get to know Dylan and for me to meet your girls. But he's lost so many people already. And I can't risk you meeting him and then disappearing, too. You're married. With a husband who still lives with you. And who didn't walk out on you one November morning. It's not a good idea, is it?'

I stretch out my hands to touch him, but I stop myself.

'Do you love him?' he says.

'I have to go,' I say, standing up and shedding the blanket. 'I need to pick up Stella and Ava.'

A muscle works in his jaw. He watches me go without saying a word and there's such sadness in his expression, I think my heart is going to break.

STELLA

maddaddam liked your photo.

maddaddam liked your photo.

maddaddam started following you.

maddaddam commented: Good to hang out with you **@thefirestation**

msrochester commented: It was fun! Thanks for the ☕

maddaddam commented: **Me** and **@neil_b3** & **@theboyz** heading **@thefirestation** on Wednesday night. Want to play? Bring **@littlemisskaylee** & **@totallygorgeousnuala**

littlemisskaylee commented: Totally up for that! 💋

totallygorgeousnuala commented: Me too. Love you guyz! 🖤

maddaddam commented: awesome

Fuck you! I think. He actually doesn't like me. It's just a way to hang out with Nuala and Kaylee. I feel stupid even for thinking I was privileged to see his Instagram profile and he wouldn't want everyone knowing all about his animal photos. Why am I even bothered? He doesn't like reading and I don't give a rat's arse about urban fucking foxes. But then I remember that he joined Book Club, even though he only likes non-fiction. I thought maybe it might have been to meet me? But now I know it was just to meet girls. Plural.

I go upstairs. Mum and Dad are sitting on the balcony, each drinking a glass of wine. It's kind of chilly and it's starting to get dark. Mum's got a thick poncho on. She looks like she'd rather be on the sofa.

'Can I go out with Kaylee on Wednesday after school?'

Mum parts her lips as if to answer and then glances at Dad.

'Absolutely not,' Dad says.

'You don't even know where I want to go!'

'I don't need to. You've got homework, and your exams coming up. If you want to trail around town with her on a Saturday afternoon, that's your prerogative. But you're not going out mid-week.'

Mum finishes her glass of wine and gives me a sympathetic look.

'So I have to go to ballet with Ava again?'

'At least you'll be able to revise, love,' she says.

She reaches for the bottle, but Dad gets there first. He puts one of those silver stoppers in it and brushes past me as he goes inside to put the wine back in the fridge. I look at Mum to see if she's going to protest, but she doesn't meet my eye. She's staring over the fields, as if, like me, she's seen something out there that eludes her.

EMMA

It's Sunday. We spend the morning wandering around Clevedon Court, a fourteenth-century manor house, as a family, much to the girls' annoyance.

'Penny for them?' asks Jack, stretching out his hand to me.

His fingers are long and thin and his hand no longer feels right in mine. Paul's hands are large, his fingers thick and strong, his palms as rough as sandpaper.

'Thinking about the beast,' I tell him, as we climb the steps to the octagonal summerhouse.

'Ah, the monster in the bakery.'

He teases me about treating the sourdough culture – the leaven – as if it's a creature. It is, though. It's millions of creatures – yeast cells all bonded into a superorganism – and if we don't feed it, it will die. It needs a mixture of flour and warm water every day. Harry, Katie and I alternate who goes in on a Sunday to feed it when the bakery is closed. Today it's my turn.

'I have to go in,' I say, trying to sound apologetic.

'That's okay,' he says. 'We've had some time together. And I need to work in the afternoon, too.'

We pause and look down at our two girls, running in and out of the box maze and, for once, looking as if they're enjoying themselves, and behaving like the children they still are. I squeeze Jack's hand. He pulls me closer and puts his arm round my shoulder.

'I can see the end in sight.'

'What do you mean?' I say, instantly worried in case he's found out.

'Stella's not going to come on our trips for much longer. And then Ava will refuse. It'll be no fun for her, with just the two of us.'

'You'll have a much better time on your own,' I say, half-teasing, as we start to walk along a path bordered by lavender. 'Think of all the medieval architecture you can see, without anyone pestering you to take them to the cafe.'

'Ah, it wouldn't be the same without you,' he says. 'I only do this so that we can spend time together. The girls might make a fuss, but when they look back at their childhoods, they'll remember these days fondly, because they're the ones when we've all been together as a family. It'll add texture to their memories – and it wouldn't hurt if they recall a little about the Tudors, too.'

I run my hand through the lavender flowers, releasing their scent. I'd thought this was another of Jack's obsessions, like his HIIT workouts or the garden, which we all had to fit in with. It hadn't occurred to me that this is what he's doing: lending structure to our lives and, all along, I've been only too eager for our outing to end so that I can escape. I crush the tiny buds beneath my fingers and release them. I feel so guilty; it's a constant dull ache in my chest. But my need to see Paul is stronger.

That afternoon I leave the girls curled up on the sofa, watching a film. Jack has already retreated to his office at the bottom of the garden, reminding me to set the alarm on the house before I go.

I sent Paul a message earlier to tell him and now, as I drive towards Temple Meads, my heart rises in my chest. I haven't seen him for a few days – since the start of the week – and I've missed him. For once, I don't change into my chef's trousers and Crocs; I won't be in the bakery long. I put an apron on over my short-sleeved dress and pin the thick waves of my hair up. I hum as I weigh out the flour and take the temperature of the water. The leaven smells slightly acrid; I can't help thinking that it really must be hungry. I pour it into the giant mixer and turn it on. I jump when I realize a man is standing next to me. I hadn't heard him come in.

I switch the machine off and he folds me in his arms.

'I scared you again.'

It's the first time I've seen Paul in normal clothes. He's wearing jeans and a T-shirt that show off his biceps. He looks too broad, too rugged to be standing in an urban cafe. I've always associated Paul Bradshaw with the hills and mountains, hidden tarns and wild weather.

'Do you miss it?' I ask him, as the jolt of my heart subsides.

'What? I've missed you!' He kisses me, long and slow.

'Your job as a ranger. The Lake District.'

'Aye. Every day. I like being outside right enough, and the woods on our back doorstep are pleasant.' He grins, and I can tell he's remembering our last walk. 'But I miss the space.' He doesn't say any more, as if he's struggling to articulate what it is he's lost.

His wife. His life; his sense of self, I think.

'Good for the lad, though. I hardly see him. He's made friends. He's out all the time. It's given him more confidence.'

I've dusted flour on him and I smile, knowing he wouldn't care if he noticed.

'What did you have in mind, Emma?'

'There's a small office,' I say, 'at the back.'

He leans against the counter and smiles.

'I won't be long. Shall I make you a coffee?'

'Please.'

It's warm in here; it's the residual heat from the ovens, which were on all day yesterday. I wipe my hand across my forehead.

'You've got a smudge,' he says. He gently wipes it away and tucks a strand of hair behind my ear. 'You look different.'

'It's having my hair up,' I murmur.

I turn away from him, so he can't scrutinize me too closely, and I begin making his coffee. Paul sits in the deserted cafe and flicks through some of the books on the shelf above the table. They're mainly cookery books that Katie bought on her trip to San Francisco, the one that inspired her to start the bakery. Harry has added some hipster ones too, like *The Curious Barista's Guide to Coffee*. I steam the milk, the way Paul likes it. Do I know this from going to the cafe at Tyntesfield? Or from before? I'm not sure. It's becoming a blur in my mind.

He scrapes his chair back and stands.

'It's okay,' I say, 'I'll bring it over. I'm going to make one for me, too.'

Why not? I think, *the caffeine won't kill me*. Paul is still walking towards me. At first I think it's because he can't wait, not even the length of time it takes to drink a cup of coffee, but something is not right. His face has a kind of blank expression – the way the sky can go neutral just before a storm. He sets down a book about tattoos by the sink. My heart clenches. I wonder if he's tried to speak to Julia.

'I thought . . . I thought I was going insane, but it *is* you.' He grabs my chin and twists my face backwards and forward. 'There's something so familiar about you, yet you look completely different. You sound different. I don't know what you've done. Your nose. Even the shape of your eyes. Surgery? I suppose you dye your hair and do something to it, to make it like this.'

He seizes a handful. The pins fall out and my thick hair, with its carefully cultivated wave, tumbles down.

'Paul! I don't know who you think I am, but I'm *me*. Emma. Emma Taylor.'

He reaches out and grabs my wrist. He yanks me towards him and runs his fingers roughly over my upper arm. There's a faint scar. It's so faint most people wouldn't notice it. The skin is a little whiter and ever so slightly raised. He drops my arm as if I've scalded him.

'You had it removed, didn't you?' He shakes his head as if he can't believe anyone would do anything so horrible. 'This is where it was, I'm sure of it!' He jabs the scar with his finger. 'You had your son's name – our son's name – removed.'

I shake my head.

'I don't know what you're talking about.'

'What the fuck do you think you're doing?' He's shouting in my face, spittle flecking my cheeks. 'Why did you do it? Why did you leave us?'

His rage is terrifying. I'm breathing so fast I think I'm going to choke.

This is Paul, I remind myself, *Paul. He'd never have hurt a woman. He won't hurt you.*

'Do you know what you did to us? Do you have the slightest idea what it was like? No, I don't suppose you do, with your swanky big house and your rich husband. You walked away from us, left me with a six-month-old baby. Dylan grew up without a mother! And I had no fucking idea – you know me, I could make a classy Cosmopolitan and pour a decent fucking pint, but purée carrots: are you fucking kidding me? He cried, every night. Straight through until he fell asleep out of sheer bloody exhaustion, and then when he woke up there'd be, oh, maybe five minutes when he smiled and then, as soon as he realized you weren't there, he'd start again.

'We didn't have enough money to live on – I couldn't work full-time because I had to raise Dylan and, if you recall, we didn't have enough even when I was doing two part-time jobs. It was why you went to work in Leeds. Did you meet someone there? Is that what happened? Did you get a better fucking offer?

'And all the time – all the sodding time – I was thinking something terrible had happened to you, that maybe you'd been mugged, or worse. Murdered. I missed you. God, I missed you so much. And Dylan, well, I've done the best I can, but he's not the boy he should have been. He's not the person he could have become, if he'd had a stable, loving home with two parents and hadn't grown up with this terrible hole in his fucking heart, because his mother left him before he was even a year old.'

He stops, as if there is so much more to say, but he's run out of the will or the energy. He's breathing heavily. I'm trembling. But I have to be strong. I inhale deeply and stand up straight.

My voice quavers to begin with, but I say firmly, 'You've made a mistake. I'm not her. I'm not Lizzie. You think about her all the time, don't you? And it's stopping you from seeing clearly. From seeing me for who I really am. A woman you met for the first time a few weeks ago.'

The colour drains from his face. He points a finger at me. 'I *know* who you are. Why do you keep denying it? And what the hell are you doing now? Pursuing me, after all this time? You're fucking insane. Keep away from me and my son.'

He shoves a table aside and bolts out of the cafe.

My hands are shaking and I'm shivering. The book he was looking at has fallen open on a double-page spread. It's a quote in exquisite calligraphy: *It isn't a question of beauty, it's only a question of truth.*

The words are interwoven with yellow roses, sunflowers and golden lilies. It's beautiful. It's a photograph of a tattoo on a young girl's slender arm. I slam the book shut and start to cry.

How the hell am I going to find Lizzie's son now?

LIZZIE

She ordered a hot chocolate; she needed something comforting and sweet. She kept her coat on, to cover her garish yellow-and-blue uniform. She glanced at her watch: her break had ended five minutes ago, and Gregor would be searching for her. He'd sack her. He didn't give anyone a second chance. Well, it saved her having to hand in her notice. What had she been thinking, saying she'd testify? She'd go back to Miriam's and get her things and catch the bus home. She'd manage. Even if it meant putting off her studies for a year or two. She longed to be with Dylan right now; she could almost feel the weight of her baby in her arms. And she and Paul needed to talk properly. Work out what they were going to do. She realized that she no longer believed her husband: it was as if the certainty that he'd betrayed her with her best friend had settled into her bones like the chill of a damp day.

She'd chosen a chair at the back of the room, so she could see anyone who came in. Simon arrived with his female partner, DS Helen Robbins – Lizzie knew her name now – who had limp blonde hair in a bun and looked worn out.

'Would you like anything? A sandwich?' Helen asked, when they came over.

Lizzie shook her head.

'Can I see the letter?' Simon asked, without even saying hello.

She handed it to him and he slid it into a plastic folder, along with the envelope, before he examined it.

'We'll dust it for prints, but I suspect we won't find any. And we'll do a search on this kind of stationery . . .' He trailed off, as if even he knew it would be a waste of effort.

'You told me I'd be safe! You said I'd be anonymous!' Lizzie burst out. 'How does he know who I am and where to find me?'

He looked up from the letter; one eye was bloodshot and he hadn't shaved for a few days. He passed it to Helen so that she could read it, too.

'I'm afraid,' he said heavily, 'it looks authentic. It's his style.'

'You've seen other letters he's written, then? It's definitely from him?'

'Aye, I'm as certain as I can be.'

She looked around. It was Tuesday morning and she was in a dismal cafe in Next in a nondescript shopping centre on the outskirts of Leeds. If she looked out of the window, she'd be able to see the sickly blue and brash yellow of Ikea. The cafe was half-filled with shoppers, bulging bags at their feet; dry cheese sandwiches and slices of cake on their plates. A full mug of cooling hot chocolate was on the table in front of her, along with an unopened packet of shortbread biscuits that Helen had insisted on buying her.

It didn't seem right that this should be the place to find out she was going to die.

STELLA

Kaylee was insufferable after hanging out with Adam and the other boys at The Station. Like they were all drooling over her and she could have the pick of any of them.

'Of course Adam paid me the most attention,' she said, and I imitated her, *Of course*, but only in my head.

They all went yesterday afternoon, too.

'You should come,' Kaylee had said, in that smug tone that meant, *Only if you want to be a fucking loser*. 'He's so fit!'

I didn't go. I didn't want to be humiliated by her and Nuala. I kept thinking about them. I imagined her and Nuala in identical clothes with Kardashian cleavages. Wondering if they were having fun. If Kaylee had kissed Adam. And I feel sick, thinking about my mocks. I spent the afternoon studying, but I couldn't concentrate. And I can't believe Dad dragged us round Clevedon Court today. Like I need a crash course in fourteenth-century architecture!

I don't know why he wouldn't let me stay at home or even sit in the cafe and work, but he said, 'You need a break. It'll help you study better.'

He's such a fucking dictator. Even Mum didn't manage to look like she was enjoying herself. She was super-jumpy and kind of absent. She's gone to the bakery to feed the sourdough culture. I suddenly feel like I need to be with her, without Dad and Ava. We never have any time alone together any more. When she's not focused on the prima donna, she's not here; she's somewhere else in her head. I never talk to her, not really about things that matter, but I wonder what she'd say about Adam and Kaylee? It feels like an amorphous mess in my mind and she might be able to straighten it out. And I'm so jittery about my mocks. She does all these breathing techniques; she might be able to teach me one. And maybe, if it's just me and her, she might tell me what's going on – what she's doing with the man from Tyntesfield. Like, you know, a proper mother-and-daughter chat.

Ava and I are watching the first Harry Potter movie, which we've seen a million times before.

'I'm going for a bike ride. Tell Dad, if he asks.'

'Hmm,' says Ava, trying to look round me as I get up.

It's her favourite film of all time, so it's unlikely she's heard a word I said. I turn off the alarm system and go and fetch my bike. Unlike Mum, I don't mind cycling to *Kate's*. It's mainly on cycle paths alongside the river. As I bump over the cobbles and seagulls wheel around me, I imagine sitting in the cafe while Mum sneaks me a lemonade from the fridge and makes me a proper cheese toastie. It's quiet when I arrive. There are hardly any cars or many people. I lock my bike up and walk over.

The bakery is in a tunnel that runs underneath the station. There's a whole series of these archways with offices in them, but the one next to *Kate's* is empty – it's where the bins are kept. The cafe's at the front, and the kitchen where Mum works is at the far end of the arch, and then there's a tiny office. When I was little, I used to sit there while she was working and watch her folding the dough and cooking caramel sauce. My stomach rumbles. The metal shutters are only half-open and, as I crouch to duck underneath, I hear voices. One of them is a man's, the other is my mother's. Until this summer I'd just have gone in anyhow, but now I stay low and peer through the window. It's the man I saw with Mum before, at Tyntesfield, I'm sure of it.

I quickly slip back out. I follow the next tunnel, squeezing between the bins and holding my nose. A little way down there's a door set in the wall, which leads into the back of the bakery. I open it a crack and look through. I can't see them, but the man is shouting. I can't make out the words, but I'm starting to feel really frightened. I reach in the pocket of my denim jacket for my phone, just in case I need to ring Dad. Or the police.

I step inside. There's the smell of coffee and yeast. I hide behind one of the trolleys, stacked with plastic trays that the dough gets put in when its rising. The shouting has stopped. I can see a tiny bit of my mum. Her hair is a wreck. The door slams and the metal shutters rattle, so I guess the man has just left. There's silence and then Mum starts to cry. Proper crying, with tears and snot.

For a moment I feel sorry for her. I'm about to go over and give her a hug, when I realize. She must have been meeting that man on all her cycling trips. That's what they were for – not for getting fit. I kept hoping he was just a friend and that it wasn't an affair, but no one yells at their friends like that once they're grown-up. And now she's even arranged for him to come here, to the bakery when she's supposed to be working, and Dad, Ava and I are waiting at home for her.

Is it over? Has he just broken up with her? I don't feel sad for her any more. I creep back out and keep walking through the tunnel, as far as I can. It grows darker as I go further in and there's green slime on the walls. In places the plaster has chipped and you can see red bricks beneath. I think of the weight of the station and all the trains resting on top of me. I stop when I reach some iron bars and there's just blackness ahead and the soft, exhaled breath of trapped air. I'm angry but I'm also relieved. He's finished with her and now she won't leave us.

EMMA

On Sunday night Jack and Stella had a huge row. I'd tried to tidy myself up as best as I could after my conversation with Paul at the bakery; I'd brushed my hair and reapplied my lipstick. In the car on the way home I went to my safe place, the one I created with the help of my therapist. It's the stream near the house I grew up in when I was a child. In my mind, it's a warm day and I sit on the bank, trailing my toes in the water. The stones are smooth beneath my soles; there's a duck on the other side, sleeping in the sunshine, her head tucked under her wing. I imagine the pull and suck of the water lapping against my ankles.

When I got in, my face was still red and blotchy. I hoped everyone would think it was the heat from the ovens and not remember they hadn't been switched on, but no one noticed. Ava was hiding downstairs in her bedroom and Stella was yelling at Jack. Apparently she'd gone out without telling him and she'd switched the alarm system off while he was in his office.

'It's not a big deal. God! Ava was in the house watching a film. You were there!'

'I was in my office. I've told you over and over again – if there isn't an adult in the house with you, you need to have the alarm on.'

'You two are so fucking weird,' Stella said.

'If someone broke in, I wouldn't be there. I wouldn't even hear. The shed is soundproof and it's right at the bottom of the garden. You know all this!'

'If someone broke in – which is so unlikely—'

'You never know!' I say, my voice shrill. 'A break-in could happen anywhere, at any time. There's fewer people around in the suburbs, the neighbours might not notice.'

'Then I'd ring the police. Like a normal person.'

'What I don't understand is why you didn't tell me?' Jack said. 'How long would it have taken you to walk to the bottom of the garden? You could even have sent me a text!'

'I don't have to tell you every fucking thing I do!' Stella shouted back.

'Did you go to Kaylee's?' I asked.

My daughter didn't even look in my direction.

'I went for a bike ride,' she said.

'Where?' asked Jack.

'Around.'

She stormed out of the room, still without looking at me. Jack held up his hands. 'I'll talk to her later when she's calmed down. How was the beast?'

'It had turned into a ravenous monster,' I said, trying to smile.

He kissed me on the forehead and went downstairs to reassure Ava. I stood at the window and looked out, over the fields and towards Tyntesfield – and Paul. Where had Stella gone? It's not like her to go for an aimless bike ride. What had made her leave? I can't imagine she'd have come to the bakery and seen us, but still . . . it's a warning. We should have been more careful. What if I slip up in one of my many lies? Stella would tell Jack. She's always got on better with him than with me. I shudder when I think what might happen if Jack found out. He'd be so hurt. I've never crossed him, but I imagine he'd be . . . unforgiving.

There's no way round it. I'm going to have to tell Paul the truth. It's the only way he's going to let me see Dylan. It's risky, but I have to do it, before anyone can find out what I've been doing. And then after that, I'll stop seeing him. For my husband's sake.

Before Jack came back upstairs, I sent Paul a message and asked him to meet me on Wednesday afternoon in the Pavilion cafe.

'I'll explain everything,' I wrote.

He didn't reply. For the next three days I checked and rechecked my phone.

It's now Wednesday and I'm on my way. I have to hope that he will turn up, even if it's only because he still loves Lizzie. After all, he keeps telling me that he only had a 'fling', as if he's still trying to apologize to his wife.

I drive. I don't want to arrive hot and flustered. I need to look as if I'm in control. It's raining and cold, so I go inside and sit at a table by the window. I order a cup of tea. My stomach is churning too much to eat anything. I dabbed the oil that Jack bought me on my wrists this morning and I inhale the scent of lavender and clary sage. I'm going to have to say things that I haven't said for sixteen years.

I close my eyes and return to my safe place. I think about that little mallard duck, sleeping by the stream, her head tucked under her wing, the sun glinting off the royal-purple flash in her wing. I dip my toe in the clear, cold water. My baby sister is lying on the grass next to me, and her gurgles mingle with the lapping of the water.

There's the scrape of a chair against the stone flags and I jump. Paul sits down opposite me. His face is hard, his expression closed.

He leans forward and says quietly but with venom, 'The truth, Lizzie. Why did you leave us?'

My voice is shaky. 'My name is Emma Taylor.'

He folds his arms across his chest. 'You can't fool me any more. It took a while, I'll give you that. I thought I was going mad. But I recognize you now, even without the tattoo, and with your dyed hair and the extra three stone.'

I twist the band round my wrist. I need to say it. I take a deep breath. It's the second-hardest thing I've had to say in my life. I feel as if a chasm is opening up inside me. It's so many years since I've said her name.

'You're right. I *was* Lizzie Bradshaw.'

Paul is still leaning back in his chair, putting as much distance as possible between us. I pour the tea. My hands are trembling and it spills on the table.

'We weren't good enough for you?'

'I was in a car accident,' I say. 'I was pretty badly hurt.'

He makes a low sound, dismissing my pathetic injuries as nothing, compared to the anguish I've caused him and our son.

'I had amnesia. I had no idea who I was. It took months to recover, to be able to walk again.'

'Broke your nose, did you?'

'I had plastic surgery to reconstruct it and part of my cheekbone, and this bit here, around my eye. When I was well enough to leave the . . . the facility I was in, I still had no memory of who I was. Or of you, or Dylan. The police weren't able to discover who I really was and they gave me a new identity.'

He doesn't say anything. He looks as if he hates me. But I've had enough counselling to know it's a defence mechanism.

'I reinvented myself as Emma James. Years later . . .' I take a sip of tea. It's too hot and I burn my tongue. 'Years later I saw a therapist to deal with my anxiety, and I started having flashbacks. I started to remember you and our son.' My eyes well up. 'But by then it was too late. I was married to Jack. I had two girls.' Tears trickle down my face. 'I couldn't go back and find you. I had to live with the memory of you and Dylan, of the life I'd lost. Julia, my sister. Mum and Dad. My friends – Miriam.' In spite of his angry silence, he looks ashamed.

'Since then there hasn't been a day that I haven't thought about you both – and now, finding out that I have two nieces I've never seen, my sister has emigrated, my parents are both dead . . . I'm losing everyone I loved all over again.' I stop and try and control myself. 'That girl – Lizzie Bradshaw – she's gone. I had to let her go. I had to pretend she never existed.'

'Clearly,' says Paul, and he looks me up and down, his gaze unflinching as he takes in my soft belly, my flawless complexion, every freckle removed, the wave set into my dyed blonde hair and the beautifully cut wrap-dress that Jack bought me and that Lizzie would have hated.

'Catching sight of you in Tyntesfield brought it all back. Everything I've been trying to suppress. And made it so much worse. I had to see you again.'

He leans towards me. 'And now that you have, how does it feel, Lizzie Bradshaw, to be married to two men?' His voice is thick with rage. 'How does it feel to be having a cup of fucking tea with your husband, while your other spouse is hard at work? How does it feel to have sex with one of your husbands and then go home and fuck the other? It's not really betrayal, is it? Not when you're legally married to both of us.'

I flinch. It's so stark when he puts it like that. And the word – such a horrible little word that I have spent so many years avoiding, not even whispering it to myself when I'm at my lowest and most vulnerable – now floats into my mind, grows larger and more threatening. I can see it poised in the curl of Paul's lips. He's ready to spit it at me. *Bigamy.* I shut my eyes for a moment and focus.

'You can't call me Lizzie,' I say. 'I'm not that girl any more.'

'You're my wife. I'll call you what I fucking like.'

'I'm also Jack's wife,' I say, a warning note creeping into my voice. He does not own me. 'I want to see my son.'

'No!' He stands abruptly.

People in the cafe are staring at us. The two young men who work here in the afternoon are glancing at Paul: he's still in his uniform. An employee losing his temper with a visitor doesn't look good. An employee having an affair in work hours is even worse. But Paul has never cared about appearances. It was one of the many reasons I loved him. I don't want to be responsible for him losing his job, though.

'Walk me back to my car? Please?'

Paul strides out and I follow him. He slows down fractionally and we continue side by side, past the children's playground and the field of calves and down the estate road towards Backwell Common where I've left my car, parked on a grass verge.

I stop beneath a copper-beech tree. Rain drips from the leaves and slides coldly down my back.

'I missed you. I love you,' I say.

For a moment he remains standing with his back to me. Then he turns and crushes me to his chest. I cling to him. His body heaves as he sobs. My cheeks are wet, and I can't tell whether it's with his tears or mine or the rain.

'I've missed you so much,' he says into my hair. 'Miriam meant nothing to me. It was just that one time, and I regretted it even before it was over. I couldn't wait to get her out of the door.'

'I know,' I say. I don't want to think about Miriam, not now. I won't let her come between us again. 'What are we going to do?' I ask him.

He pulls a hanky out of his pocket and wipes my face gently. He traces a line around my eyes and down the bone in my cheek that a surgeon once broke. He blows his nose.

'We'll figure it out,' he says, attempting a smile. 'The main thing is that we've found each other again.' He takes a deep breath. 'But it's too early for you to meet Dylan. He's never had a mother . . . that he can remember. He's angry with you, with the memory of you.

It'll take a long time to get him to change. And it's too complicated a situation for him right now. I mean, I can't get my head around you losing your memory, being married, having two girls – his half-sisters! And you know what teenagers are like. Everything has to be black and white. It would be traumatic for him, and he might push you away without giving you a chance.'

'But he's my son!'

'He doesn't feel like that,' says Paul, but his voice is gentle. 'Let's meet up again and try and work out what to do, what to tell him.'

He takes my hands in his and suddenly I'm twenty-two again. I'm passing him our baby boy and kissing Dylan's soft forehead, and saying goodbye to Paul. I'm sad because I won't see them for four days, and a small, secret part of me is relieved. For four days I won't have to think about nappies and bottle-feeds; I won't have to get up in the night or spend the entire day trying to have one single conversation. I'll be able to go out with girls my own age and get drunk and giggle, and maybe even read a book or have a meal instead of grabbing some toast when the baby isn't crying. I'll wear clean clothes that don't have sick down the back or mud around the hems. I'll be warm without having to fetch wood and scrape the hearth clean. I'll be able to have a shower with hot water and not have a cold, shallow bath with a baby crying bitterly on the mat next to me. But, of course, it wasn't like that and I felt guilty the entire time I was away. How I hated myself. How I hate myself.

'You have some serious thinking to do. About Jack. Let's both take some time, get our heads round this. I'll see you in a week.'

He kisses me and strides away. I stand in the rain and watch Paul until he disappears around a bend in the road, and it takes me all my strength not to run after him and beg him never to leave me again.

STELLA

Both Mum and Dad sent me texts today saying that he's going to pick me up after school. I'm half-suspicious and half-looking forward to it, since the last time he picked me up, I got to eat a huge quantity of cake. But he might still be pissed off. He was really cross I'd gone out on Sunday, when I cycled after Mum without switching the alarm system back on. The precious prima ballerina was unprotected and in the house by herself while Dad was in the shed.

'Where are we going?'

'You'll see,' he says.

I sigh. There's really little point in engaging anyone over the age of twenty-one in a conversation, and Dad's what – fifty-six, fifty-seven? Old, anyhow. He's got this salt-and-pepper crew-cut and he's so lean and pumped from his workouts, and with this kind of flinty look in his eye, that you don't think of him as having an age. He looks like a soldier. His dad, our Grossvater, was actually in the army. I guess Dad must have got over the alarm thing, as he doesn't mention it. That's one of the good things about Dad – he doesn't hold grudges. Part of his Dr Seuss training.

We park at Cabot Circus and I trail after Dad, across the bridge and into the shopping centre. I hate going anywhere public in my school uniform. Dad turns into the House of Fraser.

'Wait!'

'I'm not trying to buy you a dress. Come on.'

I fold my arms and don't move, aware that I'm causing an obstruction to all the shoppers trying to get past. Dad will be annoyed by the spectacle, so he'll have to listen to me. He comes over.

'I want to buy your mother a dress for the anniversary party.'

I look at him in astonishment. Dad does this Germanic high-efficiency shop twice a year for all our clothes. We go to an outlet store or he does it online. I put my foot down a couple of years ago. We had a massive row and then he backed down, and he lets me get my own now.

'So what do you need me for?' I ask, still not moving. 'You know you always "help" Mum choose her clothes. You know what size she is. And what she likes. Correction: what you like her to wear.'

Actually, if you like that kind of thing, he's got quite good taste and he picks stuff that suits her and flatters her shape.

He sighs. 'Well, as the cake outing demonstrated, I don't know her as well as I thought I did.'

Dad doesn't seem to be in the least embarrassed, standing outside House of Fraser with shoppers streaming past us and tutting because we're in the way, and now I start to feel uncomfortable.

'Since when did that bother you?' I mutter. I glance at him from beneath my hair, but surprisingly he doesn't look angry.

'I've realized,' he says, looking down at the seething mass of people three floors below us, 'that sometimes I push her in directions she wouldn't have chosen for herself. And when you love someone, you have to allow them to be themselves. You have to let go.'

He sounds as if he's giving a presentation, but it's probably as personal a revelation for his freaky nature as you're ever going to get.

'Okay,' I say.

Normally I hate shopping. As we wander between the racks of clothes, I think of Kaylee, but then I try not to. We haven't spoken that much since last weekend, when she went to The Station with

Adam and the Boyz and all the other tools she was hanging out with. This is actually going to be, well, not fun, but quite nice. We check out brands I've never really looked at before, because Kaylee would have laughed her head off if I'd tried, and I'd have felt too awkward to imagine myself in anything other than jeans. Dad does his usual thing – pulling out wraps and halter-necks with tiny patterns and lots of ruching, from boring designers, but I ignore him. I think about my mum, really think about her.

'You know,' I tell him, 'she's actually more of a trousers person.'

'Trousers don't suit her,' he says dismissively.

Eventually I find it. It's the perfect outfit: drapey trousers and a long tunic. It's elegant – you could imagine her at a garden party or in business class on a plane. The tunic and trousers will skim over her fat bits and elongate her legs. They're dark grey with a greeny undertone, which will look amazing with her blonde hair and light-grey eyes.

'Grey?' he says. 'It's a summer party.'

I hold them up against a mannequin in a swimsuit, who's wearing a straw boater and high-heeled sandals, and Dad nods.

'I see. Perhaps a silk shawl?'

Obviously he's not going to say, *Wow, you're right Stella!* I shake my head.

'A short denim jacket to toughen it up.'

He opens his mouth to protest and then he grins at me and ruffles my hair, and for once I don't make a fuss about it. We head over to the denim lab, but instead of looking at jackets, he goes straight to 7 for all Mankind and pulls out a pair of black waxed jeans in my size.

'Apparently models wear them with a simple white T-shirt at garden parties.'

'More like J Brand, but they'll do,' I say, taking them from him and heading for the fitting room.

Dad gave me a tenner to spend in the cafe while he went to choose some underwear and jewellery to go with Mum's outfit and I did some revision. When he came back, he was super-excited.

'Look! Isn't this perfect?'

'Er . . .'

'Ruby is the gemstone associated with being married for fifteen years.'

He's bought a ruby pendant, the size of a coffee bean, on a thin gold chain, with matching gold-and-ruby earrings.

'And red roses are the other symbol,' he adds.

'Well, that's pretty handy,' I say, 'since we've got a ton of them growing in the garden.'

He raises his eyebrows.

'Wait! You mean, you actually planted them because you knew . . .'

'Yes,' he says, and grins.

'But, that was like . . .'

'Four years ago, when I had the garden landscaped.'

'Wow,' I say. 'Dad, you are certifiably insane.'

Inside, though, I'm wondering if anyone will love me so much they'll grow roses, hoping to present me with a bouquet of them four years in the future. Mum definitely doesn't deserve him. And then I think that I can't ever imagine being that sure of anything. I mean, it seems like tempting fate somehow, planting flowers that have such a weight of emotion attached to them. They could get decimated by a plague of aphids. Or your partner might get, you know, hit by a bus or something.

By the time we get home I'm feeling pretty good. I've actually got a cool outfit to wear to this party. I'm still angry with Kaylee and a bit with Adam, although I don't know how I feel about him, but mainly I'm cross with Mum. I mean, Dad might be a bit much sometimes, but he really loves her. He's making such an effort. She's been sad and withdrawn all week and the bike's stayed in the shed, but at least she's finally stopped seeing that guy. She'll get over it when she realizes that me, Dad and Ava are what's important, and not some random bloke she has tea with.

As we go inside, Dad whispers, 'I'll hide these in my office, you go on up.'

I start walking upstairs to the living room, when I see Mum and Ava spinning around and flinging each other across the wooden floor in a kind of dramatic waltz. They're singing. I think it's something from *The Sound of Music*. Mum looks happy. Her skin is luminous, and she's flushed pink from dancing. She and Ava giggle and trill. They look ridiculous. I haven't seen Mum this happy since . . . And then I go cold. She hasn't got over him at all. They must be back together again. I feel sick.

I creep back downstairs before they notice me, and go into Mum and Dad's bedroom. The French windows open out onto the garden, so I'll see Dad coming back up from his office long before he'll be able to spot me. I open Mum's handbag and take out her wallet. I empty all the receipts on the bed. Still no sign of Dad. I check the dates for the Tyntesfield ones. Yeah. She's started meeting him again all right. It must be serious. Is she going to leave us?

EMMA

We've been meeting as often as we can. I cycle straight to Paul's cottage after work, so that there's no chance of anyone catching us. He doesn't even take a lunch break so that we have time to meet. It's not enough, though, for either of us, snatching a scant hour before I have to pick up the girls and he needs to return to work. We barely speak. He starts taking my clothes off as soon as I'm through the door. It's as if we're making up for all the years we've lost. Afterwards he holds me tightly, or else he explores my body gently with his fingertips, learning it anew. He's not as wiry and lean as he was; he's thicker, more barrel-chested. It suits him, as do the furrows across his forehead, the smile lines around his eyes.

We were children when we last saw each other. And I find that I can – that I already have – forgiven him his one transgression with my best friend. In fact I've never been this happy – as Emma Taylor, that is. But the happiness is short-lived, momentary. I have the rest of the day, the rest of my real life, to deal with. The guilt I feel, the indecision, the longing to see my son, the anxiety about the risks I'm taking are almost overwhelming.

Today we're lying beneath the sheets; rain is beating against the windowpane and pattering on the roof tiles. I push the covers back; I've just come and heat is radiating from me. My body gleams with perspiration. I feel strangely weightless, as if the only thing holding me down is Paul's arm anchoring me at my waist.

Who am I, when I'm with him? I introduced myself to him as Emma Taylor. Emma is in her mid-thirties and has a husband called Jack and two gorgeous girls; she has blonde hair and bakes cake for a living; she's the kind of woman who goes to the pub on Friday nights with her family. But the person he knows, the girl he remembers, is Lizzie Bradshaw, mother of his newborn baby, a slim, fit hill-walker who was halfway through her degree in Environmental Science. Emma is not the kind of woman Paul Bradshaw would be interested in. They have nothing in common. Lizzie is the woman he really wants, and I can't find her any more. I buried that girl long ago. So who does he see? Who is Paul fucking? Is he looking for his auburn-haired wife who'd race him up Langdale Pike, who campaigned against particles of plastic in the world's oceans and could tell the difference between a Heath and a Pearl-bordered Fritillary butterfly, now hiding in the body of a voluptuous middle-aged woman?

'Hey, what is it?' he asks, stroking my stomach.

I sigh. 'I have to go in a minute.'

'Yeah,' he says, rolling onto his back and releasing me.

I float then, my body rising until I'm hovering just below the ceiling. I look down at Paul. He has one hand over his eyes. The sheet is draped around him. He's tired, tired of this double-life, of trying to figure out how to break the news to his seventeen-year-old son that the mother who abandoned him when he was six months old is back, but she's turned into somebody else.

'I'm not sure how much more of this I can take,' he says.

I'm instantly next to him, in my lumpy body that has carried three children, and I'm suddenly appalled by my saggy breasts, the striation of stretch marks puckering my skin and my soft flesh. I seize the edge of the sheets and wrap myself up in them.

'What do you mean?'

I'm frightened. He can't end this – not now, not when I'm so close to seeing Dylan.

He rolls over onto his side and props himself up on one elbow. He strokes a stray strand of hair out of my face.

'I can't stand the thought of you with him.'

'Yes, I know,' I say softly, taking his hand. 'He helped me, though. I met him when I'd recovered physically from the accident but I didn't know who I was. He's part of me, of who I am now.'

'He exploited you when you were vulnerable.'

'He made me want to live.'

'Do you love him?'

'Yes,' I say.

It's true. I love Jack, and what I'm doing here, with Paul, makes me feel wretched. Jack has always been there for me. He's never once belittled me or made me feel foolish for being so over-wrought all the time. He accepted it was part of who I was, because of what had happened to me.

'I told him my mum and dad and my sister were killed in a car crash. I didn't know what else to say – I didn't even remember who they were, where they lived, what their names were,' I say. 'And then I said, when I had therapy, that I'd remembered the name of my sister. Jack put me back together. Made me whole again. '

Paul clenches his jaw. 'But you were with me first. You married me first. We have a son!'

'I love you, too!' I say. 'I do! But I have two daughters with him!'

'You can't,' he says. 'You can't love us both. You can't be married to both of us. You have to choose. I want you to leave him!'

And the words he doesn't say hang heavily in the air: *Because if you don't, I won't let you see our son.*

I get up and dress quickly. I can't be late to pick up the girls. I'm trembling. How can I choose? My husband and the son I haven't seen for sixteen and a half years, or my other husband and our two beautiful daughters? Paul doesn't know what he's asking.

The only reason I'm alive today is because no one knows who

I really am and what actually happened. I've never told Jack, and I cannot tell Paul the whole truth. I cannot tell him what happened that terrible night and the morning that followed it, all those years ago. Because if either of them ever found out, none of us would make it.

LIZZIE

Simon leaned towards her and said, 'We need to get you out of here, right now. For all we know, Lilley's men have followed you. We'll talk when we get there.' He glanced up at Helen. 'We'll take the service stairs. Bring the car round.'

Helen nodded and left.

Lizzie looked around the cafe inside Next, at the other shoppers eating vacantly. 'Talk where?'

'We're going to go somewhere safe and then we can discuss our options,' said Simon.

He took her arm, but instead of heading towards the main exit, he pulled her through a door marked 'Staff Only' and into a drab, dingy stairwell, the lino and the walls scuffed.

'You got a scarf?'

She shook her head. Her mouth was dry. She didn't know what to say, but she could feel panic rising inside her like trapped bubbles of air.

'Do up your coat and put the hood up,' he said when they reached the ground floor. 'And don't call anyone. Not until we've talked. In fact, give me your mobile.'

He peered round the door, and she heard the crunch of tyres. He pulled her outside. They were in a loading bay, a couple of Next vans parked alongside a yellow waste-skip. A dark-blue Peugeot stopped in front of them and Simon hustled her down the concrete steps and into the back of the car, placing his hand on her head, as if, she thought, she was a suspect.

In the car, Simon immediately got on the radio.

'Where are we going? What's happening?' she asked.

'We'll stop soon,' said Helen, glancing at her in the rear-view mirror. 'We'll discuss it then.'

It felt as if they drove for a long time, but she couldn't be certain. She desperately wanted to speak to Paul. It was dark when they pulled off the A1 into the car park of a rundown hotel. The room they led her into hummed with the sound of traffic, and the view from the window was of two corners of the building, air conditioning and heater vents extruding from the brickwork like black fungi. If she craned her neck, she could just see a fragment of the night sky, glowing an opaque orange from the street lamps.

Simon passed her a bottle of water and shrugged off his coat. Lizzie looked around. The carpet was a swirl of burgundy and brown; there was a TV, a kettle, a small fridge, a double bed and a table with a couple of armchairs that had wooden armrests. They looked as if they'd be uncomfortable to sit in.

'Okay,' Simon said, sinking into one of them. 'Let's talk this through.'

She joined him at the table and Helen perched on the end of the bed.

'What's going on?'

She was so frightened she could hardly speak.

'We've been trying to work out how Lilley could have found you. His lawyer will have your name, because it's on the witness statement you gave. He shouldn't have given it to Lilley, but he might have done. As for knowing who you are . . . I thought you said he didn't see you? Is there some way he could have?'

She thought of standing in Arjun's stockroom, her arms out-stretched towards the child, how Lilley had snatched him and then he'd turned and looked through the crack in the door into the darkness as the door swung open and closed and, for one fleeting moment, she'd seen his eyes. She shivered as she remembered: it was as if he'd looked right through her and yet she was sure he couldn't have seen her. Surely he'd have killed her, if he'd known she was there?

'He looked towards me, but I was in the dark, I didn't think he could . . .' And then it came back to her and she felt as if her stomach was dropping away, as if she was in a lift plummeting to the ground. 'I dropped my name badge; it must have been when I had the migraine and Arjun let me lie down, out the back. I found it on the floor, just by the door to the stockroom, when I left. I didn't think anything of it, because it was behind the counter. I didn't think anyone would have . . .'

'So it's possible he could have seen it – and it says Ikea on it, as well as your name?'

'Yes.'

'And it is an incredibly distinctive uniform.' He glanced at the yellow-and-blue striped tunic, the kingfisher trousers. 'If he glimpsed you, saw a flash of colour even, he'd be able to guess. There's only one Ikea in Leeds.'

'I need to go,' she said, 'I have to get back to Paul and Dylan. I'm sorry, I can't . . . I can't do this . . .'

Helen said, 'We understand, love, but we need to figure out how much he knows. It's not safe for you to go home right now.'

'Of course he knows. Of course he fucking knows! He says he's going to kill my entire family and all their friends!'

Simon shook his head. 'It's a threat. We have to take it seriously, of course, but look at how he's worded it. "Your family and their friends." Believe me, if he knew who they were, he'd have visited them already, or named them in this letter. And it wasn't addressed to you at home, so I think – I hope – he doesn't know where you live yet.'

'You think? You hope? What kind of protection is that?' she said. 'I'm not going to testify for you. I'm sorry, but I can't risk it.' She paused, remembering. 'In the letter, Lilley said to ask you about the other witnesses.'

She pulled her rucksack onto her lap, wondering how she was going to get home. She had no idea where she was. Maybe they'd drop her at a bus stop, and she shuddered when she thought of standing on the edge of the road by herself. Neither of the officers spoke. Helen was looking at her hands again, and Simon was staring at her, his brown eyes dark, unreadable. She sank back into the chair.

'What happened to them?' she asked again.

'Lilley killed them,' said Helen.

'What – all three of them?'

Simon reached out and seized her wrist. 'That's why you're so important, Lizzie. We've been trying to bring Lilley to justice for years. Every time we've gathered enough evidence and a witness, Lilley has got to them just before the court case and the trial has collapsed. You're our only chance.'

'What about Arjun?'

Simon shook his head. 'He won't testify. He blames himself – says if he hadn't held out, his son would never have been hurt. He says he can't risk the kid's life again.'

She shook her head. 'I won't risk my son's life. Or mine.'

'If you don't testify,' said Simon, 'Lilley will walk free. He'll continue his threats and extortions, and his reign of terror. Have you any idea what it's—'

'Spare me,' she said, standing up and slinging her bag over her shoulder.

'The thing is,' said Helen, 'the thing is . . .' She coughed and glanced at Simon and then said, 'The last witness also received a death-threat from Lilley exactly like this one, and he withdrew his statement. It was three months before the trial was supposed to take place. The case collapsed.'

'So?'

'Lilley still killed him,' said Helen. 'I'm really sorry, Lizzie, but you're not safe, whether you testify or not.'

Simon rubbed the stubble on his chin. 'Look, let's sleep on it. We'll talk some more in the morning. We'll have a better idea of the situation and we'll have figured out some options for you. Helen will kip on the floor in here, and I'll be right next door. Try and get some rest.'

She looked at him, appalled. *Lilley still killed the witness . . .* She was trembling. A phrase came into her mind, one of those old biblical ones that her granddad might have quoted: *Damned if you do, damned if you don't.* Whatever decision she made – whether she chose to give evidence or not – she was going to die. And the only person protecting her right this minute was a tired woman who was going to be lying on some cushions at the bottom of her bed.

STELLA

'What's the narrative structure?' asks Ms Heron. It's Book Club and we're talking about the second half of *Oryx and Crake*. Kaylee is sitting next to Nuala, not me, and passing her notes and they're whispering to each other. The two of them smile and giggle when Adam comes in. They've both put lipgloss on. I bend towards the desk and let my hair fall over my face. When I glance up, Adam isn't looking at me. I study his profile and my stomach does a slow flip.

'It's told by Snowman, who's really Jimmy, in the present day, when everything's gone to shit,' says Theo, 'and then in flashbacks of him growing up with Glenn and when they're older, working together at RejoovenEsense. And that kind of takes us up to the present day and explains why Jimmy, now called the Snowman, is so miserable, and most of the other people are dead.'

Ms Heron steers the discussion towards the relationship between Jimmy and Glenn and what it means. Adam doesn't join in as much as last week. He sits back in his chair and watches, like he's giving the other kids a chance. Kaylee's been ignoring me this week. I'm trying not to think about whether anything happened between her and Adam. I wonder if they kissed at The Station. I wonder what it would be like to kiss him. He's got full lips; I think they'd feel soft. Adam catches me staring at him and I blush furiously. Nuala gives a little smirk. My neck feels itchy, like I've been to the hairdresser's and tiny fragments of hair are caught in my collar.

'What do you think of the final scene with Oryx, Crake and Jimmy? asks Ms Heron.

There's a kind of visible shiver round the room; only Adam smiles gently.

'Why would Crake slit his girlfriend's throat?' asks Cian.

'She wasn't his girlfriend. Crake was using her as a prostitute,' says Nuala.

'So? He still liked her. If he knew Jimmy was sleeping with her, why didn't he kill him instead—'

'What?' interrupts Theo. 'Did he actually know Jimmy was having sex with her?'

'Jimmy loved her, you idiot,' says Nuala. 'That's why Crake killed her. So Jimmy couldn't have her.'

'He planned it,' says Adam, leaning forward. 'He'd made Jimmy promise to look after the Crakers because he knew he was going to die. He also knew if he killed Oryx, Jimmy would kill him. But if he'd *asked* Jimmy to kill him, like a mercy "murder", he wouldn't have. Oryx was just,' he waves his hand, 'collateral damage. And a way of getting back at Jimmy. Win-win.'

Everyone starts talking at once. I feel cold. I realize in that moment that I really like Adam. I want him. And I'm ever so slightly scared of him – like, the kind of person who could figure out something like that, and say it so dispassionately, has to have an icy chip in his heart.

I pack my things up slowly, thinking Nuala and Kaylee might speak to me, but they don't. They hurry after Adam. I walk as if my feet are made of lead, down the corridor and across the playground towards the car park where Mum and Ava are waiting for me. Just as I reach the gate, I hear footsteps behind me. It's Adam.

'Hey.'

'Hey,' I reply.

His hair is messy; his fringe has fallen over his eyes again. He's wearing a checked Patagonia shirt over a grey T with a whale on it. It looks sort of nerdy. I like it.

'I had a good time the other week at The Station. I thought – I kind of thought – maybe you did, too?'

'Yeah, I did,' I say, starting to feel that hot, prickly sensation again. I glance towards the car park. I hope my mum can't see me. I fiddle with my shirt cuffs. I hate being in a uniform. I must seem so young to him.

He follows my gaze. 'Right. So I asked Nuala and Kaylee along because I thought, you know . . .' He runs his hand through his hair and it stays standing on end. 'I thought it might make it easier for you to go out, if your mum is, like, protective or strict or whatever it is.'

'Oh.'

I'm blushing really hard now, my cheeks are literally burning. He did want me to go! He doesn't fancy Kaylee. And he's also being really uncool, he's actually telling me what he thinks and not acting like a – well, like a boy.

'So, do you want to go somewhere?'

'Like where?' I say and then feel like an utter idiot.

'Well, I know you like coffee,' he says, grinning, and I can't help grinning back at him.

And then I have an idea. There are no cafes in Long Ashton and if we go to either of the pubs, the bar staff will recognize me. I don't want to go to The Station. What I need right now is proof – of what my mum is up to. I mean, before I say something to my dad, I need to know she's not just meeting an old friend for tea and biscuits. I need proof of her affair and that she's getting ready to leave us. I can't ask Kaylee to get Ted to take us to Tyntesfield again . . .

'Saturday afternoon, the Pavilion cafe at Tyntesfield,' I say.

'Tyntesfield?' he says, his brow furrowing. 'Really?'

'Yeah. The National Trust place? The cafe at the bottom has really good coffee. And you can sneak in without paying, if you're not a member. I mean, our family are, so . . .' I stop, feeling stupid.

He gives a kind of shrug and smiles. 'I know where you mean. Well, if that's where you want to go. I'll send you a message in the morning. Suitably Gothic, Ms Rochester.'

I can't stop grinning all the way to the car. Fortunately Mum's right at the back of the car park and she hadn't seen me. If I time it right on Saturday, I can follow her and then meet Adam. Win-win.

EMMA

Jack has been working late. After we've eaten dinner he spends a few minutes in the garden, pulling up a weed or spraying his precious roses or edging the lawns. It's as if he's putting off the inevitable, the moment when he'll disappear into his office. We've got into the habit of setting the alarm anytime he's there; I suppose he doesn't like the idea of a woman and two girls being on their own in the house at night any more than I do. Even though I go to bed so early, not long after he's gone to his shed, I know he doesn't come back in until at least midnight, because I always wake at the first cheep of the alarm, the first chink of the back door opening.

Today I check the girls are in their bedrooms and are pretending to get ready for bed, and then I take a cold beer out of the fridge and walk through our garden in the semi-darkness. I can smell the sweet scent of the roses. Jack's office is a rectangular cube of cedar wood; the far wall, looking out over the fields, is, like the main house, made of glass. I tap softly on the door and go inside. Jack is sitting at his desk, illuminated by a single lamp on his desk that casts a small pool of light. He stretches and takes off his little round-framed glasses and rubs his eyes.

'Thank you, darling,' he says, taking a long draught of the beer.

'You look tired.'

'There's a lot to do.'

I hesitate. I hardly ever come in here. The space is austere: there's only the desk, an Eames armchair and a couple of filing cabinets.

No clutter. Jack's family travelled a lot when he was a child and, before he met me, he moved around a lot too, he said. You'd never know it, because there are no mementoes or ornaments, but I expect it explains his desire for control. You'd think there might at least be a photo of us as a family, or of the girls, but the only object hanging on the wall is a framed certificate from when he qualified as a psychologist.

'You not having anything?' he asks.

I shake my head. Jack's questions about alcohol are always double-edged. He wants me to be strong enough to have one drink and then stop, but he also knows I lack his willpower.

'Is this for your new client?' I ask, sitting down in the armchair.

Jack's told me he's restructuring the personnel system of an energy company.

'Yeah. It's a big job.' He pinches the bridge of his nose.

I realize my husband has aged. The skin below his eyes is puffy and his face has changed: the lines from his nose to his mouth are deeper, his jaw is leaner, the elasticity in his skin has gone. I never minded that Jack was older than me when we first got together: it made me feel safer. After the accident I needed someone to look after me, someone I felt secure with. But now I can see his mortality. In a little over ten years he'll be coming up to retirement.

'Can't screw this one up,' he says, smiling at me.

'How are you feeling about it?' I ask.

I expect him to give me his usual spiel, about loving a challenge, but to my surprise he says, 'A bit nervous, to tell you the truth. It's an incredible opportunity, of course, to be there right at the start and set the tone for the whole organization, but it's a little daunting.'

I feel a sharp pang below my breastbone. Jack doesn't normally show any vulnerability. If he knew about Paul . . .

'It's a nuclear-power station. Moorside. It's in the Lake District,' he adds. He looks up at me, his gaze direct, intense. It's as if he's expecting me to challenge him or argue with him about the job. I can't tell him what I honestly think, because I might give myself away. In any case, I'm so used to hiding what I really feel, it's become second nature. My lips are dry and I lick them.

'Will you have to go there?'

'Yes. Soon. I'll let you know.'

We're so distant, I think. It's like he's a friend or an acquaintance, someone I hardly know, not the man I've been married to for almost fifteen years. It makes it easier, I suppose, to feel like this when I'm cheating on him. Jack stands up and lets the blinds scroll down over the plate-glass window.

'Seeing as you're here,' he says, smiling at me, 'I could do with a distraction.'

He comes round the desk and kisses me. He strokes my bare arms. The veins in his hands are raised. His fingertips gently travel over the scar on my bicep. I shiver. Even though his body is hard from working out so much, his skin has the looseness of middle age. I'm suddenly repulsed by his touch. Jack nuzzles my neck and his cheeks are so smooth it feels unnatural, after the rough scrape of Paul's stubble; I can't help thinking about the youthfulness of his body next to my husband's. My other husband. I step out of Jack's embrace.

'I can't leave the girls,' I say.

'They'll be okay for a little while,' he says, taking my hand.

'And I've got to be up in a few hours,' I add and give my husband a small, chaste kiss goodnight, as I suppress a shudder.

I shut the office door firmly behind me and walk back towards our house. A cool breeze caresses me. I push my feelings of guilt away. Tomorrow I'll see Paul. He's asked me to meet him at his cottage. I hope, more than I've ever hoped for anything in my life, that it's because he finally wants to introduce me to Dylan.

LIZZIE

She looked down at the egg. The yolk trembled when she touched the white with her fork. The edges were crinkled, glistening with oil. The fried mushrooms were black, the baked beans congealed, the toast hard and burnt, so cold the butter hadn't melted. She pushed her plate away. Her eyes felt raw, as if she hadn't slept at all, but she must have, because she'd woken with a start when she heard the toilet flushing around seven in the morning and had sat up in bed, overcome by a wave of panic, before she saw the sheets and cushions on the floor where Helen had been sleeping and remembered where she was, and why.

Simon had brought in a chair and ordered room service. He said she wasn't allowed to leave the room, for her own safety.

He swirled a slice of black pudding in ketchup and Lizzie looked away, feeling nauseous.

'I'm done,' she said. 'I don't care what options you're going to give me. I don't want to testify and I am going home.'

'I'm afraid you can't,' said Simon flatly. He put down his fork and glanced at Helen.

His partner wasn't making much headway with her fry-up, either, and she set aside her cutlery, too.

'We sent someone round to pick up your things last night from the address you gave us in Belle Isle.' She cleared her throat. 'Lizzie, love, you can't go back there. Lilley has found out where you live. And we need to find your husband and son. The women we spoke to said Paul and Dylan weren't there, thank God.'

Lizzie shook her head. 'How did Lilley find out? And how do you know he did?'

Simon said, 'You do live in Belle Isle? One of the women said you shared a room with Miriam Cartwright, but they didn't know where Paul and Dylan were.'

'I sub-rent a room for three nights a week from Miriam while I'm working. I didn't want you contacting me at home – that's why I only gave you the Belle Isle address. You said not to tell anyone. Paul would have freaked out and sent you packing.'

'So Paul and your baby son don't live there – they're not in Belle Isle, with you?' Simon said slowly.

He looked at Helen again and something passed between them, but she couldn't read what it was. Lizzie felt her stomach contract.

'What's going on? What's happened?'

She coughed and took a sip of orange juice. She felt as if shards of toast had lodged in her throat.

'I'm afraid Miriam's dead, Lizzie,' said Helen, reaching out and taking her hand.

'What?'

'When our officers got to the house, late last night, they found her body,' said Simon.

'Oh my God. And you're sure it was—'

'She'd been stabbed. Three times in the chest and once through the eye.'

She put her hand over her mouth.

'Sounds like Lilley's sending us a message,' he said.

Lizzie's eyes filled with tears. She hated Miriam for what she'd done, but they'd been best friends for years. She thought of how Miriam must have felt in those last few moments of her life: terrified and in pain.

'If it's any consolation, it was quick. She didn't suffer for long, love,' said Helen, squeezing her hand.

Lizzie wiped her eyes. She knew Helen was lying and that the detective was only trying to make her feel better. What had happened to Miriam was her fault. Lilley's men had been searching for *her*, not Miriam, and when they hadn't found her, they'd made good on their boss's promise.

I will find your friends and I will kill them.

'We need to know where Paul and Dylan are,' said Simon, leaning towards her. 'Where do you live for the rest of the week?'

'In the middle of bloody nowhere,' she said, wiping her eyes. 'A cottage on a hillside in the Lake District. The nearest village is Elterwater. No one's heard of it. My husband is a ranger – he works out on the Langdale Pikes. You can walk for miles and never see a soul. Please, let me go home. I'll be safe there. We'll be safe.'

Simon was pale, even paler than before. He rubbed his hand over his chin and the rasp of his stubble set her teeth on edge.

'You can't persuade me to testify. I won't. I can't believe you're asking me to, after what's happened to Miriam. Look how easily he found out where I live! And I've got a baby. He's six months old! You know what Lilley's capable of. And you're still trying to talk me into this. I want to go. Please take me home.'

Helen grabbed her arm. 'Think about it for thirty seconds. We have to be sure Lilley's men haven't followed us here. We're making plans to take you somewhere else, to a safe house. But if they know you're here and you leave, they'll follow you. If they can find out your address in Belle Isle, they'll find your real home.' She let go of Lizzie, as if realizing she was being too forceful. When she spoke again, she sounded even more agitated. 'Don't you understand what a big deal this is? To us, it's crime. To Lilley, it's business. His business, with a turnover of hundreds of thousands of pounds every year. And if he goes down, he could take everyone who works with him down, too. Every single one of those scumbags will be on the lookout for you. A quick trip to the Lake District to a remote house, a young woman, a small baby, an unprotected family – it would be a walk in the park for men like them.'

'Robbins!' said Simon, a warning growl in his voice.

Lizzie sank back into the armchair. 'So what are you saying? We're all going to die?'

'Just hear me out,' said Simon, holding up one hand. 'We can protect you. We can put you into Witness Protection. But only if . . . only if you testify. If you walk away now and refuse to testify – anonymously in court, I promise you – then we can't take care of you. I'm sorry, Lizzie, I don't make the rules. And your life, your husband's life and your baby son's life are at risk. I'd go further than that. I'd say, if you leave now and go back to your cottage in the Lakes, you're signing your death-warrant, as well as your baby's and your husband's. Lilley doesn't make idle threats. He will find you. He will kill you all. And from what I've seen, he won't do it nicely.'

Lizzie swallowed hard. She was trembling.

'But if I help you, you'll protect me? Put me in Witness Protection. What does that even mean?'

'You come with us now and we take you to a safe place. Then, over the course of the next six months, we'll create a new life for you, a new identity, find you another job. You testify. We look after you. It's as simple as that.'

She looked at him in disbelief. She couldn't comprehend what he was saying. She would be someone else? They'd live somewhere else?

'I'm not sure, I'm not – I can't see Paul going for it,' she whispered. 'I mean, this is his whole life: the Lakes, the mountains; his family live nearby, they're sheep farmers. You can't uproot him from all that.' She suddenly wondered if he'd even go with her; if he could so casually kiss her best friend, sleep in the same bed as her, probably even have sex with her – when they'd only just got married, only just started a family and she'd only just begun working away from home for three nights a week – was their future together already doomed?

'Lizzie,' said Simon, resting his hands on his knees, 'I'm talking about you. *You* would have a new identity. You would have a new life. You can't go home. Ever. You would lead Lilley's men straight to Paul and your six-month-old baby.'

'What? I don't – I can't . . . Can you get them, and bring them to me?'

Simon nodded. 'We could. It would be risky, but it's possible. Lilley's men are probably nearby. They know we're cops. We send a car to pick up your husband and kid, they'll put two and two together—'

Helen interrupted, 'We can set up a secure line and you can speak to Paul and see what he – you both – want to do. But remember, you'll never be able to live the lives you have now. You, your husband and your son would have to go into hiding for six months and then they would be given new identities, too, and he would be given a different job. Nothing in the public eye. Certainly not roaming about the mountains on his own, chatting to strangers.

'They will never be able to see their friends or their family again. Dylan will grow up without grandparents, godparents, aunts or uncles. Your family will, in spite of our best efforts, live in fear for ever. Or,' she said, taking Lizzie's hand and looking into her eyes, 'you can be extraordinarily brave and allow your son and your husband to live their lives in the Lakes. Healthy, happy lives. The lives they were meant to have. Safe. They'd be safe.'

'So,' Lizzie said, 'if I agree, I'll never see them again?'

Helen's eyes were large and blue, the skin beneath them thin and puffy. She looked older than she probably was.

'It's your choice, Lizzie. We will phone them or fetch them for you, if you want us to.'

Tears ran down Lizzie's face.

'Lizzie, we have another death on our hands,' said Simon. 'Lilley killed your friend, Miriam. He tried to kill a six-year-old child. What if it had been your child? Your son, Dylan? You've got a chance to put this monster away for good. But – and I can't stress this enough – if you walk away now, we cannot guarantee your safety, or Paul's and Dylan's.'

If she didn't testify, no one would even try to protect her. Lilley had promised he'd kill her if she *did* testify, and he'd as much as told her that he'd still kill her, if she didn't. So even if she brought Paul and Dylan into hiding with her, Lilley was likely to find her and kill them, too. She looked down at Helen's hands, wrapped around her own. The detective was wearing a gold wedding band and an engagement ring with a single, small diamond. She probably had a husband and kids at home. It was easy for her to fucking talk. Lizzie snatched her hands away. The heart of it was that no matter what they said or what the police did, she was going to die. And the only choice she had was whether to risk her husband's and her son's lives, too.

'Lizzie, love,' said Simon, putting his hand on her shoulder, 'I hate to say it, but I don't see what choice you have.'

EMMA

Paul retreats into the darkness as soon as he sees me at the door. Gil wags his tail, pushes his wet nose into my palm. I'm not stupid. I've been waiting for Paul's anger. Sixteen years of hurt don't simply disappear. I step slowly over the threshold and follow him in. It's dim inside; the mullioned windows are filmed with algae and shrouded by creepers. I go into the sitting room. I haven't been in here before. It's small, cramped by a saggy sofa and two armchairs. The hearth is clogged with ash and the bookshelves are dusty. It's cool, as if it might get damp in the winter and the walls haven't quite dried out. There are towering piles of books on the floor and dirty teacups. I notice one of Paul's favourites: Henry David Thoreau's *Walden: Life in the Woods*. My heart shivers as I think of Dylan growing up motherless; his entire life filled with dust and dirt and unwashed dishes, with bought cakes and ready meals.

Paul stands in front of the window with his back to me.

'Have a seat, Emma,' he says, as if I've come for a job interview.

I move a plate and a threadbare blanket off one of the armchairs and sit down. I scan the walls and the shelves quickly, but there are no photos of Dylan here, either.

'We need to talk,' says Paul.

He sits at the far end of the room, opposite me, his face in shadows. I notice a frame on the mantelpiece and I snatch it up. It's a picture of Paul and our baby son. They're grinning, glowing with youth and happiness; Dylan has a big, gummy smile. I clutch it to my chest and sink back down. Gil pushes against my legs and sits on my feet.

'I thought, if I gave you time and didn't rush you, you would open up. You'd tell me the truth.'

'I did! I told you—'

He shakes his head. 'I haven't pushed you. I've been patient. But you've been lying to me since you met me.'

'I told you the truth, in the end, about the accident—'

'Come on, Emma, I know you didn't have bloody amnesia. When you went missing, it was the first thing I did. I checked all the hospitals, every single bloody one, and no one was admitted who looked like you.' He jumps up in agitation. 'Surely it wasn't because of Miriam. She meant nothing. Nothing!'

I grit my teeth. At the time, it wasn't nothing. I feel a flash of pain, of the betrayal and hurt I'd felt all those years ago, but I suppress it. Miriam, in spite of what she did, didn't deserve what happened to her, and I have to live in the present and be thankful for what I do have – and I, at last, have my husband back. I shake my head.

'I can't – I won't – believe that if you remembered us, me and Dylan and Gil, even if it was years later, even if you were married, you wouldn't have come and found us,' he says. 'We didn't go anywhere. We stayed in Langdale. Waiting for you. Hoping you'd come home. The truth, Emma. You owe me that, at the very least.'

'I can't—'

'You can tell me!' He seizes my arms. 'Tell me what happened!'

He gives me a little shake. I look at Paul, his face is so familiar and yet unfamiliar after all these years. To those who didn't know him that well, he always seemed easy-going, affable, able to get along with anyone, a pushover even. But I've always known that he's also one of the most stubborn and determined men I've ever met.

He folds his arms across his chest. 'If you don't tell me the truth now, I will never let you see our son.'

I feel as if he's punched me in the chest. I take a breath. 'I *was* Lizzie Bradshaw,' I say, as I said to him before.

I'm hugging the picture of the two of them so hard, the glass might crack. I force myself to continue. Only this time I do tell Paul the truth, the whole truth. I tell him about crouching in a newsagent's storeroom. I describe seeing a six-year-old boy being stabbed through the eye. How I'd thought, *What if it had been Dylan?* How I had agreed to testify against Jon Lilley. And then I tell him about the letter I'd received when I was working at Ikea. Those chilling words seared in my heart: *if you give evidence against me, I will kill you . . . I will hunt down your family and I will kill them . . . I am nothing if not a man of my word.*

'You heard what happened to Miriam?' I ask.

Paul nods slightly. 'She was in an accident. A mugging that went wrong, that's what your mum told me.'

I shake my head. 'It was Lilley. He was trying to find me. Trying to scare me. Miriam was murdered, Paul. He stabbed her in the chest and through one eye with so much force, the knife came out the other side of her skull.'

I watch my husband carefully. He looks shocked, appalled, but he doesn't act as if he's lost the love of his life, and I feel ashamed at using Miriam's memory to test him. I suppress the thought of her beautiful pale, grey eyes, that long blonde hair fanned out in the blood pooling on the linoleum of a grimy hall in Belle Isle. The police had shown me the crime-scene photographs when I'd pressed them. I'd had to be certain it was her and that it had been Lilley who'd been responsible.

'The detective in charge of the case said I needed to go into Witness Protection instantly, because otherwise Lilley's men would follow me home and kill you and Dylan. They told me that even the witness who didn't testify had been murdered. Don't you see?' I say. 'I didn't think I was going to make it; I thought he would kill me before the case even reached court. It broke my heart, but I couldn't ever go home because Lilley's men would have followed me – and found you. For your sake, for Dylan's, I had to protect you by disappearing. And that's why, now, no one can know I was once Lizzie Bradshaw. Lilley could get out early! Or what if someone who worked for him hears about me? And finds you? It was stupid of me to follow you in Tyntesfield – I couldn't believe it would be you! But I had to find out if you and Dylan were okay.

'I spent six months in hiding before the trial,' I continue, 'creating a new identity with the police. The counsellor who was treating me suggested that I start thinking of Emma James and Lizzie Bradshaw as two separate people. It would help me remember who I was – the new persona the police had given me. As Emma, I would have none of the friends, the family or even the interests that had been Lizzie's. I'd have gone mad, if I hadn't thought of her as someone else. Do you understand?' I say. 'Jon Lilley might be in prison, but the men who worked for him are not. Do you know what it's like? To live every day in fear? You can't tell anyone who I really am. Who I really was. We can't jeopardize our family. Or my new one.'

'Christ!' says Paul.

He folds me in his arms and presses his wet cheek against mine.

STELLA

I'm so nervous I burn my forehead when I straighten my hair. I put on make-up and then I rub most of it off, so it doesn't look as if I've made too much effort. I consider wearing my new jeans, but Dad would notice, so I go for grey skinny ones. I leave early, while Ava and Dad are still out – Dad's planning on taking her to buy a dress after ballet. I don't want to arrive all hot and sweaty, so I catch the bus instead of cycling.

I rest my head against the window and look out. I wonder if Adam will turn up. What will we talk about? I don't know what to say. Does he even like me, or is this a friend thing? Maybe he's lonely and just wants someone to chat to. I send Kaylee a message to see what she's doing, but she doesn't reply and I don't feel like finding out by looking at Instagram. She'll only look gorgeous and be having more fun than me. Maybe Adam wants to talk about her or Nuala or some other girl he's met and he needs some advice? Yeah, that must be it.

The bus takes for ever, stopping and starting, and loads of people get on, like everyone is heading out of Long Ashton and Failand and going somewhere interesting. I wish we didn't live here. It's a nothing kind of place, it's not a village or a town in its own right or a proper part of the city, either; we're not really part of anything. It's stuffy and my hands are clammy. I rub my palms on my jeans and bite the skin round my fingernails. Mum will be leaving work soon. I think I've got about an hour before she turns up. If she does.

The bus eventually stops outside Tyntesfield. It's a long, steep driveway down to the car park and I feel out of place; everyone else is with their family, pushing buggies or helping old people down the hill. I walk on ahead of them, trying to ignore their stares. I shiver after the heat of the bus; it's windy and the sky is grey.

It's cool in the Cowshed Restaurant, too, even a little chilly. I buy an apple juice and go and sit in one of the booths that were stalls for farm animals. It's weird, all these posh people drinking cappuccinos and buying silk scarves where cows used to shit. I get out my homework. I don't want Mum to see me, but how will I know if she's here? This was such a stupid idea. If she spots me, I'll tell her I'm meeting Kaylee later. I try and concentrate on my biology homework, but I can't fix the parts of a flower in my head. After a while I stretch and wander through the gift shop, past the jams and the biscuits and ridiculous fucking paperweights. Who uses paper? And needs to hold it down? And that's when I see them. I quickly step back. It's the man I saw before, all kind of relaxed, with his long legs stuck out, his feet crossed, and next to him I caught a glimpse of a shiny blonde head. It's got to be my mum.

They're in one of the stalls. I double-back and go round behind them, past a stone water trough and the queue for coffee. I pour myself a glass of water to give me a bit of time to think and something to do, so I won't look strange standing about. Fortunately, there's no one in the stall behind them. I go in and peek through the bars of a manger that once held hay. I can't see Mum properly, just the top of her head and one shoulder. If I go closer, she might sense my presence and look up. And that would be really bad. For both of us. But I've seen enough.

I back away. I fetch my things and almost run out of the gift shop, bursting through the doors at the far end. I jog down to the Pavilion cafe to meet Adam. My heart is beating so hard I think I might die. The man was holding her hand. And then he leaned towards her and kissed her. So now I know it's definitely back on. She's still having an affair with him. I don't know why I feel like she'll leave us, but she can't stay with both Dad and this man. And she doesn't seem as into Dad as he is into her. What with his party-of-the-century. Plus, she can't afford to look after me and Ava. So we'll end up with him. And that'll be a nightmare. But what the fuck do I do? I thought I'd tell Dad as soon as I knew for certain, but I can't imagine doing that now. He'd be so hurt. And it would be like betraying Mum, which is ridiculous, because she's the one betraying us.

I'm not sure I want to see Adam after all. I'm too wound up. I stop next to a greenhouse and lean against the door frame. I can smell geraniums and feel the sun-warmed heat rising from the cream and magenta flowers.

Pistil. Stamen. Xylem. Phloem. The force that through the green fuse drives the flower . . .

I inhale, trying to calm myself, and get out my phone to text him.

'Not cancelling on me, are you?'

I look up and he's standing in front of me, his hands in his pockets, smiling. I blush and stick my phone in my back pocket.

'Why would I do that, when you're going to buy me a double-shot mocha with whipped cream?'

'Marshmallows and sprinkles with that, Ms Rochester?' he says, and we start walking side by side through the flower garden. 'You okay to sit outside?' he asks, and I nod, even though it seems a bit cold to hang about out here.

He leads me down a little lane past the orangery and the side of the walled garden, and then into a grassy area round the back of the cafe that looks out over the fields towards Backwell Common. I sit at a wooden table, hugging my hoodie round me, while Adam gets our drinks. I feel slightly more relaxed. Even if Mum has left her bike at this end of the estate, she couldn't see me here: Adam and I are hidden. I try and blot out the images in my mind, of my mum kissing that man. And what my dad will do if he finds out.

'You seem kind of distracted,' Adam says, putting my mocha in front of me.

'Wow, an emotionally-intelligent teenager!'

'Want to talk about it?'

I shake my head.

He gets out his phone and I think he's going to show me some more photos of foxes, but instead he says, 'I saw this band at the weekend. They were so cool.'

'What kind of stuff do they play?'

'Kind of country rock,' he says, scrolling through some videos.

I stare at him in surprise. He looks up at me from under his fringe. His eyes look more blue than brown in the sunlight; there's a darker ring around the iris.

'From Nashville, Tennessee. How amazing is that? Here.' He hands me his headphones. 'Have a listen.'

They're those giant ones that go over your ears, not the little buds that Ava and I have, and instantly all the sounds around me are blocked out and I'm listening to a man's voice. He's American, slightly nasal and gravelly, like he's been out late and smoked too much. The song starts off quiet and then the drums and guitar come in with a roar. It's all about whiskey and broken hearts. I'm right there, in some booze-soaked bar, the sun's gone down, my body's moving in time with the rhythm – and all this other stuff has disappeared: my flighty friend, my imminent exams, my annoying little sister, my mother. I close my eyes. I can feel the wind messing up my hair, making my nose sting; the first flecks of rain across my cheek, but none of it matters. Adam sits next to me and lets me listen.

When I open my eyes, he's smiling at me and I feel like a tethered balloon; cut the string and I will float away.

LIZZIE

The wind caught the door and slammed it shut, but the wood was warped and it didn't quite close. The man on the other side tugged it shut and locked it from the outside. For a moment she remained in the porch, the chill seeping through the linoleum floor into the soles of her feet. She reminded herself that she had her own key, too, cold and hard and pressed into her palm. It was not a prison. She could go out if she wanted to.

It was the first time she'd been alone for four days and nights. She thought she'd feel relieved. She'd been claustrophobic in the hotel. She hadn't been allowed to leave her room; a team of police officers had taken it in turns to sit with her round the clock, offering her endless cups of tea and small bags of cheesy biscuits.

She went back into the sitting room and heard the wind keen round the edges of the house, the tyres of the police car crunch down the potholed bridle path. The loneliness was crushing. She pulled on her boots and her coat and let herself out. The house was a small bungalow, originally white, now blackened, the paintwork peeling and flaking from the rotting windows. It had a square of rough ragweed-infested grass around it, and a windblown hedge, bare of leaves, with a rusted gate set into it. The bridle path ended at the cottage, and turned into sand. Beyond were dunes covered in marram grass, the strands whipping, razor-sharp, in the wind. She pulled up her hood and dug her hands into her pockets. She'd been itching to get outside, but now, with the wind so strong it snatched the breath from her lungs, she wasn't sure. Paul would have liked to see this place, she thought; he'd be interested in the shore birds and the sea life; he'd have revelled in the bleakness. Paul. Her eyes filled with tears, but they were dashed from her face before they had a chance to fall.

They kept saying, *It's the shock, love*, until she thought she'd punch them.

She couldn't, she still couldn't believe it.

I don't see what choice you have. Simon's words echoed in her mind.

No choice, if she didn't want her husband and her son to die. But she still could not believe that she would never see them again. She felt numb, as if she were swathed in cotton wool and nothing was quite getting through. How long did she have left? A month? Six? Lilley's men would find her, of that she was certain.

She took a jagged breath of air and the cold and the salt burnt her throat. The sand was deep and powdery. She slogged through it, her calf muscles aching after nearly a week of doing no exercise. She emerged between the dunes onto a wide expanse of sand that seemed to stretch endlessly to either side of her: the grey of the sand melded seamlessly into the sea and sky, so that it was impossible to tell where one ended and the other began. The wind hit her with such force, it felt like a living thing. There was nothing between her and Norway.

Simon and Helen had brought her to this house in north Northumberland. She wasn't sure exactly where she was, but there were no villages nearby, or even any other houses. It was properly remote – safe – he'd said. She would stay here for six months. There was a lot to be done. They needed to prepare her for the trial, and the Witness Protection team would work on creating her new identity, finding her a place to live, a job.

'Do you have any ideas about what you might like to do? It's a chance to try something completely different,' Helen said brightly.

Lizzie silently told her to fuck off, but it must have been obvious what she was thinking because Simon glanced at the detective and coughed and carried on talking. He said she'd start counselling tomorrow.

'We'll come back and talk you through the trial, but the Witness Protection team will take over now, supporting you while you're here and dealing with the logistics for your new identity,' he'd told her.

She hadn't replied. After that frantic drive through the night from the cafe in Birstall to the hotel in the arse-end of nowhere and then to this place, she'd barely spoken. It was as if she'd lost the ability. Or the inclination.

Simon took her hand just before he and Helen left. He said, his voice hoarse, 'It's fucking shit, Lizzie. It's going to be hell for a long time. Through no fault of your own, you were in the wrong bloody place at the wrong bloody time. Nothing is going to make it better. All we can do is get justice, and put that bastard away for the rest of his unnatural fucking life. Pardon my French. That's how we win. We won't let what happened to Miriam happen to you. We will protect you. I promise you that.'

A flock of dunlin scuttled over the sand, like wind-up toys. She leant into the wind and concentrated on putting one foot in front of the other. Sea water oozed round her feet; the surface of the beach reflected the dark grey of the clouds in its glass-like surface. It was bisected by rivulets of water that had carved arteries, veins and capillaries through the sand. Once she'd have imagined jumping over them with her son – another six months and he'd be learning how to walk – now she stumbled straight through them, not caring that the cheap boots the police had bought her were leaking.

She wasn't sure how much time had passed, but when she finally looked up there was a black dot in the distance. She squinted. It was a person. A man. Whoever it was, he was alone, without even a dog. He was heading straight towards her, coming rapidly closer. She could already see the outline of his reflection on the waterlogged sand. She looked behind her. There was no one there. Nobody was in the dunes, either. She was on her own.

She took the mobile that the police had given her out of her pocket and held it up to the sky. There was no signal here. She felt her heart contract. She'd never been afraid before when she was hiking. Was it one of Lilley's men? Had he found her already? She headed back the way she'd come, retracing her footsteps, which were slowly filling up with water and disappearing. Soon there'd be no trace of her, nothing to show that Lizzie Bradshaw had walked this way along a beach in the very northernmost tip of England. How had he found her? She wondered if he'd followed the police; if he'd been waiting until they'd finally left her on her own in this isolated spot.

'Properly remote,' Simon had said.

There was no one – no one who could help her. The bungalow had a phone line, though. And she had the number for the Witness Protection team. She could call when she got back. She looked behind her. The man was gaining on her. She walked faster, her heart racing; in spite of the chill November day, her back was slick with sweat. How would he do it? She thought of the knife in Lilley's hand and she remembered Dev and Miriam. Her nose was running and her eyes were streaming by the time her footsteps disappeared. Now there really was no sign of her existence. And she wasn't sure how she'd got onto the beach. It was one long stretch of sand, blurring into the distance and, to her right, an unbroken line of dunes. She glanced over her shoulder. He was still there. *Would she be able to find it*, she wondered, *that narrow path between the marram grass, back to the hidden, crumbling house?* She'd have to.

She pushed on. She started to run, clumsy in the new boots, which fitted badly and slipped on her heels. It felt as if she were running in a nightmare, putting so much effort and force into her flight, but barely covering any distance. She was out of breath in seconds. She veered towards the dunes, only to realize it was a shallow scoop in the sand, not a proper path. She tried to remember if there had been any distinguishing features – driftwood or a tree, a gorse bush or a flat stone. If this were the Lake District, there'd have been a cairn. But if there had been, she hadn't noticed; she'd been so muffled in her misery, she'd barely registered her surroundings. The man was still behind her, striding over the sand, gaining on her even though she'd been jogging.

She found it, or at least a path that looked like it. The sand was deep, like she remembered, and she struggled through it and saw, thank God, the bungalow, crouched in the lee of a shallow hill, half-hidden by its barren hedge. She fumbled with the key to unlock the door and shouldered it open. The wind was silenced almost instantly and her ears rang. The number was stuck to the phone, but her fingers kept slipping on the keys and she had to dial it twice.

A woman answered immediately and, when Lizzie said there was a man on the beach, following her, she said, 'Probably out walking, pet. But we'll send someone round, just in case. They'll be there in a few minutes. They're not far away. Have you locked the door?'

She stood by the window and felt the cold draught creep round the edge of the frame. She was still there when the car eased back up the lane and the two officers who'd only left an hour ago strode back up the path towards her. As she watched them, she had a moment of clarity, sharp and hard, that pierced the fogginess of her thinking: *This is what it's going to be like from now on. I will live in fear of every man, of every stray sound, of every footstep in the dark, of every shadow in the night.*

EMMA

'More tea, Vicar?' asks Katie, and falls about laughing.
'Anyone would think you'd had a drink,' says Harry, taking
the teapot from her before she tips it over. He pours us all a cup.

The teacups and saucers are floral and mismatched; the fragile
porcelain looks as if it'll shatter in Caleb and Toby's thick-fingered
hands. I take a sip. We're drinking Lady Amy of Braganza – a peach
and white tea and vodka cocktail, although I think there's a bit of
ginger beer in there, too. It's *Kate's* monthly staff outing, and as well
as Harry, Katie and our chefs, Caleb and Toby, Nate, our driver, and
Izzy, Simone and Jessica, the baristas, are with us, too.

Katie is at home in this bar: she looks like a 1950s housewife
who's dropped a tab of LSD. She's wearing what looks like a prom
dress with gauze petticoats, decorated with a pink flamingo print
that showcases her ample bosom. Katie is my age, but the others
are all in their twenties. Toby and Caleb have beards and crew-
cuts; the three girls are beautiful, with glowing skin; all of them
have multiple piercings and tattoos. *How did I get here?* I think.
It's not something I normally allow myself to dwell on, but Lizzie
is elbowing her way back into my life. Lizzie – even younger than
my friends and colleagues – was a beer-drinking, fast-walking,
fast-talking woman who'd have debated solar versus nuclear power
until closing time. For so many years I had to think before I opened
my mouth, in case what I said would give me away, that the habit
has stuck. I appear quiet, shy, reticent, but I can feel Lizzie waiting

to erupt. I take another sip of my drink and the vodka starts to unloosen something inside me.

'Cheers!' says Katie, chinking her cup against Caleb's. 'Here's to averting disaster.'

'Christ, what was up with it this morning?' asks Toby.

'It smelt terrible. Was it hungry?' asks Jessica.

'Yeah, ravenous,' says Harry, grinning.

'Don't joke. It could have died!' says Katie.

The sourdough culture had gone flat when we got in.

'It's because it's so cold,' I say. 'It's confused by our chilly summer.'

Harry had to coax the leaven back to life this morning, which meant everything was delayed, there was nearly no bread and we had queues of people right out the door, waiting for cheese toasties.

'Never work with animals,' says Caleb, topping up our teacups.

I can feel my spiked tea coursing icily through my veins and the memory of my last time with Paul comes back, as if it's been imprinted on my body. It was the most passionate sex I've had. I can't recall any more what it used to be like with him. There was little or none after Dylan was born, that's for sure. I was sore and knackered and our cottage was so cold. I remember Paul pressing his icy feet against my shins and laughing like a drain.

Gin isn't really Harry's thing, and he comes back with an espresso Martini in a mug and I'm reminded again of Paul. He loved mixing cocktails – although back when he was working at the Sticklebarn pub, everyone wanted Cosmopolitans.

'Hey, man, can I get one of them, too?' asks Toby.

They both look wired. Harry and I have been up since four, and Caleb, Toby and Nate were in shortly afterwards. I signal to the waiter to fill up our teapot.

I hope to God that Paul will let me see Dylan now. I have to figure out how to tell our son what's happened. But what then? Once Dylan knows, nothing will ever be the same. I can't stay married to two men. I can't hide my secret family. But if I don't continue to protect my identity, I'll put us all in danger. And I don't know how I can be true to Paul *and* Jack, how to be both Emma and Lizzie. I buried Lizzie. But now she won't stay dead. She's coming back.

'You okay, love?' asks Katie, touching my arm.

I nod and chink my teacup against hers. How I wish I could tell her. Ask her what the hell I should do.

'You ought to eat something,' she says. 'You know what that husband of yours is like.'

'What do you mean?' I say.

My tongue feels too big for my mouth and my words slur a little.

'You remember the last time we had a staff outing? Jack was furious! He even sent me a text the next day, ticking me off for letting you get in that state!'

'He's just concerned. You know.'

'That was a long time ago, love,' she says, putting her hand over mine.

I told Katie, like everyone else I'm close to, that my family were killed in a car crash. And she knows I was drinking far too much when I first met Jack.

'He's got to let you have fun now and again. You're not going to end up like that again.'

Still, she waves at our waiter and a few minutes later he brings over a board of bread and cheese.

'Can't have him saying I'm "shirking my duty of care" again,' she says, winking at me.

'Not as good as ours,' I say, taking a bite of the granary, and Katie smiles.

'We need a staff trip to San Francisco,' she says. 'You'd love it there – they do mean cocktails. Best place in the world to get a Martini. And no one will be able to check up on you.'

Would I? I think. I don't know any more. I do know I would have killed myself if I hadn't met Jack. He was the first person that I talked to properly after I moved to Bristol. Or, rather, after the police moved me here. I wouldn't have chosen this city. It's a million miles from the Lake District. I told Jack who I was, as 'Emma'. That's all he's ever known, and so, without realizing, he helped me stick to my new identity, helped me become the person I am today. Jack has been my rock, my port in a storm, my saviour, my safety. For fifteen years he's loved Emma Taylor. Would he have loved Lizzie? I doubt it. She drank pints, answered back, washed her hair in the sink, wore hiking boots and didn't even own a dress. Lizzie loved Paul. I love Paul. And I can't let him go.

When the taxi drops me off, Jack is waiting. He takes off his glasses and scrutinizes me.

'You're drunk,' he says.

'I'm okay,' I say, stumbling a little. I sink down on the sofa next to him.

'Did you have a good evening?' he asks, stroking my hair.

I nod. I don't speak, in case I slur.

'You know I love you.'

I nod again.

'But it's not good for you to drink so much. Remember what happened before.'

'It was years ago,' I say, shrugging his arm off. His touch feels odd, alien, after being with Paul, and I can't stand how proprietorial he's being. 'I'm a different person. And it's not surprising! I mean, my parents and my sister had just been killed!'

There's a long pause and then he squeezes my hand. 'I know. It's understandable. I don't want you to go back to that place again.'

'I won't,' I say, angry with him now. 'It was just drinks with Katie, for God's sake!'

I get up with as much dignity as I can and stagger out of the sitting room and down the stairs to our bedroom. I think, although I can't really remember, that later that night we have sex. And I know, to my shame, that I throw up in the toilet in the early hours of the morning.

STELLA

It's Sunday morning. Dad's making pancakes when I get up.

'Where's Mum?' I ask as I slide onto my chair next to Ava.

'I'm on my second one already,' she says, pouring maple syrup all over her plate.

'Have some fruit,' says Dad. He's chopped up strawberries and bananas for us. 'Had a big night,' he tells me, grinning wolfishly.

'You mean, she was drunk?' asks Ava.

'Just a little. She'll have a sore head this morning, so keep the noise down.'

I snort. She doesn't deserve him. 'Can I have a coffee?'

He tosses a pancake in the air and slips it onto my plate. 'Only if you have lots of milk in it.'

I nod. I don't think I can eat a pancake right now, at this time in the morning, but I go through the motions of piling on fruit while I wait for my coffee.

'Who was she out with?' I ask, thinking of the man, all in brown with the dark eyes and stubble. The phrase *A bit of rough . . .* comes into my head and I close my eyes and swallow.

'Are you okay, Stella?'

'Yeah, fine. You know it's way too early to be up, if you're a teenager.'

'Ah, yes, you're like vampires. She was out with Katie and the others from work. Cain and Abel.'

'Caleb and Harry,' I mutter.

I pour a splash of milk into my cup. Dad raises his eyebrows and waits until I fill it halfway and then he tops it up with coffee. I inhale the smell. It reminds me of yesterday afternoon. Mocha with Adam. Listening to The Cadillac Three.

'I'm just going to take a cup down to your mother,' he says. 'Eat some fruit, Ava!'

Adam asked me if I wanted to go and see a band with him. I haven't told the parents yet. They'll make a fuss. And I'd have to tell them about him. Maybe I could say a group of us are going? But would Kaylee cover for me? She'd want to come along, and then she'd do her best to steal Adam. Which she might, because nothing has actually happened between us.

Dad comes bounding back in, looking pleased with himself. He likes waking people up. It makes him feel superior.

'Ready for another one?'

I shake my head and then find myself agreeing. It was actually pretty nice, for food before 11 a.m.

'Can I have one, too?' asks Ava and I manage to stop myself from calling her a fat pig. Because she's not. Obviously.

'Listen, I'm sorry, girls, but I'm going to have to do some work today.'

'So our family outing is going to be cancelled?' I ask.

''Fraid so. I know you're devastated, Stella.'

'What are you working on?' I ask, hoping that'll distract him enough so that I can help myself to more coffee.

'A presentation for my new client. I'm heading up north soon, to go through it with them,' he says, and flips another pancake, 'and leaving you in your mother's tender care for a few days.'

Tender? Yeah, right. She doesn't give a fuck about us.

'When are you going?'

I have a cold feeling. It's not like Mum is lax or anything, what with her hovercraft parenting, but still, if Dad's not around, she might go and see that man even more often.

'I'm not sure, sweetheart. In two or three weeks. Don't worry, I'll put it in the schedule well in advance,' he adds, winking at me.

I send Adam a quick text to say I'd like to go to the gig. Because I am going, no matter what. Dad washes out the pan and puts away the flour and milk. How can I tell him about Mum? He'll be devastated. He whistles as he fries bacon and eggs for himself. For the first time, I realize he could be angry with me for spying on her.

I get a text back from Adam almost immediately, saying

'Cool! 😎 Will send you a YouTube link so you can check out the band.'

I imagine Adam lying in bed typing this message. His chest is bare and his blondish stubble glints in the sunlight filtering through his curtains. I have to stop thinking about him because it's making me uncomfortable: a hot flush sweeps across my cheeks and my palms prickle; my stomach churns. I wish I hadn't eaten both pancakes.

I head downstairs and get out my journal. I start out with the facts – seeing Mum and the guy in the cafe – but it ends up as a rant, and my writing goes bigger and digs deeper into the paper as I get madder. Maybe if I don't say anything, she'll get bored and stop seeing him? Is that betraying Dad, though, if he finds out I knew? When I go upstairs a bit later and look out of the window, I can see the top of Dad's head framed in the thin window of his office. I make myself a peanut-butter sandwich. Mum still isn't up, but the light's flickering in the box by the front door, so Dad has set the alarm. Honestly, my parents are insane. I mean, he's only in the garden and Mum's downstairs. It's not like we're home alone, even if one of our primary caretakers is comatose.

I push open the door to my bedroom and find Ava sitting on the bed with my diary on her lap. I'm just about to scream at her and drag her out by her skinny little arm, when she looks up at me and her face is streaked with tears. She hands me the tiny gold key.

'I'm sorry,' she says. 'I shouldn't have read it. I was just going to look at the first page and tease you about it, but then I couldn't help it and I read all of it. Is she going to leave us?'

'How did you know where it was?'

'I saw you get it out when I was writing my Citizenship project.'

'So you've been reading it all this time?'

I sit on the bed next to her. Ava nods and carries on crying.

'What's going to happen to us?'

'Ssshush,' I say, putting my arm around her, 'Mum might hear.'

'Will we have to live with Dad? Or will the other guy be our new dad?'

'No one is going anywhere,' I say. 'It's all going to be okay.'

'You don't know that,' she says, but she wipes her face on her sleeve.

'I do. They both love us. I know Dad loves Mum. It'll all work out.'

'But you wrote—'

'That's what a diary's for. Getting all your feelings and thoughts out. It's kind of like therapy. So you don't bottle it up and get mad.'

'But she kisses him.'

'Who?'

'Dad.'

'Well, she probably still loves him, too. Adults can love two people at once, you know.'

'Oh.'

'Don't tell anyone. They don't know I know.'

'I won't.'

'Shall we snuggle up in my bed and watch a film?'

'Yeah! Can we see *Harry Potter and the Deathly Hallows*?'

'Sure,' I tell her and Ava bundles herself up in my duvet.

She looks like a child and I feel afraid, because I'm really not ready to be the grown-up around here.

LIZZIE

He was big with dark ginger hair. He spoke with a wheeze and when he knelt on the floor, struggling for breath as he did so, his trousers exposed half his backside.

'Gary's our best techie,' said one of the officers cheerfully.

Lizzie turned and stared out of the window. The man disgusted her. She disgusted herself. She'd been weak, calling the team back so quickly when they'd only just left her. If she wasn't so frightened, she'd be out there again, walking along the beach. They were here today to set up her sessions with the counsellor. The tinny sound of the phone ringing startled her. Gary jabbed a couple of keys with one fat finger and pulled his jumper over his stomach.

'Doc?'

'Yes,' came a faint voice.

'It's working. You're all set.' Gary's breath whistled as he spoke.

'I can hardly hear him,' said Lizzie, with her arms folded, remaining resolutely at the window.

Gary shook his head. 'The line is heavily encrypted and we're three miles from an interchange down a copper wire.'

'Our Gazza means,' said the officer, 'that the line is secure. No one else can trace this call or listen in to your conversation. Just check you can hear the doc on the headset, pet, and then we'll take you off speakerphone and give you some privacy.'

Lizzie reluctantly sat down in front of the phone. Gary passed her the headset, wheezing over her shoulder.

'Hello,' a man said, his voice slightly crisper now that she was nearer. 'My name is Dr Joe Wood. I'm your therapist. I'll be with you virtually every day for two hours, from ten until twelve.'

'Can you say something back?' said Gary, 'I need to check the volume on the microphone.'

'Hello,' said Lizzie, gritting her teeth.

'Can you hear that all right, Doc?' Gary asked.

'Loud and clear,' said the doctor, 'although I'd much rather be talking to Lizzie than you, Gary.'

Gary toggled the phone off speaker and onto the headset. 'Try it with the headset on its own.'

She fitted the band over her head, and Gary swung the mike-arm into place in front of her mouth. She could smell salt and vinegar on his fingers, as if he'd been eating crisps in the car.

'Hello, Lizzie,' said Joe again.

Lizzie nodded at the officer, avoiding looking at Gary.

'Right then, we'll clear off,' he said. 'Get your kit, Gazza. See you later, pet.'

Joe waited until the door slammed.

'How are you feeling, Lizzie?'

The voice wavered as the line crackled. She didn't say anything. He made no sound and she wondered if the connection had dropped out. She hoped it had.

'I imagine you must be feeling a range of emotions right now,' he said. His voice was warm and soothing, with a rich timbre. If he were telling her a story, she could have sat and listened to him for ever. But he wasn't.

'You have no fucking idea how I'm feeling.'

'Why don't you tell me?' he said.

After a few moments, when she still hadn't responded, he said smoothly, 'Well, let me tell you a little bit about me. As you know, my name is Dr Joe Wood. I imagine that you don't trust me at the moment because you see me as part of the police, and it is the police who have separated you from the life you had before. I'm a psychologist. The police have hired me to help you, but I'm not a police officer. I hope you will be able to trust me eventually.' When she didn't respond, he continued: 'Let me tell you the facts as I understand them, and then you can tell me whether I've got anything wrong or not.'

His voice reminded her of Christmas: of old movies and cigar smoke, of sweet sherry in cut-glass tumblers and the crackle of a real log fire.

'You saw something terrible. Something no one should witness,' continued Joe Wood, his voice losing and then gaining volume, as the signal faltered. 'As a result, the police have put you in protective care to keep you safe because, otherwise, your life would be in danger. But this means that you will never see your son or your husband again.'

Lizzie heard the catch in her throat, as if the stifled sob had come from someone else.

'You are grief-stricken and bewildered and lost. Soon, the enormity of what has happened is going to hit you and it will hurt like hell. But right now, it seems unreal to you. You are in shock. You feel a little numb. There is no space in your mind to assimilate a trauma as profound as the loss of your baby boy, your husband, your mother, father, sister. The murder of your best friend. You will go through several stages of grief, including anger and acute distress. The pain is going to be overwhelming. What has happened to you *is* unbearable; it is unacceptable. It's profoundly unfair and unjust. In time, the depth of the despair you will feel may diminish and become less raw, but the sadness will remain and will always be a part of you. My job is to help you find a way to live with this anguish. My job is to help you rebuild yourself.'

Lizzie found that tears were streaming silently down her cheeks. Her chest ached. She realized that the size and the shape of the pain were the exact space where Dylan would have been if she'd been holding him in her arms. For two hours she sobbed and Dr Joe Wood listened.

At a minute to twelve she said, 'I feel as if my heart is breaking.'

'Yes,' he said, 'yes, your heart is breaking. I'm here. Every day I'll be here for you. Until tomorrow, Lizzie.'

The line went dead.

EMMA

'You look beautiful,' I tell my youngest daughter.

'But I want the other one. Miss Angela said . . .'

'Miss Angela said a purple one. She didn't say exactly which one. And that one is really expensive!'

Plus it's so tacky, I think, putting the purple tutu covered with silver sequins back on its hanger. We're in the dance shop buying Ava an outfit for her *Sleeping Beauty* performance.

'I want it!'

Ava stamps her foot. She crosses her arms and pouts. She looks just like Stella. Heaven help me. Her thick blonde hair is escaping from the bun. I take a strand and try and tuck it behind her ear, but she tosses her head.

'The one you've got on is lovely.'

She's wearing a plain lilac-coloured leotard with a simple chiffon skirt. It's the least expensive item in the shop and looks gorgeous against her creamy skin. I'm afraid she'll look like a child beauty queen in the garish tutu.

'I hate it!'

'That's the one you're getting,' I say firmly, wondering what's wrong with Ava.

Perhaps the extra ballet lessons have over-tired her? I'll talk to Jack when we get home, I decide. Maybe we should scale back some of her classes.

Ava tears the straps off her shoulders and yanks the outfit down. As she steps out of it, there's a shearing sound. The skirt has ripped.

'Ava!'

'It wasn't my fault,' she says, flinging it on the floor.

I snatch up the flimsy scrap of fabric. I'm so angry, I'm shaking. When Dylan was a baby we didn't have enough money to buy him clothes. Every single thing he wore was a hand-me-down. How I would have loved to dress my son in just one sweet, brand-new outfit, which I'd chosen and which wasn't covered with washed-in milk stains. In contrast, my daughters have grown up in a modernist palace like two spoilt princesses and have never wanted for a single thing. I go and pay for the dress and buy some matching thread to repair it. I'd wanted this to be a wonderful mother–daughter occasion, choosing Ava's outfit together, for once without Stella moaning in the background and me rushing because I feel guilty for dragging Stella round after her younger sister. I was planning on buying her new ballet tights and one of those matching crochet hairnets, but now I don't.

I wait by the door for Ava, to allow my anger to subside, but she doesn't emerge from the changing rooms, so eventually I go back in. She's sitting in the corner with her hands over her face, crying quietly.

'I'm sorry, Mummy,' she says, when I sit on the chair next to her. 'I didn't mean to rip it. Did you have to pay for it?'

'Yes. But don't worry, I'll sew it up. You won't be able to tell when you're onstage.'

She bursts into loud sobs.

'Ava, love, what's the matter?'

'Are you going to leave us?' she asks, hiccuping.

I take a tissue out of my handbag and pass it to her.

'Of course I'm not going to leave you. What are you talking about?'

I give her a cuddle and she blows her nose and sighs.

'Why do you think I'd leave?'

She shrugs and looks down, avoiding meeting my eye. I help her get dressed and give her another hug.

'I'd never leave you or Stella. I love you. Did Stella say something to you?' She shakes her head. 'Why would you think I'd leave you?' I persist.

'What about when we grow up?'

'Well then, you'll be the ones leaving me and Daddy,' I say, trying to laugh.

Although I sound calm, I'm frightened. Has Stella seen something? What has she said to Ava? I take Ava's hand. It feels hot. Maybe she's coming down with something? I glance at her in the rear-view mirror as we drive home. She looks more composed now: the pink flush in her cheeks had disappeared, but her eyes are still red.

I feel as if my heart is being squeezed tighter and tighter. I love my daughters so much. I've lost almost everything that matters: my husband, my son, my mum, my dad, my sister, my friends, my grandparents, my home, my past, my own self. Was my sacrifice worth it? I did put Jon Lilley away for life.

I could have chosen not to. I could have walked away. But then Lilley would have gone free and he'd probably have murdered me and then Dylan and Paul. I wanted him to pay, for what he'd done to me, as well as for the people he'd killed, the child he maimed, the lives he blighted.

Yes, I think, *I won*. Lilley will never be released. And I have a new life, a wonderful husband, two gorgeous girls – I got away from him. And I've met my previous husband again, and soon I'm going to see my son. Could I have it all? Can I juggle both my families? Has enough time passed? Am I finally safe from Lilley and his henchmen now?

STELLA

I had my English exam this morning. I was so nervous, but I think I did okay. I love *Jane Eyre*, and *Jeykyll and Hyde* is another of my favourites. I said I'd done badly to the other kids in my class. Obviously. Kaylee is kind of speaking to me – if you didn't know her, you'd think nothing was wrong, but she's still being really cliquey with Nuala. I'm a lot more worried about next week, when I've got Combined Sciences.

When I got up this morning there was a present next to my place at the table, beautifully wrapped in grey paper with a cream ribbon. The gift tag said: *Good luck today, you'll be brilliant! Love Mum xx.*

Inside was a box set of Jane Austen novels.

I said, 'She has no idea. No bloody idea! I'm not even studying Jane Austen!'

Dad was about to reply, but instead his mouth went into a thin, hard line. And I'm glad Mum wasn't there, because it meant I was able to thank her properly when she came to pick me up, and she was so pleased, she kept smiling at me all the way home.

I told my parents I was going to The Station with everyone tonight to celebrate doing our first exam. Dad wasn't happy – he said we should wait until we've done all of them, but Mum actually stood up for me.

'Remember what you always say, Jack? Imagine you're climbing a mountain. It's important to stop halfway up and see how far you've come.'

'Celebrate the small steps,' me and Mum both said at once and laughed.

'She's been working hard. She deserves a night off,' Mum added.

He looked like he was going to carry on arguing, with it being a school night and all.

'No more timetabled lessons from now until the end of term. Just revision. You could help me? I've got triple sciences coming up,' I added.

He stopped grimacing then and basically agreed, but there were a whole lot of 'provisos' – like getting a taxi home and not leaving my drink unattended, in case someone rapes me and dumps me with the garbage out the back. Not that he put it like that.

So here I am, with some actual money in my wallet, heading to the *Thekla*, and I can see Adam standing outside the entrance with his hands in his pockets, like he's trying to look casual. It makes me feel a whole lot better knowing that he's nervous, too. Plus he's on his own. I didn't know if he'd invited a load of his mates along. So it's like a proper date. My cheeks ache from grinning before I even reach him. Damn! I'd hoped I'd be a bit cooler.

'Hey,' he says. 'Got your ticket.'

He keeps his hands in his pockets as we go up the gangplank. I'm beyond excited. The *Thekla* is a ship moored off the harbour. I've never been before. I've only seen live music with my parents, and their taste runs to classical concerts. Well, Dad's does. Mum listens to the same stuff as me and Ava. Inside it's dark and panelled with wood. You can see the curve of the boat's sides. It's starting to fill up already, and Adam chooses a spot for us on a balcony overlooking the stage.

'Don't want you getting crushed down there,' he says, nodding to the pit in the ship's bowels below us.

He goes to the bar to get the drinks and I suddenly feel alone, even though there's tons of people here. I've thought of literally nothing but Adam for days. Maybe weeks. I don't really know him. I know almost nothing about him. I watch him, as if he's a stranger. It's like there's a spool of thread between me and him and it's unravelling, but we're still connected. It tugs at my chest and it's hard to breathe, as if it's attached by a barbed hook. I want him to look at me. He reaches the bar and turns and smiles and a tremor runs through my legs.

When he comes back, his hands are wet where the drinks have spilt. Thank God I'm not with Kaylee or I'd have to get some alcopop crap. Adam wipes his hands on his jeans and leans down to me.

'You know that band we were listening to the other day – The Cadillac Three? The guy we're going to see lives next door to the lead singer! How cool is that?'

He smells like newly planed green wood and forests, like he's being lying in the woods and then quickly put aftershave on. I can feel the heat radiating off him. I want him to be closer to me. I want him to put his arms around me.

And then they're bounding onto the stage: Tyler Bryant & The Shakedown, all the way from Nashville, Tennessee, to a boat in Bristol. Adam's excited, but he stands almost completely still. I sip my wine, and the music and the alcohol pulse through my body and the world cracks open like it's full of possibility. Tyler Bryant is skinny and pretty with high cheekbones and long shaggy hair. He's wearing black jeans and a loose shirt open at his throat and loads of long necklaces. The music is raw and rocky. Someone pushes me and I fall. Adam catches me and he leaves his arm around me for a moment longer than he needs to.

When it's over, he says, 'We can get the bus back. Want to walk the long way round to the bus stop, along the harbour?'

I nod. I can hardly speak. I feel unsteady, like I'm drunk, although I only had one glass of wine. The music is still tingling through my fingers.

'I never had the chance to see big bands like this before,' he says. 'It was just, you know, guys with guitars in the local pub.'

'Where did you live before you moved here?'

'The Lake District,' he says with a laugh. 'A tiny village. You'd never have heard of it.'

'Do you miss it?'

We cross over Pero's Bridge and stop for a moment to lean over and look down at the black water. The stir of the sea water fragments the reflection of the lights.

'I can do a lot more here, go places on my own, go to gigs and out with friends by myself, without asking my dad for a lift all the time. But yeah, I do. I miss my best mate, Nick, and the mountains. Like, you can walk for half an hour and you're away from everything. No people. Just space and wilderness as far as you can see. Ever heard of Scafell Pike?'

I nod. 'Yeah, even I've heard of Scafell,' I say.

I know nothing about it, but the name conjures up danger and isolation.

'That's my local hike,' he says.

He smiles at me and then he pulls me towards him and kisses me.

I was worried he wouldn't want to. I was worried he would and it would be awful, our teeth would clash and my nose would get in the way and I wouldn't know what to do. But it's not like that. It's so right. I slide my hands beneath his jacket and pull him tighter. Our bodies fit together like they were meant to. It feels as if we kiss for ages.

He pulls away and says, 'Should get you back. The farmers back home all had shotguns. But I'm guessing your dad's not like that.'

'Nah. But he'd probably knock you out with one of his kettlebells if he got mad,' I say.

Adam takes my hand and we walk slowly back along the harbour. When we're on the bus he puts his arm round me and sticks his legs out into the aisle. I can see he's smiling, by looking at his reflection in the windows. He seems a lot more mature than the boys in my year, or else he's just old-fashioned from living in the countryside. I think he's going to get out in Long Ashton when I do and walk me home, but he doesn't.

He puts his lips close to my ear and whispers, 'I'll see you very soon, Ms Rochester.'

I watch him, a haloed silhouette, as the bus disappears into the darkness. It's the Clevedon one, and I wonder where he's going,

LIZZIE

'I can't imagine what he thought. What he thinks, what he must be going through. I mean, what does he know? I never came home. I never came back from Leeds. Maybe he thinks I left him because of Miriam. But I would never have done that! I love him so much. Perhaps he thinks I died? But he'll never know the truth.'

'Yes,' said Joe Wood. 'It's unbearable for you, but it's also unbearable for him. He will never know what happened, and both of you have to live with that.'

'And Dylan . . .' She started to cry.

Joe said nothing. He waited for her to stop and then he said, 'You were going to tell me about Dylan.'

'He'll be missing me,' Lizzie said. 'He'll wonder why I never came home. They'll both think I abandoned them. I wouldn't . . .'

She choked into a tissue. She didn't think she had ever cried as much in her life. Her eyes felt perpetually raw, as if she'd rubbed sand from the beach into them.

'And I can't help thinking about what's going to happen now.'

'What do you mean?' asked Joe, his voice growing faint.

She hoped the line wasn't going to drop out again. She listened and she could hear a faint hum and the sound of him breathing. He was still there.

'I mean, Dylan is going to grow up without a mother,' she said. 'How is that going to feel? To suffer this terrible loss – knowing that his mother left him, thinking that maybe he isn't good enough . . .'

'You mean subconsciously, because he will believe he was abandoned, he'll blame himself and think he wasn't good enough for his mother, and therefore he won't be good enough for anyone else?'

'The damage – it's just going to go on and on . . . And I worry that Paul won't look after him properly. He'll love him, but will he do all the things that I do? That I did. Cut his toenails, and hunt for second-hand Babygros in charity shops. Cuddle him, instead of throwing him in the air. Hug him when he cries in the night. Will he hold his hand on the way to school, or remember to hide his teeth for the tooth fairy; will he bake him birthday cakes, and teach him about love, not just sex; will he ask about his first girlfriend, not slap him on the back?'

'You mean, will Paul be a mother and a father to your son?'

She said nothing because the answer was obvious. Paul would do his best, but his best would not be good enough. It would never be good enough to repair the hole that would open in her child's heart.

A couple of minutes later Joe said, 'Tell me something.'

'Tell you what?' she said dully.

'Whatever you like. About your day.'

She was about to snap that her days were mindless, locked up on her own in this cold, dreary house in the middle of nowhere, with a rotating team of police officers for company, and how some days the only thing that kept her sane was knowing she would be able to talk to him; that some days she only managed to get out of bed in the morning because she knew that he was waiting for her. She wanted to wrap herself in that disembodied voice, feel its strength and warmth.

'The birds,' she said instead.

'The birds?'

'Yes. Brent geese from Svalbard and bar-tailed godwits from the Arctic tundra. Thousands of them, loads of different species.

They've flown from Scandinavia to spend the winter here. At night, I can hear them honking. Pink-footed geese from Iceland, barnacle geese from Norway. When I lie in bed at night, I imagine I can hear the beat of their wings.

'Yesterday I walked along the beach. It was clear, for once, and the sun was starting to set. I saw a murmuration of plovers. Hundreds of them, making these strange, unearthly shapes across the sky; the light caught their wings, and the whole flock shone like gold.'

'A murmuration,' he said softly. 'That sounds beautiful.'

'Sometimes,' she said, 'sometimes I see something like that and it is the only thing that holds me here – those moments. I want to die, Joe. I spend all my time working out how I can do it, how I can kill myself. The police won't let me have razor blades, and the knives are blunt. They don't even leave paracetamol here overnight. I'm not allowed a belt for my trousers or even a cord for my dressing gown. There's no kettle and I don't own a hairdryer, so I can't electrocute myself in the bath. My only option is to drown myself. Every day I think about filling my pockets with stones and walking into the sea. I will aim for Iceland. I will never stop. But then I see a flock of golden plovers wheeling in the sunlight and, for a few brief moments, I forget who I am and why I'm here and what I've lost.'

Joe said nothing, and when he finally spoke several minutes later he said, 'Maybe you should.'

'Maybe I should commit suicide? I'm not sure that's what you're meant to say to me,' she said. There was a tremor in her voice. 'Shouldn't you tell me how wonderful it is that I'm "taking joy in the everyday", and "time heals" and one day my life will seem like a bed of fucking roses?'

'I mean,' he said, 'maybe it is time to let Lizzie Bradshaw go. The police have almost finished creating your new identity. Soon you'll need to learn who you are and think about what you're going to do with the rest of your life. Not you, Lizzie, but the woman you will become. You will be forced to leave Lizzie Bradshaw behind. I say, let her go now. Say goodbye to Lizzie, the girl you once were, for ever. Because that girl has got to die so that you may live.'

EMMA

'It doesn't seem real, does it?'
'No. A stage set that might get wheeled away. Or CGI. Any moment now we're going to see catering behind a green screen.'

We're walking in the woods behind Paul's cottage. It's a beautiful day in the middle of June. Gil is following scent trails, giving low growls and huffs beneath his breath as he senses where badgers and voles have passed.

'That's not what I meant,' I say.

'I know. The whole thing . . . it's unreal.'

The paths are easy to follow: neat bridleways through wide-spaced beech and oak, but the incline is steep and I'm out of breath. You'd think I'd have muscle-memory, or something. I used to be able to keep up with Paul. Although I'd never have gone for a walk in a rose-patterned sundress.

He must be thinking along similar lines because he says, 'Do you remember the first time we climbed Scafell Pike?'

I laugh. 'You nearly killed me.'

He grins. 'It was our first or second date, wasn't it? You dragged me up there in the middle of winter.'

'It was like something out of *Gormenghast*. A castle of ice and snow. And I made you climb up the second peak—'

'Literally climb up the rock face with a frozen waterfall down the middle of it. You were okay, you had crampons. But I couldn't let on how scared I was, in case you didn't fancy me any more.' He stops laughing abruptly. 'You've changed, Liz – Emma.'

'I had to,' I say simply.

'Aye. I don't know if I could, if it had been the other way round. Too set in my ways, maybe.'

'I was young. I was able to.'

I think back to the first time Jack and I went out together and I remember standing on the deck of the *Thekla*, looking out over the marina, feeling the music hum through the boards below my feet and he said, 'So, Emma, tell me about yourself.'

My throat was suddenly dry.

'What do you want to know?' I asked, my voice hoarse.

'Everything. Anything,' he said, smiling at me. 'Let's start with your full name. Your family. Where you come from. I want to know all about you.'

He was asking me exactly the kind of questions I'd rehearsed so many times before, when I was in Witness Protection. But I'd never had to tell a stranger who I was, or pretend to anyone other than the deli staff, who'd seen my made-up CV and didn't really care. And my counsellor hadn't warned me that the person who asked first would be so handsome, so charming and would hang off my every word as if it really mattered.

'My name is Emma James,' I said, and I started to grin nervously, as it sounded as if I was at a job interview – only one that my life literally depended upon – and Jack smiled encouragingly. I took a swig of perry for courage and continued with my legend. 'I was born in Bath and grew up here – in St George's in Bristol.'

'You don't have much of a Bristolian accent.'

'All reet, my duck?' I said, and he laughed.

'Go on. Tell me more, Emma James from St George's, Bristol.'

'I had a mother and a father and a sister – Julia – but,' and here

I faltered, as one might, 'they were all killed in a crash on the M4.'

'I'm so sorry,' he said, but he didn't look embarrassed or awkward, only genuinely sad. 'How old were you when it happened?'

'Seventeen.'

'That's terrible. No other brothers or sisters?'

I shook my head. 'I . . . I went off the rails a bit,' I said. 'Dropped out of school.' I gave a half-laugh. 'And here I am. Working in a deli.'

It seemed only natural then that he took me in his arms and kissed the top of my head, and a few moments later I felt his breath against my neck and then he bent and kissed me on the lips.

Jack has a phenomenal memory. I've never had to tell him anything twice. He asked me a little more about myself on our first dates – what I had been studying for my A-levels, what school I went to, when the accident happened – and he didn't forget these details. I saw myself reflected back in his eyes. As we built our lives together, the person I was going to become – Emma James – solidified; she became real. And it all happened so quickly. I fell in love. Or at least, I thought I did. Maybe I was just filling a void. Maybe it was gratitude. I got pregnant with Stella. We moved in together. We got married. The legend, once so insubstantial, was now tangible. I was Emma Taylor. I was in love with Jack Taylor. And Jack helped me, although he had no idea that was what he was doing.

We see ourselves as others see us, I think.

Jack constantly reflected my new image, my new self, back to me. He reinforced the person I was becoming, the person I became to the outside world.

Paul and I are now in a tight tunnel of hazel that arches over our heads; the banks are dense with hart's tongue ferns and there's the smell of crushed moss. He doesn't look convinced.

'People don't normally change.'

'Maybe only on the surface,' I agree. 'Just because I once drank beer and climbed mountains and now I drink Pinot Grigio and go for leisurely bike rides, it doesn't mean that deep down I'm a different person. Why do you think you connected with me so quickly, when we bumped into each other here?'

'I'm not so sure,' he says. 'You seem, I don't know . . .'

I lace my fingers between his.

'I'm losing her,' he says. 'I'm losing sight of Lizzie.'

'That might be a good thing,' I say gently.

'You don't even sound like her any more.'

'Elocution lessons.'

'Bloody hell. They thought of everything, didn't they?'

'They had to.'

We turn and face each other and he runs his finger gently down my nose. 'I miss your freckles,' he says softly.

I wonder what's going to happen now. Whether we'll peel off each other's clothes here in the middle of this wood, or whether we'll start to fight about Dylan. I've waited long enough.

He must have seen the determined look in my eye, because he says, 'I've brought you a photo.' He takes it out of his wallet and passes it to me. 'I don't know how to tell him,' he adds.

I hold the photo with my fingertips. It's Paul and Dylan. They're standing at the top of a mountain. I recognize it: it's the Pike of Stickle, a cairn balanced precariously on the top, Harrison Stickle and Thorn Crag beyond, and then rolling hills on and on, all the way to the sea. But, of course, it's not the mountains I'm looking at. It's my son.

I start crying. He is beautiful. Perfect.

The photo's not close enough, though. I can't see his eyes, but I can see how similar he is to Paul – the same jawline, the heavy brows, the blond-brown tousled hair. He's finer, slimmer and he has my nose: my old nose.

'It was a couple of years ago,' says Paul.

There's a slight roundness to his cheeks; I imagine they'll be more chiselled now that he's on the brink of being a man. I have missed his entire childhood. He's grinning, elated at being on top of the world. If my life had been different, if I hadn't gone into that newsagent's that night, if there had been no Jon Lilley, then I would have been standing there too, on that mountain peak, with my arms round my son, celebrating his achievement with my husband.

I've wondered so many times what Dylan looked like. I have imagined over and over seeing him in a crowded square, walking on a hillside and, in my dreams, I've always known it was him, and I've run to him and hugged him tightly and whispered, 'My son, my son.' In my dreams, he hugged me back and wept, 'Mummy, my mummy.' But as I look at this boy, this teenager, I can feel a horrible, dark chasm opening up inside me. Because the terrible thing is, if I passed him in the street, I wouldn't have recognized him. I wouldn't know my own son if I met him today.

My husband is walking a little way ahead of me. I stumble after him, through the wood, sobbing and tripping over tree roots, clutching the photo.

'Paul!' I shout.

He stops for a moment and holds out his hand as if he might be about to quieten a horse.

'I can't, Emma. I can't do this. The thought of you with him – it's fucking torturing me.'

'I need you,' I say.

I can hardly breathe. Gil comes trotting back and nuzzles my hand. As we reach the cottage and the turn in the track that will take me down past the Pavilion cafe and back to my car, and my other life – my other marriage – Paul comes striding back.

'I love you,' he says, gripping me by my upper arms. 'I've fallen in love with you all over again. But I can't do this any more. I want you back. I want us to be a family. You've got to leave him. Please. Let's start over.'

'You know I can't,' I say. 'What if—'

'Then you shouldn't have this. What if someone finds it?'

He snatches the photo from me and walks away, whistling for Gil, and I am left, weeping and clutching my hands to my chest, where for a few minutes I held a picture of my son for the first time in almost seventeen years.

I've stopped crying by the time I pick up the girls, but when I catch a glimpse of myself in the rear-view mirror, I look a mess. My eyes and nose are red and my make-up has smudged, leaving me with dark shadows beneath my eyes. Neither of them seems to notice. Ava talks excitedly about her ballet performance; Jack is taking her to the dress rehearsal this Saturday morning and the show is on next week. It'll be an intense few days, as most of Stella's mocks are then, too. My oldest daughter looks almost comatose. She had her English exam yesterday and went out to celebrate with her classmates. I couldn't sleep, so I got up and waited for her to come home – although I didn't tell her that – and now I'm not sure which of us is more tired.

'How did your revision go, love?'

Stella looks at me sullenly.

'Fine,' she says, and folds her arms.

I sigh. Surely a son would be easier? More straightforward.

I make them toast and they sit side by side on the sofa, hunched over their screens. I get out my laptop. I hesitate for a minute. I do know how social media works. I want to protect my daughters and so I follow them, a silent cut-out figure of a woman with an alias and privacy settings locked down more tightly than a portcullis.

I delete my viewing history every day and I have never searched online for Paul and Dylan before, even though, some days, I would have chewed off my own fingers to find out where they were; how they were.

But today – today is different. I've reached the end of something. Maybe it was actually seeing a photo of my son aged fifteen, or maybe it was my husband walking away from me when I needed him most, or perhaps it was simply Paul's ultimatum. I look around me, at our spacious kitchen and living room, the giant TV screen on the wall, the muslin curtains drifting in the gentle breeze, the view across the valley that an estate agent would give his Lamborghini for – and I know I could walk away from it all with a moment's notice. But I can't leave Jack or my daughters.

I log on and begin to look for Dylan Bradshaw. My heart constricts. It's as if I can feel Jon Lilley's cold, empty gaze settling on me, the stealthy shuffle of electronic footfalls as he follows me. I search for my son on Facebook, Instagram, Twitter, WhatsApp. I google him. Nothing. Paul's Facebook profile is private, so I can't tell if our son is one of his friends. I want to throw up my hands and ask my girls for help. I know they'd be ten times better at this than I am. I start deleting my search history and logging out of all the applications, while I'm thinking what to do. And then I notice something.

It's Stella's Instagram account. She's been liking a lot of photos recently, all from one person's profile. They're mainly of animals, which is odd. She's never shown the slightest interest in wildlife and, much as I've wanted her to, I've never been able to openly encourage her. The pictures are by MaddAddam. The most recent ones were taken in Bristol. There's an amazing photograph of a fox at dusk standing on top of a rock, and behind it, blazing with light, is the Clifton Suspension Bridge. A boy at school that she's friends with? Her boyfriend? There's no profile shot, only a green eye in a blue face. I glance up at her, but she's engrossed in her revision. I hope she knows him in real life. What if he's a stalker? An older, predatory man, preying on my daughter?

I wish we were getting on better. When Stella was a baby I imagined years of intimacy ahead of us, sharing our thoughts, feelings, baking, shopping, going on trips together . . . but she's never been the kind of child to confide much in me. And recently she's been more aggressive than usual. I expect it's the stress of exams. *I'll ask her this evening when Ava's not around*, I think, as I turn back to my laptop and my fruitless search. *Why isn't Dylan here?*

STELLA

It's Friday night. Adam's asked me to meet him. He's been really secretive about what we're doing. He messaged me to say it's going to be a late one, but he'll make sure I get home safely and he was a total tool for not walking me home last week.

'Dress warm!' he'd added and, 'Laters, Ms Rochester.'

So my usual clothes are pretty much going to be fine for this, with a thicker hoodie than normal. I'm pleased I don't have to agonize about what a freak I look like. I know Mum and Dad would completely lose it, if I said I was going on a date with a boy they don't know at night in a secret location. I'm going to have to sneak out. I lie in bed and wait until it grows dark. There are butterflies in my stomach and I keep checking my watch. Dad is still up; I can hear him wandering around upstairs, but I don't think he'll look in on me. I shove a couple of rolled-up towels in the bed and pull the duvet over them, just in case.

When it's time, I dress and open the window and climb out. Because my bedroom is on the ground floor, it's not far to jump. I push the window so it's almost closed and stand there for a moment, looking back at my room. There's a chink in the curtains and I can see my bed. Someone standing here, on our driveway, could watch me sleeping. I have a cold feeling in my chest. I always thought our house was super-safe, what with the parents being so terrified of everything and having this state-of-the-art security system. But now I see there's nothing that could stop anyone who's determined enough. Especially now I've left the window open.

I start walking up Providence Lane, and I'm even more jittery than I was before. I wonder if this is what love feels like: a cross between nervous palpitations and a tummy bug.

Yesterday Mum came into my room before she went to bed and asked me about MaddAddam on Instagram. I didn't want to tell her anything, but I needed her to get off my case, so I said, yeah, I did know him. He's a boy at school.

'Is he your boyfriend?' she asked.

'No!' I said, like that was a disgusting idea. 'Just a friend.'

'What's his name?' she asked, like she was going to trick me into admitting he's a forty-two-year-old stalker.

'Adam,' I told her

'Adam,' she repeated and then she sat there for a bit and didn't say anything. 'How do you know him?' she asked eventually. 'Is he in your year?'

'Book Club,' I said.

By the time she left, I was fizzing with hate. What the fuck does she care whose pictures I like? It's none of her business, and besides, all she's thinking about is Mr Bit-of-Rough.

I feel even stranger, walking up this hill in our dark and silent suburb, wondering whether this weird and intense feeling I have about Adam is how *she* feels when she's cycling to Tyntesfield to meet her bloke. I nearly double up then, like I'm going to be sick; it's as if we're sharing something, when what she's doing is so wrong . . . A man steps out of shadows and I scream.

'Whoa!'

It's Adam.

'Hey, sorry I scared you. I thought I should meet you, instead of leaving you to walk all the way there on your own.'

He doesn't touch me and we're awkward with each other, like that kiss never happened. He's got a large rucksack, with a flask in the side pocket. He falls into step next to me. We cross the road and duck into the woods at the back of Ashton Court.

'What the fuck are we doing?' I ask and it comes out wrong, all snappy and miserable.

'Thought you might like to see what I get up to at night,' he says, but his voice is terse.

Fucking teenagers. Like Dad says, they don't give you an ounce of leeway. He always adds, 'Or twenty-five grams,' which is not even funny. So it's going to be up to me to be moderately grown-up. I attempt to sound nice, although my heart is bumping and my skin is still crawling, thinking of Mum.

'Are you going to show me then?'

I'm glad it's dark, because that sounded flirtatious, and I start blushing.

'It's my Urban Fox Project,' Adam says. He stops and takes off his rucksack and starts emptying it, and suddenly everything is back to normal because he's so enthusiastic. 'It's for Bristol University,' he tells me. 'I'm radio-tracking foxes they've fitted with collars. We're creating a map of where they live and how far they range.'

He fits bits of kit together and there's a crackle. He swings the antenna round and the static noise gets louder.

'There's one over there,' he whispers. 'Come on.'

If anyone had asked me a few weeks ago if I'd willingly go for a walk in the woods after dark, stalking foxes, I'd have said there'd be no way on God's green earth you'd make me do that. But with Adam, it's kind of fun. It's a clear night and there's a thin crescent moon; I can see the Milky Way sparkling through the leaves. Adam grabs my hand and tugs me after him.

'It's how I get photos of the foxes,' he says. 'I know where their dens are and where they go. I can lie in wait. They're still shy, but they're getting used to me. And this one, AC3125X, has cubs!'

'Cool name,' I say, but he ignores my sarcasm.

He stops suddenly and holds up his hand as if to shush me. We're right on the edge of the wood. On our left is the high metal fence surrounding the deer park, and in front of us is open grassland. We edge slowly forward until we're beneath a chestnut tree. Adam points and then suddenly I see them. The mother's sitting a few metres away from us and there are three cubs right in front of her! They're rolling and play-fighting in the long grass and chasing each other round a fallen log. They're adorable, little fluffy balls with short snouts and tiddly ears. We slowly crouch down and lean against the trunk of the tree.

'They know we're here,' whispers Adam, his breath hot against my neck.

Occasionally the mother fox flicks one ear towards us. She stretches and yawns and her sharp teeth glint in the moonlight. The babies make funny little sounds, almost like they're muttering at each other. I can't believe it: that practically next to us is a family of foxes and, on the other side of the fence, there's a herd of fallow deer; their eyes glowing green in the starlight. The sky's a deep plum-purple and everything smells fresh and sharp. It's like the wood is pulsing with energy. Adam is pressed against me and my whole side tingles as if it's electrified. I can't quite breathe. An owl hoots softly, and sharp tree-bark digs into my spine. None of it seems real. It's like one of those magical moments you see in a film.

But then the mother hears something and almost immediately the cubs snap to attention and they all race off into the wood. I expect Adam to leap up and chase after them, waving his radio-tracking thing, but he sinks back into the tree and looks up at the stars.

'Don't you have to—'

'Nah. It's not one of my data-collection nights. I just wanted to show you.'

He pulls out his flask and pours us both a cup. I can smell it's coffee but when I take a sip, I nearly choke. Adam grins and his teeth gleam in the darkness.

'Thought we might need something to warm us up.'

The whiskey sings through my veins and the stars seem to blur and sharpen.

'But maybe we don't,' he says.

He kisses me, ever so gently, just touching his lips against mine. He moves away and the heat rushes from my body. I wonder if I've done something wrong, or if he's changed his mind.

'Just got to put this stuff away in case I accidentally sit on it or something. It cost a fucking fortune. My dad had to do some fast talking to persuade the Prof at Bristol Uni to lend it to a seventeen-year-old.'

This time, when he kisses me, it's long and slow. He cups my face in both hands and there's something unbearably sweet and tender about it. I expected that my first proper kisses would end up with me pushing the guy away, to stop him groping me, like the boys in my class try to do at every party when they've had a drink to make them brave. But I didn't realize how much I would want it, how much I'd ache for him to slide his hands beneath my top. I'm desperate for him to touch me all over. Just when I can't bear it any more, he breaks away.

'I should get you home, Ms Rochester,' he says, and his voice is hoarse.

It's colder and the moon is hidden. I stumble as we walk back through the wood. Adam takes my hand. He seems totally at ease here. For the first time he tells me more personal things about himself – somehow it's easier to talk in the dark.

'You live at Tyntesfield?'

'Yeah,' he says, and I can tell he's smiling. 'That's how I knew we'd get on – when you said you wanted to meet there.'

'Oh. But why, I mean, *how* can you live on a National Trust estate?'

'My dad's a gardener.'

His tone is harder and I don't know why. My dad says sometimes if you shut up and don't say anything, people feel so awkward with the silence that they start telling you what you want to know.

We continue walking and, after a few moments, Adam says, 'He was a ranger in the Lake District – we've lived there since I was born. But he wanted me to have more opportunities and independence. You know, meet people, go to a good school, maybe study at Bristol Uni, if I can get in. So he took this shit job. Well, it's not bad, and the house we get to live in is cool – it's in a wood. But, it's not him.' He struggles to explain. 'My dad doesn't like being cooped up, you know? He's happiest in the mountains, fixing a wall or building a path or catching a stray sheep.'

I squeeze his hand. I get it. That horrible feeling of shame because you're responsible for their unhappiness and they've made that sacrifice for you, and you're meant to be, like, intensely fucking grateful without actually saying it, when maybe you never wanted it or asked for it in the first place.

'What about your mum?' I say, because he's never, not once, mentioned her.

'She left.' And now his voice really is bitter. 'Walked out when I was six months old. Can you believe it? Dad's never got over it. He says he thought they were happy.'

'Wait,' I say, not paying proper attention to what he's just said. 'Your dad is a gardener at Tyntesfield. Does he have a girlfriend?'

'No,' Adam says, and he sounds slightly annoyed that I haven't picked up on this major revelation about his mum, but I can't, because I've got the taste of bile in my throat. We've reached the edge of the wood. I stop walking.

'What is it?' asks Adam.

There are street lights here and I can sort of make out his face, but I can't look at him. I take both his hands in mine.

Say it. Just fucking say it, I tell myself.

Adam steps down off the curb so that he's almost the same height as me. He waits. It must be a skill, I think. Good with animals and teenage girls.

I grit my teeth and take a breath. 'My mum's having an affair, and I think it's with your dad.'

'What?' He lets go my hands and reels back into the road.

I'm suddenly frightened, like I'm making it real by saying it out loud. I stretch out my hands towards him and he comes back to me.

'How do you know?'

'I've been following her,' I say in a small voice.

He chuckles. 'Maybe you'd make a good animal-tracker after all.'

'I've seen her with a man at Tyntesfield. A gardener. He wears a brown uniform.'

'What does he look like?'

I describe the man I've seen and Adam says quietly, 'Does sound like Paul, my old man. The bugger!' He looks at me then, really looks at me, and then he grins. 'Maybe we'll end up as stepbrother and sister. Just think what we could get up to, if we were in the same house.'

And he pulls me towards him and kisses me.

EMMA

For the next few days I monitor Stella's Instagram account, but she's not using it much. She's wound as tightly as a bow – she's had three exams this week. It's Book Club today. Ava doesn't have ballet because her performance is on Friday and the girls are 'resting'. I drop her off at a friend's house and go to pick Stella up. I want to be early. I'm assuming there'll be no 'MaddAddam'. If he were her boyfriend, she'd be in constant contact with him. In any case, the Instagram photos seem too well composed to be a teenager's. And it's not typical teen behaviour – waiting patiently for hours to get the perfect photo of a wren. I know the pupils who go to Book Club by sight, so I'll notice if there is a new boy with them.

It's a warm day and the sky is a brilliant blue, with a soft breeze. I sit on a bench outside the entrance to the school and wait. Just after 4.30 a few of them spill out of the door, pushing each other, their bags slopping off their shoulders, their ties askew. Nuala and Kaylee are next, heads bent close together, in conversation with each other. I expect to see Stella at any moment, but she's not with them. I wonder if she and Kaylee have fallen out? I've never really liked Kaylee that much, she's so self-absorbed. As if to prove me right, she flicks her thick mane of hair to one side and she and Nuala pose for a selfie. But she has been Stella's best friend since the start of secondary school. Perhaps that's why Stella is so upset at the moment?

A couple of girls come out – Fee and Khadijia, I think – and then Stella. Her hair is down and it's long and straight. It shines in the sun and she looks beautiful. She throws back her head and laughs. I almost do a double-take. Stella? Laughing like she's carefree? She's talking to two other kids – Theo and Cian from the year below – and a sixth-former. She's goofing about and she's not touching him; surely she would, if she were going out with this boy? So, just a friend then. And then I grip the bench hard. I freeze. It can't be. But it is.

It's Dylan. He's unmistakable from the boy in the photograph that Paul showed me: older, taller, his jaw is squarer, his cheekbones are more defined; he's a boy on the brink of being a man. My son. This is not how I imagined it would be. I thought if I saw him, I would run and fling myself at him, scoop him up in my arms, tell him he was mine. But we're outside a school. He's much taller than I am. And he's with my daughter.

I stand up slowly. My legs are shaking. I feel as if I'm on the verge of tears. I pull my spine straighter and walk towards them. They look up as I approach. Dylan has shaggy hair that covers his eyes, and my heart trembles when I'm reminded, yet again, of all the years he's had without a mother to care for him.

'Hey, Mrs Taylor,' says Theo in my direction, and he and Cian slouch off.

I want to grab hold of Dylan to stop him leaving, too, but he shows no sign of going. Stella scowls at me and then recovers.

'Mum,' says Stella, 'this is Adam. From Book Club.'

There's a gleam in her eyes as if she knows I'm here to try and prove she was lying.

'Adam?' I stutter.

I hold out my hand and he grips mine. I hold his fractionally too long and he looks up at me from beneath his fringe, like a horse about to shy or bite. I grip my wrist tightly to stop myself from asking him why he's not calling himself Dylan. It explains why I hadn't found him online, though.

'Yeah. MaddAddam. Remember?' Stella prompts.

Dylan grins.

'Yes, I do. Stella showed me your photos on Instagram. They're brilliant.'

'Thank you, Mrs Taylor,' he says.

'Please call me Emma. I was taken aback at seeing you. Your profile is a blue person.'

'A Craker,' he says.

His voice is soft and deep. He's not a child any more.

'From *Oryx and Crake* by Margaret Atwood,' Stella tells me. 'We've been reading it in Book Club. Adam's just started coming.'

'I love her work,' I say.

'Really?' Stella sounds disbelieving.

I want to slap her. She thinks I'm uneducated. Stupid. Sometimes I want to shout at her that I have twelve GCSEs, four grade-A A-levels and was planning on doing a Masters in Environmental Science, before Jon Lilley derailed my life.

'*Cat's Eye* is my favourite. The one about the girl whose parents are zoologists?'

'Yeah, I liked that one, too,' Dylan says. 'But I prefer the MaddAddam trilogy.'

Stella looks impatient.

'Can I give you a lift?' I have to remember to call him Adam.

He glances at Stella who shrugs, and then he says, 'Yes, please. Thank you, Emma.'

Paul has brought him up well. Stella sits in the front. I can't stop staring at Dylan in the mirror. Adam, I mean. I suppose he wanted to make a fresh start when he came here. I'm touched he's chosen it. It was my father's name. His grandfather. But the memory is bittersweet: it reminds me I'll never see my mother or father again. I realize I have what I always thought I wanted – my husband and my son. My son is sitting in my car. Yet I cannot touch him. I cannot tell I love him. That I've always loved him. That there hasn't been a single day when I haven't thought of him.

Adam has noticed that I keep looking at him. He flushes and stares out of the window, hiding behind his fringe again, just like my daughter does.

'You can drop me at the lay-by,' he says. 'The bus stop's over there.'

I want to ask him to come home with us for a cup of tea, to prolong the time I have with him, but I know I mustn't. I don't look at Stella, but I can feel the static charge of her animosity. She's probably completely embarrassed that I've given a boy a lift and all her other friends will have seen. I hope they don't tease her.

'Is here okay?' I ask pointlessly, as I pull in.

'Thank you, Emma,' he says. He merely nods at my daughter and says, 'See you later.'

Stella doesn't say anything. I wait too long, far too long, after he's gone, before I turn the car round and drive up our road.

'How did your exam go?' I ask her.

She still doesn't speak and, as soon as I pull into the driveway, she gets out and slams the door so hard, the whole car shakes. And then I can't help myself. I stay sitting in the car, bent over the wheel, and I cry and cry.

It's Friday afternoon and the performance of *Sleeping Beauty* is about to begin. We're in the dance studio, in one of the larger rehearsal rooms, which is packed with parents on hard chairs fanning themselves with the programme.

I squeeze Jack's hand and he reaches his arm round me and pulls me in towards him. Stella angles herself away from us, hunched up, her hoodie stretched tightly around her, even though it's hot inside. She didn't want to come, but she's got no more exams left to study for and Ava begged her to. I think Jack had a word with her as well. I've tried to talk to Stella over the past couple of days, but I've given up.

The music is delicate, spring-like. It's Princess Aurora's christening and the fairies are bestowing gifts on her. Ava is in the purple dress – I mended the tear – flitting round the stage with the other girls in her class; they're all acolytes of the Lilac Fairy who, I'm guessing from the programme notes, is going to stop the wicked fairy Godmother from allowing the Princess to die after she pricks her finger on her sixteenth birthday.

I feel as if my heart will burst, watching my youngest daughter. I know I'm biased, but Ava has such grace and poise already. Tears of joy spill from my eyes. *I'm so lucky*, I think; in spite of everything that happened, I have two beautiful daughters and a loving husband. Jack is strong, kind, handsome. Of course one's feelings will ebb and flow – that's what being married is about. But I do love Jack and I'm thankful for what I have: an amazing home in a beautiful part of Bristol. I enjoy my job, too, even if the pay barely covers the bread I buy. It's as if Jon Lilley made a pact with the devil and I was the recipient: this is what I get, my wonderful life and, in return, I forfeit my family, my former friends, my first husband, my baby boy. And now? Now I've found my husband, my son. What the hell am I going to do? I don't have the strength to leave them again, to spend the rest of my life mourning them. But I can't lose my other husband and my girls.

'You okay?' mouths Jack, and I nod and mime wiping my forehead. He smiles and plants a kiss on my hair. His eyes are moist as he turns back to watch our daughter.

There's a slight hiccup as Miss Angela tries to project a picture of tangled brambles against the wall and the focus slips. For a moment Ava and the other fairies are bathed in green light, spinning in consternation, like butterflies beating their wings against a window.

The image sharpens into thorns and thick, sinuous stems. Princess Aurora flutters into their midst: a vision conjured by the Lilac Fairy to show the Prince his prize.

Is there a way I can have both? I wonder. After all, I don't want anyone to get hurt, and so far no one knows. No one even suspects. An hour a day with Paul – would it be enough? And if he won't tell Dylan or, rather, Adam, then I will. I feel a frisson of excitement, a little bubble of hope. Now that I've found my son, maybe I really could have it all.

The music swells and builds as the Prince sees the beautiful, sleeping Princess and kisses her on the lips. The boy playing Prince Désiré must be about fourteen and he surreptitiously wipes his mouth. The Princess rises from her century-long slumber and spins between his hands. It's as if he's moulding her into a shape of his choosing. She falls into a grateful, graceful curtsey at his feet. Thankfully the performance is highly edited and this is our cue to begin the applause.

Ava is still on a high, dancing around the rattan sofas we're reclining on. We're in the Ashton Gate pub garden. We're surrounded by lavender blooming in pots and the scent envelops us. It's still warm and the sky is the colour of a faded hyacinth. I'm wearing a white broderie-anglaise dress that Jack bought me last summer, with a cerulean silk scarf. I feel, as I bask in the heat, that I've found my way back to Jack, to my other husband, even if my relationship with him is not as passionate as it is with Paul.

'A toast,' says Jack, holding up his glass of wine. 'To our two beautiful, talented daughters.' He chinks his wine glass against mine. 'Well done, Ava, you were superb. And well done, Stella, for getting through your exams with aplomb.'

She snorts. 'You don't have a clue how I've done.'

'I'm sure your results will be excellent,' he says.

It sounds more like a warning than an affirmation. I turn back to Ava.

'You were wonderful,' I say, catching her and giving her a quick hug, before she pirouettes away.

'Next time I'm going to be Princess Aurora,' she sings.

I take a sip of my wine and then another. and my muscles melt into the cushions and I start to relax. My mood lifts. *Yes*, I think, *it can happen.* Jon Lilley has no idea where I am or who I am now. I can have all three of my children around me. I smile at my husband.

'Are you okay?' I ask Stella quietly. 'It's just, I noticed that Kaylee came out of Book Club with Nuala instead of you. You two are normally inseparable. Is everything all right between you?'

'Mum! Kaylee talked to Nuala for, like, a nanosecond.'

'So you're still friends,' I say, passing her the bread basket and filling our glasses with water.

'Jesus!' she says, and rolls her eyes. 'Stop trying to make a big deal about everything.'

She snatches a roll and starts tearing it into bits and scattering them on her plate as if she's about to feed some ducks. I sigh and sink back into the sofa. *It's just a phase*, I tell myself. *She'll grow out of it.*

'You know,' she says, continuing to shred the bread, 'it's such an unhealthy message to promote.'

We all look at her.

'I mean, leaving aside the impossibility of making an entire castle full of people go into suspended animation for a hundred years – the Prince only hacks his way through the undergrowth because he's heard she's *pretty*. Not, you know, *intelligent* or a great conversationalist. And when he sees her, he kisses her. That's not consensual, is it? So she wakes up, sees him and falls in love with him, like, that second, when he could have been a rapist, and then they get married. They don't know each other. It's all based on how they look. What's going to happen when they find out what they're *really* like? And they have to spend the rest of their lives married to each other?'

Ava bursts into tears.

'That's enough, Stella,' says Jack.

'It's a fair point,' I say, 'but let's not spoil it for Ava.'

'Every fucking thing is about Ava,' she says.

She shoves the table back, spilling our drinks, and stomps inside. I exchange a look with Jack, but we let her go. He gives Ava a hug, and refills my wine glass.

'I'll go and talk to her,' I say to Jack. 'Let's give her a minute to calm down.'

But as I sit and sip my wine, I can't help thinking about my son instead of my daughter. I need to decide what to say to Adam, how to tell him so that he'll understand, to make him see how much I have always loved him and what it cost me to leave him. Somehow I have to find words with enough weight to carry my love – and ensure he continues to keep my secret safe.

LIZZIE

'Okay. Let's go through this one more time. Hi, my name's Joe. Pleased to meet you.'

'Hi, I'm Li— Emma. Oh my God, this is so bloody ridiculous,' she said.

'Shall we try that again? Hi, my name's Joe. Good to meet you.' Joe's voice was warm and enthusiastic, as if he really had bumped into her for the first time, instead of spending two hours a day for the past five months talking to her down a crackly phone line.

'Yeah, I get it,' said Lizzie. 'I'm Emma James, blah, blah, blah.'

There was a long moment of silence and she wondered if the line had dropped out. It was unreal, pretending that her name was Emma, and so stupid going through these role-playing games with her therapist who, although he'd never set eyes on her, knew her better than anyone ever had, possibly even better than her mother or her husband.

'No, you don't,' he said, and it sounded as if he was talking to her through gritted teeth.

Joe had never been anything other than kind and patient, no matter how awful she'd been or how harshly she'd spoken to him. There was a bang as if he'd thumped the table. Her heart gave a little jump.

'You really don't fucking get it,' he said, and she stiffened. She hadn't even realized he was capable of losing his temper. 'In a month – in one fucking month – you'll be living in Bristol, on your own, without twenty-four-hour police protection,' he shouted down the phone. 'This identity that you find so ridiculous will be yours. You *will* be Emma James.' He took a breath and his voice became slightly quieter, but the anger was still bubbling underneath; he spoke as if forcing the words out, his jaw tightly clenched.

'Don't you realize: although Jon Lilley has been in custody all this time, his men are not? They've been looking for you. They are monsters. Now that their master is in a cell, they're unemployed monsters. And what do you think will happen after the court case? Either Lilley, for lack of evidence, will be a free man – and what is the first thing he's going to do, do you think? Or, by the grace of God, he's convicted and he'll spend the rest of his life in prison – who do you think he'll blame? He has an entire criminal workforce who are no longer on the payroll, thanks to what you've witnessed and your willingness to testify. Either way, you are going to be in danger for the rest of your life.' Joe lost the battle he was fighting with his temper again and yelled at her. 'This is why your identity, how you look and how you act, has to be a fucking flawless performance, the performance of your life. If you slip up, even once, Emma, you will die.'

They were both silent. She could hear him breathing heavily down the phone. Tears ran slowly down her face. She looked round at the cold, draughty sitting room. Rain spat against the window and the pane rattled. Outside she could hear the sea crashing against the shore, the wind moaning round the gable end of the house. She'd never felt so alone in her life, even though the police came every day and she spent two hours talking to Joe each morning. But he was right, of course. In a month she'd be in a city she'd never been to in her life and, if she felt alone now, it was nothing compared to the isolation she'd feel when she left Northumberland. Worse, she'd be living in fear for the rest of her life. Every time she opened her mouth to speak, it would matter what she said and how she said it.

'I'm sorry,' he said after a minute. 'I shouldn't have lost control like that. It was unprofessional, and I apologize. It's just that,' he took a gulp of air, 'I care about you. I want you to be safe. I want you to live.'

She wiped her eyes. 'I'm sorry, too,' she said, and she was.

The enormity of not taking this seriously had hit her hard, but it was more than that. She'd hurt his feelings, and she hadn't known she had the power to do that or that she would mind so much.

'We need to keep rehearsing this until if feels normal. Until it's natural. As natural as breathing to say, "Hi, I'm Emma James."'

She blew her nose and dried her eyes.

'Let's start again,' she said.

STELLA

'Come on, girls. It might even be fun!' Dad says, as he pulls up in the car park.

Of all the places he could have chosen, it had to be Tyntesfield. It's Saturday and Mum's at work. There's no ballet because of the big performance yesterday. Neither me nor Ava says anything.

'I'm going away for a few days for work – I'm leaving tomorrow – so I want to have a special day with you.'

We still don't say anything. Ava and I walk really slowly behind him.

'Where are you going?' I ask, as we pass the piggery, now converted to a solar-power centre.

'Up north. Putting in place a personnel structure for my new client.'

God, grown-ups lead such dull lives. We drag our heels, going slower and slower, as the path winds steeply down through the ironically named Paradise, with its tree ferns and palms – all part of the Victorians' plunder of Third World countries, to bring back rare stuff and show off. Everything is ornate. Even the benches are made of stone and carved with Tudor roses. All those poor people, chipping granite just to get some stale bread.

And then we see one of them. He accosts us, waving a pheasant, and Ava screams.

'Don't be alarmed, young lady. I'm the gardener.'

Ava grabs hold of Dad's hand. The pheasant's head nods with

a sickening looseness and its tiny eyes are squeezed shut, the skin all crinkly around the socket.

'I've been ridding the woods of these here varmin, for the master, Mr Gibbs. I reckon my missus will make me a nice pie with this one.'

If I weren't afraid of bumping into Mum, I'd have walked off by now. The man, dressed in pantaloons and a necktie, has the chubbiness of a modern-day volunteer. He slings the bird over his shoulder, holding it by its feet, and the bronze and russet feathers glint in the sunlight.

'Sorry, mate, we're on a tour of the house,' says Dad.

The Victorian gardener tips his cloth cap to him.

'Quite all right, sir. I should take a peek at the treasures Mr Gibbs has brought back from his travels.'

'You do know that Gibbs made all his money – which he used to build this monstrosity – from selling bird-poo?' I tell my father as he marches us ever closer to the mansion.

'Yes, Stella, I did, although technically it's called "guano". But I'm glad you're showing an interest.'

I sigh. Sometimes I think Dad has taken lessons in how not to get wound up by teenage girls. We pass an aviary. It always reminds me of *Hansel and Gretel*: there are little cages inside a replica woodsman's cottage, and it gives me the creeping dreads.

As we're standing outside the house waiting to go in, Ava murmurs, 'What if she's here?'

It's exactly what I've been thinking.

'Don't say anything,' I whisper back.

I look up. It's like the architect was on crystal meth: there's turrets and battlements everywhere. Silhouetted against the perfect blue of the sky, a griffin leers down at me from above a window covered with yellow birds painted on the stained glass.

'But what if she is? And he sees her?'

Ava is hopping about from one foot to the other with anxiety.

'She hasn't finished work yet,' I say, looking at my watch. Nervousness is making my stomach cramp.

The massive doors swing open and we follow Dad inside. The library is pretty cool. There are 2,900 books here. I'd love to take them off the shelves and check out what the Victorians were reading, but Dad would have a fit if we touched anything. He wanders into the study – a whole room just for one man to chill out in, when he got bored of reading in the library!

'She said she won't ever leave us,' whispers Ava.

'What? You *told* her?'

Ava shakes her head. 'No. But I asked her if she was going to leave us and she said, "No."'

'You idiot! She'll wonder why you were asking her.'

Ava's big brown eyes fill with tears. 'She didn't! She just gave me a hug.'

'What are you two muttering about?' asks Dad, coming back into the library.

'Have you seen this inscription?' I say. 'It's Latin for *The spoken word flies away, the written word remains*.'

Dad refuses to be distracted.

'I hope you're not upsetting your sister, Stella. Remember our talk?'

Ava loyally shakes her head and the movement scatters a tiny tear onto her cheek.

We peep in the games room. It's where the men used to hang out and smoke and drink brandy. The stuffed stags' heads hung all the way around the walls freak Ava out, so we go and wait for Dad in a little sitting room.

'This is where the ladies would take tea and do their sewing,' one of the volunteers tells us. 'It was really quite cosy.'

I give her my best teenage-girl stare and she shuts up and backs off. I'm examining an intricately carved applewood tile of a persimmon when Ava says, 'Why are you always so mean to me?'

'I'm not!'

'You hated *Sleeping Beauty*.'

I'm about to tell her how shit the story is – light on content, completely implausible and totally unfeminist – when I see her lip quivering. I was being mean because I'm worried, just like she is. And I feel even worse now. What if Dad sees Mum and finds out? What if Mum *does* leave us? And if I'm being honest with myself, I'm pretty wound up because this is Adam's house, sort of, and I might bump into him, and then I'd be utterly humiliated, as I'd have to introduce him to my dad and my little sister, and I'm not ready for that.

'Sorry,' I say. 'I thought you were amazing. You're such a good dancer. I've got two left feet, you know that. I'm just not very good at appreciating, you know, stuff like that. But I loved you in the performance and if you want to be Princess Aurora next time, I bet you will be.'

Ava smiles and flings her arms around me, stopping an elderly couple from getting past us. They beam in delight at her. Sometimes I wish I was a bit more like my little sister. I don't think I can blame it all on hormones.

We go up the grand staircase, passing a host of interlinked rooms for the ten children – or however many Mrs Gibbs had – and sit on an upholstered velvet bench. My skin is crawling with a weird combination of boredom and fear. Dad carries on alone.

'Imagine if you were in a long dress and you lived here,' says Ava, looking up at a painting of one of the Gibbs family in an old-gold dress with a diaphanous blue scarf draped around her arms.

Now *that* I can do. I picture myself as Jane Eyre: 'Suppose you're the governess and you're a bit shy, and you've only got one dress and it's dull grey and you look a bit plain. But inside you're secretly burning with—'

'And you really want to wear a dress as yellow as a lemon and stitched with precious jewels—'

'But no one notices you. So you go down the wide staircase—'

'And out to the orangery, where they grow real lemons in pots—'

'And you're so poor you've never seen one before—'

'But you meet a handsome man—'

'Who can see your intellect shining in your eyes and knows you're his perfect match, even though your situation in life is so different from his—'

'And he gives you—'

'There you are!' It's Dad. He stands in front of us for a minute, as if he's assessing us. 'I don't suppose I can tempt you to look around the chapel? Even the crucifixes are covered in jewels!'

We shake our heads in unison.

Dad sighs. 'Since you're clearly not interested in Gothic Revival interiors, shall we go to the cafe?'

I guess he's expecting us to leap up at once, but we both hesitate. *What if she's there?* This is about the time she arrives, and I've seen her in both the Pavilion and the Cowshed.

'Okay,' I say with a shrug, and the two of us get to our feet like little old ladies. I hold Ava's hand and she squeezes mine hard.

Dad looks perplexed. 'Are you ill? Tired? I expect performing onstage and in the classroom has taken it's toll.' He nods to himself, satisfied he's worked us out. 'Well, girls, if you can stagger as far as the Pavilion, I might buy you an apple each.'

I snort. 'Why do dads think they're funny?'

'That's more like it,' he says.

Ava and I hold hands all the way there, as if we're children, and then I remember that Adam might be here, so I let go just as we reach the first greenhouse. Ava races off to the Orchard playground. I force myself to look around – at the orangery, at the other people sitting in the sunshine, but I can't see Mum. Or him.

'Keep an eye on your sister,' Dad tells me. 'What would you like?'

'Anything big with lots of icing on it.'

'Heaven help us,' he mutters. 'You do know sugar is terribly bad for you, don't you? It'll give you spots, and you could end up with Syndrome X.'

I ignore him. How odd that this is kind of like Adam's garden. If it were me, I'd avoid it – all these strange people here every day. On the other hand, I could sneak down here and read and eat cake, without anyone making comments about acne. I notice a tiny room, literally built into the corner of the walled garden. The square window is boarded up with shutters. It's like *The Secret Garden* meets *Narnia*. I wonder what's inside. I wonder if Adam could get a key? I start to send him a message via Instagram and then I stop, in case he can tell where I am from the location settings.

Dad and I sit on a bench and I eat a huge slice of chocolate-fudge cake as we watch Ava doing somersaults around bits of rope strung between the apple trees. Dad has a banana, which is really pushing the boat out for his carb intake.

'So how's the party-planning going?'

I don't actually care, but if I'm going to have to be there, I might as well know what I'm letting myself in for.

'Good,' says Dad. 'I've ordered a cake. Victoria sponge, as instructed. And I've hired a caterer. Plus a marquee. Bought alcohol, of course – we know your mum loves it – and orange juice for the kids.'

'What about Coke?'

He ignores me and continues to check things off on his fingers. 'I've got all of our outfits and your mum's present, as you know. And I'm compiling the guest list at the moment.'

'Will Grossvater and Oma be there?'

'Naturally. I'm thinking about a band. You might have to help me choose.'

I stop myself from rolling my eyes. Old people have such appalling musical taste. The choice is bound to be between one shit group or another.

'You don't seem that excited about seeing your mum and dad,' I blurt out.

'Hmm. Interesting you should say that,' says Dad.

Ever Dr Seuss. Any other father would have got annoyed.

'Well, I love them, obviously.'

'Obviously,' I say, through a massive mouthful of cake.

Dad makes a face at me because of my bad manners. 'But your grandfather was a bit of a disciplinarian.'

I laugh, showering myself with chocolate crumbs, because that's the understatement of the century. I remember Grossvater telling me in his funny German sergeant-major accent that *Children should be seen, not heard.* I must have been about five and Ava was two. I was totally bemused even then – I mean, how do you get a *toddler* to be quiet?

'We moved around a lot when I was a child,' Dad says. 'Your granddad was in the army, so he got posted all over the country and to various places in Europe. I went to a couple of international schools and then to boarding school. Nowhere felt like home. Every time I came back for the holidays we'd be in some estate with all the other army families, which looked identical to every other place I'd ever lived, except when you walked outside, and then you'd find yourself in Switzerland or Bavaria.'

'Hmm,' I say, thinking that sounds really crap. Apart from the cheese and the sausages. I knew he'd lived abroad before our grandparents settled in Ireland, but Dad's never said how he felt about it.

'So that's why I was determined to create a stable home for you two. And I try not to travel much. I'll miss you while I'm in Moorside. But I bet you won't even notice I've gone.'

'What do you want: sympathy?' I suppose it explains why he's such a control freak and big on Family Outings and Family Nights at the Pub. 'Hang on a minute. Moorside? Where's that?'

'It's a nuclear-power station in Cumbria.'

Before I can think of any more questions, Ava comes running over, all hot and sweaty with her hair sticking to her face. Dad passes her a slice of carrot cake.

'Part of your five a day,' he says, but she just stares at him as if he's a total freak.

'Ask Ava,' I say.

'Ask me what?'

'She's got a much better idea about crowd-pleasing music than I have.'

Ava looks delighted, and I take the opportunity to leave them to some father-and-daughter bonding. I want to double-check that Mum isn't here. And maybe I will send Adam that message after all.

EMMA

Jack told me he took the girls to Tyntesfield yesterday.

'Oh,' I said brightly, trying to look interested, instead of anxious. I could feel my pulse quickening. 'Did you have a good time?'

I hardly took in what he said. Thank goodness I didn't meet up with Paul. What if we'd been there? I could have talked my way out of it, if we'd been in the cafe. I'm good at lying, after all these years. But if he'd noticed us before we saw them, our body language might have given us away. And what if we'd been strolling back from the cottage, our arms around each other? We'll have to be more careful.

I think about what my therapist told me when I was practising telling the lies that would become my truth, the truth of who I am now: Emma Taylor, neé James, whose mother, father and sister were killed in a car crash on the M4 and who never went to university. He said it was a myth that people look to the right when they're telling a lie. Instead, they make more hand gestures; sometimes they shrug, or they nod their heads whilst saying no. There's no single behaviour that can give a liar away. It's all the little tics that make others suspect. In short, he told me, liars act differently from the way they normally do.

So I smiled at Jack and pulled a face. 'I bet the girls hated it,' I teased him. And then I kissed him and told him I'd miss him while he was away.

He left early this morning. I woke as soon as he got up, but I forced myself to relax, to lie back in bed and take slow, deep breaths.

He kissed me on the nose and said he'd put the alarm system on as he left.

'You can go back to sleep,' he said. 'I'll miss you. I love you.'

And I closed my eyes and I did sleep. Without Jack to get us up and cook us breakfast and hustle us out of the house to some historic estate or other, we rose late and stayed in our pyjamas. We ate cereal with the radio on and read books at the table. Now Ava is playing the piano or, rather, playing with the piano. There's no one to make her practise scales or stick to set pieces, and I love the way the scattered notes hang in the air. I open the French windows and the scent of lavender drifts in from the garden. I make a pot of Earl Grey and sip my tea on the balcony.

Jack will just be arriving in Cumbria around now. He's heading to the west coast, to Moorside, a new nuclear-power station that's opening shortly. I'm envious. It's not far from there to the Lake District, to the mountains where Lizzie – where I – once lived with Paul. I doubt I'll ever go back again. The memories would be too painful and it would be too risky. I don't suppose Jack will even look up from his meetings to take in the view, though.

After a little while, Stella joins me. I beam at her. She gives me a wan smile and takes out her battered copy of *Jane Eyre*. She always rereads it when she's upset or unsure of herself in some way. She appears so grown-up, so confident, I have to remind myself that she's still a child.

'Are you okay?' I ask.

'Yup,' she nods, and hunches over her book.

I stop myself from rephrasing the question. She hates it if I push her. I hope she'll say there's something she wants to talk about, but she doesn't. And I can't help myself.

'That boy, Adam – is he a sixth-former?'

'Yes.'

'When did he start school? He's new, isn't he?'

'I only met him this term, when he began going to Book Club.'

She looks at me impatiently, as if she's desperate to get back to *Jane*. She must know the story off by heart by now.

'Do you think maybe he'd like to come to our house? For dinner? Or, you know, a glass of juice and a slice of cake?'

'Are you kidding?'

'No, Stella, I'm not kidding.'

I'm annoyed with her attitude and frustrated: how can I get in touch with a seventeen-year-old boy without raising anyone's suspicions, or his dad or her father finding out?

'Seriously, you want to ask a boy you've seen once over to our house for a "glass of juice and a slice of cake". You've never invited any of the other boys in Book Club over. So why him? I mean, Kaylee is hardly even welcome here.'

'That's not true. Kaylee and all of your other friends have always been, and will always be, welcome.'

'Right. You just manage to make them feel so awkward, by hovering over us and checking we don't "get into any harm", they never want to come here. And as for Adam,' her voice rises, 'why would *he* want to visit, when you were so goddamn creepy when you gave him a lift? You couldn't stop staring at him!'

'You should think about how you speak to people,' I snap at her, finally losing patience.

'And you need to think about who you're fucking.'

We both freeze.

'What?' I say, aghast.

She blanches. 'I'm sorry, Mum, I didn't mean . . .'

She gets up. I grab her wrist.

'How dare you speak to me like that!'

She shrugs. 'I said I was sorry.'

She shakes her arm, trying to loosen my grip as if I'm a bramble inconveniently snagging her path.

'Do not walk away from me when I'm trying to talk to you!'

I yank her arm, pulling her towards me. I'm dimly aware that inside the music has stopped and Ava has slipped away so that she doesn't have to hear us arguing.

Stella faces me defiantly. She's almost as tall as me and now, in spite of her pallor, two pink spots have bloomed in the centre of her cheeks.

'Apologize for speaking to me like that, and then tell me what you're talking about!'

This is no way to engage with a teenage girl – but I'm too wound up to back down. My heart is hammering. Stella folds her arms.

'I'm not going to apologize to you,' she spits at me. 'You're the one who's behaving badly.'

'I have no idea what you mean,' I say, putting on my best poker face, although inside I'm trembling. Could she have seen us together? No, it's impossible. We've only ever met at Tyntesfield, and that one time in the bakery.

'You know exactly what I'm talking about.'

There's a long moment of silence as we both stare at each other. In the distance I can hear the hum of cars on the Long Ashton bypass, the low of cows in the fields below us. I look away first.

'If you're insinuating . . .'

'Adam's dad,' she says.

And now I reel back and cover my mouth with my hand. How did she know? How has she found out?

'It's meant to be a secret, but Dad is organizing a surprise anniversary party for you. It's a big fucking deal. With a marquee and a band. Because he loves you. And look what you're doing. How you're repaying him.'

She's nearly crying now. She backs away and I stretch out my arms, but she shakes her head.

'You're a hypocritical bitch!' she whispers, and the fact she says these words so quietly makes it much, much worse.

I stand on the balcony, trying to gather myself. Ava comes out after a few minutes and puts her arms round me.

'Are you okay?'

'I'm fine, darling,' I say, blowing my nose.

'Are you going to leave us?' she asks in a small voice.

'Of course not,' I tell her, cuddling her. Does she know, too? Has Stella told her? 'I will never leave you. Your sister and I were just having an argument. Everything will be fine. Don't worry.'

But it isn't. Stella refused to come out of her room for the rest of the day. I'm on my own with her for a week, without Jack. And although I'm dreading having this out with her, a small, nasty part of me thinks that it's a good thing he's away, because I'll have time to talk to her properly and make sure she never tells my husband.

LIZZIE

The birds were starting to leave for Scandinavia and Siberia. Long V-shapes trailed across the sky and, at night, flocks of bar-tailed godwits wheeled above the beach. The icy wind, straight off the Arctic tundra, had abated slightly, and the days were growing longer. One night there was a storm, and in the morning the beach was littered with debris: eel grass torn from the beds around Holy Island, bladderwrack encrusted with barnacles, scraps of fishing net and opaque plastic bottles. She took it as a sign and spent the afternoon gathering driftwood, dragging the branches further up the beach towards the dunes where the sand was drier. She covered them with bin bags weighed down with rocks and left them for a few days to let the sea water drain from the sodden timber. At the back of the bungalow was a padlocked shed, but the wood was rotting and the door sagged on its rusted hinges. Lizzie unscrewed the latch with a teaspoon. Inside there were some shears, a pair of secateurs and an old lawnmower. She tipped it on its side and drained the petrol from the tank.

Around a week later, she was ready. She'd lost track of dates and even days. She finished building the bonfire in the late afternoon. It was beautiful: she'd placed shells and cuttlefish casings and shards of glass worn smooth by the sea around it. She carried her sleeping bag, the one she'd used when she'd slept at Miriam's, to the beach. Inside it she put her possessions or, rather, Lizzie's possessions. There wasn't much: a pair of North Face trousers and a Trespass fleece, Salomon trail shoes, her essay on *Renewable Energy? The Environmental Impact and Sustainability of Electricity Generated by Nuclear-Power Stations, using the proposed Moorside power plant as a case study* and her notes. Two textbooks. Her favourite novel: *Prodigal Summer.* The police had already destroyed her bank cards, her mobile and her laptop. She draped the sleeping bag on top of the pyre and poured the petrol from the lawnmower over it. When she lit it, the flames were a ghostly blue and an unnatural green as they consumed the ink in her books, the plastic in her polyester sleeping bag.

Lizzie loved beer; Emma, she thought, would like wine. She drank the cold, pale-green liquid straight from the bottle, wincing at the astringency. She walked once round the bonfire and then she stood as close as she could, the heat searing her skin, her back cold. The blaze roared, orange and amber and red; sparks danced in the darkening sky. In the distance, the sea pounded on the shore and the wind wheeled about her; a curlew keened, calling like a lost child.

She thought about Lizzie and what her short life had been like. She remembered one of Lizzie's happiest memories from her childhood. It was a hot day in August and her mother had taken the afternoon off work. They'd walked to the meadow below the ruined abbey where the river meandered in great loops, its shallow bends edged by pebble beaches. Lizzie must have been about four or five. She'd found a tiny tributary running from the Strid and had sat on the bank and dipped her toes in the water. Julia was just a baby and she lay under a white parasol and kicked her fat legs and arms. Lizzie had looked round and seen her mother sunbathing amidst a sea of buttercups. The water was shockingly cold, the sun hot on the back of her neck because she'd refused to wear a sunhat; an ice-cream van was playing a tune, and the much-anticipated picnic was in a cooler by her mother's feet. And then she'd looked across to the other side of the stream and had seen a duck – a female mallard – sleeping, barely a metre away from her. The duck had tucked her beak under her wing and Lizzie was so close she could see the striations of chocolate-brown and biscuit-yellow in the bird's feathers, the flash of royal-purple on her wing; the way droplets of water glistened like crystals scattered across her back. It was a perfect moment: her joy in seeing the bird, the trust the creature had in her, how beautiful her mother looked amidst the flowers; her baby sister gurgling and the soft murmur of the water; the certainty her mum would buy her an ice cream later: she could almost taste the vanilla on her tongue and feel the rivulets of melting ice cream running down her wrists.

Emma took the last remnant of Lizzie's life out of her pocket. It was a picture of her with Dylan in her arms, and Paul standing behind her, hugging both of them. The blaze had died down a little, and Emma dropped the photograph onto the glowing embers at the edge of the bonfire and watched the picture bubble and char and turn to ash. She said out loud:

'Though the radiance which was once so bright
  Be now for ever taken from my sight,
  Though nothing can bring back the hour
  Of splendour in the grass, of glory in the flower;
  I will grieve not, rather find
  Strength in what remains behind.'

And she bowed her head and said goodbye to Lizzie Bradshaw.

STELLA

The key doesn't fit. Adam tries another and then another. The noise of them jangling is so loud in the quiet. I glance behind us, but we're alone. Some of the keys are modern, but a few are like the keys you have in a dream – long stems and chunky bolts, a loop at the top. I imagine it's one of those keys that we need. It's strange being at Tyntesfield at night, standing where I stood yesterday, but in the dark and without the noise of children playing, the bustle of the cafe. There are other sounds, though, which make me jump: a kind of a rattle, a rustle in the bushes, an owl hooting. We're in front of the secret room set in the corner of the wall around the Kitchen Garden. Adam knows which keys open the potting sheds, the ones with spades and plant pots in, but I don't want to go inside them. I want to know what's in this one. He stole the keys from his dad, he told me. I cycled here and he met me on the back road. We left my bike leaning against the bins round the back of the cafe, in case anyone sees us.

But there's no one around. There are holiday cottages in the woods, but nobody lives in the mansion any more, and the other buildings by the orangery are offices, so if anyone were here, they'd be at least a mile away. I still feel nervous, though. Adam seems totally at ease – but then he grew up in the country without street lights and loads of people, and this is his garden, kind of. Even so, the back of my neck is prickling and I can't stop looking behind us. Adam swears under his breath. I'm just about to say we should give up and go, when the bolt clicks in the lock. Adam pushes the metal handle down and the door opens. He grins at me. There's a soft breath of air on my face, like the room has exhaled. He goes inside, disappearing into the darkness.

For a moment I hesitate, standing outside. I've spent the day in my bedroom, seething. I was so angry with Mum, literally shaking with rage. Dad works so hard and this is what she does! Fuck around with someone else, without even a shred of remorse. I kept thinking about Adam and why she wanted to ask him over. It makes no sense! I was careful not to act like he was my boyfriend and I don't think she thought he was, either, or she'd have had a million questions. And then I thought: maybe she's trying to get to know him because he's Paul's son. She's wants him to like her, for when she leaves Dad and moves in with Adam and Paul. After she went to bed, I made myself a peanut-butter sandwich and sneaked out of the window. I wanted to meet Adam to teach Mum a lesson, but now I'm here, I don't feel so sure any more.

Is he my boyfriend? Does *he* think he is? I bite the skin around my fingers and wonder if I should go back. A soft light appears.

'Come on,' says Adam.

I step over the stone lintel. The secret room is L-shaped, following the line of the stone wall. It's darker than outside because there are wooden shutters over the window, but Adam has lit a candle. There's a round wooden table and a couple of old armchairs, the seats ripped, leaking stuffing. He closes the door behind me and lights more candles, setting them on the windowsills. The walls are raw brick, the plaster has chipped off and the floor is stone. It's very dusty. There's a short shelf on metal brackets, covered with cobwebs, and some scrunched-up plastic bags in the corner, like the kind that might have had compost in. I'm worried a bat will fly out of the low roof and into my hair. I'm also disappointed. I thought it would be more interesting. And then I look at Adam and my breath catches in my throat.

He's staring at me intently. The candlelight emphasizes his cheekbones, the set of his jaw. He's on the verge of being a man. And although no one has ever looked at me like that before, like he's hungry, I know what it means. I want him, too, but I'm not ready. It's too soon. I don't know what he thinks of me, what he expects. Has he had sex before? How many girls has he had? Does he think I'll sleep with him? And if I do, will he stop speaking to me? Will it hurt? Did he bring condoms? The air feels thick, full of tension. I came here because I was angry and I didn't know what to do with that feeling, that energy – but it's gone now.

Adam smiles and takes out a flask and something wrapped in foil. I breathe again. I sit in one of the armchairs and a cloud of dust erupts into the air and makes me cough, and we both laugh. Everything is suddenly normal again. He pours me coffee and I can smell the whiskey in it. I take a sip. It burns and it's like something melting me inside. Lava. Igneous rock. Maybe it is the right time. I don't want to be a virgin for ever. Kaylee isn't. She says most of the girls aren't. Adam peels off his jumper and I catch a glimpse of his stomach, flat and muscled, a line of dark hair running upwards towards his chest. He pulls his T-shirt back down. I have an image of myself getting up and walking over to him. I straddle his thighs and he leans back, looking up at me from beneath his fringe, and then he slides his hands beneath my top . . . He opens the package.

'Oh!' I say in surprise.

He grins. 'Yeah! Not bad. I made it,' he adds, tearing a chunk off and handing it to me.

It's like a giant Chelsea bun, the bread sweet and warm, scrolled around currants and sultanas with cinnamon and sugar over the top.

'That's so good,' I say, my mouth full. I suddenly realize how hungry I am. I barely ate all day. 'My mum's a baker.'

His expression darkens. 'Yeah, I always wanted to come home to the smell of cake. You know, gingerbread hot out of the oven, or biscuits, or home-made apple tart. My mate, Nick, his mum baked a lot. She's a farmer's wife, so they're all big eaters in their family. I'd go round there and she'd feed me. I think she felt sorry for me. But it made it worse coming back to our house. It was always cold and messy and muddy, and Dad can't cook for shit. I ate fish fingers and beans on toast for most of my childhood.'

I tear another piece off, the dough squidging between my fingers.

'Then one day – I was about eleven – I thought, "Stop feeling sorry for yourself, Dylan, and just fucking get on with it." So I did. I asked Nick's mum to teach me how to bake. Nothing fancy: I can do cakes and pies and all that. And I'm bloody good at making bread.'

I swallow. 'Dylan?'

'Yeah,' he smiles at me. 'Didn't mean to let that one slip, but I guess you'll find out soon enough, when you meet my dad. Dylan's my real name. I changed it to Adam, after my granddad, when we moved. He and my grandmother died when I was a baby, not long after my mum had left. So I kind of wanted to honour him, you know? Didn't say anything to my old man, just told the school what I wanted to be called. I filled in all the forms – he hates doing that kind of shit. I've been forging my own sick-notes since I was ten,' he laughs. 'Anyhow I wanted a fresh start, you know? I can be whoever I want to be here. New life. New girlfriend.'

He stretches out his hand and grips mine. My head is reeling. Dylan? He makes cake. He called me his girlfriend! He wants me to meet his dad? Adam – or is it Dylan – is pulling me towards him.

'Wait,' I say. I wipe the sugar and crumbs off my lips. I hesitate. I want to know so much more. I feel sorry for him, growing up in the middle of nowhere with ready meals and an empty house. I think what it would be like if I'd only had my dad and no mum. I love my dad, but he's not exactly soft and cosy. He'd have had me on a diet of spinach and chicken breasts, and interval-training in the park. I shudder. 'That sucks,' I say. 'I mean, about your grandparents and your mum.'

'Yeah,' he says. 'Dad got drunk one night and burnt all the pictures with her in. But I rescued this one.'

He gets his wallet out of his rucksack and takes out a photo. I can tell it's old, it's so battered and creased that the shiny surface has become matt, and there's a black-and-orange bubble in one corner where the fire must have singed it. I take it reverently. My heart is beating so fast. In a minute, I think, we're going to be kissing – kissing properly – and maybe more, and I do want it. I want him. I'm his girlfriend. I'm Adam's girlfriend. He hasn't told anyone here but me his real name. And now he's sharing his only photo of his mum with me! It's, like, a big moment. I hold the photo beneath the candle and bend over it so I can see it better.

It's of a man and a woman on top of a mountain. Adam's dad looks younger than the man I've seen – his face smoother, rounder, and he's a bit thinner. He's grinning and he's got baby Adam on his knee. There's a sheepdog sitting at his feet. I get a bit distracted by the view – range after range of mountains – like they could go on for ever, and where they're standing is unearthly, all rocky and barren like something out of *Gormenghast*. It makes me think of that other lonely boy, Titus Groan, and I remember a line from the book:

> *He had no longer any need for home, for he carried his Gormenghast within him. All that he sought was jostling within himself.*

I look at Adam's mum then. She's smiling, too. She's slim and pretty. Like his dad, she's in full walking kit, waterproofs and those trousers made of weird material with unflattering zips at the knees, so you can make them into shorts if you get hot. I'd never wear anything like that, even if you paid me.

And then I inhale sharply. There is something familiar about Adam's mum. I hold the photo closer to the flame.

'Hey – careful!' says Adam.

'What was your mum's name?' I say, holding the photo firmly, so he can't snatch it off me.

'Lizzie,' he says, his brow furrowing.

Okay, so this is not a photo of Julia, my mum's dead sister who, for all I know, might have looked like this woman.

'Your mum . . .' I say, and then the words stick in my throat.

Of course this woman is young – the photo was taken sixteen years ago. And she's different, so I can't be certain. But there's something about her that's familiar: perhaps it's the way she's standing?

'What's up with you?' asks Adam. 'You're creeping me out.'

I put the photo down carefully and I sit back in the armchair and stare into the darkness. The flickering circle of light around the candle makes my vision pulse, purple and orange. My tongue feels as if it's swollen and I won't be able to speak. My heart is racing and it's not just because I'm so close to Adam, or because of the whiskey or the caffeine or the sugar. I look back at him and I can't see him, he's just a blur; and then my eyes adjust, and he leans towards me out of the darkness, his expression a mixture of annoyance and concern.

'My mum,' I stutter.

'What are you on about?' He relaxes a little and gives a half-smile. 'You worried she's going to discover you've sneaked out?'

'No,' I say and I point at the photo. 'I think . . . I think this could be my mum.'

He shakes his head. 'It can't be. I met her—'

'Yeah, she definitely doesn't look like this now.' I gesture at the picture. 'She's fatter and she dyes her hair blonde and does something to it. She has tons of secret appointments at the hairdresser's that she thinks I don't know about.' I examine the picture again. 'The shape of her face, or something, I can't work out what it is, what's altered – maybe her nose? It could be because she's old. Your features change when you age.'

'Nah, I don't believe you,' he says. 'It can't be.' He gets up and paces round the cramped space.

I stare at the woman again and I have a cold feeling around my heart. The person taking the picture has captured her perfectly. It's one of those fleeting moments – as if she was looking at something else and she's just turned to him and smiled: it's a smile of love and delight, a smile that says you're sharing a secret so special, only the two of you know about it. My mum has given me that smile almost every day of my life.

'It is,' I say. I know it now, with absolute certainty.

'Why would she . . . leave us? Marry your—'

"That's why she couldn't stop staring at you!' I say, and then I put my hand over my mouth and double over. I think I'm going to be sick. 'You're my brother.'

Adam yanks open the door and jumps out, over the stone lintel. I hear his feet crunch on the gravel. I stay where I am. I'm trembling. Water is leaking out of my eyes as if I've no control over my own body any more. After a few moments I get up and drag my sleeve across my face. I know it, but I don't believe it. It's too big a thing – because it means – my *brother*. I retch. I go outside. It's cold. It must be nearly midnight. The sky is bright with stars and the moon is three-quarters full. There's no sign of Adam. I walk round to the front of the cafe, but he's not there. I call his name. I go back the other way, through the flower garden, brushing past dahlias and towards the greenhouses. The sweet smell of jasmine lingers in the air and a small cloud of moths rise from the flowers. The word *incest* whispers in my mind, over and over, until I want to scream. I still can't see Adam. I walk through the archway in the wall and stop at the entrance to the vegetable gardens, but he's not here, either. The moon is bright enough to illuminate the paths and glint on the pond in the middle, but there's not enough light to see the edges. I shiver and stumble back out.

I run towards the cafe and scream his name. My voice bounces around the old stone walls, and the echoes make me even more scared. I'm crying properly now. How could he just go off and leave me? The pain drowns out my shame, just for a few moments. I take out my phone, but there's no signal here. I'm starting to feel really frightened. I'm on my own in the dark, and no one knows where I am. I run and get my bike and wheel it past the Orchard playground and up onto the lane. I stand there for a moment, beneath a beech tree, looking across the fields and up towards the woods where Adam's house is. He doesn't appear. I get on my bike and cycle home as fast as I can.

EMMA

It's chaos when I arrive at work. Izzy, Simone and Jessica are working flat out and there's a queue of customers right through the bakery and out the front of the shop. I let myself in the back entrance. Katie's face is bright red and she looks as if she could murder someone. Probably me. There's flour everywhere, and the bread dough in the bannetons, which are stacked up in trolleys, is bubbling over and escaping in long, stringy fingers.

'Afternoon,' says Harry, winking at me.

'The oven's not hot enough,' snaps Katie, as if it's my fault. 'We haven't been able to bake any of the bread or pastries.'

Everywhere I look there are trays of over-risen puffy croissants oozing butter, sausage rolls splurging their filling, and Danish pastries popping their sultanas through bubbles of leaking custard.

'Someone didn't put the oven on early enough,' says Caleb and ducks the lump of dough Katie chucks at him.

It's so loud; there's lots of people inside the cafe, trying to order and vigorously complaining about the lack of toasties, when their train is about to leave any second now. I grab an apron and check the oven. It's finally reached the proper temperature. The oven is temperamental and you have to start it early and gently, before cranking up the heat. Harry and I begin sliding in the loaves. The other oven's not warm enough, but the pastries will be ruined if they're left any longer. I take a risk, and Caleb and I get them all in the oven.

'We can always sell them with a ten per cent discount,' I murmur, and he nods.

Jessie looks as if she's about to cry, but I can't send her for a break just yet. I steer Katie into the office and tell her to write a sign saying there'll be no bread until 11 a.m. She's such a drama queen, she's been making everyone else tense. I need to check on the cakes, but I suspect Katie hasn't managed to make any, and there's nothing left over from Saturday. I assume Nate must have taken what there was when he took the delivery to Tyntesfield. I start tidying up the mess – it's not good for the customers to see, and it means I'll be able to check what else needs to be done.

Katie had agreed to cover for me this week while Jack is away, so I could get the girls up and drop them at Breakfast Club. It's just after 8 a.m., so Katie's only worked the first three hours of my shift, and I'd said I'd finish late to prep for the following day. But because the sourdough culture is a living thing, you can't suddenly change the times it eats and rests and rises. Finishing later also means I'll have to go straight to pick the girls up from school and I won't have a chance to see Paul this week. I didn't see him on Saturday as I'd hoped to, and I'm missing him already. My body aches in a way it hasn't since I was a teenager.

I finish sweeping the floors and cleaning the surfaces. Now everything is semi-tidy, I notice a massive bowl of chocolate-cake mixture.

'Caleb, lovely, do us a favour and get this into some cake tins. Don't forget to line them.'

'What the fuck are we going to do?' mouths Harry.

'Why didn't you tell her?' I say, meaning tell Katie that she needed to make five different kinds of cake before 7 a.m., but he raises his eyebrows.

'He's too much of a coward,' says Caleb.

'Or too fucking sensible,' says Harry.

'I'll make some muffins, and you could do some friands. They're both fast, and we'll at least have a gluten-free option.'

The day hadn't begun well at home, either. Ava was in an uncharacteristically bad mood at being made to get up early and go to Breakfast Club, and Stella flat-out refused. She pulled the duvet over her head when I went into her room.

'I can go on the bus,' she said. Or at least, I think that's what she said.

'I've already booked you into Breakfast Club. Come on!'

'No! I don't have to be in school yet. And there's no other kids my age there. And I don't have any timetabled lessons.'

'I can't leave you here on your own, Stella. Please be reasonable. I have to go to work, and you know I'm already going in late.'

'You can! I'm old enough!' She threw back the duvet. 'For fuck's sake, Mum, in a year I could leave school. Get a job. Vote. Legally have sex.'

'In two years,' I say.

She did look really pale, with dark rings under her eyes. She mustn't have slept, after our argument. God knows what she's been thinking and feeling. She opened her mouth to scream at me, and I held up my hands.

'Okay. Go back to sleep and catch the bus later. Text me when you get to school. And you and I need to have a talk tonight.'

I had a horrible sick feeling in the pit of my stomach as I remembered what she called me, and what she knows. She couldn't look me in the eye. I wanted to kiss her goodbye, but I was afraid she'd push me away. I remember when she was little and I put her to bed, I'd kiss her goodnight and then I'd walk backwards out of her room as we blew kisses at each other. How did we end up here, barely speaking civilly to each other? She nodded and sank back into bed, pulling the duvet over her face.

The rest of the day is a frantic blur. The bread is far from perfect, but I hope only our regulars will notice. The chocolate cake doesn't rise, so Harry and I rescue it by soaking it with an espresso-rum syrup and layering it in tiers with salted-caramel butter cream. The blueberry muffins and plum friands sell out as fast as I can make them. I bake tray after tray of chocolate-orange brownies, and a cake that I invent using the glut of courgettes that Katie picked up from the market. I decorate it with a cream-cheese frosting and scatter it with rose petals and rosemary. I'm exhausted by the time I pull up in the school car park. I haven't had a chance to sit down all day. It's too early to pick my girls up, but there's not enough time to go anywhere else. I push the seat back and wind the windows down, let the cool air slip through the car, and slide my sandals from my feet.

A shadow crosses the window and I look up. For a moment I feel as if my heart has stopped. It's my son. I sit up and shove my feet back into my shoes.

'Adam?' I call out of the window.

He walks on, as if he hasn't heard me. Maybe he didn't see me, slumped in the car. Or recognize me. After all, I am only Stella's mum, the woman who gave him a lift. Not his mother.

'Adam?' I call again, and scramble out.

He hunches his shoulders and starts to walk faster. In a moment he'll have reached the end of the car park. I begin to jog. I'll catch up with him when he gets to the bus stop, but I don't want to lose sight of him. This could be my only chance to speak to him without Stella, Paul or Ava seeing me.

'Adam!' I shout as loudly as I can.

My son veers suddenly and sharply to the left. He pushes through a gap in the hedge and vaults over the fence. I run after him. I'm out of breath when I get there. On the other side is a path that cuts diagonally across a field.

I lean against the fence and scream, 'Dylan!' And now he starts sprinting, pumping his arms as if he cannot get away from me fast enough.

He's heading towards Tyntesfield, and when he reaches the end of the fields, he'll disappear into the woods. There is no way I can catch up with him. My chest heaves and my heart is heavy, as I watch my son grow smaller and smaller as he races away from me. Why is he running? Has he somehow found out who I am? Paul must have told him – there's no other explanation for it. So I can't blame him. But I wish he could have given me a chance. Just one chance to explain how much he means to me, how much I've loved him every single day of his life.

STELLA

I couldn't sleep. My thoughts were going round and round like an animal in a cage. Like one of the birds trapped in the Hansel and Gretel house in Tyntesfield, banging its head and its clipped wings against the bars. I kept checking and rechecking my phone all night, in case Adam got in touch. I finally fell asleep in the early hours of the morning, and then Mum came in and fucking woke me up. I can't believe she'd dare show her face. I feel as if I'm going to be sick. She must have noticed, because she actually said I could stay here and catch the bus later for, like, the first time in my life. She and Ava banged around the house and then I fell asleep again after they left. At about nine I woke up for the second time, when a message came through. It said:

> Sorry. Shouldn't have left you on your own. Hope you got back ok. Couldn't handle it. MA

I guess MA is MaddAddam. No kisses or smiley emojis. I lie there looking at the ceiling, trying to get my thoughts in order. So basically, Mum married Paul and had baby Adam. Then, when he was only six months old, she left them. Adam's seventeen. Mum and Dad are celebrating their fifteenth wedding anniversary. So, a year and a half after she walked out, she married my dad. Fuck! Did she even get divorced? You can't do it that fast without your husband agreeing, can you? Could she actually be married to two men at once? That's disgusting. And wrong, obviously. Whatever. Me and Ava are Adam's half-sisters. So that means I kissed my brother. Aren't there laws against that? Am I weird? There must be something wrong with me, if I wanted to have sex with my own brother. But what I *do* know is that it's my mum's fucking fault.

I get dressed and go upstairs. There's no way I'm going to school. I send Mum a text saying I'm there, though, so she won't ring me. I can't bring myself to eat anything. I keep thinking I'm going to vomit. I try and call Adam, but he doesn't reply. The third time I leave a message asking him to call me back. My voice is all croaky, like I've been drinking whiskey or something. Then I send him a text, saying:

What the fuck? We need to talk. Call me, Ms R. x

Adam doesn't reply to that, either. I want to phone Dad, but a) he'd be pissed off at being disturbed at his big client shakedown; and b) what the fuck would I say?

Hi, Dad, It's me, Stella, your fourteen-year-old daughter. I almost slept with my brother and, by the way, did you know your wife is married to another man?

I cave in and send Kaylee a message, even though she's been ignoring me for weeks. I make myself a really strong coffee, with about ten teaspoons of sugar in, and sit drinking it and staring at my phone. I go out onto the balcony where the reception is better, in case Adam calls but I can still get Wi-Fi if he sends a message. It isn't that warm and there's a low mist covering the fields. The sky is milky-white. I wrap myself in my hoodie and then I yank it off and fling it into the garden, because it smells of him. Kaylee doesn't get back to me and neither does Adam.

I go and have a shower as hot as I can bear, and scrub and scrub my skin; I feel as if insects are crawling all over me. I wish

I could scrub my insides. And rinse out my head. Because even now, whenever I think of Adam, I still get that feeling, like molten lava, and I know it's wrong, it's so fucking wrong.

In a few hours Mum is going to come home and make up some bullshit excuse about why she's got two husbands, and try and persuade me not to tell Dad. She's a lying bitch. But the truth is, I haven't got anyone to talk to about it or help me figure out what to do. It's not like I can have a cosy chat with Grossvater or Oma, and Mum's relatives are dead. Or are they? I mean, she's changed her name. She left her own baby. She's lied about everything. She might not even have had a sister called Julia. And if Kaylee does get back to me, she'll only laugh and make me feel even more ashamed than I already do.

I go downstairs and pack my rucksack with some clothes and wash stuff, *Jane Eyre*, my journal, money – including all the stashes that Mum keeps hidden round the house and thinks I don't know about – plus my phone and laptop. I sit on my bed for a bit and look round my bedroom. What do you take, when you have to leave everything you've known and all the people you once loved? What's important? I look at the small pile of things I've gathered. It's not much, for fourteen years of life. I don't have any hobbies other than reading. I don't collect anything. I don't need a hairdryer because my hair is straight as a ruler. There's pretty much nothing you can't buy or get online, if you had to. My photos, books and music are all on my phone. My friends are a waste of fucking space. There's just Ava. She's the only person I'm going to miss. But she's the star of the whole fucking show. Mum would never leave her, so she'll be okay.

I decide to write Ava a letter to help her understand the situation, because Mum will put some spin on it. I put it in the bottom of my wardrobe, where I used to hide my diary. And then I leave. I don't set the alarm.

LIZZIE

DI Simon Duffield did a double-take. She recognized his expression. Sometimes she caught the same one on her own face, when she glimpsed her reflection in the mirror or in a pane of glass. Who was that woman? It was a strange sense of dislocation, as if she didn't quite inhabit her own body.

'You look . . . they've done a good job – I wouldn't have . . .'

He gave that nervous cough that she remembered from their previous appointments and held out his hand to shake hers, as if she were a person he was meeting for the first time.

'Did it hurt?' he asked, rubbing the stubble on his chin.

'I can see why celebrities hide. It takes a while for the bruising to go down. I looked like I was in a car crash.'

'And how are you feeling, Emma?'

'Nervous,' she said automatically.

Nervous didn't quite cover it. She felt sick, thinking about returning to Leeds, combined with a fragile hopefulness. She knew she wouldn't see Paul or Dylan, but it was the closest she'd been to either of them for the past six months. And, of course, she was petrified.

Simon hastened to reassure her. 'He wouldn't recognize you if he saw you; but he won't,' he said. 'You'll be brought in through a back entrance, like we talked about, and you'll be behind a curtain the entire time.'

'He'll hear me, though.'

'Aye, but you don't sound like you – I mean, like you did.'

'He'll know who I am.'

'He has no idea where you live or who you are now,' cut in DS Helen Robbins. 'You'll be safe.'

But at what cost? thought Emma. *And for how long?*

'Just remember what we practised,' said Helen. 'The defence will try and claim you're lying. Just answer truthfully – yes or no – don't elaborate, and be firm.'

'We're going to get him this time, I can feel it,' said Simon, holding the door open for her and squinting up at the sky. 'It's going to rain,' he muttered.

She took a last look at the bungalow, before she got in the back of the car. She wouldn't miss it, this damp, cold place, the loneliness and the isolation, but equally, starting her life over again as someone else entirely in a city she'd never been to, doing a job she'd never done before, was a terrifying prospect.

The journey was long. It drizzled during the entire drive. They swapped cars twice; the last one had blacked-out bulletproof glass in the windows, and they drove almost right to the back door of the Crown Court. Simon shrouded her in a black drape until she was inside. No one but Simon and Helen and the usher were allowed in the witness room with her. He paced and Helen made cup after cup of tea while they waited. She read. She was used to being still now. The books were fluffy, lightweight holiday reads, nothing that would upset anyone. The kind of books Emma would like, she thought, and then mentally corrected herself: *That I like.*

She could hear Joe's words in her head: *Take deep breaths. Go to your safe place: your most serene childhood memory. Think about that little duck, sleeping calmly opposite you; your baby sister is gurgling on the grass next to you; your mother is sunbathing; the buttercups catch the light and send dancing golden spots across her calves. You are happy. You are safe.*

She felt calm when she stepped into court. As Simon had told her, there was a curtain that ran around the witness stand, so that most of the court was screened out. She angled her feet towards the jury, as Simon had asked her to, so that she would remember to address them, and she looked across at the panel of men and women who were staring at her, the clerk and two barristers and their legal aides, their solicitors behind them, and felt her throat tighten, her palms prick with sweat.

Lizzie would have been fine, she thought. *She'd have treated it like a tutorial, as if she were giving evidence on nuclear power, or plastic in the sea. She'd have relished the opportunity to do the right thing, to put her argument across.*

She took a deep breath and looked at the prosecution barrister. She needed to borrow Lizzie's strength. If she was going to die, better to put Lilley away for life first, and to do it with dignity. The barrister was in his fifties, with sharp blue eyes, receding hair and a hooked nose. He was wearing a pin-striped suit and, as he stood up, his cufflinks caught the light and she closed her eyes and swallowed hard. He sounded kind, though, and he gently coaxed her through the statement she'd given to the police. She managed to recount what had happened right up until the point when Lilley had seized the child, and then she broke down and started to sob. She was crying for Dev, of course, but also for her own lost son, for Paul, for Arjun, for herself. Even for Miriam. The usher brought her a glass of water and some tissues. Just before the judge cleared the room and ordered a ten-minute recess, she saw that a few members of the jury were looking visibly distressed. A woman in her twenties wearing a white blouse with blue flowers wiped her eyes as she stood up to leave.

Lilley is barely more than a couple of metres away from me, Emma thought. *There is only this flimsy fabric and a pane of glass between us.*

Once the jury returned, the barrister for the defence rose. She was tiny, a thin, slight figure in her sixties with a craggy face; brittle, ash-blonde hair peeking out from beneath her wig. When she spoke, her voice was sharp; her accent that of a woman with a public education who'd led a life of privilege. Emma instinctively disliked her.

'It seems most odd that a young woman like yourself would be hiding in a storeroom belonging to an Asian newsagent.'

'I wasn't hiding,' said Emma, her voice becoming more clipped, her vowels elongated in response, as if she really was from the south of England.

Don't overdo the accent, Helen had warned her. *The jury won't like you.*

'As I said earlier, I had a migraine, and Mr Kumar was kind enough to let me lie down on the camp bed his six-year-old normally slept on.'

'And are you usually in the habit of lying on camp beds in dark rooms owned by strange men?'

'Mr Kumar was not a stranger. I didn't know him that well, but I spoke to him every week. And you've obviously never suffered a migraine.' She remembered Arjun's words, as he talked about his wife. 'They are debilitating.'

'M'lud,' the prosecution barrister said, getting to his feet, 'The hospital records clearly show that the witness was treated for a migraine immediately after the incident.'

'The witness could have suffered a migraine after the alleged incident.'

'The hospital records speak for themselves,' said the judge. 'Kindly move on.'

'I put it to you that you were having an affair with Mr Kumar, and that was why you were in the stockroom.'

Emma twisted the skin around her left wrist with her right hand, to stop herself from speaking rashly.

'I was not having an affair with Mr Kumar,' she said firmly. 'I was lying on his son's camp bed, talking to him about Spider-Man, while Mr Kumar fetched ibuprofen for me.'

She looked up at the jury. A woman in her forties gave her a tired half-smile, soft and sympathetic.

'In your statement to the police you described a man, fitting the description of the defendant, Mr Jon Lilley, grabbing the child, Dev Kumar, while you were attempting to call the police.'

'M'lud,' said the prosecution barrister, 'the call records from the night in question show that the witness did ring the emergency services and request police and an ambulance.'

'Please refrain from using language that undermines the witness's statement,' said the judge to Lilley's barrister.

The woman seemed undeterred. 'You claim the defendant pulled Dev Kumar into the main part of the newsagent's. You described what Mr Lilley was allegedly wearing, and then you allege the defendant took a knife and stabbed Dev Kumar.'

A man in the jury winced.

'I put it to you that the defendant could not have known the child was there, or dragged him through a closed door. And it is an awful lot for you to have seen, when you have told the court that you were in a dark room behind a shut door.'

'Jon Lilley would have known there was a child because his associate would have told him,' Emma said. 'Arjun often had the boy with him in the shop.'

'Conjecture!' interrupted the barrister.

She ignored her. 'That night Dev Kumar was pressed right up against the door, which was ajar. I tried to make him come away, but he wouldn't.' Emma took a sip of water and rested her fingertips against the wooden stand. She focused on keeping her voice even. 'Lilley was able to see him through the gap. And when his associate hit his father, Dev cried out. Lilley was standing on the other side of the door, so he would have heard him.

'Lilley reached in, through the slightly open door, and pulled the little boy into the shop. I saw Lilley's arm as he seized the child. That is how I know he was wearing a suit: a navy suit with a white shirt and gold cufflinks. The door swung closed again. I staggered backwards. Because the room was dark and with no windows, he didn't see me. The door was on a hinge and could swing backwards and forwards, and it swung a little way open again. It was through the gap, at that moment, that I saw Jon Lilley's face, and that's how I was able to identify him from the photographs of suspects that the police showed me.' She looked across at the jury, appealing to them. 'I saw Jon Lilley hold Dev Kumar, a six-year-old child, by the throat and take a knife and stab him through the eye.'

She was breathing heavily now, pinching the flesh around her wrist.

'I put it to you that have lied, from start to finish, about this whole incident, because of your friendship with Mr Kumar.' The defence barrister's tone was triumphant, but even Emma could see it was a last-ditch attempt to discredit her.

'Why would I lie?' she said, struggling to suppress her anger. 'It's true Mr Kumar was kind to me, but I only saw him once or twice a week when I did some shopping, for the three weeks before Jon Lilley attacked his son. I'm in Witness Protection because of what happened that night. I've lost everything. My family. My friends. My career. My home. The person I once was. I hope Jon Lilley goes to prison for what he has done, but I'm already there. I'm already serving a life sentence, because I happened to be in the wrong place at the wrong time on the wrong day.'

'No further questions,' said the prosecution barrister, and Emma felt herself collapse backwards, as if the woman had been tugging her forward by a leash around her neck and had now released her.

She pictured Jon Lilley, sitting silently and still on the other side of the court room, his eyes dead and cold, half-smiling as he considered the ruin of her life. She imagined he was planning how he might destroy her further. For surely, even if he went to prison for the rest of his life, he would spend his time thinking about how to take hers – and who could be persuaded to do it for him.

EMMA

Ava and I sit in the car waiting for Stella. I'm clutching my phone – I sent a message to Paul asking what the hell he was thinking, telling Dylan without warning me. We should have all sat down, the three of us together, and talked it through. If Paul hadn't been so bloody stubborn, holding off from letting me see my son . . .

'Where is she?' I say out loud.

I'm on edge. My wrist is throbbing and is a dull pink where I've been letting my hairband snap against it. The skin is smooth and shiny from the old scar, but no longer raw. I haven't done this for weeks, but now my old anxieties have come surging back. The last few pupils are hanging out in the playground; no one has come out of the main doors for the past ten minutes. I call Stella, but it goes straight to her voice message. I send her a quick text. I take a deep breath. What would Jack say?

He'd be reassuring: *Don't worry. There must be a rational explanation.*

I check my calendar, but she doesn't have anything on after school. She never does, apart from Book Club. Have I been ignoring her? I've been so focused on Ava's needs that I haven't paid Stella enough attention. I squeeze my eyes tightly shut as I remember her face, white and pinched, spitting out the word *Bitch* at me. Better, I suppose, than *Bigamist*.

'Did you see her at school today?' I ask.

Ava shakes her head, her eyes wide.

'I'm sure she'll be here soon,' she says.

The soothing sentiment sounds fake in her childish voice. I twist the skin round my wrist. My constant neuroses have pushed my eldest daughter away and made my youngest one grow up too soon. All I've wanted to do was keep them safe, but I can see now that I've made mistakes. I ring Kaylee and she answers straight away.

'Emma?' she says in surprise, her husky voice deepening.

'Hi, Kaylee. Sorry to bother you, but have you seen Stella? It's just . . . we're waiting for her in the car park and there's no sign of her. Is she with you?'

'No. I'm with my dad. We're back home already.' There's a short pause and then she says, 'She didn't come into school today.'

'She texted me to say she was there this morning. She caught the bus.'

'Right.' There's an even longer pause and then she says more firmly, 'She definitely wasn't in registration or her tutor group in the morning. She could have come in late, but I didn't see her. And we're in the same study group.'

'Oh. And she's not with you now?'

I say it flatly, although I know it'll wind Kaylee up. I've seen some of her legendary tantrums; another reason why I wasn't that keen on her friendship with Stella. But when she replies, Kaylee's voice is small and a little ashamed.

'We fell out – over nothing. I should have made it up to her. She's been my best friend for years.'

'So you have no idea where she is?' I press the point before Kaylee can become tearful. Or before I start thinking about my own so-called best friend and how what happened to her was my fault.

'No, but I'll let you know as soon as I hear anything.'

I'm not sure I believe her. Those two constantly messaged each other. I'll ring Ted, Kaylee's dad, if I can't get hold of Stella. He always let Kaylee walk all over him, but he'll be able to see how serious this is . . . I try my daughter again, and then the house, but there's no answer. Ava and I try and get into the school; the door is locked, though, and the receptionist has left for the day. My call goes straight to the school's answerphone.

I take Ava's hand and say unsteadily, 'Let's go home. She might be there, waiting for us.'

'I hope so, Mummy,' says Ava, squeezing my hand.

I drive back as fast as I can. Ava's face is white beneath her summer tan. I think of Dylan. I'm certain he knows I'm his mother. He's angry, resentful, hurting. He and Paul are the only people who know my true identity. Could Dylan – or rather, MaddAddam – have posted something online? That's all it would take for Jon Lilley's men to track me down, to find my family. To find Stella.

I pull into our driveway and run across to the house. When I unlock the door, there's no telltale peep from the alarm. My heart rate shoots up. Anyone could get in, and I have a sickening feeling as I think about leaving my daughter asleep alone in the house on the ground floor . . . Someone could have broken in through that window. It would take a lot of force – it's triple-glazed – but even so . . . I can see her unmade bed. A man could stand here and watch my daughter sleeping. Why didn't we realize? Putting the bedrooms on the ground floor now seems like an insane idea. Lilley's words echo in my head: *I can assure you that, as well as killing you, I will hunt down your family and I will kill them, and then I will find your friends and I will kill them, too.*

'Stella!' I shout.

I check upstairs and then I run downstairs and slam open her bedroom door. Her room, as I'd seen from the outside looking in, really is empty. I search the other bedrooms and the bathrooms.

Ava is standing in the middle of the sitting room. She looks like a broken doll whose batteries have run down.

'Should we ring the police?' she says.

For a brief moment I'm aware of how it might look from the outside. Stella is fourteen. School only broke up an hour ago. How many other parents would go into a ridiculous panic this soon? But then, our family isn't like other families. We've never given Stella much freedom. Jack, at heart, is a disciplinarian like his military father; and I – well, I have always known the consequences of losing sight of my girls for even a short time.

The phone rings, making us both jump.

'Probably one of her friends,' I say, grabbing the handset. 'Hello?'

'Hi! I thought you'd just have got home from picking up the girls. I'm on a coffee break. It's so beautiful here – you'd love it! Did you survive getting them off to school? Practically a lie-in for you!'

It's Jack. The cheeriness of his words is in such a stark contrast with what is happening here that for a moment I'm speechless.

'Emma?'

'It's Stella,' I say. 'She's gone.'

'What do you mean?'

'I left her to take the bus this morning,' I say, my throat dry and scratchy. 'She texted to say she was at school. But when I went to pick her up, she wasn't there. Kaylee says she didn't come in.'

'Who've you called?' he asks, immediately businesslike.

'Kaylee. The school. There was no answer. I'll ring a few of her other friends and Kaylee's dad in a minute. I thought she might be here . . .'

'With any luck she's in town with her mates. She's not answering her phone?'

'No.'

I wonder if she's with Dylan. There's a ping as a message flashes up on my phone.

'Hang on,' I say, snatching up my mobile.

I haven't told him yet. Still waiting for your decision . . . I love you.
Paul x

I swallow uncomfortably. 'It's nothing, just a text about work,' I tell him.

'Check if any of her things are missing,' says Jack. 'Then ring the police.'

'You mean . . .'

'Well, what might she have taken, if she went into Bristol?'

'Or if she's run away,' I whisper.

'Did you have an argument?'

'Yes,' I say.

And if nothing is missing, what then? Could someone have abducted her? If he'd had a knife, there would be no sign of a struggle . . .

'I'll get off the phone,' he says. 'Call me. I'll come home tonight. I'll wrap things up here.'

I don't say anything.

'Emma?'

'Yes?'

I expect he's going to say something kind and supportive, to reassure me like he always does when I get anxious, to tell me that the argument was not my fault; to reiterate that he loves me and misses me, and he'll be there soon. After all, he doesn't know that I have always been – and now Stella could be – in grave danger.

He says, 'The police won't take this seriously at first. She's a teenager, not a child, and they won't respond straight away. You have to find her. Now.'

The fact that Jack thinks this is serious, too, makes my heart rate soar. I turn in a half-circle, about to do something, but I'm not sure what. What should I do first? Call Stella's friends? Kaylee's dad? Check Instagram? Search her room for missing possessions?

Call the police? My brain feels foggy but my pulse continues to rocket. I once heard of a man who had a congenital heart defect – I think the guy was a footballer. He was rushed off the pitch because everyone thought he was going into cardiac arrest. His heart rate was 260 beats a minute. He said you could literally see his heart pounding through his chest. That's what mine feels like now. I put my hand over my breastbone.

'Has Stella run away?' asks a small voice.

'I'm sure she hasn't,' I say, suddenly remembering my other daughter, still standing behind me, who's just heard everything I said to her father. 'She's probably just with her friends. Do you know what she would have taken with her, if she was going out?'

Ava's face clears as she realizes she can help. 'I'll go and look in her bedroom,' she says.

As soon as she's out of earshot, I ring the police. As Jack predicted, the woman taking my call didn't sound too concerned. She said to do all the things my husband had already told me and, if I still can't find Stella, to call back and she'll send two officers to the house.

'Hopefully she's with her friends, letting off some steam after the exams, love. I'll log your call now. Can you take down this reference number, if you do need to ring us back? Have you got a pen handy?'

I stifle a sob as I hang up. I check Stella's and then MaddAddam's Instagram accounts, but neither of them have posted anything for the past couple of days; there's no mention of where she might be, or, thankfully, anything about me. There's a sharp wail and I feel a stab of fear. What has Ava found?

I run downstairs to find my youngest daughter in tears, clutching a piece of paper. *At least it's just a bit of paper*, I think, and then I remember the other piece of paper I received all those years ago.

'She's gone,' she hiccups through her sobs.

I give her a hug and try to take the sheet from Ava, who clutches it to her chest. It's already damp with her tears, but I can see it's Stella's handwriting.

'It's okay, Stella won't get into trouble,' I say as soothingly as I can, when what I really want to do is snatch it out of Ava's hands.

'Is it true?' she says, looking up at me with her big, brown eyes.

She hands me a letter, torn out of a notebook, the paper smooth and thick and creamy. I smooth it flat; apprehension makes my hands tremble. I can't look Ava in the eye. I read:

Dear Ava,

Whatever happens, please remember that I love you. I don't want to leave you, but I don't know what else to do. Mum and Dad love you so much. Everything will be okay.

Lots of love,

your big sister, Stella xxxxxxxxxo

'It's true, she's really gone,' cries Ava, and flings her arms around me.

Thank goodness it is from Stella, and it wasn't written with Lilley's men standing over her. She hasn't said anything about Paul, either. I'm relieved at first, then panic-stricken. She hasn't been abducted, but wherever she is, she's vulnerable. If Paul and Adam know who I am and where I live, and if Adam has told anyone, then it's possible that Lilley's men might find out, too. I have to find her.

I can't send MaddAddam a private message, so I risk posting a public one:

I know you don't want to speak to me right now, but we need to talk. It's about Book Club.

'Where would she go?'

I feel paralysed. I should be making phone calls, sending messages, trying to track my daughter down, but I have a strong suspicion that she isn't with any of her friends. She's gone somewhere else and she hasn't told anyone.

MaddAddam sends me a friend request. When I click on the link, I get a private reply.

I've nothing to say to you.

I type: Stella is missing. Help me find her.

No idea where she is, he replies.

A moment later another one comes through: Have you tried The Station? We went there sometimes.

The Station? This is the first I've heard of it. She and Dylan have been going out together? A cold, sick feeling engulfs me.

He's her brother – and she didn't know.

What else has my daughter been doing that she hasn't told me about?

Ava peers at the screen. 'Yeah, The Station,' she says, 'She could be there! It's, like, a kind of cafe for teenagers to hang out.'

'Let's go,' I say, taking her hand.

I pull up on the double-yellow lines outside the converted fire station. I catch sight of the words *Cake, Baking!* and *Sexual Health*, as I run inside. Everyone looks up, their expressions hostile. They're all teenagers and I feel immediately uncomfortable and out of place. Not that I care at this precise moment. Ava must feel the same, because she leans into me.

'I'm looking for my daughter,' I tell the barman. 'She's fourteen. She's missing.' I shove my phone towards him, a picture of Stella on the screen.

He shakes his head and goes back to scooping ice into glasses.

'Who's in charge?' I shout.

He looks up at me sharply and says quietly, 'I would tell you, if I'd seen her. We take safety very seriously here. My shift started at twelve. I definitely would have noticed her if she'd come in.' He pushes his order pad towards me. 'Tell you what. Write your number down. I'll call if I see her, and I'll inform the staff coming for the changeover at six. What was she wearing?'

I'm about to describe her school uniform, when I realize I've no idea. She wouldn't have been wearing it, if she'd been planning on running away. I admit I don't know, but add, 'Probably Converse, black jeans, a T-shirt or a plaid shirt and a grey hoodie. It's all she ever wears.'

After I've given him my contact details, I grab Ava's hand.

'Where are we going?'

'The bus station,' I say. It's just across the road. Ironically, the police station is in between the two buildings. I'm so enraged that the police haven't taken me seriously, I want to spit at the panda cars parked outside as we pass.

There's no sign of her there, either. The men at the ticket desk and the woman in the information booth tell me they haven't seen Stella. Her hair is a striking feature – but if she had a cap on or the hood of her sweatshirt up, would they really have noticed her?

I'm just about to walk through the station again and check the toilets, when one of the men at the counter says, 'Only National Express here, love.'

'What do you mean?'

'Well, kids go on Megabus, don't they? Cheaper. You can travel for a pound.'

Oh, of course, I think.

'Goes from outside Colston Hall, love, but it's just a stop. No ticket desk. If she's on a bus already, she's gone.'

My heart sinks. We walk round the block to the music hall, its green-gold façade glittering dully in the late-afternoon light.

'Where would she go?' asks Ava, her forehead crumpled with worry.

'I don't know,' I say, and it's true, I don't. I'm sure she wouldn't try to visit Jack's parents in Northern Ireland. They're not exactly the warm type. *Jack*, I think, *she might try and find him*. But that doesn't seem likely, either. I'm pretty sure she's run away because she doesn't want to tell him what I've been doing. Guilt courses through me. Where *would* Stella go?

There's a straggly line of people waiting for the Megabus. Stella isn't amongst them. I walk along the queue and show every single person the photo of my daughter; my phone keeps going into screensaver mode and I don't know how to stop it. Most people look bored. Only an older woman with dyed henna-red hair and three inches of white roots shakes her head sympathetically and says, 'Och, she's a bonny lass. Hope you find her, pet.'

No one says they've seen her.

'How would we know if she'd got on a bus before we arrived?' asks Ava in a small voice.

'I'll phone head office. I'm sure they'd have a record if she bought a ticket,' I say, with an optimism I don't feel. Ava's right. Stella might have been on a bus first thing this morning. She might have paid for her ticket in cash. She could be in Scotland or France by now, for all I know. 'Let's try the train station.'

It feels odd walking through Temple Meads, knowing *Kate's* is beneath us; the sourdough leaven living, breathing, growing in the dark tunnel below our feet. Above us pigeons coo and seagulls screech. The Transport Police start checking through CCTV footage, and Ava and I walk from platform to platform until Ava bursts into loud, noisy sobs.

'But where would she go? She's got nowhere to go!'

I realize Ava hasn't eaten since lunchtime and it's now nearly seven o'clock, so she's probably having a blood-sugar low. I buy her an orange juice and a cheese sandwich. I feel too sick to eat, although today was so busy, I missed lunch. We return to the Transport Police's office and sit on hard plastic chairs attached to the floor. I recognize the officers on duty: they're in *Kate's* every day for a coffee and a croissant; the male officer always orders a sausage roll on Fridays. I give the sausage-roll man the reference number from my earlier phone call to the police.

The idea of Stella being on her own at night is terrifying.

'Maybe she wants to be Jane Eyre,' I say to Ava, more to try and make her feel better than because that's what I really think. 'Maybe she's gone up north to find a vast Gothic mansion.'

'That doesn't make any sense,' says Ava, resolutely refusing to play along.

I text Jack, and then Paul.

'No sign of her, Mrs Taylor,' the police officer tells me. 'I've called it in. Best thing you could do is go home, in case she's there, or she returns. I'm sending two officers round. They'll arrive in half an hour.'

In the car I send Dylan a message.

Are you sure she isn't with you?

He doesn't reply. I'm certain he's found out who I am, even though Paul says he hasn't told him. I send him another message and this time I try and provoke him.

We have to find her. She's your sister.

He responds almost immediately: I fucking know that. Now.

I type back: So help me. Help her.

Have you tried Tyntesfield?

I start driving back towards our house. If she's playing *Jane Eyre*, Tyntesfield *is* a large Gothic mansion, albeit in the South-West. More importantly, it's where she's seen me and Paul – I'm guessing – though how she did, I can't imagine. And a tiny voice whispers, *And maybe that's where she's been meeting Dylan.*

I switch on the voice-recognition software and dictate a message to my son.

It's shut now. How would she get in?

Same way you did.

Why would she go there?

'Who are you talking to?' asks Ava from the back of the car.

She looks slightly more composed, now that she's had something to eat, but she's still pale.

'Dyl . . . Adam, Stella's friend. I'm sending him a message.'

Adam doesn't reply. I slow down when I reach our house, but the police haven't arrived yet. There's a ping and a text from Jack arrives.

Just finishing my presentation. I'll set off in half an hour. Call me as soon as there's news. x J

'Why aren't we stopping?' asks Ava.

'We're going to Tyntesfield,' I say. 'In case she went there.'

I look at my youngest daughter in the rear-view mirror, but she doesn't protest. If she thought it was a stupid idea or out of character for Stella, I'd be able to tell. Maybe Ava knows more than she's telling me. I remember that day she and Jack and Stella went round the mansion. What do they know? What have they seen?

I think about my eldest daughter. She's not an outdoorsy person. In another life, if she'd been Paul's daughter, she could have become one. But we've always lived on the outskirts of the city. She's never been into sport or hiking, and Jack and I have never tried to persuade her to try those pursuits. So if she did go to Tyntesfield, she'd have gone somewhere indoors. A vivid image comes into my mind of Paul, of a room with yellow birds at the window, of carved wooden pomegranates . . . I suppress it.

Can you get the keys? I dictate.

We'll meet you by the dog cage.

I can't help shuddering. He means the large, curved metal cage in the courtyard near the servants' entrance that Paul and I used to get into the house. It's large enough for a child to stand inside and, like the aviary on the other side, reminds me of something sinister out of a fairy story. I think of the network of cellars below the house . . .

My heart starts to thump again. I'm going to meet my son and my husband with my youngest daughter. It's what I've always wanted, yet not like this. Never like this. What the hell am I going to say to them when we're all together?

It's dusk and the giant Douglas firs are silhouetted against the plum-bruised sky. Bats fly round the trees, tiny shards of black, like optical illusions. I can smell cut grass and shaved wood.

'Are we allowed to do this?' asks Ava nervously.

Her hand is cold in mine.

'We're members, aren't we?' I tell her, although I'm as anxious as she is. What if someone has followed us? We're alone, it's night and there's almost no one around for miles, and the son who doesn't want to speak to me is the only person who knows we're here. I remember what DS Helen Robbins once said to me: . . . *an unprotected family – it would be a walk in the park for men like them.*

We reach the house, all spikey turrets and row upon row of dark windows. I scan the ones I can see. As we reach the courtyard, Paul steps forward and hugs me tightly. I fold into him, let him take my weight, just for a moment.

'We'll find her,' he says.

'Ava, this is Paul,' I say.

She looks at him warily, curiously.

'And this is Dylan,' Paul says to her. 'Although I've just found out he's been telling his Bristol mates he's called Adam.'

Adam doesn't say anything. He glares at me from under his fringe and, with an effort, pulls himself off the wall he's been leaning against.

'I've checked a few places already,' he says gruffly. 'Places we went.'

I choke back my response. Paul squeezes my hand and his look says, *Now is not the time.*

He lets go swiftly, but Ava has already seen.

'She's been trying to get hold of me, so I thought maybe – maybe she'd come here looking for me. She knows I live here,' Adam adds. He stares at his trainers when he speaks rather than meet my gaze.

'I've been walking round the estate since I got your message, and I can't be sure, but I don't think she's in the grounds,' says Paul. 'I mean, the gardens – the estate is vast, and so's the wood. I can't search it all. I thought maybe we should start with the house? It's possible she could have gone in, and then hidden when the place closed.'

'What would she do that for?' mutters Adam.

'I don't know. I doubt she'd hang around outside, though,' I say. 'Let's just have a quick look, and then I need to get back home. The police are on their way.'

Paul nods. He unlocks the servants' door and steps into the darkness. He switches off the alarm system by the door.

'Are you going to get into trouble?' asks Ava in a breathy voice.

'Probably,' Paul says. 'It'll be worth it if we find your sister.'

He hands a torch to Adam, who disappears into the darkness, and then gives me one.

'I'll take the first floor. Why don't you and Ava go to the top floor?'

Ava and I follow the narrow flight of stairs up to the servants' quarters in the eaves of the house. Ava starts to cry.

'I'm scared.'

'There's nothing to be frightened of. There's no one here – apart from us, and maybe Stella. It just seems a little creepy,' I say, as a stair creaks under my foot and Ava yelps. I try and suppress my own rising panic.

We reach the landing. This floor is closed to the public. The carpet muffles our footfalls. I try each door in turn. Most of them are locked. One opens and I stand in the doorway and shine my torch around it. It's shrouded in white shapes. Ava gives a little scream.

'Only sheets,' I say, hugging her to me. My heart is pounding.

'William Gibbs, the owner of Tyntesfield, amassed a fortune and spent some of it on treasures he collected from around the world,' I say. 'That's what your dad told me.'

His collection of curiosities is stacked up and draped in sheets, but my torch picks out a few that haven't been covered up: a glass dome with tiny, stuffed hummingbirds, the smooth carapace of an ostrich eggshell, a jade-green ammonite. This would be the perfect place for someone to stalk us. There are so many hiding places. Even if Paul heard anything, it would be too late by the time he reached us; and surely, if Lilley's men were here, they'd kill him and Adam, too, as Lilley always promised.

I am nothing if not a man of my word . . .

Vast shadows loom over us as I swing my torch across the room: only an elk's antlers, I reassure myself and Ava.

We back out and I call Stella's name softly. If she is here, I don't want to frighten her. Below me I can dimly hear my husband and son doing the same thing. The need to find my daughter is overwhelming. I check my phone but there's no signal. This is stupid. I have no idea where Stella is, and breaking into a mansion and searching the attic is insane. We should go back and talk to the police. Perhaps it's time to tell them – not who I am, but that I was in Witness Protection. They'd have to take my concerns seriously then. I hesitate when I reach the next door. This is the door to the room that Paul and I made love in. I take a deep breath. I'll quickly look inside, just in case, and then go home and make the police ramp up the search for her.

The door suddenly jerks open and Ava and I both shriek.

'What the fuck are you making so much noise about?' says Stella, blinking in the glare of the torch.

We lurch at her and hug her at the same time. For a moment she's rigid, and then she hugs us back and bursts into tears.

'Thank God you're okay,' I whisper into her hair.

'I saw the stained-glass birds in this window when I came here with Dad. I wondered what this room would be like.'

I look behind her at the four-poster bed with the imprint of her body in the centre of the damask throw; the turret in the corner; the glass birds glint a frosty-yellow. I shiver.

'I got as far as the Megabus, but then I didn't know where to go. So I came here. I thought I'd hide tonight and by the morning I'd have figured out what I was going to do, where I was going to go.'

I take her hand and she doesn't protest.

'Let's get you out of here.'

The four of them – Ava, Stella, Adam and Paul – walk in a straggly line down the road. I lag behind, calling the police to say we've found Stella, leaving a message for the school, for Kaylee, another one for Katie, to tell her I won't be into work the next morning. I sent Jack a text earlier, asking him to pull over, so we can talk.

'She's okay?' he says, when he rings.

'Yes,' I say. 'She's fine. I haven't talked to her yet. I'm just so relieved. I want to get her home and warmed up first.'

'Go easy on her,' he says.

'Where are you?'

'Not that far from Moorside,' he admits. 'I'll get home as fast as I can. The roads should be clear.'

I watch my family for a moment. Adam looks intensely awkward. His shoulders are hunched, his body is angled away from the others and he's walking as far away from Stella as he possibly can. Now that we've found Stella and she seems to be unharmed, the nauseous feeling in my stomach returns, as I wonder what has happened between my son and my eldest daughter.

'There's no need,' I say to Jack. 'This is a really big job for you. You were meant to be there for the week. If you pull out now, they'll let you go and hire someone else instead. We've found her and she's okay. I'll take the rest of the week off. We can manage. Go back and finish the job, and then come home when you can.'

'No, I need to be with you. With Stella.'

'Honestly,' I say, 'we're okay. I'll talk to her. We're safe. She's safe. Don't worry.'

I need the chance to talk to Stella on her own before Jack gets here. I hold my breath, waiting for his response.

'Well, it is a huge contract. And even though I told them it was an emergency, you're right, they'll call someone else in to set up the personnel structure. They even asked me for a recommendation!'

'You see.'

'All right. If you're sure. But call me if there's any problem. I'll try and get this over with as fast as I can and come home early.'

'Take your time,' I say. 'Better to do the job right.'

'And you're okay?'

'Yes.'

'I love you.'

'I love you, too,' I tell him, and then I hurry after Paul and my children.

'Do you want to come back to our house and have a cup of tea?' asks Paul.

'Do you have any hot chocolate?' asks Ava.

'I'm sure I can rustle up hot chocolate. And Dyl . . . Adam made a fruitcake today. Do you like cake?' he asks Ava, who nods vigorously and starts to tell him what her favourite kinds are.

I interrupt. 'We need to talk. All of us,' I say.

We sit in an awkward circle on the sagging sofas and armchairs in Paul's front room. Adam passes us each a plate with a thick slab of fruitcake, the butter in uneven lumps. I set mine down. I still can't manage to swallow anything. Adam's face is fixed in a perpetual scowl. His body is tight with barely suppressed anger. Stella has her head forward, her hair hanging over her face. Ava tucks into her cake with huge, ravenous bites.

I clear my throat nervously and glance at Paul, who's perched on the arm of the sofa, next to Adam. 'I think everyone apart from Ava knows this, but I'm going to say it, so there's no confusion.'

'You're having an affair with Paul,' says Ava, through a mouthful of cake.

I stop, my mouth open. This wasn't how I imagined telling them.

'She read my diary,' says Stella.

'Well, technically it's not an affair,' I say. 'Paul and I are married.' I hurtle on, speaking faster and faster. 'We met and married when we were at university.'

'What? You didn't even manage to get A-levels!' says Stella.

That's so typical of her, I think, *to focus on whether I have any qualifications.*

'Actually, your mother has four,' says Paul, 'and she had a place to do a Masters in Environmental Science at Leeds University.'

'I got pregnant. With Dylan. Adam, I mean. Adam's my son. Your half-brother,' I say, keeping my gaze firmly focused on Ava. 'Then, when Adam was six months old, I was forced to leave. And after that I met your father, Jack, and had you two.'

'I don't know why the fuck you're still speaking to her,' shouts Adam, jumping to his feet. 'She shouldn't even be in our fucking house.'

'Sit down,' says Paul. He stands up. Adam is as tall as him, but Paul is broader. 'Please listen to what she's got to say. No one is asking you to forgive her for leaving you, only to hear her out.'

'I'm not listening to her crap excuses,' he yells and pushes past Paul.

I get up and stand in front of the door. Adam towers over me. I don't touch him, although I yearn to take him in my arms.

'I'm afraid you can't go,' I say. 'If you do, you'll put all of us in danger. Everyone in this room. Please sit down.'

Adam breathes heavily, glowering at me, then throws himself back on the sofa. Ava, who is sitting at the other end, bounces into the air and spills hot chocolate on her knee.

'I don't understand,' she says. 'Why did you leave your baby? Did you get a divorce?'

'No, she fucking didn't,' says Stella. 'It's called "bigamy" and it's illegal as well as being immoral.'

Ava screws up her face as she struggles to understand Stella.

'I didn't choose to leave my son and my husband,' I tell them, 'I had to. I saw something terrible – an awful crime – and I had to go into Witness Protection.'

I'm sure Stella and Adam have a hazy idea of what Witness Protection is, even if it's called something different these days, and would be insulted if I tried to explain it to them, so I continue to focus on Ava. I tell her as much as I can about what happened, what it meant to go into Witness Protection and how I had to change.

'I wore a wig at first, until my hair grew long and I could dye it and straighten it permanently, to take out the curls. I had my freckles removed, and plastic surgery on my nose and round here . . .' I run my fingers under my eyes and across my cheek-bones. 'I even had special lessons to change how I spoke and stop me sounding like a Northerner.'

For the benefit of all three of my children I add, 'So, no one must ever find out who I really was, or the bad men who committed the crime might come and find me. And if they find me, they might find you. It's horrible and frightening, but I need you to understand how serious this is. You have to think of me as Emma, not Lizzie. You must never tell anyone what I've told you. Adam,' I say, turning to my son, 'I have always loved you. I always will love you. I've thought about you every single day of my life. I never wanted to be apart from you. Because of the sacrifice I made – and you had to make – Jon Lilley went to prison for the rest of his life.'

'And we were safe,' says Paul.

'It doesn't make it right. Or bearable,' I add. 'You lost your mother. I lost you. Nothing can ever make up for that.'

Adam doesn't say anything. He remains sprawled on the sofa, gazing straight ahead, so that he won't have to look at me or Stella.

Ava's eyes are round.

'So you're kind of on the run? You had a nose-job? I've got a big brother?'

'The car crash was a lie then?' says Stella. There's a sneer in her voice. She tosses her hair over her shoulder as if she's imitating Kaylee.

'In a way, it wasn't. Paul's just told me that your grandparents – my mum and dad – died shortly after I went into Witness Protection. My sister is alive, but she's in Australia. I knew, though, I would never see any of them again, so I had to pretend they were dead because otherwise . . .'

I stop and look down at my hands. The adrenaline has left me. I found Stella. My first husband is by my side. My children are all here, yet this is not the joyful, tearful reunion of my dreams. My eldest two are looking at me as if they hate me.

'What about Dad? What about my dad?' yells Stella, jumping to her feet.

'He doesn't know,' I say.

'I'm going to tell him,' she says. 'He deserves the truth!'

'Stella—' says Paul.

'Get out of the way!' she screams at him. 'You're not my father!'

'Why don't you all stay here tonight?' Paul says. 'We can talk about Jack in the morning, and what you want to say to him.'

'What? Like one big, happy fucking family?' she spits in his face.

He puts a hand on her shoulder as if she's a colt about to buck. 'Let me show you the spare room. You and Ava can share.'

'I want to see, too,' says Ava, and follows them.

In spite of how I'm feeling, I give a half-smile. Paul has always had that ability to soothe frightened animals, nervous hikers, irate drinkers. I look over at Adam, hoping to see a softening in his features, the beginnings of an understanding. How I long to hold him. My son. His face is impassive. He gets up with as much dignity as he can and strides out of the sitting room. A couple of moments later I hear his bedroom door slam.

Stella and I have a lot to talk about, I think. I rub my eyes and blow my nose. I hope nothing has happened between her and Adam. I blame myself. I should have seen it, although she hid her feelings for him. Even so, I should have guessed.

Paul kneels down in front of me. 'They're beat,' he says. 'They'll sleep pretty well.' He runs his finger down the curve of my cheekbone. 'Give Adam time. He'll come round.'

I nod.

He takes my face between his palms. 'I love you,' he says. 'I am so sorry about what happened to you, what you've been forced to go through. Everything, and everyone, that you lost. And that the last time we spoke, it was about Miriam.' His eyes glisten. 'I'll do anything you want. Whatever you need. I promise.'

'I love you too,' I say, realizing that I've finally made a decision. 'I never want to leave you again. Will you have us? All of us.'

'All of you,' he says, and kisses me gently. 'One big, happy family.'

I wake early. Force of habit, I guess. I ease out of Paul's embrace and check on the girls before I go down to the kitchen. There's a note on the table:

Dad, Gone out for a bit. Back later. MA 🙂

I'm not surprised, but it still hurts. I'd hoped we could talk, have breakfast together. Much as I've loved the excitement, the frisson of danger with Paul, I've also craved domesticity. I measure out flour, drop eggs in a well in the centre, stir in the milk. I fry a stack of pancakes, caramelize pears and bananas in honey, set out orange juice and coffee.

Paul comes in and kisses me on the cheek. 'Smells good.'

I show him the note.

'MA?'

'MaddAddam. It's his Instagram name.'

'Oh. Sorry.' He gestures towards the pancakes. 'I should find Adam and check he's okay, and I need to walk Gil, and I've got to get to work. Save me some?'

I suspect the girls were waiting on the landing because, as soon as Paul leaves, they stumble downstairs and sit blearily at the table.

'Ava snored and kicked all night. I didn't get a minute's sleep,' says Stella through a curtain of tangled hair.

I pass them a plate each.

'Yuck! What's that? We always have strawberries with our pancakes,' says Ava.

'That's all Paul had,' I say.

She puts her fork down. 'Are we going to live with him now?'

'I don't know. We need to talk about it.'

'I don't want to. I want to go home.'

'Me, too,' says Stella.

'Okay,' I say, defeated, my dream of a happy family meal evaporating. It was stupid of me even to think it would be a possibility this soon.

I text Paul to tell him we're leaving and we'll talk later, and then ring the school to let them know that the girls are both ill.

'Some bug they've caught,' I say cheerily, and then remember the phone call I made last night. It would have been better to sound downbeat and leave a message saying we need to have time to bond and heal as a family. My ability to lie convincingly is slipping.

The girls are unnaturally quiet in the car.

'Is there anything you want to talk about? Anything you want to ask?' I say, dreading what their response is going to be. 'I know it was a lot to take in last night.'

Neither of them responds. As soon as we're back in the house, they both slip away to their bedrooms. I make Stella a cup of coffee and take it downstairs.

'I'm sorry,' I say. I move a pile of T-shirts from the armchair in the corner of her room and sit down.

'For what?'

'Everything. But mainly, I'm sorry about Adam. Did anything happen between you?'

'Mum!' She blushes and ducks her head.

I wait. Jack has told me I talk too much, I rush to fill the silence. Hold back, he'd said, and the other person will want to fill it instead.

After a couple of moments she says, 'Nothing happened.'

Relief floods through me. But then I think of what a teenager's 'nothing' really means.

'That's good,' I say, as evenly as I can. 'Even if something did happen, it's not wrong. You don't have to feel bad. You didn't know he was your brother. Sometimes brothers and sisters who don't grow up together are attracted to one another. It's because they look alike and maybe their personalities are similar.'

'I look like Adam?'

'Yes,' I say, 'and you got on well with him, didn't you?'

'Yeah, there was a connection. Even though we don't have much in common.'

She is scarlet with embarrassment now, staring hard at her duvet cover and blinking furiously to keep her tears at bay.

'It must feel strange. Confusing.'

'Yeah,' she says. 'I thought he got me, you know? Like we were soulmates.'

'Oh, sweetheart,' I say.

She's sitting on the bed, her knees drawn tightly to her chest. I go over and hug her, until gradually she unwinds and hugs me back and starts to cry.

'What's going to happen now?' she asks eventually.

'I don't know. I'm going to talk to your dad. I'm guessing you ran away because of your feelings about Adam, and because you felt you should tell your dad what's going on, but you didn't want him to get hurt and you didn't want to betray me. And I shouldn't have put you in such an impossible position. It's not your fault or your responsibility. I have to tell him what I've done. But whatever happens, we both love you.'

'Yeah. The party-of-the-century he's planning . . .' She takes a deep, juddering breath and dries her eyes on her sleeve. 'It explains a lot of things.'

'What do you mean?'

'Like why you're such a freak.' She's smiling at me, though.

Stella puts on one of the Harry Potter films and she and Ava curl up on her bed, the duvet wrapped around them, sharing a big bowl of popcorn. I make myself a cup of tea and take it into the garden. I stand in the middle and look around. I'm on a path of Cotswold stone chippings, bordered by a miniature box hedge. The hedge and the grass are neatly trimmed, hardly a blade out of place. Halfway down there's a sundial, and beds radiate from it like the spokes of a wheel. They're filled with roses: deep red and creamy white; each bloom is perfect. The scent is intoxicating. The edges of the garden are planted with shrubs. Some of them are blooming, although I know Jack planned these borders to give 'interest' throughout the year. Now, a lilac-coloured climbing rose and a jasmine that wind along the fence are looking stunning.

As I follow the path I notice, for the first time, an inscription on the sundial. It's in Latin and runs round the edge of the clock face: *Omnes vulnerant, ultima necat.* The sundial is still so new there's no lichen or moss growing on its surface. Curving in the opposite direction is the English translation. It's carved into the stone in beautiful flowing calligraphy: *All hours wound; the last one kills.* I wonder if my husband chose these words when he had the garden redesigned four years ago. Why would he have had a bespoke sundial inscribed with that particular line?

I shiver. I feel childlike and out of my depth, standing here in my blue dress. It's as if I've strayed into someone else's domain and it is as foreign as Wonderland was to Alice. I half-expect to see the Red Queen striding towards me through the roses, the White Rabbit tutting and inspecting his watch before disappearing behind the shrubs. I look back at our house. It appears like a normal 1930s town house from the front, but here, at the back where it's private, it's a cube of glass, the transparent walls glistening in the early-morning summer sunshine.

I thought I loved this house. It's Jack's creation, and therefore Emma liked it. Lizzie would have felt uncomfortable here. The garden is sanitized, segmented, ordered. Nothing is allowed to be wild or free. Below me are fields grazed by cows, a playing field, the edge of a golf course, the last stretch of the suburbs. There is no wilderness here where one can walk for hours without seeing a soul. But I *am* Emma, and I once was Lizzie. Is Lizzie still there inside me like a small, cramped Russian doll? If I remove the façade – the coils of blonde hair and the artfully applied lipstick – will she emerge, unfettered and righteous? *I can't suppress her any more*, I think, but equally I'm no longer that young girl. I need to stretch and grow, to allow room for Lizzie to be me, for me to be Lizzie. I might have literally buried the girl I once was, but now I must acknowledge that she's there, that change is natural. I need to hold the multiplicity of all my selves within me.

But what the fuck am I going to do?

I'm not the girl who once married Paul. Neither am I the kind of woman who would, in another life – in my own, original life – have married Jack. I thought I loved Jack, but what I really felt for him was gratitude. I mistook that feeling for love. He saved me. He kept me safe. And now I need to let him go.

I start to feel the familiar anxiety rise within me, the tension locking my muscles, turning my spine rigid. I take a deep breath and smell one of the roses. The fragrance immediately calms me. I start walking towards Jack's office. I don't know how I'm going to do this, but I can do it. I will do it. I have to have all three of my children by my side. Questions flutter around me like the Queen of Hearts' cards: where will we live? Will Adam ever speak to me? How will the girls get on with Paul? Can we survive on a gardener's and a baker's salaries? Will Jack continue to support us? Will Adam and Stella ever talk to one another again? I try and bat them away. I have no idea about our finances. I let Jack handle all of it. I was in no fit state at the beginning, when we first met, and then I got pregnant so suddenly and I couldn't think straight. This house and the renovation were Jack's project and he dealt with it all. I can't even remember if I'm on the title deeds – if the mortgage is jointly in our name or not!

Why did I allow myself to drift through my life and my marriage? I think, annoyed with myself, as I follow the path to the end of the garden and Jack's office. I key in the combination for the lock and let myself in. There's no paperwork in the house, apart from the pile of letters from the school and from Ava's various clubs. Knowing Jack, everything will be filed here in a neat and orderly manner. I can't see him quietly leaving the house that he built, though, or Paul and Adam wanting to move in. And clearly there's not enough room in Paul's cottage for all of us. I sigh. Am I procrastinating, trying to find out if I'm even legally entitled to half this house, when I should be figuring out what to say to Jack?

It'll give me ammunition, I think, *to know, for once in my life, what my situation is.* I'm going to leave him, I've decided that much, but I don't want it to be too big a wrench for the girls, and if they have to share a room and a bed in Paul's cottage, then Jack will fight hard to keep them, and the girls are likely to side with him.

I stand in the doorway for a moment, letting my eyes adjust. I've rarely been in his office, and never on my own. I feel like an intruder. It's a stunning view: it's as if I'm perched on the edge of a soft, green cliff. If I pressed myself against the window, I'd imagine I could fly. It smells of sun-warmed wood, a resinous tang of the cedar mixed with a hint of Jack's aftershave: the smoky, earthy essence of vetiver.

There are two filing cabinets in the corner. They're both locked, but the key is still in one of them. When I turn it, the drawers slide open easily. The first has hanging folders with all of our household bills, each utility awarded its own separate space. In the second drawer down, I find what I'm looking for: our mortgage statements and, towards the back, several folders whose contents relate to buying the original house on this plot and renovating it. I remove all of them and lay them on Jack's desk. In one of these folders I'm sure I'll find the deeds, showing whether we own the house jointly or not.

The front of Jack's office has narrow slits for windows, making it quite private. Jack has fitted blinds, too, perhaps to stop any glare from hitting his computer monitor. I lift one slightly and peer towards the house, but I can't see the girls in either Ava's bedroom, which is next to ours, or upstairs in the sitting room. I imagine they're still tucked away in Stella's room at the front of the house. I glance at my watch. The film's only been on for half an hour. I didn't set the alarm, but I did lock the front door. I'm only going to be a few minutes and then I'll go and check on them. Perhaps we should have a chat, all three of us, over lunch. I wonder whether I ought to ring Jack and ask him to come home early, or wait until he returns?

An architect's drawing slides out, and I have a sudden memory of sitting in the Bird in Hand, breast-feeding Ava, and trying to stop Stella, who was eating an enormous ice-cream sundae, from covering herself and the table with cream and chocolate sauce, while Jack was talking to the architect. I was supposed to be part of the meeting, too, putting forward suggestions and checking that I was happy with the progress of the plans, but I had no capacity to join in – Ava was a contented baby as long as I held her in my arms and fed her for eight hours a day, while she stared adoringly up at me with her large, brown eyes; and Stella was a complete handful, playing up because she was jealous of her new baby sister. I was so tired! I'd have said yes to anything. As I look at the original plan, starkly etched on shiny card, I can feel the tug on my nipple as Ava sucked, smell the stickiness of the chocolate syrup, taste the sharp grassiness of the glass of Pinot I was drinking, even though my husband disapproved of me having alcohol whilst I was breast-feeding. Jack smiled at me, with both fondness and exasperation at the fuzziness of my thinking, and made all the decisions by himself.

I can't afford to be nostalgic now, I tell myself, but I can't help it. Even though I'm meant to be doing a quick search for the paperwork – which is unlikely to be in this folder, with the architect's plans, if I know anything about the precision of Jack's filing – I get distracted. There are floor plans, and a mood board. I didn't even know he'd made one. Photos, too, of the original house, and the chaos when the builders moved in and gutted it. The new one, rising Phoenix-like from the rubble. Me and the two girls in the overgrown garden

with its mad Seventies crazy paving and leylandii. I'm wearing
Jackie Onassis-style sunglasses and a scarf around my throat; my
sandals are mustard-yellow, and I'm in a navy-blue sundress with
a pink wrap-cardigan. It was the first outfit Jack bought me – and,
in hindsight, I can see it was the start of the Emma Taylor uniform.
It'll be a relief to revert back to wearing fleeces and cargo pants.
Or maybe *I'll* decide what my new look will be. I push the photos
back and spread the other folders out on the desk.

As I do so, I see the corner of a file, poking out from behind
the architect's paperwork. It's different from the others, which are
all identical: the colour of oatmeal, with crisp white labels. This is
a faded lilac, the card so old that it's soft and dog-eared. There's
some writing on the top corner in marker pen, the black now grey
with age. I pull it out. It says, *Elizabeth Bradshaw.*

Adrenaline surges through me. Why does Jack have this? Why
is it here, hidden at the back of his filing cabinet? Just as quickly as
the heat rushed through me, I'm filled with an icy fear. My heart
contracts. I open the folder and take out the yellowing sheets inside.
The top one is a police file. My photo is attached with a paperclip,
although I hardly recognize myself. It has all my details on it: my
original details, as Lizzie Bradshaw. Stapled to it is a photocopy
of my statement, the one I gave DI Simon Duffield, my signature a
weak scrawl at the bottom. I remember I was so relieved when it
was over, I could barely hold the pen.

And then there is what looks like a report. My hands are shaking.
I put everything on the desk for a moment and wipe my palms on
my dress. It's written by Dr Jack Taylor for Leeds Metropolitan
Police Force. My eyes blur and the letters dance across the sheet.
That it is about me is clear, though. I turn over the title page and
words leap out at me: *racketeer, Elizabeth (Lizzie) Bradshaw, Witness
Protection, trial, identity.* I turn the pages faster and faster, unable
to take it in. *Distress, depression, Recommendations, identity, legend,*

surgery, and then, jumping off the page as if it's been branded there in fiery ink, my name – my *new* name: *Emma James.*

I think I'm going to be sick. I drop the report and put my hands over my breastbone. I can feel my heart pulsing. So he's known – he's known all along? But when I met him, he wasn't working for the police. Unless he'd been undercover? Was he spying on me? Or lying? Is he with Lilley? I can't think. My brain is dissolving, my thoughts disintegrating.

I have to get the girls away. We have to get out of this house – now.

I start to shove everything back into the folder. I will look at it all later, when we're well away from here.

The door clicks and slides open almost noiselessly. I spin round, hoping it's Ava or Stella, wanting more popcorn, or to tell me the DVD has stuck. But I know it won't be. Neither of them knows the code to access the office. The man is a dark silhouette in the doorway. He shuts it carefully behind him. I clasp the folder to my chest. It's Jack.

He knows. He knows.

The words run though my mind, leaving no room for anything else.

Who is he?

'Don't you remember me?' he says.

I want to ask questions, but my mouth has gone slack, I can't form the words I need.

'Take a deep breath. Think of that duck, the little female mallard, asleep on the bank, its beak tucked under its wing. Imagine your toes, trailing in the stream. It's cold, it's the north of England after all, but it feels good against your skin, on that hot summer's day, the sun beating down on your back, your sister lying in the grass by your side, your mum sunbathing between the two of you, taking a moment out of her busy day. You were safe and all was well.'

I'm trembling. It's as if his words are in my own head, the words

I hear when I'm anxious and I need to return to my safe place. He smiles.

'I spent so long talking to you. Every day for six months. Do you remember now?'

I do, I know exactly who he is. Or who he was.

'You were my psychologist. But – you were Joe, Dr Joe Wood.'

'I worked as an advisor to the police. When they offered me your case, they suggested I create an alias for myself. Just in case. It did help me to have sympathy for your predicament. It's odd changing one's name, isn't it?' I'm speechless, and Jack continues to talk. 'Your situation sounded intriguing. Unusual. Devastating for you, of course. I wanted the challenge – to help someone to start again. You were practically a blank slate. What an opportunity! So many people would welcome a second chance, to begin again, to do things right.'

'I lost everything! I had the life I dreamed of. I didn't want to "begin again".'

'I could see that. It was hard for you. But I helped you. Talked you through the grief, the anger, the loss. I invented your new legend. I created you – Emma James.'

I remember what he said to me the very first time we spoke:

My job is to help you find a way to live with this anguish. My job is to help you rebuild yourself.

'But how—'

'How was I able to find you in Bristol? I was working with the Witness Protection team on the logistics. I made some suggestions about where you should be relocated, what kind of work you could do. Once they'd moved you to Bristol, I resigned. And I came here,' he says. He puts his hands in his pockets. He appears perfectly relaxed. But with Jack, appearances can be deceptive.

I think about the kind, attentive man who bought a coffee from me every single day.

'Were you really working as a counsellor when we met?'

'Of course. I set up a private practice so that I could pay the bills while I re-trained.'

'You manipulated me! You engineered the whole thing!'

'I helped you. Can you think of any other man you might have met at that stage in your life who would have been so patient, so understanding? To anyone else you'd have seemed unstable, erratic, irrational even. Who else would have put up with that? But I've supported you every step of the way. Cemented your new identity for you. Protected you. I knew your fears were real, and I did everything I could to keep you safe. Anyone else who didn't – who couldn't – know your past wouldn't have been so accommodating. Who but me would know how well we need to protect our daughters? Just in case.'

I can't pretend any more. In a way, it's a relief. No more lies. I summon Lizzie, I summon the woman I once was, who was strong enough to walk away from her husband and her baby son in order to save their lives, who stood up to a known murderer and helped put him in jail for life. Whoever Jack really was, whatever hold he thinks he has on me, I – Emma Taylor – can deal with it. I've faced worse. I stand up straighter, pull my shoulders back.

'You're a monster,' I say.

'Emma! How can you say that?' He stretches out his arms towards me, but I back away. 'We spent a long time talking to each other. I knew you inside out before we met in person. I fell in love with you. I didn't plan to! I gave up everything for you. My job. My house. I re-trained. I reinvented myself for you. I did all of that so I could be with you. Because I loved you.'

I swallow. My throat is so dry it's painful. My fingers leave sweat stains on the pale-lilac folder.

'You were a professional hired by the police.'

'Come on, Emma. You're really denying you felt nothing for me?'

I think back to that voice, soft and resonant, a voice I listened to every day for six months; a voice I drew strength from, a voice that got me out of bed in the morning when I had nothing else to live for. It's no wonder that, when I met him, I felt so at ease with him almost immediately.

'It's natural to grow attached to one's counsellor – even to fall in love with him or her,' I say. 'It's called transference. It's the redirection of your feelings for the person you really love, to the person who's helping you. You knew that! You abused your relationship with me to get close to me when I was at my most vulnerable.'

'I loved you. I love you. And you love me. We've been together for fifteen years. We've built a wonderful life. We have two beautiful daughters. You're happy here, with me. You're safe.'

'I'm leaving you,' I say.

Jack stands in front of the door.

'You can't,' he says.

'You can't stop me. Please let me past.'

Jack's office is claustrophobic. Perspiration trickles down my chest, pools in the small of my back; my scalp prickles. The smell of wood is overpowering; it's so hot it's as if it's smouldering.

'Sit down, Emma. Let's discuss this like rational adults.'

'I'm going, and I'm taking the girls with me.'

My husband's hands are loose at his sides. I recognize the body language: he's pretending to show warmth and vulnerability; in contrast my posture is defensive, my arms hugged tightly around my chest, clasping the pale-lilac folder. I remember him telling me this, warning me against letting my body betray me, once I was out of Witness Protection. But now I notice tiny telltale movements: the way a muscle jumps in his jaw, how his biceps flex. His body is hard, solid, menacing. He seems unfamiliar, like a man I've never met.

'You can't leave,' he says quietly, 'because if you do, I'll tell the police your identity has been compromised.'

'What?' I set the file on the desk. I will wrestle my husband out of the way if I have to. 'You can't do that!'

He leans towards me slightly, as if he's having a friendly conversation.

'If I tell the police that you've told someone what your true identity is, you'll never see your children again. They wouldn't be safe, would they? The police will be forced to step in. They'd give you another identity. I'd have sole custody of both girls. We'd be relocated. You'd never see any of us again. You'd never even know where we were or what our names were. Our new names.'

'You wouldn't! How could you—'

'It's true, though, isn't it? At least one other person knows who you really are, don't they? You've compromised us. All of us.'

'What do you mean?' I whisper.

'You remember I said that I understood your fears? I took your anxiety seriously because I know what Jon Lilley is capable of, even from prison. It helped, though, being an ex-police psychologist: I picked up some tips when I was with the force. As well as installing the alarm system, I monitored the girls' social media and I cloned your laptop. I put tracking devices in both our cars. I even put one on your new bike. I wanted to protect you . . . but, well, I'm sure you can imagine what I found out. I also kept an eye on your former husband.' He says quietly, 'You told Paul Bradshaw who you really were. And maybe Dylan, too. Or should I say, Adam.'

I step backwards and sink into the armchair. He perches on the edge of the desk. And although we never had a face-to-face session when I was in Witness Protection, this feels as if we're back in that space – as if, once more, he's my psychologist and I'm his patient.

'If you stay, you can have the girls with you. I'll even let you see Adam – once he's started talking to you again. We can pretend he's your nephew. We'll say that when your sister died in the car crash, her husband went off the rails. He blamed you and wouldn't let you see your sister's son. But now, all is forgiven. You've been reunited with your sister's husband and your nephew. In fact, why don't we invite Adam and Paul to our anniversary party? I presume Stella has told you about it. After all, the two of them live so close to us now. Obviously you'd have to stop seeing Paul. Privately, that is.'

He stands up. Stretches. Picks up the documents that describe the life that once was mine.

'This was my insurance policy, in case anything went wrong. I thought it was about time you found it and we had this little chat.'

'What? You planted it there? But—'

He shakes his head. 'It's been there all the time. I left the filing cabinet unlocked and moved it from the bottom drawer into the folder about the mortgage. I know how your mind works, Emma. I knew that if you felt things with Paul might get serious, you'd realize that you have no idea whether you own this house or not. You don't, by the way. It's solely in my name.'

I take a sharp inhalation of breath and tears prick my eyes.

'I assume I don't need the police report any more, now that we have no further secrets between us. I'll get rid of it, although maybe not just yet. I've also taken the precaution of cloning your phone. I'm sure you won't betray me again, though; not now, not once you've thought it through. I'll go and check on the girls.' He glances at his watch. 'The film should be finishing soon. Take your time – I'll make them lunch.'

My husband opens the door and strolls out into the garden, the lilac folder tucked under his arm. He stops briefly, to smell one of the roses he planted four years ago, and then he follows the path, his feet crunching on the butter-yellow Cotswold stones, to the house that he built.

EPILOGUE: STELLA

I lean against the door frame. My bedroom looks both familiar and unfamiliar.

'Hey,' I say.

'Hey,' Adam answers.

He doesn't look up, though. He's sitting on the bed – my bed – puffing something out of a canister with a straw in it at his cameras, and polishing the lenses with a cloth. If you'd said Adam would be in my bedroom a few weeks ago, I'd have been so excited, even a little nervous. But it's like living with a moody teenager. And every time I see him, my stomach does this little flip. Not in a good way, though.

'What are you doing?'

'Your dad asked me to take some pictures.'

I thought Adam would go out, to avoid it. I mean, why would you want to go to the anniversary party of the man who'd married your mother fifteen years ago, when she was still married to your dad? Even I want to fucking avoid it, and I live here. I've got what feels like worms wriggling through my chest. Last night Oma and Grossvater flew in from Belfast and came over for a meal. They're staying at a hotel, as Adam is here and I'm already sharing with Ava, so there's no room for them. They'll be back in a few minutes.

Adam looks up. 'You look nice.'

He says it in a flat, neutral way, but I still blush.

He sets down the camera he's cleaning carefully on the bed and says, 'I had a talk with your dad about it. About it all.' He turns red and ducks his head. He can't hide under his fringe any more because Mum took him to a hairdresser's. 'He said it'll take time, and we'll feel ashamed and bad and strange. But he says how you think about something determines how you feel about it. The more I think about you as my sister—'

'Cousin.'

'Yeah, my "cousin" – the more I'll feel like you are.'

'And are you starting to?'

'Well, you're pretty annoying to live with.' He grins at me, a big, goofy grin. 'And you really do look nice.'

I drop my head, so my hair hangs in front of my face. I feel this odd mixture of relief and mortification. I mean, not very long ago this boy looked at me as if he could eat me alive, and now there's a blankness inside him. Whatever he felt hasn't been replaced by brotherly love yet.

'Your dad is actually pretty cool. He says he's going to help me set up an infrared camera-trap in the woods, so I can video the foxes. And we've started doing interval training. He says it gets you fitter much—'

'Speak of the devil,' I mutter, starting to feel cross. Dad is so not cool.

He bounds in. He's even more full of energy these days.

'Hey, you two!'

He's wearing dark-grey chinos and a black, short-sleeved linen shirt with his round-framed wire glasses in the pocket. You can see the muscles in his arms. He looks like Steve Jobs on crack.

'It's arrived,' he says, handing something to Adam.

'Excellent! So we're all set for next weekend? What about . . .' He inclines his head towards me, as if I'm a kid and he mustn't mention ice cream in front of me.

Dad turns and stares at me. It's like the two of them belong here and I'm the outsider, leaning against the door jamb.

'She can come, if she wants to.'

'What are you talking about?'

'We're climbing Snowdon.'

'It's just a baby,' says Dad, smiling at Adam, who waves his new map at me, 'but it's the highest mountain we can get to in a day.'

'What? You're not going to take your "nephew" to visit an old church?'

'I knew you'd be disappointed, Stella. Adam's persuaded me of the joys of hiking and we have so much to explore. The Brecon Beacons are right on our doorstep. Just think, we have thirty-four furths in Britain.'

'That's a mountain over three thousand feet,' Adam says.

I'm not sure what happened, but shortly after I ran away and Dad came back unexpectedly, our parents said Adam was going to stay with us for a few weeks while he waited for his exam results. Paul had to go back up north, apparently, some emergency on his dad's farm, and he had some things to take care of in the Lakes. I haven't seen Paul since that night we spent at his house. I still haven't got my head around it. I mean, Adam. Some days it's okay, and other days I want to die, the shame is so intense. The worst of it is I can't even talk to anyone about it – someone professional, that is, not Kaylee, obviously – because then I'd be giving away Mum's secret.

Adam is out a lot, with his fox project and his friends, which helps. But it's odd coming home sometimes and finding him slumped on the sofa, checking his Instagram feed or watching endless wildlife documentaries. I know more about fucking falcons and fiddler crabs than anyone should ever have to.

I also can't get my head around the idea that our mother is his mother, too. They're wary of each other, kind of circling one another like, I don't know, lionesses, maybe. She's desperate to give him a hug and I think he's desperate for her to hug *him*, but they're both afraid the other one's going to bite. It's *all* different. My room certainly smells different.

'Sweetheart, would you go and check on your mum? Our guests will be arriving soon,' says Dad.

I knock on my parents' bedroom door and let myself in. I don't see my mother, but I notice something shining on the chest of drawers. It's caught the light and it's practically glowing. It's a glass paperweight with a dandelion clock inside. I turn it over. It feels smooth and comfortingly heavy in my palm. As I do, I notice a tiny crack at the edge of the base, as if it's been dropped or thrown and it's chipped.

'I bought it as an anniversary present for your dad,' my mother says, and I jump.

I hadn't noticed her. She's standing at the far end of the bedroom, staring out into the garden, half-obscured by the curtains. Just standing there, not doing anything.

'But then I saw the flaw in it and I didn't want to give it to him.'

I turn it over and put it back on the chest.

'You can't tell,' I say, 'and I'm sure he'll love it.'

I wonder what her inner forecast is for today: cloudy with showers at intervals? She's wearing the clothes I helped Dad choose and she looks really elegant. She's lost a bit of weight recently. She says she's cut out cake, and she's been running in Ashton Court after work. She's straightened her hair, too; it hangs to the middle of her shoulder blades, thick and smooth and the colour of set honey.

'Are you okay, Mum?'

'I'm fine, love,' she says, smiling at me. She's wearing the necklace Dad bought her; the ruby lies in the hollow of her throat. 'You look beautiful, Stella. Thank you for choosing this outfit. I love the denim jacket. It goes with it perfectly.'

'Well, it was Dad's idea to buy you something,' I say.

'Actually, I was wondering if you could help me. I want a new look. New clothes. Do you think you could come with me and help me choose?'

'I'm not really the right person for that job,' I say, indicating my jeans and T-shirt, even if, today, they're posh ones.

She takes my hand in hers. 'Please,' she says, and her grey eyes are bright with tears.

'Of course,' I stutter, appalled at how upset she looks.

I want to ask what happened with Paul. All she said was that Dad knew everything we did, and then she never mentioned 'it' or him again.

'Thank you,' she says, squeezing my hand.

She blinks and the tears are gone. And just like that, it's impossible to believe she was ever unhappy. I feel lost, like someone has pulled the chair away from me that I was just about to sit on. My mum smiles widely, throws open the French windows and steps out into the garden before I can say anything. The band is setting up at the far end, next to Dad's office. I say 'band', but it's just two guys – twins – who call themselves The Blues Brothers. I guess it's meant to be funny.

When I catch up with her, she says, 'Did I ever tell you that the first date your dad and I went on was to see a blues band? It was on a boat. You know, the *Thekla*?'

'Yeah,' I nod and swallow. My throat is dry, as I remember my own first date.

A few people have arrived already. Dad is standing by the marquee – it's more of a glorified canvas shelter – marshalling the catering staff and issuing directives to the twins, who nod slowly as if they're still hungover from last night's gig. There are cut-glass bowls of blood-red roses on the tables, and the cake, a five-tier Victoria sponge, is decorated with a thick swirl of them.

A waiter comes over and Mum takes two glasses of champagne and passes me one.

'We need to celebrate,' she says, chinking hers against mine.

'Oh, yeah, sorry, Happy—'

'No, not that,' she says impatiently. 'I've got into college to do my A-levels. If you were me and had four A-levels you couldn't tell anyone about, would you repeat the ones you'd already done or would you do new ones?'

'I'd do the same ones again,' I say.

'I thought I would, too. But when I had to fill in the form, I chose new ones. So I'll be studying something completely different when I get to university.'

I look at my mother's eyes, glowing sharp as flint in the sunlight, and wonder why I never realized she was intelligent.

'You know,' she says, 'I've been using what happened to me as an excuse. Feeling sorry for myself. I've let myself coast through life. And the thing about you, Stella, is that you've never coasted. You've always worked hard and been determined, and known what's important to you. I admire you.'

I don't know what to say and I blush. My mother has never spoken to me like this before.

'But now we have to think of the future. Our future. Come on, let's go and talk to our guests,' she says and she takes my arm.

'There you are, darling,' says Dad, putting an arm around Mum's shoulders. 'You look beautiful.' He kisses her cheek. 'Your crew have just arrived.'

It's the guys from *Kate's* – Caleb and Toby, Nate, Harry, Jessica, Simone, Izzy and, of course, Katie in some monstrous fucking frock with three billion petticoats. They surround Mum, Katie screeching like a toucan. Mum doesn't look as if she belongs with them any more.

Dad takes a couple of canapés from a waiter and passes them to me.

'Did you know,' he says, as I inspect them to see if I remotely want to eat some twiddly bits of toast, 'that these were made by the deli where I first met your mother? She was working there. I used to go in for a coffee every single morning, just to try and get to know her. Cost me a fortune in Americanos before I had the courage to ask her out.'

Jesus, I think, *I don't want to hear another thing about how my parents met.* I see Adam on the other side of the rosebed and I head over to him. I rub my arms, which are a bit goosebumpy. Even though it's late August, it's not that warm, and I'm going to have to find my hoodie. Adam's carrying a camera bag and he's got his Nikon on a strap round his neck. I wish I had a camera – you can be here but not here, if you know what I mean, concealed behind the lens. And then I wonder if that was Dad's plan – Adam might not have stayed for the party if he didn't have a job and somewhere to hide.

I pass him the canapés and he wolfs them down in two bites.

'This is where the extension is going to be,' he says.

'What?'

'Yeah!' He gives one of his old, slow smiles. 'I've got into Bristol Uni!'

'Oh! Um, congratulations.'

'Jack says there's no point in spending a fortune on crap student accommodation. So he's going to add an extra room onto the office and that'll be my pad, and I'll be able to come and go as I please, and he's going to put an extension here and that'll be his office. He says it was stupid to put it so far from the house. Shame about the roses, though.'

I look at the four-year-old red and white roses, all blooming perfectly, and perfectly on time for my parents' wedding anniversary.

'They've served their purpose,' I say. 'Least I'll get my room back. I'm going to have to fumigate it, though, before I can move in.'

He grins and punches me – *quite* gently – on the shoulder. I rub my arm and try not to think about the last time he touched me.

'Hey, it's the little princess,' he says, as Ava comes running over.

She's wearing a pink-and-gold dress, with matching bows in her thick, blonde hair, and she looks really pretty. Adam gives her a one-armed hug, holding his camera with the other hand so it doesn't swing forward and hit her in the face. Ava adores him and he's really nice to her. I guess it's a lot less complicated when you find out you have a secret sister but she's only eleven. Weirdly, it makes me feel jealous. They're in profile and then, at the same time, they turn and grin at me, and it's like they're mirror-images of each other. Same chin, same smile. If I go back and look at the selfies I took of me and Adam, would I see a similarity, too? I feel as if I'm in a great glass elevator and I'm plummeting to the ground because I know the answer already. We might have different hair and eye colour, but we do look like brother and sister.

'Look, there's Oma and Grossvater,' I say, before I can start freaking out.

Our grandparents have just arrived. Oma's wearing a floaty white dress befitting a summer party, but since it's Bristol, it's highly likely it's going to rain. Grossvater has a shock of white hair and he's standing to attention. He's got a kind of khaki suit on, which makes him look like he's on a military op in the Maldives.

'When I was little, I couldn't say "Grossvater",' says Ava, starting to giggle, 'so I used to call him "Gross Farter".'

Adam snorts. 'That's actually pretty funny,' he says and even manages not to sound condescending.

'I suppose we should go and talk to them,' I say. 'You can take their photo.'

Adam's expression changes, the way camouflage colours flush through a cuttlefish. Yeah, I know this kind of shit now: first shock, then delight and then he looks aghast. I spin round to see what he's looking at. Yup – OMG all right. It's Paul. He looks out of place. Like he's left the mountains for a day in the big city, but didn't quite get the dress code right. He's striding through the garden, straight towards our mother and father.

'Your dad's here!' says Ava excitedly.

My sister is so unsophisticated.

We head over as quickly as we can, given that the garden is now full of adults who are already a little drunk.

'Hey, son!'

Paul throws his arms round Adam and gives him a massive bear hug that ends up with that man-thing of slapping each other on the back, but they don't make eye contact.

'Wow, you look so pretty,' says Paul, crouching down to talk to Ava. He looks up at me and hesitates. 'Hi, Stella.'

Why does no one know how to talk to me? I might want to be spun round like a kettlebell or told I look pretty, too. I nod back at Paul. He looks different. His nose is a bit red and his eyes are bloodshot. Mainly he looks – diminished, somehow.

'How's he been?' he asks our parents.

'He's a joy to have,' says Mum seriously, and I splutter.

Dad puts one arm round Mum, and now *he* slaps Adam's back with the other. 'He's eating us out of house and home,' he says, and the grown-ups give fake laughs.

'He's got into Bristol University,' says Dad proudly, like Adam's *his* son. 'Did he tell you?'

'Yes, he sent me a text this morning.'

'It's great news,' Dad continues, as if Paul hadn't spoken, somehow managing to keep a hand on both Mum and Adam at the same time. 'We've been saying: it would make sense for Adam to stay here. I'm going to fit out the office for him, so he's got his own space.'

A muscle tightens in Paul's jaw and he glances at Mum, but she's looking away, as if she doesn't really want to be here at all, having this conversation.

'Did you get everything sorted?' Dad says to Paul.

I keep looking at Mum, hoping she'll give me a clue about what's going on. Paul nods curtly.

'That's fantastic,' says Dad, and he lets go of Adam and puts out his hand to shake Paul's. 'It's agreed then.'

Paul slowly, as if he's utterly reluctant, takes Dad's hand.

'What's agreed?' I ask.

'One big, happy family,' says Paul, but so quietly I can hardly hear him.

'That's right,' says Dad, equally softly.

'What is going on?' I ask again.

Everyone but my mother looks at me, and for a moment I think no one will answer.

'Mum?' I say.

But it's my father who replies. 'Adam is staying here with us while he's at university, and the National Trust have kindly given Paul his old job back and his home in Langdale.'

There's a long moment of silence, although all the guests are talking and laughing really loudly. Paul is looking at my dad like one of the stags in Adam's documentaries, like he might bellow and charge. I reach out and take Ava's hand and squeeze it tightly. My mother finally looks at Paul. Her grey eyes still have that steely glint.

'Paul,' she says, 'you made me a promise. You said, *I'll do anything you want. Whatever you need.* Remember?'

'But I meant—'

The first few bars of gentle guitar chords drift across to us and gradually grow louder and deeper in power.

'I think it's time for you to leave now,' my mother says.

'Ah,' says Dad, smiling at Adam's father, as if apologizing for his wife's behaviour. He tilts his head to one side. 'This song was a hit the year Emma and I got together. Please excuse us. Darling?'

He takes my mother in his arms and they start to dance. The guests move back and our parents are in the middle of a circle of people who are smiling and swaying to the music, as The Blues Brothers belt out 'Breathe' by Faith Hill. Adam begins to take photos and Ava lets got my hand and does a little pirouette. When I glance over to where Paul has been standing, he's no longer there. I look around, but I'm hemmed in by our guests and I can't see him any more.

Katie sticks two fingers in her mouth and does a wolf-whistle and suddenly the beautiful barristas, Jessica, Simone and Izzy, are shimmying on the lawn, and Caleb and Toby and Nate, all buzz-cuts and beards and tattoos, are jumping and jiving along with them. More people crowd into the middle and start dancing, and at the centre is my father, who is still smiling, as he twirls my mother round and round.

ACKNOWLEDGEMENTS

In spite of its dark side, I've loved working on *My Mother's Secret*, for many reasons, but in particular this novel has allowed me to indulge my obsession with cake. Some might say it's a vicarious fantasy, as I'm gluten-intolerant and have rarely eaten refined sugar since writing a non-fiction book about its impact on our world. My Instagram feed, though, is full of pictures of cakes and Prosecco, even if the former are largely made out of nuts and dates. Another reason I've loved writing *My Mother's Secret* is because of Stella. It's been an absolute dream and pretty darn therapeutic to write as an angry fourteen-year-old. Someone cuts me up at the lights? A car nearly wipes me out when I'm on my bike? No problem! I can come home and slip right into the head of an angry, sweary teenager.

No writer writes in isolation; when I was doing my tax return, I discovered that I'd spent a small fortune in *Hart's Bakery*. Run by Laura Hart, this 'secret' bakery is hidden beneath Temple Meads train station. Not only does *Hart's* sell the best coffee in Bristol (from *Extract Coffee Roasters*, which conveniently happens to toast its beans at the end of my road), but also the best sourdough. I am beyond disappointed that I can't eat much of it. Laura kindly agreed to let me spend some time behind the scenes in the bakery, quizzing her staff about what it takes to be a professional baker (special thanks to Jodie and Simon). *Kate's*, where Emma works, is modelled on *Hart's*. In fact, quite a few of my favourite cafes feature in *My Mother's Secret*. Stella and her dad discuss what cake to buy for Emma in *Ahh Toots*, a stall in the charming St Nicholas Market, run in real life by cake artist Tamarind Galliford. Tam made the stunning bourbon and chocolate cakes we had at the book launches for my last two thrillers, *The Stolen Child* and *Bone by Bone*. *Toots* is opposite *Lucy Anna Flowers*, a gorgeous florist, who supplied the flowers for my book launches. Another favourite is *Cox and Baloney*, a perfect example of a quirky Bristolian hangout and the ideal place to have afternoon tea or teapot cocktails, and is where *Kate's* crew go for their boozy staff outing. Last but by no means least, *Papadeli* is the delicatessen where I imagined Emma working when she first met Jack – and is where I spent many mornings when I was writing *Bone by Bone*.

On a more serious note, this book would not have been possible if it were not for Paul Whitehouse, who helped me with the logistics of the police procedure and also brainstormed the initial synopsis with me. We sat in the Ashton Gate pub (which also features in the novel), with me acting a bit like a recalcitrant teenager, metaphorically stamping my foot and clinging to my plot, hoping Paul could help me figure out how to make it stand up factually. Thank you also to Tom Abbott for his insights on counselling. I've been lucky enough to have had some amazing and talented people on my side: my editors, Sara O'Keefe, Louise Cullen and Susannah Hamilton; Jamie Forrest, Marketing Campaigns Director; the publicity has been brilliantly masterminded by Kirsty Doole; Vanessa Kerr has handled rights; and Francesca Riccardi is a digital wizard who shares my love of dinosaur necklaces (but the whole team at Atlantic Books is, indeed, awesome). Special thanks to Mandy Greenfield, who fielded my errant commas and wonky hyphens with aplomb and stopped me making a complete idiot of myself on numerous occasions, in print at least. My two writing buddies, Emma Smith-Barton and Claire Snook, have been there for me whenever I've needed a laugh, a cry or a triple gin and a slab of sugar-free cake. Most importantly, they've pushed me to become a better writer.

Huge thanks to my agent, Robert Dinsdale of Independent Literary, who has been with me for the whole rollercoaster psychological-thriller ride and absolutely gets what it's like to be a writer, whilst nailing the agenting aspect of the business, as well as being one of the most insightful editors around.

Thank you to my family: my mother, Rosemary O'Connell (who I'm *quite* sure has no Emma-like secrets!) and my siblings, Sheila, Dee and Patrick, and their partners, Simon, Ian and Emma, for always being there for me whenever I emerge from the depths of a book; my husband, Jaimie Rogers, who pretty much keeps the show on the road, and without whom none of this would be possible. Our daughter, Jasmine, is utterly adorable and, thankfully, has not yet become a teenager and is still willing to hold my hand in public.

Finally, I'd like to thank the National Trust. Tyntesfield in Bristol and Langdale (including the Sticklebarn pub) in the Lake District are owned by the National Trust, a conservation organization that preserves vast tracts of our countryside and many historic buildings and estates, as well as providing some exceptionally fine cafes (back to cake!) and its knockout Sticklebarn gin, brewed from its own spring water and acorns. To me, the National Trust is the best part of what it means to be British.